Aren & Élise

Pathways of the Soul

ETTENIG SAYAM

BOOKSIDE Press

BookSide Press
877-741-8091
www.booksidepress.com
orders@booksidepress.com

CONTENTS

DEDICATION

To Alys, my constant muse and guardian angel.

Forty is the old age of youth. Fifty is the youth of old age.

—Victor Hugo

PROLOGUE

◇◇◇

VESPERS

◇◇◇

Pétion-Ville, *Haïti 1965*

> *Little Boy kneels at the foot of the bed,*
> *Droops on the little hands little gold head.*
> *Hush! Hush! Whisper who dares!*
> *Christopher Robin is saying his prayers.*

Ghislaine was reading Élise's favorite poem: "Vespers" by A.A. Milne. The fact that Élise did not speak English, did not prevent the toddler from loving the sound of her mother's voice when she said "Hush, hush." Oh, how she loved that sound.

Just then, there was a terrible sound of forced entry coming from the front gate. Ghislaine and her husband Christian had just returned from their vacation back home in Saint Martin. It was the start of the school year. They debated whether they should return. President Duvalier renewed Christian's visa, but things were so different now.

"It's not safe," Ghislaine tried to warn her husband. So many of their friends were leaving—going to France, Canada, and the US—even Africa. Anywhere, but away from Duvalier's craziness and Tonton Macoutes. Duvalier was a distant relation from Guadeloupe. That's probably why Christian was allowed to return. "But why, chéri?" Ghislaine insisted. "We could go to Montréal or New York. Castro's Cuba would be better than this."

Christian placed his tapered fingers over his wife's well-formed lips. Of course they were going to go back. Christian was loyal to his friends, members of Jeune Haïti, and Haïti Littéraire. But not even his gifted friends like Anthony Phelps and Louis Depestre or even the one who was part of that Tuskegee airmen corps in America could outsmart Duvalier. His Vodou gods, the *loas*, were powerful. *Bon Dieu*! If Duvalier thought eating the brains of his precious wife or children for breakfast would give him superhuman strength, he would do it. Was he evil? Maybe. Crazy? Paranoid? More like it.

Boom!

Ghislaine heard the front door forced open. Joseph, their caretaker, was yelling and then a horrible sound silenced Joseph.

The house was filled with the sounds of rapid-fire kréyol as the Tonton Macoutes demanded Christian Douchet surrender himself to their authority. Ghislaine was paralyzed with terror. The book she had been holding fell to the floor.

Christian bounded up the stairs before the Tonton Macoutes could notice him. His first thought was to protect his family. He cried out for Maudette, affectionately called MoMo by his daughter Élise and increasingly by the rest of the family.

"MoMo," Christian's calm voice reverberated on the second floor. "*Viens vite*! *Come*!" Normally, MoMo would appear instantly at the sound of his voice. Where was she? He frantically searched through the rooms and found her hiding in the hallway closet. He had to drag her out of the closet she was hiding in—the smell of fresh urine was overwhelming.

"Go hide Élise and Ghislaine!" Christian ordered.

Somehow, Ghislaine snapped back to reality. She grabbed her baby girl and ran to the hallway to meet her husband, who just then was being manhandled by the Tonton Macoutes.

MoMo was keening or was it Ghislaine as she handed Élise to MoMo and tried to rescue her husband. The Tontons punched her. She staggered to the floor. When Christian struggled to help his wife, they assaulted him brutally.

Élise started to scream. "Papa! Papa!"

That's all Élise could say. MoMo held Élise tight against her sagging breasts and muttered "Tonton Macoutes." Élise struggled out of MoMo's arms in the direction of the men who were now taking the stairs.

That terrible night, someone else was in the house who witnessed everything. BoBo the houseboy was a child, barely ten years old. He was trained to not be seen or heard, but to respond on demand. In the midst of the commotion, BoBo, who had just finished filling the water tanks, let himself into the house through the kitchen. He noticed the Tonton Macoutes as they approached the front gate. Who could mistake the tell-tale signature straw hats and the sunglasses even at night? It didn't matter if you were dark or light-complexioned, educated or not. Haitian or foreigner. They would come for you in darkness. Sometimes, if you were lucky, you spent a few days in prison—beaten up, but alive. Other times that would be the last anyone ever heard of you. Members of his family were joining up with the Tontons. Duvalier took care of them. That's what he heard them say.

For a moment BoBo thought the Tontons might be going to the neighbor's house. Maybe he was praying for that to be the case. But from the courtyard, he could see they passed the neighbor's house and were approaching the iron gates. He was already in the house when he heard one gunshot. BoBo didn't flinch when he saw Ghislaine and Christian brutalized by the Tonton Macoutes. He ignored MoMo's hysterical screams. He saw Élise wailing and heading toward her parents. He had no time to lose. He quickly scooped up Élise. They were friends. She always smiled at him and gave him hugs and kisses. He scooped her up and ran like the wind, escaping notice from the Tontons. He sang her favorite song in kréyol to calm her. He would go to the neighbors, the Syrians, M. & Mme. Raymond Malouf. They would know what to do.

.oOo.

Forty Years Later
Green Hills Prep School
Boston, Massachusetts
2005

In the school...headmaster's expansive office, Élise Douchet sat in the comfortable chair smiling politely as he explained his decision to promote the Assistant Director of the History Department to Director of Development, Major Gifts.

"You understand, Élise," the headmaster began. Élise kept the smile plastered on her face. She didn't hear what he said. Something about connections, legacy interspersed with "You understand."

"Excuse me, what did you say?" Élise asked. The headmaster had asked a question that she was supposed to answer.

"Élise," said the headmaster. "You are a valuable and trusted member of the community."

Élise started to squirm in her seat. This was usually a prelude to exact some kind of favor or concession from her. She felt trapped.

"Yes, John," Élise said quickly, hoping to cut him off.

"We would really hate to lose you. Our board members and trustees rave about how you have really breathed life into the French and Spanish Department with your inclusion efforts. The students adore you."

Élise sighed. She looked at her hands so the headmaster wouldn't see the tears brimming in her eyes. She wasn't promoted to French Department Chair. Actually, there was no French Department. They decided to combine the French, Italian, Portuguese, and Spanish Departments into the Department of Romance Languages and have division heads for each language group. Spanish and Portuguese were rolled into one division. Élise taught as many Spanish introductory and advanced classes as the Spanish Head. She was the French Division Head, but it did not carry the same weight as Department Chair. The person who was given the title of Department Chair of Romance Languages was actually the head of the German Department, but then German was rolled into the Classics Department and he neither spoke nor read Latin or Greek. The school was focusing on Arabic and Mandarin as language offerings.

But I speak and write Arabic, Élise thought to herself. She sighed more heavily.

"Élise," the headmaster said, "I know how dedicated you are and how frustrated you are at your lack of career growth."

Élise now directed her gaze toward the window.

"Élise," he said, "my hands are tied. But I do have some good news."

Did he say something about good news? Élise looked at the headmaster. "What is that, John?" Élise asked warily.

"Well, starting next term you will no longer be required to do weekly dorm checks."

"Oh?" *That's an improvement.* Élise mused.

"Well, you will do them, but I was able to reduce them to once a month."

Élise rolled her eyes too quickly for her to stop it. The headmaster laughed.

"That's what I appreciate about you, Élise. You're so transparent. You must be a terrible poker player."

Indeed, Élise was a terrible poker player, but was that the reason? "Élise, we can offer you a raise. It's not as much as you would get if you were Department Head or if you had gotten the Development job." Élise scrutinized the headmaster's face. She narrowed her eyes.

"There's a catch. What is it?"

The headmaster laughed nervously. "Well," he sighed, "in addition to being Division Head for French, we thought we would free up your time from some of the more onerous aspects of your job so that you can publish and present papers."

He paused to gauge Élise's reaction and then continued. "Someone from the board suggested this. We want you to attend conferences and present papers. It's a win-win. You keep up your academic credentials which are stellar, and you promote the school's profile."

Élise bit her lip. "The board is impressed with my 'credentials,'" Élise said using her hands to form air quotes. "But they're not confident I could be an effective Development Director. And you're not going to compensate me at a level that would be competitive with the other positions I was applying for."

The headmaster looked deep into Élise's eyes, but said nothing. Élise sighed. She bit her lower lip. "Am I free to move off campus?" She asked.

"Yes, of course," the headmaster said.

"All right then," Élise said with resignation.

They both stood up. The headmaster escorted her to the door. They shook hands. As Élise exited the administration building, she thought about her apartment. She started to formulate plans. She would start making arrangements to stop renting out her apartment. Maybe she could finally do some renovations. Apartment therapy. That's what she needed.

.oOo.

Quebec, Montréal,
Canada Winter 2010

Élise was sitting in her mother's spacious and elegantly appointed duplex. This was the place her family fled to after the attack of the Tonton Macoutes. Élise did not recall the details of that event. She remembered Mme. Malouf showering her with different treats and hugging and kissing her a lot and calling her "*ma petite chérie*" or sometimes "*Doudou*."

Over the years, Élise would try to seek professional counseling for what some insisted was PTSD. But the minute the events were recalled she would shut down. She did not want to go there. She did not ever want to go back there. BoBo came with them and so did MoMo. She of course remembered her time in Saint Martin with her grandfather.

Those were happy memories. But her real childhood memories began with arriving in a snow-covered Quebec where everyone was dressed from head to toe with fur and goose down. She remembered squealing with laughter at the mist, the precipitation from people's mouths when they spoke. Canada was home. Other than the Haitian community in the neighborhood, Canada was as far away from Haiti as possible.

Élise heard the upstairs door open and close. The footfall of the doctor was carefully navigating the stairs. She heard the doctor entering the kitchen. She turned around.

"How is she, Doctor?" Élise inquired.

"Oh," he said, "you understand with older people, shocks are harder to absorb. I never met BoBo and M. & Mme. Malouf but she has spoken of them so much that I feel like they are my old family friends. It's heartbreaking that they died in the earthquake. What a tragedy. Your mother is funny. She resolutely refuses to step foot in Haiti, but all of her memories are of her past in Haiti and Guadeloupe and Saint Martin. It sounds magical."

Élise maintained a flat expression. She identified with Haiti but at the same time, she didn't claim it.

"Doctor, my mother just recovered from a stroke." She could feel herself choking up. She continued. "She looks so frail. She's only seventy-two. That's not so old, but she seems—"

The doctor reached out his hand to hold Élise's. He looked at her with compassion.

"Élise, I have done all I can medically for your mother. She's resting comfortably. That's the best medicine. If you can take some time from work to spend time with her, I would say that would be a good thing."

.oOo.

Jamaica Plain, Boston
Winter 2011

Élise sat patiently on the edge of the clinical couch while her acupuncturist Felicia Soltero examined her tongue and checked her pulse.

"Your tongue has a nice red color, but your pulse is really deep. Is everything all right? I mean with work? Life? Have you gotten your period? You've been slacking off on your regular appointments you know."

Outwardly, Élise was the picture of robust health. She didn't share her feelings of stress and anxiety. She sighed deeply, a sigh that was consistent with what her acupuncturist sensed.

"Oh, it's probably menopause. Hormones are supposed to go crazy, right?" Élise said.

"Hmm, well that could be it."

"That was the risk I took, right? All those fertility treatments. My body finally said 'Hey, I'm outta here. Time to close up shop!'"

Felicia chuckled. "Well, at least it decided to leave you with your sense of humor."

Élise sighed again and then lay down and rolled up her sleeves so her acupuncturist could insert the needles in the appropriate pressure points.

"You know, I'm going to use the infrared heat lamp to stimulate your qi. It should help stimulate blood flow and circulation and help improve your mood. You might get your period back."

Élise turned her head toward the wall and away from the acupuncturist's gaze.

"You're not old, okay? Your body is just going through its natural changes."

"Whatever you say," Élise said in a monotonous tone.

Felicia looked at her patient and knit her brows with concern. "Maybe you need to go on vacation." She picked up Élise's chart to make notations and then she paused to look at Élise. "Ah, you have a big birthday coming up in a few months, huh: Fifty."

Élise let out a huge gasp as if someone had just punched her in the belly.

"I guess I found the source of your angst. Hey, fifty is the new forty."

"Really, I don't want to talk about it."

"All right, I'll let you rest. You're okay with the cliché classics? The New-Age CD got badly scratched and that is all I have available. We're talking about maybe installing Pandora or Spotify. Thanks for the suggestion."

Élise was looking up at the ceiling. "You're welcome," she said sullenly.

Felicia was focused on inserting the needles in the appropriate acupressure points. "Perhaps a retreat would help," she suggested. "There's a great one in Western Mass near Tanglewood. There's also a really interesting hiking spa in Vermont."

Élise turned her head to look at Felicia. "Hiking spa?"

"Yeah, I mean I think they probably offer yoga and Pilates and such, but the focus is hiking in the mountains. I've heard really great things about it."

"Hmm, I'm not outdoorsy. I mean I get winded after three laps around the Jamaica Pond by my house."

"I'm sure they tailor hikes suited to each guest's level of ability," Felicia replied. "Check it out. I may have a brochure. I'll bring it in for you when your session is over."

Felicia surveyed her handiwork. "All right, now I'm really going to let you go. Relax, okay?" she said. "Let whatever is bugging you go. This is your time." Felicia switched on the music. She shut off the lights and closed the door behind her.

Élise lay on the treatment bed in darkness, listening to the familiar strains of Pachelbel's Canon in D Minor. Yes, it was a cliché classic, but it never failed to soothe her. She took deep breaths and then another. She closed her eyes hoping that the feeling of sedation would take hold. Alas, not this time. A wave of dizziness hit her. *Did I not get enough sleep?* She took another breath. She was hyper-aware of the stale clinical smell of the treatment room. She could feel each and every insertion point on her arms and hands. She could hear someone tapping on the computer keyboard in the cubicle just outside the room. Memories, some of them deep and some of them fresh. She lost her good friends Jean Henri to the Haitian earthquake and his wife Zora who died of cancer two years before that. She thought about her mother's death last year and about the funeral of her nanny, MoMo who died a few months ago. She thought about BoBo, the boy who had worked in her parent's house so many years ago. He died in the 2010 Haitian earthquake while visiting friends. They had lost contact for many years and only reconnected when Élise transitioned from being a college professor to teaching at the prep school where she now taught. Memories of her childhood in Haiti she thought were lost, resurfaced. She remembered the sound of BoBo's cheerful voice singing a folksong in kréyol while he did his chores. She remembered the way his brow glistened with sweat in the heat of the day. Of that terrible night, she remembered the way he held her tight to protect her when the boogeymen came. He was just a boy, but he was an angel. Sometimes when she had nightmares, she thought of BoBo's arms and that soothed her.

Tears started to stream from her eyes. *What's wrong with me?* She wiped her eyes with her hands, taking care not to disturb the needles. Lately, she found herself crying all the time for no reason at all. She didn't feel like playing violin anymore much to her friend Antonio's consternation. Even her girlfriend Fanny complained that she didn't return her calls. She had no patience for her students. She hadn't gone to mass in weeks, or maybe months.

"Snap out of it!" Fanny would say if she were in the room with her.

Élise sighed. Sighing seemed to be the only thing she was capable of doing.

Hiking Spa. Well, maybe that's what I need. She also was considering a lave tête. MoMo, before she died insisted that Élise do a lave tête to help clear the negative energies. When Élise was going through her fertility treatments, MoMo said that the treatments wouldn't work until she appeased the loas, the Haitian gods, and ritually cleansed her spirit. "I'm not *haïtienne*," Élise said dismissing MoMo's words as typical Haitian folklore.

"Ah, that's what you say. But I know. I took care of you with the loa Erzullie's help."

"Yeah, yeah," Élise said during that conversation.

It was MoMo who on her first and last visit to Élise's Boston apartment set up a shrine in Élise's hallway. She had intended to get rid of it, but kept it and maintained it.

Antonio liked to pray the rosary sometimes in front of the icon. For Élise, it was a symbol of divine protection. Most people, if they weren't familiar with Caribbean culture, just thought it was interesting to see a Black Madonna and thought no more of it.

Élise's eyes felt heavy. *Oh, finally a little rest. No more thinking.* Her last thought before that blissful feeling of nothingness took hold over her was hiking and maybe a lave tête, a ritual head washing to enter the fifth decade of her life.

.oOo.

When Élise returned home from her acupuncture appointment, she decided to go through old files. She still wasn't sure if it was time to throw them out or perhaps archive them digitally. She found the folders containing her fertility charts. She went through the last five years of her charts and noted the pattern of irregularities in her rhythm. In those days, she made comments on what was going on in her life. It astounded her now, almost ten years later that she had not grasped the enormous stress she was under and how that affected her fertility. In 2001, she had attempted in vitro fertilization after undergoing laparoscopic surgery to correct the fibroids and endometriosis she had suffered. Her long-term boyfriend and fiancé had left her and married a woman who was fertile and younger. At forty, she wanted to make a last-ditch effort to get pregnant using advanced reproductive technologies. She was fortunate that as a single woman she could even afford these extensive treatments thanks to her generous insurance plan. She had expended so much mental and physical energy to conceive and what resulted was four miscarriages.

The last attempt was in 2003. She was able to get pregnant at the age of forty-two, but the pregnancy failed in the sixth week. The medical board discouraged her from trying again with her own eggs. She didn't want to try surrogacy. That ended the chapter in her life when she was trying to conceive. At the same time, her aunt, whom she always called her mother, was grappling with advanced Alzheimer's and diabetes, and she died that same year.

Élise took a three-month sabbatical and traveled to Kerala, India, did some volunteer work, and also joined a spiritual group. It changed her life. Her brother Fred would write to her, begging her to come back. At one point he even sent detectives to track her down, convinced she had joined a cult. She smiled quietly remembering those turbulent, yet oddly serene periods in her life. But when she did return, she found peace.

In 2005, Élise began publishing again. She started alienating some of her colleagues who suspected her of trying to make a play for becoming the Romance Languages Department Chair. That wasn't really her intent, but what did it matter anyway? She made traveling a regular part of her life. When she wasn't traveling, she was taking all manner of classes on a wide range of topics. She became a studio rat and learned just about every kind of dance. That was her social life. And even though she didn't attend mass regularly anymore, she joined a group of lay nuns affiliated with the Sisters of Saint Francis in Jamaica Plain. She liked to work with incarcerated women and help them get a new start in life when they got out.

In 2006, at the urging of her friend Zora, she began renovating her apartment and splurged on an interior decorator. Her friends gagged at the money she was spending to remodel.

"What's wrong with you?" one friend asked.

"Nothing is wrong with me. I just want to be surrounded by beauty. I don't have a man. I don't have any children. I'm not that materialistic. I just want to live in a beautiful place."

"But you could be donating the money to charity and doing good works."

"Well, I'm selfish."

And that was that. Her friend Zora died of cancer, but she was able to see the finished results and approved. Zora's daughter Marie Ange would often come to her apartment. There were little touches here and there of Zora they could both enjoy.

Her last act of pure self-indulgence was cosmetic surgery. She made a pact with her close friend to go to Venezuela. Her friend got a tummy tuck, butt lift, and lip enhancement. Élise took the extraordinary step to get a breast lift.

"Élise, are you finally trying to get a man?" her friend Fanny Gonzalez teased.

"No. I'm doing it for me. I'll be looking at my boobs for the rest of my life. They may as well look pretty," Élise said in her inimitable deadpan. It always amazed Élise that she took enormous satisfaction in the look of her breasts. No one ever saw them except her when she would step in and out of a shower and catch sight of her reflection in the mirror. Even in the women's locker room at the gym or in the sauna, she made sure she was covered with a towel wrapped around her body.

Élise put away the files. She reached for a post-it notes and wrote: To review in 2012.

The Hiking Spa brochure was sitting on her desk. Élise walked over to the desk and sat down. She opened her laptop and typed in the website address and began to register for a spot during the May session.

.oOo.

Élise surveyed her apartment one last time. The cleaners did a great job. The apartment smelled wonderful. When she returned from her trip to Vermont she would come home to a clean and immaculate place. She would begin her life milestone with a clean home. A soft knock on the door brought her out of her reverie. That was her friend and neighbor Antonio Sanchez. He would be driving her to the bus station. She would be taking a tourist bus to the hiking spa resort in Vermont. She opened the door and the friends' exchanged kisses.

Antonio noticed the travel bags neatly arranged in the hallway, including Élise's purse.

"You're early," Élise said. "The bus doesn't leave for another two hours."

Antonio chuckled. "Well, you know how I feel about 'better to be too early than late.' But yes, we have time. I thought you could come over and have a café and some fresh dulce con leche with just a dash of rum."

"I guess this will motivate me to really detox when I get to the spa, hein?" Élise said.

Antonio looked at Élise with tenderness. He brushed his knuckles against her soft cheeks. Élise for him was the most beautiful person inside and out. But he also knew she carried a lot of emotional baggage. Oh, he was not one to pry. He listened if Élise wanted to talk, but she was not one to talk or reveal. In the neighborhood, they referred to her as Doña Élise as a sign of respect, but also because she did put on airs, perhaps unintentionally, or maybe that's how others perceived her.

When Élise announced she was going on a hiking spa vacation, Antonio was shocked. The spa part made sense. If she had said she was going to New York or Paris or even Brazil or somewhere in the Caribbean for a beauty spa vacation, he would have understood perfectly. But trudging through mud and rocks with a bunch of strangers seemed like an odd choice for Élise. The most athletic thing she did was ride her bicycle to the park. She didn't wear the whole biker's outfit. She wore her normal clothes.

"*Querida*, you know I don't understand this hiking thing. But if this is what you need to accept turning fifty, then I support you. You're young. I know you don't think so, but you are. I'm almost seventy. I know it's different for women, but I promise you there is still so much of life ahead of you."

Élise nodded with resignation. Antonio cupped her chin.

"I pray for you every day. God is with you. I can't say that about a lot of people, but I know with you, that is the case. The Lady protects you. Fanny and I love you so much. We know you're lonely. But I'm telling you. God works on his own time clock, okay? No more tears. Maybe that fresh air will dry it out of you. Okay?"

The friends hugged each other.

"Come on," Antonio said. "We can have our cafecito and flan and leave in thirty minutes. Sound good?"

Élise smiled. Antonio opened the door and walked out. She took a final look at her apartment and focused on her shrine to the Lady. She prayed for strength to start a new decade in life with optimism and purpose. She started yoga and Pilates and embraced a holistic lifestyle when she turned forty. Maybe with fifty, she would turn into an outdoors woman. Ha!

CHAPTER ONE

THE FALL

On a warm and sunny day in May, Aren began his hike, his daily morning constitutional, two hours later than his usual time at Mount Tom. He overslept. The relentless pounding of his head wouldn't allow him to hit the trail before eleven in the morning. He came to his cottage to work on the scientific paper he needed to submit for publishing. He was supposed to commune with nature. Why did he go out the night before and get talked into a night of poker, whiskey, and cigars until 4:00 a.m.? Although official hiking season wouldn't really begin for another couple of weeks, Aren was annoyed when he parked his Prius and found the parking lot full. Of course, he knew if had gotten up on time, he would have had the trails to himself. He steeled himself for the endless perfunctory "Hey" greetings he would have to endure during the hike.

Aren trudged along the path. "Oh!" he yelled as he stumbled over thick tree roots. He had a few more stumbles and kept cursing himself that he didn't have a hiking stick as he navigated his way up to the top. What was he thinking? The sun blazed. He pulled on his Ray-Bans.

.oOo.

Aren

It took a few minutes to work up to a comfortable stride. There were a lot more dogs out at this hour than I would have liked, but they were reasonably well-behaved. When I reached the top, I noticed the loud group of hikers taking a break before heading back down. I went off to a corner and ignored them. I stretched and used the time to collect myself and enjoy the view of Killington Ski Mountains now covered with green leaves. I ate my apple and drank some water. I was finally starting to feel like myself again. Phew! When I was ready to make my descent, I was relieved to be alone at the summit.

There were two ways up to Mount Tom. The easy way was serviced by carriage trails so it wasn't too steep. The other way, the route I took, Precipice Trail, was the fastest way and the steepest. I would be able to make it back in less than twenty minutes. I noticed the group had split off: one taking the easy way and the other group took the more challenging trail back down to the base. There were a few stragglers. I waited a little to put some distance between us. There still were a few muddy patches which made the way back a little treacherous and challenging for my knees. But it was manageable. Just a few hundred yards ahead of me, I noticed one of the stragglers from the group leaping from rocks. It looked like she was trying to avoid the tree roots which were unavoidable. All I could see of the hiker was her gray ponytail tied with a scarf. Seeing her gray hair and watching the hesitant way she moved, I got the feeling she might be elderly. She kept tripping over rocks and tree roots. *Why is she alone?*

I was gaining on her and was going to pass her. I could smell a distinct but subtle fragrance of flowers. Suddenly, she veered sharply to the right. Perhaps she was trying to let me pass. Who knows? She tripped over something and went careening down a ravine several feet with a swift "Oh!" as she fell and then silence. The way she arched her back as she slid down was terrifying.

Oh God! The terrain was tricky so I couldn't just sprint to help her. I navigated my way to a spot a few feet away from where she slid down. I reached out my hand while holding onto an evergreen branch for support. I widened my stance.

"Are you all right?" I called out to her.

Her hair covered her face as she focused on her ankle. She had a thick mane of silver and dark brown hair that brushed past her shoulders in an iconic Jackie Onassis hairstyle. Then she looked up at me with a gentle smile. The sun's rays struck her light brown almost hazel eyes framed in a very pretty cinnamon-brown complexion.

"I'm fine really," she said breathlessly, "I'm sorry to trouble you like this."

She spoke with a delightful lilting accent. She had a charming way of enunciating every consonant. She folded her legs underneath her and jackknifed to a squatting position and then stood up cautiously. She held onto my hand to support her as she climbed back to higher ground where I was standing. She lifted her arms and did a few knee bends. She walked a little away from me to do her own diagnostics of her body and wipe away the glaring evidence of her fall. She uttered "Ouch!" a few times and "Oh, I'll need that hot tub tonight." She turned around to face me again and said, "Oh, I'm okay. I'm just clumsy."

Her accent sounded French. It wasn't very strong, but still noticeable. It was pleasant. There was something surprisingly sweet about the way she was apologizing for something that wasn't really her fault. Although if she had been wearing the proper shoes, she may not have slipped like that. She was wearing the ubiquitous suede Merrill moccasins. If she had taken the other path, she would have been fine. What possessed her to get on this trail?

"Let me see your hands," I said. "On the way back, you'll have to use your hands for support. You'll be miserable if you have open cuts and wounds. I have some Band-Aids if you need them."

She let me turn her hand over and examine the palms and the outside of her hands. I could see the fine blue veins beneath her delicate brown skin. The lingering floral scent I picked up earlier was a little more intense now that I was physically close to her. *Definitely roses, maybe mixed with jasmine and bergamot but now mixed with her natural scent or sweat.* It had a tantalizing appeal. She had a tiny patchwork of scratches and welts, but nothing too scary. She had very soft hands.

The nails were nicely filed and buffed to a natural polish. I hesitated before releasing her hands.

She fluttered her long lashes rapidly like a hummingbird's wings. "You see, I'm okay. I feel bad that I have interrupted your hike." She let out a heavy sigh. She looked flustered.

"Isn't that your group a little way ahead?" I asked. "What are you doing so far behind? Is this your first-time hiking? You should have a guide," I said. "You shouldn't push yourself beyond what is appropriate for your level on a mountain. It always spells disaster for everyone."

"Yes, well, clearly, I took the wrong path. I got confused," she said primly.

I chuckled internally at her feistiness. She turned away from me to brush off the dirt from her still neatly ironed pants and her red anorak. There was a dried leaf and some debris in her hair. It made her look as if she had had a nice romp in the middle of the forest.

I let out a chuckle. She looked at me with her mouth slightly open. "Oh, you have some dead leaves and debris in your hair."

She instinctively reached her hands up to her hair and raked her hands through it, but the leaf and the debris remained.

I drew closer to her. Her forehead brushed my nose.

"Here, wait, allow me," I said. I removed the offending leaf and picked out most of the moss and dried forest treasures from her hair. But my goodness her hair had a delightful nutty scent like macadamia nuts or was it coconut? Divine. Her hair felt like finely knit cashmere. It was different. I was surprised. I don't know why. "All gone," I said, "and I didn't notice any ticks."

"Ticks!" she said, opening her mouth wider in horror.

"Well, what do you expect? You're in the woods," I said, finding the conversation comical.

She started to look around her on the ground. "Where's my scarf?" she asked.

A few feet from where we stood, I spied a silk scarf lying in a mud puddle. She bent down and retrieved it, sticking it inside a pouch of her very small daypack. She let out another big sigh.

"Well, thank you again," she said. Before I could say "You're welcome," she began walking off the trail and through a thicket of trees. "Hey, you're going the wrong way!" I yelled. I caught up to her easily and steered her back to the main path.

"This is the path?" she asked incredulously. It had a much steeper slope than where she had just been. She gasped. "Oh my God!"

"It's a little tricky, but most people can get down in less than half an hour."

She was shaking her head.

"Come on, I'll walk with you," I said.

"Oh, no, that's not necessary. I'll just stay on this path, now that you've pointed it out to me," she said, her voice trembling. For some reason, I seemed to be making her really uncomfortable. *Did I reek of tequila or something?*

I extended my hand in a handshake. "By the way, my name is Aren Karajian."

She hesitated. "My name is Élise Douchet," she said in a solemn voice. *What an alluring name and perfectly suited to her.*

"Pleasure to meet you," I said. "I hope you don't mind my asking, but are you from Jamaica? I noticed you have an accent."

"Oh, no, I'm from Saint Martin, the French side and Haiti. I left many years ago. I actually grew up in Quebec. I guess I still have a bit of an accent."

"I think it's charming."

She didn't say "Nice to meet you too." In fact, her sunny warm complexion went a little ashy, like the color of the dried dead leaves on the ground. She pulled out her phone and fumbled in her bag and then pulled out a card and started to press numbers with unsteady fingers. She threw another nervous smile my way and then waited. No connection.

"My phone gets really good connection even on this trail. Do you want to use my phone? I'll dial the number for you."

Her lashes fluttered wildly again and then she handed me the card. It had the name Jake Leeds and a cellphone number. I dialed. It took a few rings before he picked up. I introduced myself and told him, where we were on the trail. Élise was looking at me as if I were faking the entire conversation.

"Hold on a second," I said, and then turned my attention to Élise. "Do you want to speak to him?"

"Oh, yes," she said perking up a little. Of course, she had nothing to say to the guide other than apologizing profusely for being, in her words, "such a bother."

She ended the call and handed the phone back to me.

"Shall we?" I said leading the way back. She nodded and followed close behind me.

The sun was streaming in between the trees. Élise removed her red anorak and wrapped it around her waist. We continued walking in silence for a while. I was surprised she made no attempt to initiate small talk. So I got the proverbial ball rolling.

"So what group are you with?" I asked. "Oh, it's a hiking spa near Killington."

"How did you find out about it?"

I knew the spa she was referring to. The word around town was the so-called spa had a reputation for attracting people who professed to want a "holistic" outdoor experience, but it wasn't very rigorous. The spa facilities weren't even that great. Yet, it attracted a lot of people and got rave reviews. Go figure. It was probably the first time she had ever seriously walked a good distance, much less hiked.

She kept her eyes directly forward and answered without looking at me. "Oh, I just liked the description and decided to try it out. I'm, well—I just wanted a retreat."

If she wanted a retreat, she could just stay with me. "Are you enjoying yourself?" I asked.

She stumbled as we approached some difficult terrain, but she recovered quickly.

"I suppose," she sighed. "I'm not disappointed."

"You might want to consider getting a walking stick next time," I said. I wanted to add, *and you might consider getting appropriate shoes.* But why pile on?

She smiled serenely.

"Do you like to hike? I mean, would you like to try it again?" She cast her eyes downward. "Yes, I guess that's why I came."

I noticed Élise's one-line answers. She was pleasant, but she was not inviting more conversation. *I must be flashing an intense expression.* My daughter Lily always complained about my intensity. She said I scared people. Maybe Lily was right. Élise didn't want to look at me. Maybe Élise was shy and reserved, but whatever it was, her standoffishness annoyed me to no end. It occurred to me that if she really disliked me, I should just take off. We were about fifteen minutes from the end of the trail. She would be fine. And then I thought about the very end of the trail. *No way. She'll do something stupid, unintentionally because she doesn't know the terrain and hurt herself.*

I slowed my pace so Élise could continue to walk alongside me. At one point, she stopped to admire the wildflowers.

"Are those lilies?" Élise said excitedly.

It was an unguarded moment and she looked like a woodland fairy, albeit with an iconic Jackie Onassis hairdo.

I smiled at her enthusiasm. I bent down and plucked a flower and handed it to her. "They're called trout lilies because of their mottled leaves."

"Oh, how sweet! Thank you, Aren." She looked around and noted the different varieties of flowers on the forest floor. "Do you recognize the other flowers?" she asked.

I smiled. "So you like wildflowers? The white flowers with the red inner rim are called Dutchman's breeches."

Élise giggled at the name. We continued to walk but now we talked to each other about the forest and hiking. I pointed to a cluster of white flowers with purplish-pink streaks.

"They look a little like orchids, don't you think?"

Élise followed my gaze and agreed. "Do you know what they're called?"

I smiled sheepishly. "They're called spring beauty."

Élise pulled out her camera. "Aren, why don't you pose next to the flowers? You don't mind, do you?"

I must say I was floored when she asked me to take a picture of me with wild flowers. She noted my look of surprise.

"Don't be shy, Aren," she said. "I want to be able to show people the man who scooped me out of the ravine and taught me about beautiful wildflowers in the forests of Vermont."

I made a little bow and said, "Of course, my lady," and obliged Élise by posing next to the flowers so she could take a picture. She took a second picture and insisted I remove my Ray-Bans. I realized then she didn't really know what I looked like. I hesitated. I felt better than I did an hour before, but I still felt haggard. Oh well, the lady asked me to take off my glasses. I obliged.

By the time we reached the end of the trail, she didn't seem to flinch from my touch when I helped her over a glacier rock or steadied her when she stumbled.

"I think I can handle his one," she said with a glint in her eye when we approached the last obstacle.

"Go for it," I said.

I stood back and watched her scale a rock and hoist herself over without sliding.

"You see," I said, "there's hope. You just need the right equipment."

"All right, all right," she said good-naturedly. "I'll get proper shoes."

"And a walking stick," I insisted.

She rolled her eyes in exasperation. I laughed.

Jake and a few hikers were standing outside the bus when Élise and I reached the parking lot. She turned to me and held out her hand warmly. So different from when we began our hike together.

"Well, this is it. Thank you, Aren, for taking the time to show me all this abundance in nature," Élise said. "I learned so much from you. It was wonderful!"

She turned to walk towards the bus.

The horrible headache, queasy stomach, and sore muscles from this morning had gone. I felt all right. Good even. I didn't want to say goodbye to Élise.

"Élise," I said. She stopped walking and turned to look at me. "Yes?"

"I'd like to see you again," I blurted out without thinking.

Her eyelashes fluttered rapidly. She seemed genuinely surprised. *Why is this such a surprise?* I wondered. "Oh, um."

We had not exchanged any personal information. Was she hesitant because she already had someone in her life? Maybe that's why she was so aloof in the beginning. *God, I'm such an idiot. That must be it.*

"Are you traveling with someone?"

"No," she said.

Maybe it was her body language or the faraway look in her eyes or maybe the dryness in her tone, but I understood she was single or at least unattached.

I fished out my wallet from my pocket and pulled out my card. I walked toward her and handed it to her.

Silly me, I thought she would do the same and hand me her card, but she didn't. Instead, she focused on the card and avoided my gaze.

"I'm not a scary person. I'm respectable. Really," I said.

She smiled. Now that the sun was at its mid-point and streaming down upon us, I realized she reminded me of the Marvel Comics X-men character Storm—minus the imperious look. I realized then, giving Élise my card meant nothing. She would most likely file away my card and forget about me. I had to think of something. What would a proper lady appreciate?

"You know there's a wonderful tea salon near where you're staying. The Dobra Tea Room. Why don't we meet for tea this afternoon? Three o'clock?" She hesitated.

"You do drink tea, right? Or, I'm sure they serve something else if you don't like tea."

She was smiling with amusement. Her lashes were fluttering but not wildly like before.

She was studying me.

"I don't know, Aren. I'm—"

I fixed my gaze on her. "It's just tea and conversation," I said.

She was appraising me the way I had appraised her. Shit! Were my eyes still haggard and bloodshot the way they were this morning? Oh, and I was wearing my Yankees baseball hat, backward of course. No wonder she treated me like a goofball. I was a goofball. Shit! Shit!

She bit her lower lip and blinked a few times thinking.

"Wait, can you give me back the card I gave you? I'll write down the address."

She handed me back my card and I pulled out my phone and searched my address list and copied down the information on the card before handing it back to her.

"A tearoom," she repeated.

"Tea and conversation," I said and made the sign of an X on my chest. "Cross my heart."

"I've always liked that expression. It's so wonderfully American," she said.

"So, is that a yes?" I asked gingerly.

The bus driver honked, startling Élise for a moment. She looked back at me: a pinch of flesh was being pressed down by her teeth. She did the blinking thing again, but it was more subtle.

"All right. Three o'clock. But, if I change my mind, don't take it personally, okay? I don't really make it a habit of going on a date with a stranger."

"It's not a date. It's tea and conversation."

"It's a date," she said.

"And so it is. I'll see you at three," I said.

She laughed this time flashing the whitest smile. The bus engine started.

"Oh, Jake is going to be really angry with me," Élise said walking backward in the direction of the bus, still facing me."

"Oh, he's just a kid. I'll slap him around and set him straight," I said jokingly, but the look of fright on Élise's face put me on the alert. "Just kidding. It's just an expression. Go, they're waiting. I'll see you at three o'clock."

She didn't answer. She boarded the bus and it drove away immediately. I couldn't tell if she waved. I certainly wouldn't know if her fellow hikers would give her an earful and discourage her from going out with the stranger she met on a hiking trail.

I walked to the end of the lot and found my car and got in. I didn't look at myself in the mirror. I called my barber and said, "Hey, can you fit me in today for a special?"

CHAPTER 2

THREE O'CLOCK AT THE DOBRA TEA ROOM TERRACE

Aren

Wharhat is that French word for wily and tricky? *Malin*. Élise is *malin*! After the bus took off, I didn't know whether she agreed to meet me at the Dobra Tea Room. At two o'clock, I received a text message that simply said, "Okay." Malin Élise, I could deal with. A *méchant*, wicked Élise, I wasn't sure about. I guess I would find out which one I was having a date with when we met. But we did have a date.

.oOo.

Aren arrived at the terrace of the Dobra Tea Room fifteen minutes early. He wanted to secure a table and in general, make sure the venue for his date with Élise was suitable. As he sat in a far corner of the terrace with his chair backing the glass window and facing the street, he was feeling self-confident. His barber had given him a nice steam facial along with a shave and applied special aftershave cologne. He decided not to have his hair buzz cut the way he normally did. Actually, it was the barber's daughter who cut his hair and suggested to leave it a little long but with a shape.

And so he sat in his leather bomber jacket, Italian gray wool trousers, red silk jersey, and black leather loafers, drumming his fingers a little compulsively on the bistro table while waiting for Élise. With each passing moment, he grew more confident she would come. Maybe late, but she would come. He was confident because as he sat and waited for her, he made up an algorithm to configure a profile of the woman he met on the trail. The end result was that while Élise was prickly, she was polite to a fault. Even if she decided she couldn't or wouldn't go through with the date, she would have left a message and presented her excuses. He checked his watch. It was twelve minutes past three.

Where the hell was she?

.oOo.

When Élise walked into the tea room at a quarter past three, she had a moment of panic. She scanned the room quickly and didn't see Aren amidst the chatting customers engaged in their respective private conversations. Everyone was dressed casually in jeans and shorts. Some people were even wearing flip-flops.

I'm so stupid. Where did I think I was? England? Invited to tea with the queen or something?

She didn't need to consult her watch. When she slammed the doors of the taxi, she already knew she was fifteen minutes late.

Maybe he didn't come after all. What am I doing here?

When Aren caught sight of Élise, he stood up immediately and strode toward her to pre-empt any fleeting thought she might have about running away. He kissed her on both cheeks, *bises à la française*. Élise felt a firm hand at her elbow and then the most butter-smooth cheek caressed hers. She took a good look at Aren and marveled that this was the same man who hiked along with her earlier.

"Élise, I'm glad you came," Aren said.

"Hi," she said in a soft voice that was slightly breathless. She found it hard to move. Her feet felt like they were glued to the floor.

"You look wonderful, Élise. Come, I already have a table for us out back on the terrace," Aren said.

He placed his hand on the small of her back ever so lightly. Her back was rigid with tension.

.oOo.

Aren

Élise had changed into an orange sleeveless silk dress with soft pleats in the front. The dress fell mid-calf. It had a delightful desert motif, with palm trees and camels. She had paired the dress with low-heeled black boots. Around her neck, she had a hand-painted silk scarf in hues of yellow, orange, and red. She had pushed her hair behind her ears to expose small silver hoop earrings. She looked modern and retro at the same time. I loved it. The fragrance she wore was clean and subtle, floral and woodsy. I was glad she didn't opt for an overpowering scent. As soon as I seated her at our table, I signaled the waiter to pour the hot water into the waiting teapots and bring the selection of teas and scones. In my business and traveling abroad, there wasn't anything that couldn't be discussed or resolved over a few cups of tea. "I'm so sorry I'm late," she said.

I appreciated her apology. But the truth was I was elated she actually came. I loved the care she took in getting dressed up. She was worth the wait. I reached over and placed my hand lightly on top of hers.

"You're here. That's what matters," I said. "I hope you don't mind. I went ahead and ordered a sampling of teas and some light food fare. I can ask the waiter to bring a menu if you decide you would like something else."

Élise beamed. "That's great," she said.

She had such beautiful teeth. Being toothless and forced to wear dentures was one of the things I always feared about getting older.

Maybe because I had to spend a fortune to get mine fixed, I noticed things like that.

"So, Élise, tell me about yourself," I said.

Élise glared at me. It was the kind of look a mother gives her child when the child does something rude or impolite.

"Oh," I said. "Did I say something to offend you? I just want to get to know you."

Élise's lashes did a little flutter. "Yes, I understand, that. But we just sat down and you launch into an interrogation as if I were applying for a job or those dreadful speed dates." She paused to catch her breath. "You didn't ask if I recovered from my fall or if I did something fun when I got back to the hotel. I didn't even get a chance to take in the Bohemian décor of the Tea Room." She sighed, heavily. "Maybe it was a mistake to come here, after all."

She looked like she was going to burst into tears. I couldn't have been more stunned than if she had slapped me in the face. I looked around me. For the first time, I registered just how quirky and otherworldly it was with the core yellow walls and the myriads of pictures and shelves filled with assorted teapots and cups. It had a very North African vibe—conversation starter all unto itself. She was right. The Dobra had a fantastic backstory that traced its roots all the way to Prague. There was also a gift shop where she could buy tea and ornate teapots. This was the kind of place she might like to linger in. Why do I have to launch into a speed date in a place that's designed to relax and enjoy the surroundings? I started laugh.

"If this is your way of putting me at ease, it's not working," Élise croaked.

"I'm a jerk. *Ich bin ein Dummkopf!* Forgive me. You're right. Would you believe I am so delighted you decided to join me that I forgot my manners? I just wanted to find out more about you. Would you prefer I start?"

Élise's expression softened. "No, that's all right."

We stared at each other. Her expression changed. A thought came to her.

"Do you like riddles?" she asked.

I wasn't sure where she was going with this, but I answered, "Sure."

"Good," she said. "That can be our ice breaker. That's much more interesting than exchanging our curriculum vitae, don't you think?"

"All right," I said. "Do you want to go first? I have to think about mine. You look like you have one lined up. Fire away."

"Okay," she said. "Riddle me this," she said dramatically. "A woman shoots her husband. Then she holds him underwater for over five minutes. Finally, she hangs him. But five minutes later they both go out together and enjoy a wonderful dinner together. How can this be?"

I laughed. "Honestly, Élise, for a polite person you have a serious dark side."

Élise grimaced. "Is that your final answer? You're stalling."

I vaguely remembered coming across this riddle on my favorite riddle website. Aha! Mme. Douchet and I shared something in common. We like riddles. She took a sip from her teacup and waited for me to answer.

I smiled. That connection we developed toward the end of our walk was coming back.

"All right," I said. "I have the answer." I cocked my head as if a great revelation was coming to me. Élise was laughing. "Ah yes, the woman, why she is a photographer. The shot refers to the picture she shot of her husband and developed it. She hung it up to dry, literally."

Élise applauded happily. "Bravo! *Bien Joué*," Élise said

"I have one for you," I said. "If the day before yesterday is the twenty-third, then what is the day after tomorrow?

Élise made a face. "That's too easy, Aren."

"You're stalling. Just answer the question. It's supposed to be an ice breaker, not a test."

"The twenty-seventh," she replied. "Wonderful!" I said.

The waiter came and deposited more savories along with hummus and Syrian bread. Élise was enjoying her jasmine pearl tea. At Élise's urging, I tried an oolong tie guan yin tea which had a marvelous fragrance instead of my usual Darjeeling tea.

"Thank you for suggesting this place. It's perfect," she said.

We talked about our travels, the books and movies we liked. I learned that she was a professor of languages, French and Spanish and that she taught at an independent school in the Boston area. She happily talked about her childhood in Saint Martin and Quebec, but she was a little evasive about her Haitian background. I didn't know very much about Haiti. I remember learning about the brutal dictatorship under "Papa Doc François Duvalier" and of course the voodoo. But that was forty or fifty years ago. *How old is she?*

"If you don't mind my asking, how old are you?"

She smiled wistfully. "Today is my birthday. I am fifty," she sighed.

Apparently, turning fifty was a huge deal to her. She didn't look a day over thirty-five, with the exception of her hair. In fact, it was shocking that someone who looked as young as she didn't color her hair. But her silver strands were stunning.

"That's young. I'm sixty-two, and I have a thirty-four-year-old daughter," I boasted. "Are you married? Do you have children?"

"No, I never got married, and I don't have any children." She choked on the last part. I decided not follow up with, *How is it possible you never got married?* Clearly, this was a sore subject.

"Well, happy birthday. Have you received your AARP card yet?" I teased.

She sighed. "Oh, I guess it's on the way. I'm in no rush."

"You know, Élise, I think you're going to have a fabulous future.

Just don't get so worked up about numbers." I got a tentative smile out of her.

The rest of the conversation went more smoothly. An acquaintance of mine noticed me and approached our table. I made the introductions and I got roped into a much longer conversation with the person than I intended. I pulled out a notepad from my jacket and tore a sheet of paper with roughly sketched out schematics and handed it to him.

"All right, thanks, Aren," the man said. When the acquaintance had left, I turned my attention back to Élise. She looked at me as if she had caught me in the act: of what, I had no idea.

"Is there something wrong?" I asked. "That wonderful smile of yours has thinned to a straight line on your lovely face."

She let out a fake laugh. *Uh-oh.* "What was that you wrote about me?"

"What? What are you talking about?" I said.

"While you were talking to that man, I noticed my name and some text written in columns in your notebook. I would like to see it, that paper."

I felt like I was back in elementary school getting caught passing a note in class. I fumbled inside of my jacket and pulled out my notepad.

"Let's see it," she insisted.

I handed it over to her. My handwriting was not the best, but she could make out my words.

"Are these talking points?" she asked. She looked down again on the paper and then looked up. I squirmed as she read aloud from my notes.

Two spots of color appeared on her cheeks.

"Goal three: Invite Élise over for drinks. Loosen up. Probability 75 percent. Are you some kind of nut?" she said.

"It's nothing," I said.

"Oh, it's something, all right."

I let out a breath I only realized now that I was holding.

"Élise, please. Don't get upset."

"How could I not? I'm looking at a blueprint for seduction."

"Oh! Do you think the plans are good?"

"I don't believe you. You're not even going to apologize."

I pointed to our teacups. "For what?" I asked. "I'm enjoying a drink with a good-looking woman who is a little, shall we say, self-contained. I have to proceed cautiously. I can't keep all this stuff in my head anymore. I forget."

Élise was panting—but not in a seductive way. She was still mad. "Yes, but you act like I'm some kind of machine that you can program to do what you want."

I never noticed how immaculately groomed her eyebrows were. They really did look like knitting needles. I much preferred the smile over the scowl she now had on her face.

I reached out to touch her hands. At first, she withdrew them. I looked at her and mouthed the word "Please." She hesitated. I reached further and gently pulled her hand back on the table and kept mine over hers. My gaze did not stray from hers. Such a lovely triangular-shaped face. Strong jaw. A spitfire. Change topic.

"You like flowers," I began.

She turned her head to avoid looking at me. "Was that on your list of talking points?"

I looked at my notes. Well, indeed I had listed topics of conversation. "As a matter of fact, it is. See?" I said showing her my notes. "You liked the wildflowers while we were hiking. Do you have a garden? I love gardens. My grandmother had an amazing rose garden in Armenia. I still remember it."

Élise didn't say anything at first. I kept talking about the gardens I loved to visit when I was traveling abroad. She listened and then eventually she contributed her own experiences with gardening. We were talking again. We learned we both loved to travel. We both loved Chilean wines. I talked about my work.

"So, do you specialize in solar photovoltaics or concentrated solar power technology?" she asked.

I looked at her in astonishment. "Did I get the terms wrong?"

"No, you have them down precisely. It's just uncommon that someone knows the difference. How do you know so much about photovoltaics? You're a language teacher."

"Why do you have to be so dismissive about my work? An important part of being a teacher is being curious and instilling curiosity in my students. As it happens, I was staying at a friend's house in Spain while my friends were installing solar panels. Solar technology is pretty big in Spain, as you know, and I just talked to the installers. And then later I helped out on a translation for a business proposal in Venezuela that didn't work out. Anyway, that's not important. You don't seem to have a high opinion of my intelligence, do you?"

Actually, I had the complete opposite opinion.

"Élise, I didn't mean to offend you with my comment. Most people, even professionals, have no clue about solar technology."

"I am a professional, Aren. I teach."

"Clearly, I am putting my foot in it. You know, I have classmates from MIT who have no clue about what I do. That you could even right off the bat engage with me by distinguishing between the two concepts shows you pay close attention to details. Ever think about a second career?"

"Hmmph!"

"Is that a yes?"

We both laughed. She didn't answer my question.

"It's a pity the government over-panicked about the economy and ended the subsidies," she said finally. "Spain is a fantastic market for solar technology."

I nodded in agreement. "Thank God I was able to pull out of the Solyndra venture in the United States before it tanked. I had seen the writing on the wall with Spain pulling out of the solar technology market in response to the 2008 financial crisis and the decrease in the prices of fossil fuels."

"Maybe," she said. "But I don't see the Eurozone being overly sympathetic to Spain's financial woes at the moment. Austerity is de rigueur these days, even if in the long run it's short-sighted."

"Ah, do I detect a raving liberal political bent?" I asked.

"At this point, I think it's best if I just observe on the sidelines," she replied.

"Why don't I believe you?"

Élise shrugged and then she smiled as she brought the cup to her lips to sip her tea.

Her phone rang. She stopped the conversation to look at the caller

ID. Her eyes lit up with glee in a way that she had not in reaction to me.

"Oh, do you mind if I take this call?"

I had actually switched off my phone so I could enjoy her company. I was annoyed she had actually kept hers switched on—not even on vibrate mode. I must have been flashing an intense expression because she said, "I won't be long."

"Antonio!" she said with an unreserved smile. She rambled back and forth between English and Spanish. It wasn't Spanglish. Whoever Antonio was they had some kind of bilingual relationship. Relationship. Holy smokes! She said she was traveling alone, but she never said that she was "available." Maybe the whole cat-and-mouse game between us was part of some kind of buffer for her relationship with this Antonio. "*Si, si, gracias, ciao,*" she said and then sent loud kisses over the phone forming perfect red puckers with her lips. I glared at her when she put her phone away.

"Oh, that was my friend Antonio. He was calling to wish me happy birthday," she said breezily.

"Your friend?"

"Yes."

"As in your boyfriend?" I asked.

"Not that it's any of your business, but Antonio and I have known each other for over twenty years. He is one of my oldest and dearest friends. And he lives across the hall from me."

"So is this a kind of friendship with benefits?"

She had just started to pick up her cup to take a sip of tea and then she set it back down on the saucer fixing me with a stony look.

"You know this conversation is rude and inappropriate. I don't appreciate your casting aspersions on my friend's character or mine for that matter."

She started gathering up her things.

"Oh no wait, I have done it again. I'm sorry. It's just—"

"No, Aren, it's just—not acceptable. You invited me for tea and conversation. I don't believe I have behaved in any way that would lead you to suggest I engage in tawdry conduct."

"What is so tawdry about two people enjoying each other if they're attracted to each other?" I asked.

She started to say something and then stopped and pursed her lips together. She looked at her watch—a sporty Movado stainless steel and diamond case with a leather lizard strap. Interesting. A birthday present perhaps from this Antonio?

"I should be going. There's a Pilates class at five that I'm supposed to go to."

"Élise, I would like to take you out for a birthday celebration. You'll be done by six, so why don't I pick you up at seven?"

Her eyelashes were fluttering rapidly, but she said a firm "I don't think so."

I thought about our time together. I thought about my initial schematics of trying to figure out what kind of person she was. The way she called me out over her friend Antonio suggested she was fiercely protective of people she cared about. She was someone who was polite, but direct, and didn't like to waste her time. Somehow even though I put my foot in it, she didn't just get up and leave, well—not immediately. We spent a little over an hour together. I annoyed her. I pissed her off, but she still remained engaged. Élise liked me. But she was being malin not méchant. It was my move.

Come on big guy, take your best shot. You have nothing to lose. It's now or never.

"Élise, I like you. I really like you. You're cute as hell. You're smart and you're funny. Is there something about me that displeases you? I mean besides my opinionated self."

"Ha!" she said.

"Well? Are you going to turn me down because of my age, my race, my ethnic background, my professed sexual orientation, my socio-economic status, or my profession? Or am I too metrosexual or insufficiently metrosexual? By the way, my hair is real. I'm not wearing a hairpiece. And my teeth are mine—I paid a lot for them. Oh, and

I guess I'll fess up to a knee and hip replacement. But that was only because of a nasty ski accident I had a few years ago."

She gasped. "*Bon Dieu!*" She fluttered her eyelashes. I waited for her answer.

She looked at me. Really looked at me. I was grateful for all the sprucing up I did for the date. Yes, indeed it was a date and a kind of job interview. Was she going to invite me to the second round of interviews? But for what job? Even I couldn't really answer that question. I liked her. I probably, no, I really wanted to have sex with her. I just had the feeling we would really connect. A guy can dream, right? I relaxed the muscles in my face and unclenched my teeth. Wow, I was nervous. I didn't honestly know what she would say.

"Aren, I came up here for a retreat. I'm not interested in well, you know. You seem like a nice man."

That should have been the end of it. Why was I insisting? I had no fucking clue. I was readjusting my algorithm in my head. The probability of this woman having sex with me was dropping precipitously below 30 percent. That was being optimistic. At that moment the frosty vibes she was sending out were formidable. Yet, I continued to press her.

"Come on, it's your birthday? What, you would prefer to sit around at the hotel with people you don't know? Eat tasteless vegetarian food and bland carrot cake for dessert while watching a slideshow on the Missisquoi tribe basket weaving techniques instead of coming out with me?"

Ah, the corners of her eyes were crinkling. "Actually, they're going to offer a lecture on woodland flower arranging."

I burst out in laughter. She smiled sheepishly. "Come on, Élise. Say yes. Please."

"I don't know, Aren," she sighed.

I signaled the waiter to bring the check. I folded my napkin and placed it on the table. I fixed her a hard look. "Well?"

She rolled her eyes. I laughed in triumph.

"Fine," she said. "But you have to be patient with me. I don't sleep with men on the first date," she said with deadpan humor.

I did my Groucho Marx eyebrow routine. "Ah, there's hope, then," I said. "We got through our first date. At least you will consider sleeping with me on our next date. Progress."

We both laughed.

"Come on, let me drive you back and then we can figure out the logistics for our date tonight."

"So more than just tea and conversation?" she said as I put money on the table to pay for the tea and steered her out of the building and toward my recently detailed Porsche Boxster.

"Let's just see where things go, okay? No demands. No promises."

"You listen to Pat Benatar?"

"I'm surprised you know who she is."

"You're incorrigible," she said.

"I try. It keeps me young," I said. "Sixty-two is not so young," she teased.

"Well, didn't you hear? Sixty is the new forty-five."

She laughed. Really laughed. "You're sixty-two," she said. I shrugged.

As I opened the door to my sports car, she gasped.

"I don't believe you. You're involved in renewable energy technology and you drive a gas-guzzling sports car?"

I smiled sheepishly. "What can I say? I'm complicated."

I stood back and watched Élise position herself in the passenger seat and then swing her long shapely legs inside. As I shut the door, I caught a brief moment when she winced in pain and reflexively rubbed her knees, and let out a long breath.

When I got into the car, I took her hand and kissed it. "Thank you," I said.

She looked at me and blew a raspberry. I laughed and then turned on the ignition.

.oOo.

Élise

I sat in the Jacuzzi for a few minutes after my Pilates class. The stretching and then the heated water soothed my aching muscles. My knees still felt a little tender, but there was no swelling. Thank goodness! Fanny called me as I was getting dressed for dinner with Aren. I didn't fill her in on the details about my meeting with Aren. I just said I ran into a friend who invited me for dinner. She didn't buy that story completely, but she was happy that I had an excuse to get dressed up and look glamorous on my birthday. We talked about hair and make-up. I sent her a picture of my outfit on my phone. She approved of my flowing patterned silky trousers and a purple ruffled top with long bell sleeves. I felt happy. She picked up on it and said, "I guess that hiking spa has done you some good. I'm glad. Love you," she said.

I was feeling despondent in the months, weeks, and days leading up to my birthday. I was crying myself to sleep every night. Even today before I decided to join Aren at the Dobra Tea Room, I had a good cry and indulged in self-pity. And now at the close of my fiftieth birthday, I was feeling okay. My life didn't change dramatically when I turned fifty. It was the same as it ever was like Talking Heads says in their song "Once in a Lifetime." Maybe I would have another meltdown when I turned sixty but for now, I was feeling a little more hopeful about the future.

Was Aren in my future? I had no idea. I could see us spending some time together during my stay in Vermont, but after that? I couldn't imagine how we could continue any kind of relationship once I returned to my life in Boston. But meeting him did force me to evaluate and re-evaluate what I want to do with the rest of my life. Is fifty too old to change careers? I would never leave teaching to return to my life as a college professor. I did the right thing by leaving. Now that my mother was gone, my life was in Boston. Fanny and Antonio were my family. I couldn't imagine moving far away from them.

I looked at the digital clock in my room. Aren would be waiting outside in fifteen minutes. I went to the mirror and applied kohl and mascara to my eyes and shimmering bronzer to my cheeks. I spritzed a new perfume I bought, Jo Malone Velvet and Rose Oud. Just the name of the perfume made me feel exotic and beautiful. I took a final look at myself in the mirror. I felt elegant and comfortable. When I passed my fellow spa guests on my way out, I ignored any comments they made about my not joining them for the evening's activities. I had much more interesting plans. Thank God!

.oOo.

Aren took Élise to a trendy Italian restaurant for dinner. If the date at the tearoom was a little piquant, dinner was much more calm and relaxing. He let her do most of the talking. It was safer that way, he gambled. He need not have worried. Élise was just thrilled to be going out and enjoying a pleasant evening. She made it a point to be extra charming and gracious.

.oOo.

Aren

After dinner, I took Élise to Woodstock for an evening of stargazing. During our date at the Dobra, she had mentioned how her grandfather used to sit with her and teach her about the stars when she was a little girl living in Saint Martin before settling in Canada. I thought bringing her to the park would be a good way of earning her goodwill. I brought a warm blanket. I wanted to set the right mood. Maybe for Élise "No," meant "I could change my mind." The evening temperature was mild and thankfully not windy. I loved the way the breeze played with her hair without really disturbing it and the way the moonlight made her skin shimmer. She was all smiles.

We sat huddled together looking up at the night sky along the banks of Kedron Brook at Teagle's Landing in the quaint village of Woodstock. The fragrance she was wearing was warm and inviting. She let me hold her hands. Kisses weren't on offer—yet, perhaps. Oh, well. "You know I remember my nanny, MoMo, telling me stories about the stars," Élise recounted. "The best part was that there were variations. I could choose which one I felt like hearing."

"Do you remember any of the stories?" I asked.

"There was one about the sun and the moon. I think she got this story from my grandfather who traveled a lot to Africa as a diplomat."

"So tell me."

"It's kind of sick."

"Oh now, I'm all ears."

Élise smiled, maintaining her gaze upward. "Well, once upon a time the Sun and the Moon were good friends and they shined equally. They even vacationed together with their families."

I started to laugh. Even in the dark I could tell she was scowling. "I'm sorry. Continue."

"As I was saying, the Sun and the Moon were best buddies. The Sun says to the Moon: 'Hey, let's go swimming in the river.' The Moon agrees. They couldn't both go in at the same time."

"Why not?" I asked.

"I don't know. I'm just telling you the story."

"Well, the details don't make sense."

"Do you want to hear the story or not?"

"Sorry. Proceed," I said.

"They agreed to take turns getting into the water to assure each family had privacy."

"Why do they need privacy? They're friends."

"Are you listening?"

"Yes, yes. Go ahead."

"Anyway, the Sun says to the Moon, 'When you see the water boiling, you'll know we're in the water.' The Sun takes his family upstream, but doesn't get in. Instead, he tells his family to cut dry branches, set them on fire, and cast them into the river. The Moon sees the steaming water and thinks the Sun has been in the water and gets in. But of course, the water wasn't really boiling. When the Moon comes out, he's cold and pale. He didn't get the benefit of the boiling water. He's angry with the Sun and swears revenge. Sometime later when there is a great famine, the Moon says since there is no more food to feed their families, the Moon and the Sun should kill them. The Sun says, 'Okay.'"

"What kind of half-ass story is this? Your nanny told you this story? I'd fire her ass," I said.

Élise sighed. "Let me finish, all right. Now, the plan was that the Moon would go upstream and kill his family. When the Sun would see blood in the river that would be the signal to kill his family."

"Oh, God!" I muttered.

"The Moon goes upstream, but instructs his family to throw red clay into the river to trick the Sun. The Sun sees the red river and kills his family. And that's why the Sun is alone when he rises and sets, but the very pale Moon is surrounded by his wives and many children."

"Is the moral of the story that the moon is a Mormon? What kind of crazy story is that? I cannot believe your nanny told you this story."

"Well, she wanted to explain why the moon appeared with the stars."

"Oh, you poor child. No wonder you're so messed up."

"Ha!" Élise said.

We continued to snuggle and enjoy each other's company. I caught a glimpse of a falling star, but it was gone before I could warn Élise. I didn't even have time to make a wish, not that I would know what to wish for. But I kissed Élise's forehead.

"If you could wish on a star and change the course of your life, what would you like to do?" I asked.

"Hmm, you know, I often wish my life had taken a different turn. But once I start thinking about changing certain things, I don't like what I have to give up. So maybe I wouldn't change the past. As for the future, I think I would love to work in a humanitarian organization and do development work. I like the idea of working to improve fair trade in the third world or helping women start companies. I would love to be able to use my contacts or write grants to get funding for worthy projects. After the civil war in El Salvador, I spent a summer working with the Fenastras labor union helping to organize field workers."

"Wow, why doesn't that surprise me? Why didn't you pursue that?" A faraway look flashed across her face and then it was gone. "I don't know," she said. I guess I wasn't passionate enough about it. Maybe that's why I would have to wish on a star to make it happen now. How about you?"

"If I want to do something, I just do it. I don't wish on stars."

"I see. Well, that frees up your mind from useless longing, huh?"

"Élise, did you really study to become a French and Spanish teacher?"

"Well, not exactly. I thought I would end up working as an interpreter and translator at an international organization."

"Ah, again, that seems like you. Where did you study?"

"I did my undergraduate work in Montreal, and then I went for a master's in Geneva at the interpreter school. At the time I had a huge interest in media. Maybe more so than politics."

"So what happened?"

"It's not so important. I received a full-paid scholarship to pursue my doctorate at NYU. My academic adviser encouraged me to go into teaching. It didn't turn out so bad, actually."

"That's all you have to say about your chosen career? That it didn't turn out so badly?"

She shrugged her shoulders in an exaggerated way with her open palm showing.

"You're funny," I said.

Élise struck me as someone who was capable of doing extraordinary things. I had a hard time believing she was content to be a teacher. If she had said, principal, headmistresss, or dean of students, that I could see. Élise and I were having a truly lovely evening together. Whatever

I thought about her career ambitions or lack of them, it didn't deserve any further consideration—at least not now. I was thankful for the fresh crisp night air that kept Élise close to me. I loved the feel of her silk blouse and the smell of her hair and perfume. She did something with her eyes that made her enchanting. I traced the contours of her face with my finger. I gently lifted her chin to bring our faces closer. I felt her soft warm breath on my face. Her eyes were closed, but her lashes were fluttering. I paused and then kissed the tip of her nose. She smiled. *So far so good.* Shall I go *for it?* When I moved my lips to kiss hers, she jerked her head back. She didn't do it violently, but she made it clear she didn't want to be kissed. I sighed and then moved my head to look into her eyes.

WTF? All right. Round 1 goes to Élise. *I'm gonna try for Round 2.*

"Maybe you should bring me back home… now," Élise said. I touched her shoulder. "Do you really want to go?" I asked.

"I—Maybe it's the best that way. I don't want to complicate things."

Things are already getting complicated mighty fast. "Okay," I said.

She released her hold on the blanket and started to get up. We packed up our things and started walking to the car side by side rather than hand in hand the way we did when we arrived.

Just before I put the keys in the ignition, I turned to Élise and brushed her cheek with my fingertips.

"Why don't you come over for coffee? I even have a little birthday dessert. It's a chocolate cupcake."

She laughed.

"Aren, you're a sweet man. I—"

"Come on. Say yes. You think you should say no. But evidence shows when you say yes to me, you have fun. Go on, admit it."

"Admit what? I have spent the evening with a pushy engineer?"

I laughed. "Oh, I'm not so bad. Besides, you said you're interested in green technology. I want to show you my cottage. And I'll make you a killer Turkish coffee with cardamom."

"Aren—"

"Please, Élise. You know, you're terrible. I have never had to beg a woman for anything as much as I have had to plead with you for the simplest thing. I'm not going to ravish you or compromise your modesty, okay? Scout's honor."

"Were you a boy scout?"

"No."

"So, why should I accept your scout's honor?"

"Oh, it's just an expression."

"Yeah, well—"

.oOo.

Élise

I accepted Aren's invitation to his cottage. How did I go from being rescued from a misadventure on a hiking trail to a delightful tea date to stargazing to following a man back to his place? What was I doing? What am I doing? Honestly, I don't know. What door was I opening? Aren always referred to his "cottage." So I was shocked when we drove up the winding gravel drive and stopped in front of an imposing three-story wood, steel, stone, and glass modern house. The entrance had heavy double wooden doors inspired by an Armenian monastery as Aren would later explain. Each door panel was carved with a full-length half cross. Together when closed, the doors formed a single *khichari* or medieval Armenian Christian cross-stone. I loved the idea that the doors separated the outside world and provided an entrance to a sacred space: Aren's home.

I was learning from our conversations that Aren was very proud of his Armenian heritage. I probably won brownie points (not that I was looking for any), for my knowledge of Armenian culture. It wasn't in-depth, but I knew about the 1915 genocide of Armenians in Turkey. I could name a few Armenians in French and American literature and culture like the French singer Charles Aznavour, tennis player Andre Agassi, Cher, best-selling American author Chris Bohjalian, and Pulitzer Prize winner playwright and author William Saroyan.

We had a vigorous debate about whether Steve Jobs, the founder of Apple/Mac, was Armenian.

"But his biological parents were Syrian," I said.

"Yes, but the people who adopted him, okay his adoptive mother, was Armenian," Aren said with pride.

The way Aren passionately advocated for the significance of the Armenian heritage of Steve Jobs' adoptive mother and the influence it had on him was endearing.

Aren's cottage had a very utilitarian feel to it, similar to the designs of American architect Frank Lloyd Wright because of the abundance of steel, glass and concrete, solar panels, and rainwater catch basins. But inside the rooms were oriented to maximize natural light and views of the lake and hillside and radiant heated marble flooring. The soaring ceilings were paneled with maple. I loved the wraparound decks, the outdoor kitchen, the intimate blue stone patio, and the lush moonlight garden.

The décor brought warmth and personality to the cottage. It was an eclectic mix of Scandinavian style and Armenian design with Kilim weave patterned rugs and cushions, smatterings of Jerusalem pottery, little touches of Morocco with a Moroccan leather pouf, raffia potted plant covers, and modern lighting. There were lots of little touches but overall, the feeling was minimalist and uncluttered. The kitchen was white and gray except for a large colorful mosaic tile mural behind the stove and the sink and the high gloss polished painted red floor.

I didn't want to tour Aren's bedroom. I didn't want to give him any ideas. But he insisted. The master bedroom had a magnificent balcony overlooking a private courtyard with a water feature. *How wonderful!* The covers of the bed were turned down. *Is he expecting me to spend the night?* I tried to play it cool and restrict comments about the bedroom to neutral topics like, "Oh, I love the wood flooring!"

After the tour, we shared an espresso with cardamom out on the patio. We sat on the ornate sofa in front of the fireplace.

I stood up suddenly. "Oh, will you excuse me for a moment?" I asked.

"Sure," Aren said. "You remember where it is on the first floor, right?

I nodded. Fortunately, the cottage had an open floor plan, so even if I didn't remember exactly where the bathroom was, I would be able to find it easily. I really needed to relieve myself so I didn't remember switching on the lights. They were on when I entered the bathroom. When I went to flush the toilet, I realized the handle was not where I expected it to be. It wasn't on the top of the tank or on the side. I started to panic. Thank God it was only pee! I looked around to see if there was a chain like with Turkish toilets. Finally, I noticed a panel with different buttons. I guess I overlooked it at first because I thought it was another light switch. I pressed one button and a wand came out magically and spritzed water inside the toilet bowl, but it didn't flush. Another button I pressed sprayed deodorizer.

The knock on the door startled me. "Élise, are you all right?" Aren asked.

Oh God. How embarrassing. Why does he have to have a complicated toilet?

"Oh, how does the toilet work? There are so many buttons."

"Yes, I should have said something about my newfangled Japanese toilet. You can flush it manually by pressing the top button just behind the lid. And if you follow the diagrams, you can activate some of the other bidet functions."

I pressed another button and it sounded like a tornado had sucked up the entire contents of the toilet bowl. I backed away instinctively. And then there was a series of whirrs and buzzes that sanitized the bowl. I screamed "Ay!" I could hear Aren laughing on the other side of the door. My face felt like it would turn to coal. It was burning.

"Okay. I think I figured everything out now," I said totally mortified. "You can go away now."

I waited until I could hear Aren walk away. I went to the sink and turned on the faucet. At least the sink operated in a straightforward manner. I hoped the water could drown out Aren's laughter. I took a moment to check my face in the mirror. I looked normal, but I felt so awkward. I did a final check to make sure I was leaving the bathroom in good order and then I walked out. The light switched off as soon as I opened the door.

"So how did you like the bidet functions? Cool, huh?"

"Fine," I said quickly, wanting to change the subject. "You're funny," Aren said.

I rolled my eyes. *He really thinks that was funny? Good grief!*

"I'm sorry, Élise. Don't be mad. Come sit down. I'll put on some music. You know when I was growing up in Chicago, my parents always had dance parties. Even though I grew up listening to the Rolling Stones and the Beatles, I still associate bossa nova with fun and intimacy."

A sultry flamenco guitar instrumental started to play. I was still a little grumpy from Aren laughing at me, but the uplifting tones of the guitar shifted my mood.

"I like it," I said. I had heard this music before.

"Isn't this Govi?" I said. "I can't think of the title of the song." Aren held out his hand to me.

"Come dance with me," he said.

I stood there at first not completely registering what he said and then I felt his right-hand press against my upper back, pulling me close to him face to face. But we maintained an open frame. We glided around the patio in a box step rumba pattern with promenade walks, chassés, and spins. Sometimes Aren threw in a drag side step and appel to show off. My goodness! He knew how to dance. Aren leaned forward and whispered in my ear: "The song is 'Rising in Love' from Govi's *Seventh Heaven* album."

We continued to dance. It was a test for both of us—getting a sense of how our bodies responded to rhythm, I suppose. But I was actually enjoying the dancing. We weren't pressed up close to each other. I still had my personal space, my frame, even within the partner dance. Aren was studying me. Maybe he was making sure that I was enjoying myself? I smiled back at him.

"Hmmm," Aren said, "how about some Leonard Cohen,"

he announced, suddenly, breaking away from me to change the music selection.

"Wait! What are you doing?" I complained.

"Ah, sweet Élise," he whispered. "I fear you need some more direct cues."

"What?" I said.

Heavily synthesized strings with a strong beat of the drum began. The gravely and growling bass alto of Leonard Cohen's opening lines of "I'm Your Man" started.

"But why, Aren?" I asked. I was annoyed that he was changing the music. I wasn't a big fan of Leonard Cohen.

If you want a lover
I'll do anything you ask me to
And if you want another kind of love
I'll wear a mask for you

"Oh, brother," I groaned. "What?"

"He can't sing! He's like Dylan. It's awful!"

"You young'uns are all alike. No appreciation for complex music. He's a genius."

"Well, I didn't say he wasn't a genius. Just that he can't sing."

That open frame we maintained while dancing was gone. Now Aren pulled me into a tight embrace and we were slow dancing. Our posture changed. My arms were around his neck and his arms were around my waist. I had a flash image of the senior dances I had chaperoned over the years. *Where's our chaperone?* Aren's lips were pressed to a spot just above my brows. I could feel him firmly applying pressure on my back bringing me closer to him, so I could feel him and the contours of his body. I resisted. I didn't want to melt into him. I danced as if there were a plane of glass between us.

And if you want to work the street alone
I'll disappear for you
If you want a father for your child
Or only want to walk with me a while
Across the sand
I'm your man

We kept dancing in a closed position, our lower bodies pressing against each other. Things were moving so fast. Yet the feel of his arms around me was really nice. I had forgotten what it was like to be in a man's arms even for a dance, albeit an intimate dance. And then we swayed as one to Leonard's hypnotic "By the River's Dark."

By the rivers dark
Where I could not see
Who was waiting there
Who was hunting me.

Did I say Leonard Cohen couldn't sing? I listened to the exquisite poetry of the lyrics. He had a lush female backing vocal which perfectly complemented his raspy voice. It was beautiful. If I wasn't a fan of Leonard Cohen before, I was now. I thought for a moment maybe Aren would succeed in getting me. Oh no!

I could feel myself falling into Aren's seduction trap. And then the music switched to the popular bands of the 1980s. I liked Spandau Ballet very much, but it was far from hypnotic. I don't think Aren did this on purpose. The spell was broken, however, and I was grateful to escape Aren's trap. Billy Ocean's "The Going Get Tough" started to play and we weren't touching anymore. We recreated our favorite disco moves and lip-synched to our heart's content. We laughed. That was good.

The drive to my hotel began in silence. I didn't really feel like talking. Aren asked if he could put on some opera. He let me choose which one, and I chose Mozart's *Magic Flute*. With the grand overture of the Mozart opera, the music filled the car with buzzing energy. We didn't talk, but we listened together.

When Aren drove up to the entrance of the hotel, Pamina, the kidnapped daughter of the Queen of the Night was just about to begin the love duet with Papagaeno, the bird catcher. I didn't immediately get out of the car because I wanted to listen to the duet. Aren let me have my driveway moment. When the duet was over, I kissed him on both cheeks, bises à la française—and said good night. I pulled the handle to get out of the car.

"Élise?" Aren called out. I turned to look at him. "Yes?" I answered.

"I would like to see you again tomorrow. Is it a date?"

I spent a truly lovely time with Aren, but it didn't really occur to me that there would be a second date, especially since we didn't have sex. That was the whole point of his seduction, right? My holiday would be ending soon. If Aren had been aggressive, the answer would be an automatic no. But he was really sweet with me. I liked him. I started to chew on my lip nervously. I wasn't sure what to do. I thought about how miserable I had been before today. Aren was right. When I went along with his suggestions, I didn't regret them. I always enjoyed myself. We had known each other less than twenty-four hours and already we had a pattern. I paused to offer a small prayer of thanks to The Lady and Bon Dieu.

"All right, Aren. I would like that too. I have my morning Pilates class—"

"No worries. Three o'clock at the Dobra Tea Room? I'll pick you up."

.oOo.

Aren

I was learning Élise wasn't that malin and not méchant. I wouldn't say she was shy, but, sexually liberated she was not. I was beginning to wonder if she was just coming out of a nun lifestyle. I exaggerate but not by much. I liked her. I think she liked me. I just couldn't figure out how to crack that shell of hers. *Why do I bother?* Maybe it was simply that I was enjoying the effort. To be around Élise, I have to be alert and on my toes. I truly enjoyed her company. There was no doubt in my mind that if she opened up, we could have a really good time together. But I was running out of time. She would be going back home to Boston in a few days.

.oOo.

Élise

Aren brought me to his Zen tea garden by the lake. It was initially designed as a pool house. Inside there was a cozy fireplace and full kitchen and bar and a Jacuzzi. We were playing Scrabble on the low Japanese coffee table sitting on floor cushions. Aren was studying the remaining letters on his tile grid. This was the fourth round. I had won the first two rounds and Aren won the last round. We had only known each other for less than forty-eight hours and here I was sitting across from him in this lovely place playing a game, listening to music, as if it was our routine. I didn't want to get used to this feeling. I reminded myself this was just a pleasant evening—a nicer alternative to hanging out alone at the resort. Of course, Aren was pushing for more. Was I playing with fire?

"It's your move, Aren."

"I know. I'm thinking," he said. He pulled out his phone. It wasn't immediately clear to me what he was doing until I caught the Google Search engine logo.

"Aren, that's cheating," I said.

As annoying as Aren could be with his pushiness, it was entertaining to watch him justify his mischievousness. His eyebrows went up and down and the cleft in his chin seemed a little more prominent.

"Hey, it's just us. We can make up our own rules," he said with an impish grin. "And we didn't expressly forbid the use of a dictionary. So, there ya go."

He set out the letters on the table to form a word I had never seen before. I gave him a serious eye roll in response.

"Aren, 'cucoloris' is not a word," I scoffed. "Oh, yes it is."

I narrowed my eyes. "Really?" I challenged.

"Some linguist you are. It means a perforate material used to break up light."

"Is this a technical word?"

"Maybe."

"In what language?" I asked suspiciously. He smiled with a sheepish grin. "Klingon."

I clicked my tongue. "You're an ass! You do know that, right?"

I won that round. "I win. I win," I said doing a seated end zone dance.

"Yeah, yeah. I let you win out of politeness."

Aren picked up the remote to change the music selection.

"Do you mind if I cut the opera short? I want to listen to some jazz. Herbie Hancock, okay?"

"Oh, okay," I said. I started packing away the Scrabble board and tile pieces. A familiar repetitive jazz piano riff began to play.

I smiled. "Oh, I like this one. I used to hear it a lot on National Public Radio as background. I didn't realize this was Herbie Hancock."

"Well, now you know," Aren said. "I thought with you being an island girl you might appreciate 'Cantaloupe Island.'"

Aren could be painfully corny sometimes. I think that's what I liked about him. He was shamelessly corny and annoying when he wanted to be. I sat back against the sofa, still sitting on the cushions. He pulled his cushion over next to mine. I didn't understand at first what he was trying to do until I found myself being pulled into the V-shape between his legs, flush against his chest and I could feel his bulge. I froze.

"Aren," I said.

"Why are you surprised? I'm attracted to you. We've got sexy music, a fire, we're alone—"

Panic. That's all that went through my mind. What had I let myself in for?

"Relax. We're just cuddling. I like touching you. It doesn't have to go any further than what you feel comfortable doing. All right?"

I let out a sigh. It was like the moment your head is still above water. The bottom dips suddenly and you take in some water. Time to hold my breath and tread water. Aren tightened his arms around my waist and waited until I stopped being so stiff. He was playing with my hair. I had tied it back in a ponytail with a scarf. He loosened the scarf.

"Wh-what are you doing?"

"Relax. I just want to play with your hair."

"N-no."

"Why not?"

"I don't know. Except for my hairdresser and my acupuncturist, no one touches my hair."

"Well, somehow, I think massaging your head is way more pleasant than having the acupuncturist stick scary needles into your head like a pin cushion. I'm not hurting you, am I?"

"No. It's just—I'm not used to it."

"Just relax and listen to the music."

.oOo.

Aren

I was really digging the clarinet solo on Herbie Hancock's "Butterfly" track: sexy, smooth, scintillating. If I had said those words out loud, would Élise have poked fun at my use of the word "dig"? Probably. But it made so much more sense than saying "I like that solo." So what? To say Butterfly "sends me" was perhaps the most apt description of what I felt. And right then with a divinely scented creature in my arms, well, she was also sending me somewhere like a hit from a good joint.

Like floating on a crescent moon and waving to the stars passing by while. I took her hand and played with her fingers and drew designs on the palms of her hands to make her giggle. My hands then traveled to her feet. They were bare. She was sporting a clean pale blue pedicure with decorative stencils on the tips. Not that I cared one way or the other about pedicure designs, still, I thought, *What really pretty feet.* Maybe it was the silver curly wire toe ring on her second toe that I thought was so sexy. Maybe she sensed my arousal because she started to withdraw her feet.

"I'm just giving you a massage. You walked a lot today."

"Yes. But maybe I'll just sign up for a massage tomorrow at the club after the hike."

"Why don't you come out with me tomorrow?"

"For tea?"

"No, for a hike and then we can make dinner here. Come on. It'll be fun."

"Oh, I don't know. I paid for a hiking experience and spa food."

"Then you shall have it, my lady. Plus, I'm giving you extra special attention."

"I think that's the problem," she said.

"No, you know what your problem is? You're ungrateful." Élise laughed. I pouted.

"Aren, what will people say?"

"Who cares? You're not going to see them anyway."

"I don't know. It doesn't seem right."

"You know, I'm not going to say anything. I'm going to trust you're going to do the right thing."

Élise cocked her brow. "And by right thing you mean I ditch my group and come with you."

"I'm not saying anything. I'm just proposing that you do your qigong thing in the morning, take a pleasant morning nature walk, have your breakfast, do your yoga, get a spa treatment, and then come out with me. We'll go hiking in the afternoon and we'll cook together."

"I feel like you've taken over my life."

Ah! She was finally catching on. I shrugged exaggeratedly. I looked at my watch. It was eleven o'clock.

"All right, I'll drive you home so you can get your beauty sleep."

.oOo.

Élise

When Aren drove up to the hotel entrance, he insisted that I wait so he could open the door for me. I laughed thinking this was so unnecessary. But I stayed seated and waited for Aren to get out of the car and open the passenger door for me.

"Thank you," I said.

He hooked his arm through mine and said "You're welcome" while escorting me to the door.

It was midnight. We were both tired.

"Are you going to be all right driving back?" I said. Even to my ears, my accent was more pronounced. I needed to go to bed.

Aren then flashed a smile. "If I say I'm too exhausted to drive home, does that mean I can spend the night with you?"

"Ah, non."

"Sheesh! So, does no mean yes in your language?" Aren asked. "No means no, Aren. But we could see if there's an available room for you. I feel bad. You're tired."

"Ugh! I'll be all right."

"Call me, okay? Let me know you got back safely."

"If you're really concerned, you'd make space for me in your bed."

"No, Aren," I said firmly.

Aren pouted. "Fine. Although for the record, I have no objections to spending the night with a woman who snores."

"Oh!"

"It's true, isn't it?"

I shook my head in exasperation. "Good night, Aren," I said. Aren laughed. "I'll see you tomorrow?"

I placed my hand gently on his arm. "Just call me to make sure you're okay. I don't care what time it is."

Aren pulled me close to him. He pressed a kiss on my cheeks. "À demain, j'espère. See you tomorrow, I hope."

I smiled. Aren released me and I walked inside of the hotel.

.oOo.

Élise

On the third day of my spa holiday, I ditched my group and went hiking with Aren. He took me to the Railroad Bed Trail near Hancock.

"It's a good general level six-mile trail," he said.

"Six miles! I don't know, Aren, I think that's a bit ambitious for me. I mean the Precipice Trail was only two miles and I almost killed myself."

Aren rolled his eyes. "Honey, don't exaggerate. You can do this." He made a picnic for us. We stopped at a store along the way so that

I could pick up "proper" hiking shoes and then off we went. No drama. I made it. Afterward, we went kayaking—my first time.

.oOo.

Aren

Over a candlelight dinner at my cottage, we enjoyed a hearty mushroom risotto with arugula salad, marinated lamb kebobs, and a lemon olive oil cake with fresh berries. We followed the recipe from the spa cookbook she purchased from the resort. We ate in the kitchen instead of the dining room at Élise's insistence. I liked that. It made it seem like this was an ordinary thing: for me and Élise to enjoy a meal together. She raised her wine glass to mine.

"Thank you so much, Aren. I have had the best three days in such a long time."

There was something about the way she said it that made me sad. She kept so much to herself, which gave her a very dignified air. Yet it was clear to me she carried a lot of regrets. I reached out, stroked her hands, brought them to my lips, and kissed them.

.oOo.

Élise

Sitting in Aren's kitchen, I felt as if we had known each other for a long time. I felt at home, like I belonged there. In some ways, it felt more like home than my apartment or my classroom. I felt at peace in Aren's cottage.

Aren was looking at me strangely.

"Oh, did I say something wrong?" I asked.

He reached out for my hands. I smiled. He stroked my hands, brought them to his lips, and kissed them. I froze.

"Élise, are you going to spend the night with me?" he whispered. I let out a huge sigh. And then I made up my mind.

"No," I said.

"Why not?" he asked. His tone wasn't whiny or petulant. My answer apparently didn't make any sense to him, I guess.

"I don't feel right about it."

"Why not?" he insisted.

I could feel myself getting emotional. I was on the verge of tears. "Aren, you have been really wonderful to me. But I'm too old—I can't—" I couldn't think of anything else to say. "Nonsense. Are you afraid I won't satisfy you?"

I could feel the blood draining from my face. I started to cough. I drained my water glass. In all of my life no one had ever asked me that question. It's not even a question I asked myself. *Oh, I feel so uncomfortable. This is too intense.*

"Why are you so shocked? You're a beautiful woman. Why wouldn't you be concerned about how much pleasure I can give you?"

That sound when the arm of the record player skips, that's what my head felt like. I stood up. My legs felt wobbly.

"Maybe I should go."

Somehow, I managed to grab my things and just leave.

I didn't realize I was standing at Aren's car until I felt his arms around me. I was sobbing uncontrollably.

"Élise, talk to me," Aren said.

I couldn't look at him. I had so many emotions and thoughts I couldn't name. I just wanted to find a hole and crawl into it and cover myself up so no one could find me.

"Élise, when was the last time someone touched you?"

I tried to step out of his arms, but he held onto me even more tightly. I dried my tears and tried my best to speak calmly. *I didn't want to answer his questions. Why does everything have to be about sex?*

"No, Aren. I—I should go," I said.

He still held onto me. He buried his face in my hair and then he lowered his face to kiss me, to comfort me, I guess.

"Élise, tell me. How long?"

"I don't know. A long time ago, okay?" I snapped.

"It's taken you a long time to get over this guy, huh? I'm sorry he shattered your confidence. I wish you knew how beautiful you are."

I wept for a thousand reasons. Aren wanted me to confess a boogeyman that no longer existed, at least not the way he imagined. Fresh tears started streaming down my face. I watched Aren catch droplets on his fingertips. We stood there silently.

"Come on, I'll take you back."

Beethoven's *Moonlight Sonata* played as Aren drove me to the resort. I selected it. We didn't speak. We drove in silence back to my hotel. Aren parked in front of the entrance and got out of the car quickly so he could open the door for me. We stood there under a full moon, facing each other, serenaded by cicadas. He caressed my face tenderly. I didn't trust myself to speak.

"Élise, when you get back to Boston, I'd like to see you."

I sighed deeply. "Why? We want and need different things."

Aren cupped my chin gently and gazed into my eyes. He kissed my nose.

"Maybe I want a chance to meet you in your territory. I have been pushing to have things play out my way. So let's try meeting up in Boston? You'll have home court advantage. There is something good between us that is more than friendship. I want to have another shot at exploring that."

I sniffled. "I don't know Aren," I said wearily.

"I have some good friends in Boston. We get together to go sailing and take in some 'culture' from time to time." He held up his hands in air quotes to emphasize culture.

"Are you teaching during the summer? What are you doing?"

"I'll be working on a paper I need to deliver in the summer. I will also teach a summer translation class at BU. I have projects. I'll be around," I said noncommittally.

"Okay. We know how to contact each other, then." I nodded.

Aren leaned toward me to kiss my lips. I could feel my back growing stiff. I didn't want to kiss him that way. Mercifully, he kissed my cheek instead.

"Goodbye, Élise,"

"Goodbye," I said.

I walked straight through the entrance of the resort building. I didn't turn around to wave goodbye.

CHAPTER 3

❖❖❖❖❖❖❖❖❖❖❖❖❖❖❖❖❖❖❖❖❖❖❖❖❖❖❖❖❖❖❖

SO, CALL ME MAYBE?

❖❖❖❖❖❖❖❖❖❖❖❖❖❖❖❖❖❖❖❖❖❖❖❖❖❖❖❖❖❖❖

Aren

To the exasperation of my daughter Lily, I had refused to join Facebook. I was an intrepid holdout. "What a waste of time," I complained.

I tried reaching Élise on her cell phone. She would talk for two minutes and then suddenly announce she was on her way to some place or to a class whether to teach or attend and had to hang up, promising vaguely, "I'll catch up to you later." She rarely called me back. Finally, I broke down and joined Facebook and friended her. She accepted immediately—after the tenth consecutive request, I might add.

We exchanged casual emails and information on Facebook. I saw the travel photos she had described for me of her trips to Kenya, Senegal, Cameroun, Thailand, India, Chile, Argentina—even Cuba. I read some of her published books and articles on comparative literature, and she read some of my work on photovoltaics and sustainable development in the emerging market.

After one week of exchanging polite texts and Facebook posts with Élise, I was fed up. But God decided to be nice to me and threw me a lifeline. In early June, my friends in Boston invited me to go to David Maxwell's Maximum Blues Band performance at the Regattabar Lounge in Cambridge, Massachusetts. Perfect! Now I had to figure out how to get Élise's immediate attention. If I emailed her, she could very well ignore the email or wait forever to respond. I certainly wasn't going to ask her out on Facebook for the world to see. I could have called, but I was afraid of an immediate rejection. Hmm, texting. In general, I got more of an immediate response from her if I sent a text message. Besides, she could think about the message—and spare my feelings. So I sent a brief text to say I was coming to Boston to see friends and that I would love to see her if she was free. I wasn't a great fan of texting. I hated pressing those tiny keys to compose a message in shorthand text speak. Ugh! The things I had to do for this woman.

É—*Coming down to Boston 2 see friends this weekend. Would love 2 see you. R u free?*

Her response:

s

I paused for a moment.

Is that a yes? I wrote.

Yes, Aren. Ok, she texted back.

We made a date to visit the Museum of Science. Not my idea of a fun date. I would have preferred something more romantic, frankly, or at least not overrun with noisy children. But I was happy she was willing to see me.

Afterward, we strolled along the Public Garden. When we walked out of the Metro T Station, we walked side by side just chatting about the weather, the garden, little things. She had a lot of different tactics to avoid holding my hand. I was positioned on her left side. She was right-handed. Crafty malin Élise now used her left hand to arrange a scarf or dig through her purse for ChapStick or point out something trivial. She did anything and everything so that her left hand was not free to hold my right hand. This was maddening and comical.

"Are we really going to play this game, Élise?" I asked. "What game is that?" she asked innocently.

"Fine," I said.

We came to the dock for the Swan Boat rides. The last time I was on a Swan Boat was probably when Helen and I brought Lily for a day trip to Boston. She must have been five or so.

"Let's take the Swan Boat," I suggested. "Have you ever been?" I asked.

Élise fluttered her lashes. "You know I have been in Boston for over twenty years." She laughed to herself. "I guess I never really got around to doing the touristy things. No, I haven't."

The six boats were filling up quickly. They consisted of several rows of benches to accommodate roughly twenty-five passengers. The pontoon was powered by a driver who was manually peddling while seated behind an enormous Swan cover. We were hemmed in by other passengers so I casually draped my arm over Élise's shoulder.

"Oh, Aren, it's so hot. Don't do that," Élise complained.

I looked at her and chuckled. "I know honey," I said. "But it's not my fault that you're so hot that you're burning up the boat." I reprised my Groucho Marx impersonation. "I might have to throw you into the water to cool you off."

Nearby passengers overheard our conversation and snickered. I smirked. Élise had nothing to say. She stopped squirming. As soon as the boat approached the beautiful flowers, she was all smiles.

I escorted Élise to Back Bay Station. This time we walked arm and arm along Boylston Street. She didn't want me to accompany her home. I took her hands in mine and held them.

"Did you have a good time with me?" I asked. Her face lit up with a smile.

"I love your smile," I said. "Okay, chérie. I'm going to go back to my friend's house and crash for a bit. I'll see you at nine, okay?"

She nodded.

"You're not going to run away, right? Or make an excuse not to show up?"

"Oh, I don't know. A little bit of drama makes life interesting, non?"

"Well, please do me a favor and just promise to come and be your beautiful charming self without the drama. Deal?"

Élise wobbled her head. "Oh, all right." She smiled. "See you later."

Later, we met up with some of my friends at the Regattabar in Harvard

Square. Élise insisted on taking the T, despite my offer to pick her up at her place.

.oOo.

Aren

I was about to open the door to the club when I saw Élise approaching. "Perfect timing," I said.

"Yes," she said breathlessly.

She was wearing a purple chiffon dress with soft ruffles at the bottom. The V in front of her dress revealed a generous mound of rounded breasts encased in some kind of corset or bra. She smelled like fresh lilacs. She had styled her hair in an elegant up-do, and her lips looked especially inviting with the deep wine-red shade of lipstick. Her cheeks were flushed from her walk from the T-stop. I kissed them. She beamed at me. I don't know—there was something especially cute about the way her nose crinkled that made my heart skip.

"Allow me," I said as I opened the door for her and then offered her my arm.

"We're joining some friends," I announced to the hostess. I quickly scanned the room and found my MIT classmates Nick Saunders and his wife Cynthia and Jim Ketseas and his wife Maureen. Cynthia spotted me and waved.

"Ah, I see them," I said.

I navigated Élise expertly through the room to the group table and made the introductions. I had said nothing to my friends about Élise other than that I was inviting "a friend" out with us. I was a little nervous. I don't know why.

"So how did you two meet, Élise?" Cynthia asked.

"I fell into a ditch while on a hike, and Aren helped me up," Élise explained.

Cynthia laughed. "You're joking," she said.

"No, I'm afraid not. And then he yelled at me for not having a walking stick and trying to exceed my nonexistent hiking ability."

The table roared with laughter.

"That sounds like vintage Aren," Nick said jovially. "He tells us you're a teacher. Well, has he already redesigned your curriculum?"

"What?"

"Stick around, and he'll tell you how to teach your class and insist you get rid of your teaching manuals. He'll design a whole new program and demand you update him on how well his idea worked. Watch out for his apps. He has an app for everything."

Everyone laughed knowingly.

"Thanks, man. Remind me never to bring a date near you," I said in a huff.

Élise recapped our "exciting" venture at the museum. I said very little. I was content to observe how Élise navigated the prickly personalities of my friends with panache.

"So Élise," Cynthia began to say, "what's it like to teach in the Boston public school system?"

"Excuse me?" Élise replied with confusion.

"You teach bilingual education at the public school, right?"

"Er, no. I teach French and Spanish at a prep school in Newton. Chestnut Hill to be exact."

"Actually, Élise left a tenure-track position at BU to teach at a prep school," I added. "She still serves as an adjunct professor during the summer."

Élise glared at me. "What?" I mouthed to her.

"Stop," she mouthed back to me. What was her problem?

"I wasn't aware I needed to present a curriculum vitae in order to go out dancing," Élise said under her breath so that only I could hear her. "Oh, all that publishing. I know. Nick and I have a friend who teaches at Harvard. And he's always stressing out about publishing. Still, it must be a real come down from being at a university," Cynthia opined. "Yes, well, I guess for me publishing is not what pushed me to find something else. I was lucky. I had a very good salary and mentors, but the environment wasn't right for me. I like teaching, being in front of a class and introducing a slice of the world to young minds. And we have a close-knit community," Élise said.

"So you live on campus? I guess that's one way to compensate for the lower salary," Cynthia mused.

Élise flashed one of her enigmatic smiles as if she had heard these questions before. Actually, I had not really thought about her work in terms of advancement and salary or her lifestyle. I had forgotten it was common for faculty to live on campus at boarding schools.

"Élise, so you never lived on campus?" I asked.

"Oh, initially, I did, and then I followed my friend Antonio to Jamaica Plain when he bought his condo. I did have to rent it out in order to stay on campus. Now I'm back in my apartment full-time."

All eyes turned to me with a knowing look. Was Antonio her friend the way I was her friend? They probably wondered.

Élise stood up.

"If you'll excuse me for a moment, I need to powder my nose," she said and then started walking towards the door. I heard Cynthia and Maureen giggling over the "powder the nose" line. For a second I panicked that she was walking out, but instead she went in the direction of the restroom. I stopped her just before she went in.

"Are you all right?" I asked.

"If I have to do battle with your friends every time you invite me to go out, maybe I think twice before accepting. You understand?"

I nodded. In truth, I had never seen Cynthia and Maureen behave the way they did toward Élise. I expected them to be curious and ask questions. But tonight, they were like vultures circling her. But I wasn't going to let them ruin my evening with Élise.

"Promise me a dance?"

She blinked with one big sweeping motion of her lashes. "Are you sure your friends can handle us dancing?"

"Don't you worry."

When Élise returned to the table, the interrogation resumed. "You know, Élise, my production team did a documentary on bilingual education in Boston's public schools. Did you see it?" Cynthia said.

Élise fluttered her eyelashes. I could tell she was confused by the question. Frankly, I was too. Other than Élise living in Jamaica Plain, I wasn't sure I saw the connection.

"Oh, no, I'm sorry. Was it on the local news? I don't really watch television or the local news," Élise said.

"Oh, that's too bad, I would have loved to get some feedback, you know from teachers like you. I'm surprised we didn't do an interview with you."

"I don't understand. I don't teach bilingual education at a public school.

"Oh, you don't? I'm sorry I misunderstood."

"Cynthia," her husband Nick said, "Élise teaches at a prep school at Chestnut Hill."

"Oh," Cynthia said. "Well, whatever makes you happy, dear. Although I wonder how much use there is for French these days. Spanish is much more useful I suppose, but it doesn't quite have the cachet that French does. I remember doing my junior year abroad in Aix en Provence."

Oh, god, there she goes. We'll have to listen to her tales of being an American in the South of France.

"Humph," Cynthia, said. "I guess teaching at a high school offers more benefits than being a lecturer. Smart move, that way you can provide for your children. You know working mothers who have to balance work with making sure their children go to safe schools."

"But I don't have any children and I don't teach at a public school," Élise clarified.

"Oh, right. I'm confusing you with one of Aren's other girlfriends."

"Ah!" Élise said fixing her attention on me.

I shrugged.

After the interrogation of Élise, Cynthia launched into her latest documentary film projects. That was fine. I was happy to tune her out so I could focus my attention on Élise.

While we sat and talked, I tried to stroke Élise's bare legs. She grabbed my hand underneath the table and removed them from her legs, putting them firmly back on my lap. I tried this about half a dozen times. I felt like a mischievous child who keeps ringing the doorbell to annoy the neighbor. I laughed. Élise grudgingly smiled as well. My friends looked at us.

"Want to share?" Nick asked.

"No," I replied, smirking. Élise rolled her eyes. Maureen had a delightful way of isolating her facial expressions and cocked her eyebrow, which made me laugh.

"So Aren," Maureen said, "did Jim tell you that we had dinner with Catherine a few weeks ago? She looks fantastic. She was asking about you. You should call her," Maureen said.

Élise shot me an accusatory look.

"Oh, you should meet her, Élise," Maureen exclaimed. "She's the most extraordinary woman. She's just one of those women who has her act together, you know?" Maureen said looking at Élise.

"Ah, so what does she do?"

"Oh, she used to be an investment banker on Wall Street for Goldman Sachs. When the economy crashed, she got laid off and then started a consulting business for women entrepreneurs. She was giving a lecture at Babson College and we met afterwards. Truly lovely woman. She and Aren used to be an item."

"I see," Élise said.

Maureen looked at me and Élise and then put on a look of surprise. "Don't take it the wrong way, dear. It's best to hear these things plainly and out in the open. You're not Aren's type."

"What?!" I sputtered. "What is your problem, Maureen?" Élise grew silent. So did everyone else at that moment.

The music started to play and I held out my hand to Élise. "Shall we dance?" I asked.

The band was playing a danceable jazz rhythm. I stood up and extended my hand to invite Élise to dance. I was grateful for the slow dance music that let me hold her close so I could whisper in her ear. Her smiles were incandescent.

"I'm in heaven …" I was singing softly.

She rolled her eyes. Her lashes fluttered dramatically. I laughed. She was enjoying herself.

"Tell me Aren, did you sing that song to Catherine?"

It was difficult to read Élise. I sighed. "Actually, she is more of a heavy metal fan."

"Aren, are you and Catherine serious? Couples sometimes need a break—"

I placed my hand over her mouth to stop her from saying anything more.

"Look, we dated. Maybe it was a little more serious than some other relationships I had—"

"You introduced her to your friends."

"Yeah, well, big deal. As it happens, she and Maureen were college classmates. Anyway, we broke up over a year ago, okay? It's over, really."

"Aren, you don't owe me any explanations. I'm having a great time."

"Are you?"

"Yes, I would have an even better time if you would keep your hands to yourself."

We did a little rock step and I spun her around and then brought her back.

"I like you Élise," I said.

She looked at me but didn't answer. In fact, we continued dancing without saying anything more. We slow danced, but she wasn't sending me those "Baby, I'm yours" vibes.

"Thank you for coming out tonight, Élise," I said softly in her ear. She smiled elegantly. "Thank you for inviting me," she said.

"Are you having fun?" She laughed.

"With the exception of the investigation from your friends, yes."

I sighed but retained my smile. Another spin and then back again. "Did I tell you how gorgeous you look tonight?" I said whispering in her ear.

"I didn't think you noticed."

"Oh?"

"You seemed so determined to get your hands under my dress."

"Correction, between your legs," I chuckled.

"Aren, why do you always ruin a perfectly lovely moment with crassness?"

"It's not crassness to want to be intimate with you. Sexually intimate."

"Why can't we just be friends and enjoy each other's company?"

"What are you so afraid of, honey? That's what it's supposed to be about: the man and woman thing."

Élise looked up at me as we shifted our weight from side to side in time to the music. With one palm of my hand on her mid-back, I pulled her hand against my chest and pressed a kiss to her forehead. There was a fine mist of perspiration that smelled like flowers. I moved my lips to the tip of her right ear. She shivered.

"Don't, Aren."

"Don't what? Don't try to make you feel good? Don't try to let you know how good I feel being here with you?"

"Aren, I can't give you what you want."

"You can, but for some reason you won't."

"I'm not a comfort girl, Aren. I'm not here for your gratification."

"All right. How about your gratification? I can be really generous."

"Be serious."

"I am serious. Or maybe not. Why do we have to be serious? Why can't we just have fun?"

I caressed the small of Élise's back. She arched it instinctively. I was enjoying the feel of her body in my arms. I could feel our hearts beating as one. I kissed the inner folds of her ear and held her tight. "I feel you," I declared.

She sighed. "I need to go," she said. She disentangled herself from my arms in the middle of the song and headed back to the table. She grabbed her purse.

"Leaving so soon?" Maureen asked.

"Yes, I must be going. It was a pleasure meeting all of you," she said flatly. She extended her hand in a handshake to Maureen.

"*On fait la bise*," Maureen said a little tipsily. She had downed quite a few cocktails while we were dancing. Élise brushed her cheek against Maureen's.

"Wow, your skin is so soft, like a baby's," she said in surprise.

Élise looked at me in horror. I grabbed her elbow and spun her away from the table. "We really must be going," I announced.

"Well, maybe we'll see you again," Maureen said gaily. Élise and I hurried out of the club into the fresh air.

The drive to Élise's place took about thirty minutes during which we didn't say much to each other. I lay my hand on her knee and squeezed it. She didn't push my hand away, but she didn't respond either.

Instead of dropping her off in front of her door, I drove a little further and I found a parking spot a few doors down from her building.

She owned a one-bedroom condo in Jamaica Plain with a view of the Jamaica Pond.

I shut off the car engine.

"Are you going to invite me up?" I asked.

"I don't want to sleep with you," Élise said defiantly. "How long are you going to keep saying that?"

"I don't know. As long as that's the way I feel." In the tight confines of my car, I could feel the intensity of her gaze on my face. "Are you okay with that?"

"No. But if the condition for getting an invitation to your place is that I have to be on my best behavior, then I promise you won't be disappointed."

We walked side by side up the wide spiraling staircase with my arm hooked through hers to her apartment. When we got up to her apartment, she sent me back down again with a visitor's parking card so my car wouldn't get towed.

In the narrow hallway, I hung up my jacket and rolled up my sleeves. She had opened the windows and turned on the ceiling fans so there was a gentle breeze that I found pleasant. On the wall of the entryway leading to the kitchen, I noticed a painting of the Virgin Mary holding the baby Jesus. She was dressed in blue robes bordered by gold embroidered filigree. On her head was a gold crown with a halo hovering behind her. The baby Jesus wore a pink robe with a halo hovering behind him. Interestingly, both of their complexions had a bluish brown cast and on the Virgin Mary's right cheek were two long dark lines, like scratches. The painting hung above a table adorned with candles and beautiful arrangement of fragrant roses and dried jasmine flowers.

"Oh, that's interesting," I volunteered, not really knowing what to say.

"Yes, that's the Haitian protectoress of women and their children. In Santeria, she is also known as Santa Barbara de Lucumi. She is the goddess of love, beauty, art, and business. She's fierce and doesn't put up with nonsense. In her arms she is holding her daughter Anais, who acts as her mother's translator since Erzulie cannot speak."

"Hmm, I see." Of course, I didn't. Her explanation of the meaning of the picture made sense. What I didn't understand was whether she was telling me she practiced vodou or just happened to collect an artifact associated with vodou. *Was Élise a witch, priestess of some sort? Or, was Élise just like many Catholics who had a devotion to the Virgin Mary?* Élise didn't add anything more to her explanation.

Her apartment was surprisingly large and spare. I think I expected lots of pretentious Louis XVI period furniture and French toile wallpaper. In reality, the walls of her apartment were painted in the white color palette. Above the white painted non-working fireplace was a stunning painted portrait of a little girl, her complexion reminiscent of my grandmother's nazook and nutmeg cake, dressed in her First Communion dress complete with the veil and the rosary bead wound around her small hands that were pressed together in piety. The little girl had large chestnut ringlet curls that reached her shoulders, luminous eyes, and a perfectly shaped mouth. Was this Élise?

On the opposite wall hung a few black and white framed photographs of Élise with her parents, when she was a baby. I lingered over the photograph, studying the elegant beehive updo of Élise's mother and her father who was dressed in a suit so reminiscent of the 1960s. Élise sat perched on her father's lap with her mother holding her hand. I chuckled at the sight of baby Élise's plump legs peeking out from underneath the frilly dress. She was a happy baby. There was one other photograph that surprised me. It was a family portrait. Her parents seemed much older. Élise looked to be about nine or ten and she was holding the hand of a little boy, a toddler. Was this her brother?

The only color photograph hanging on the wall was one where she had her arms around an older man with snowy white hair. It was not her father. It was signed by Anthony Phelps with the inscription written in

French: Haïti Littéraire - *Nous sommes les araignées du soir et nous filons l'espoir.* In English it translated as Literary Haiti: We are the spiders of the evening and we spin hope.

What did spiders have to do with a literary group?

"What does the inscription mean?" I asked.

She explained Anthony Phelps had been part of a progressive intellectual group called Haïti Littéraire, and through their writings they wanted to give hope to Haiti. Like spiders, they wove the fabric of hope through their poetry, their fiction, and their essays.

Of course I had heard about Papa Doc and the horrors of Duvalier and the Tonton Macoutes. Who hadn't? How interesting that we were both survivors of political violence: her family during the time of Duvalier and mine, the Armenian genocide. And yet, we didn't really talk too much about it. Of course, for me it was mostly my grandparents who endured the oppression and were forced to flee to Kazakhstan and Syria before landing in the US. For Élise, the terror was a little closer.

It had to have been taken a few years ago, because Élise's hair was chestnut brown with only vague whispers of gray at the temples. Her face had not changed much except that she was heavier then, but still beautiful.

The furnishing of her apartment had the ubiquitous urbane look you found in most upscale Boston apartments: comfortable sofa and chairs placed just so around the glass coffee table. Although she did seem to favor wooden carved masks. They were everywhere.

She had a few pictures of family members on her piano in a nook between the kitchen and the living room. Her extensive library of books was cleverly staged throughout the apartment. I only caught a glimpse of her bedroom, but the lion share of the books was in there.

I loved her bathroom. Maybe because I spend a lot of time in the bathroom, I have come to appreciate the subtle aesthetics of a bathroom. Hers was recently remodeled and very European with a wall-mounted toilet, bidet, and sink. There was a rectangular bathtub with German fixtures. I had the same thing at my place. She also had a compact washer and dryer hidden behind a closet. The bathroom connected to Élise's bedroom and also had a separate entrance.

Élise had her work desk in an alcove off the kitchen, which I think was endearing. The kitchen was perhaps the liveliest room in the house. Artwork and assorted photographs snapshots competed for space. The kitchen was painted a bold yellow with red laminate doors and had a big Viking stove and other impressive appliances. It was soulful. That's the Élise I wanted to get to know better. In this kitchen, she had landscape paintings of her homeland, the island of Saint Martin—her *isla negra*. That was her pet name for her homeland, inspired by her favorite Chilean poet, Pablo Neruda, whose beachfront property he also called isla negra.

"Would you like to see my garden?"

"Sure," I said.

Élise led me by the hand across the hall and up a narrow set of stairs to the roof. When she opened the door, I was treated to a sensual display of moonlit flowers and the smell of jasmine and lavender. The experience reminded me of passing by austere buildings in France and then opening the door to a beautiful courtyard. This roof was her personal paradise.

"I love it, Élise."

She smiled. "Want some mint to take back with you?"

"You're a nut. Sure."

She went and plucked a handful of mint from her container garden of aromatic herbs, tomatoes, peppers, cucumbers, and squash. I held the door open for her, and we went back inside of her apartment, where she found a sack and gave it to me.

She offered me coffee, and we sat in her kitchen talking about my grandmother's garden in Almaty, Kazakhstan. She was a captive audience.

It was past one o'clock in the morning when I realized I wouldn't be able to keep my eyes open any longer. I stood up to leave. I would be staying the night at a friend's condo in the Back Bay.

I turned to leave.

"Good night, Élise. I had a wonderful time tonight. Thank you for coming out with me."

"Aren," she said. There was a catch in her voice that made me turn around and look at her. She was doing the funny thing with her lashes again. *Uh-oh.*

"Um, would you like to come over for breakfast? Maybe we can go cycling? Antonio has an extra bicycle we can borrow for you."

"I'd like that," I said. "Great. nine-ish?

"Nine-ish it is," I said. I walked out the door without receiving even a kiss on the cheek. Oh well.

My Sunday date with Élise felt like a glorious long goodbye. Everything was perfect. What a dazzlingly beautiful early summer day. Élise and I breakfasted on her rooftop garden. French pressed coffee with evaporated milk, freshly baked croissants and bread from the nearby bakery, exotic fruit like star fruit and dragon fruit and botanical motif china were arranged on the table. We talked about literature and politics. She was the most relaxed I had ever seen her. She was wearing a long-sleeved red T-shirt and slim-fitting capri pants with espadrilles. Her hair was loose, but she had tied a scarf around her neck. We could have been on some terrace in Spain or the south of France. It was magical being with her on her rooftop garden overlooking the Jamaica Way Pond. We packed a picnic, got on the bicycles, and rode on the bike path to Concord. We found a quiet spot to park our bicycles and enjoy our picnic, watching people lazily paddle their canoes and kayaks on the murky Charles River. We then walked through the quaint downtown, where I showed her my favorite toy shop.

It was five o'clock when we returned to her apartment. We dined on callaloo, a spicy soup from Saint Martin with chicken stock, okra, kale, onions, and hot peppers. Apparently, she skipped the salt pork for my sake. She served the soup with olive loaf bread, fresh sliced tomatoes, and avocado. For dessert we feasted on the yogurt I had picked up from the Armenian store in Watertown and the fresh strawberries we picked up from the farm stand we passed while cycling. I also plied her with lots of Chilean wine. She was giggling and effervescent.

I kissed her. The first peck took her by surprise. Okay, if it weren't for the wine, she would have resisted. I kissed her again, but she didn't really respond. I kissed her again, this time really slowly, teasing her lips with my teeth and rubbing her back. Finally, I felt her. She was kissing me back.

"Now, that wasn't so hard, was it?" I said against her lips.

She smiled and then started biting her lower lip and fluttering her lashes. My lips opened wide, my tongue in search of hers. I felt her squirm and try to close her mouth. Good grief! I reached for her breasts and caressed them. She melted.

She broke from our kiss.

"Aren't we kind of old for this?" she said breathing heavily. "Absolutely not." I kissed her again. She was going to say something else, and then I murmured against her lips: "Please stop talking."

We made out for several minutes. As much as she was enjoying this, I knew she was going to refuse to make love with me. I didn't have any energy to argue. When we were finished with the chaste love play, I laughed at her hair, which had morphed into an extravagant bird's nest. She tried her best to smooth her hair, which made me laugh even harder. At that moment, I felt a lot of tenderness toward Élise. I really enjoyed being with her, but I didn't like all this chaste and modesty stuff.

"Listen," I said. "I need to get back tonight. Come up to Vermont, okay? Stay with me. We like each other. Stop the bullshit already."

Ugh! Again with the fluttering eyelashes and the lip biting. But she didn't respond.

We exchanged our goodbyes quickly. I pressed my lips to her forehead. "Thank you for a wonderful day today and for a fun weekend," I said. She smiled.

I waved to her from my convertible and drove away. My part was done. The ball was now in her court.

.oOo.

When Élise woke up the next morning after Aren's visit, she was happy to find a text message from Aren that said:

Fantastic time. Thanx

Even for a text message, it was briefer than she would have liked. She quickly got dressed and headed out the door for her yoga and Pilates classes. She would be meeting her friend Fanny later on for lunch. Fanny worked part-time as a pediatric nurse. Now that Élise was on her summer schedule, it was easier to schedule time with her friend. They would have lunch and then go to Zumba class together.

"You look different, girl. What's going on?" Fanny asked at the end of the Zumba class.

Élise smiled sheepishly and then shrugged her shoulders dramatically, the *Kanye shrug*. Fanny's teen-aged son Jorge had taught her the *Kanye shrug* and she in turn had taught Élise, but Élise had learned it from her students. Either way, they loved using any opportunity to do the *Kanye shrug* and on this particular day, it was Élise's turn.

"Oh, nothing," Élise said with a smile.

"Fine, but I'll find out. Antonio cannot resist my methods of persuasion."

The friends giggled.

When Élise put the key in the lock to open her door, Antonio opened his and stepped out carrying a beautiful arrangement of flowers. "Oh, Antonio," Élise said, "What a lovely bouquet of flowers. I see you have an admirer with good taste," Élise said good-naturedly.

"Ah, *corazon*, I'm glad you think so. But they're for you," he said. He handed her the flowers and opened the door for her so she could step inside.

"Wow," she said, sniffing the flowers.

"So," Antonio began, "it seems the lovely Élise has an admirer perhaps. Aren't you going to open up the card?"

Élise blushed slightly. To anyone who didn't know Élise, it would have passed unnoticed. But Antonio knew her well. He watched closely as she set the flowers down and took the gift card out of the envelope. She read it and fluttered her eyelashes and let out a sigh.

Curious, Antonio thought as he watched his friend's reaction. "Something, wrong?" Antonio asked hoping Élise would elaborate. "Oh, no. It's from Aren, my friend who borrowed your bicycle yesterday. Thanks, by the way. It worked out really well."

Antonio had had a chance to examine the flowers when he received the delivery on Élise's behalf while she was out. He figured the flowers had come from her visitor. It wasn't unusual that Élise received flowers. Her students did that all the time, but since school was out, and it wasn't her birthday, he concluded it must have come from her gentleman caller. Élise loved exotic flowers, and this arrangement did not disappoint with an arrangement of fragrant sweet peas, yellow garden roses, purple dendrobium, yellow mokara orchids, bird of paradise, red halo berries, and a luscious red anthurium flower with lots of ferns, fragrant jasmine vine, mint, and baby's breath. But what drew his attention was the single red artichoke-like king protea flower with vibrant pin cushion spikes surrounded by clusters of yellow- orange flame calanthea flowers with ribbed leaves. Antonio interpreted the king protea as code for love and passion, but more importantly, daring and transformation. *Does she understand the message?*

Antonio watched Élise give the flowers a fresh cut and add the packet of nutrients to revive the flowers. He plucked one of the calanthea flowers and a jasmine vine and set it on a small dish he had taken from her kitchen cabinet. He set the dish on the shrine altar in the hallway. "It's best to share your good fortune with the Lady," he said ominously.

Élise chuckled. "I suppose you're right," she said.

Antonio came back and stood with his arm around her shoulder. Antonio and Élise had a very warm and affectionate friendship. So it was with surprise when he realized her body was rigid with tension. She was fluttering her eyelashes. She was thinking. About the gentleman? About the card? He didn't know. She didn't say. He pressed a kiss on her forehead.

"Come over. I was thinking of making some platanos maduros. I also picked up some fish at the market today. The beans are already boiling so you can make the rice. Sound like a plan?"

Élise beamed. "Perfecto! Gracias. I'll be right over, okay?"

Antonio nodded. He pressed another kiss on her forehead and then left, pausing briefly in front of the shrine on his way out.

Élise looked at the flower arrangement with a sense of unease. She picked up the envelope and looked at the card once more. It said:

Your move.

That was it. That was all. She sighed and picked up her keys and walked out the door.

CHAPTER 4

THE GLORY AND SACREDNESS OF THE WELL-MADE WOMAN

Certitude

> *Si je t' étreins c'est pour me continuer*
> *Si nous vivons tout sera à plaisir*
> *Si je te quitte nous nous souviendrons*
> *En te quittant nous nous retrouverons.*[1]
>   —Paul Eluard

A week had passed since Aren's visit. Other than the brief text message, she hadn't heard from him. In the beginning when he pursued her, she was annoyed by how persistent he was. It had felt like he was browbeating her into talking to him. At least that was how she remembered it. And now his silence was tormenting her.

Now that school was out, Élise had time to focus on her projects. She worked on her paper. She worked out and attended Zumba classes with Fanny more regularly. She took walks with Antonio in the afternoon and practiced the piano and violin. She attended her garden. If she

---

1   If I embrace you it's to widen myself
     If we live everything will turn to joy
     If I leave you we'll remember each other
     In leaving you we'll find each other again.

66

wasn't traveling, this was how she would spend her summer.

Another week went by and still no word from Aren. She checked his Facebook account and was both relieved and annoyed that there was nothing "new" to report. When she was on her computer, doing work, she would sometimes notice his Skype account flashing at the bottom of the screen indicating he was online. It would have been easy to just initiate a video call, but she didn't, and neither did he. The flowers he had sent lasted over a week. Now what was left were the ferns and the baby's breath. She was having a difficult time throwing even those out. The jasmine vine and the calanthea on the altar were holding out, however. Antonio had made a cutting out of the vine and sprouts were forming. Life continued. She worked on her paper. She attended mass with Antonio on Sunday. She tutored. She visited the young mother she was mentoring in prison as part of her church's social outreach group. Her life was full. Yet the sense of panic was slowly creeping within her. Panic, over what? She chided herself. She had one of her recurring nightmares of that horrible night in Haiti when her parents were attacked and her father was taken away. After all these years the horror never left her. The smells were just as potent now as they were that night. The only difference this time in her dream was that instead of feeling BoBo's protective arms around her, it was Aren's.

What's happening to me? She panicked over her panicking. *Over a kiss?*

.oOo.

Aren

Aren stood outside the West Hempstead subway station on his way to a meeting to plan for an upcoming conference. He glanced at his watch to check the time. The meeting wouldn't start for another thirty minutes.

It would take five minutes to get to the office building. As he walked, he passed a street corner where an older man was singing a Billy Joel song. "Pressure." He stopped and listened for a while.

You have no scars on your face
And you cannot handle
Pressure

Aren observed the scenes of life around him: skateboarders, young couples walking hand in hand, individuals hurriedly getting to their next destination while talking on their headsets, homeless people napping on benches or on the grass, policemen on horses or bicycles. Even the buskers had somewhere to be, somewhere to go. He was surrounded by humanity and yet he felt so alone, lonely. When he hiked alone, he didn't feel the loneliness. Maybe it was because here in the city, people seemed to belong.

That's right I don't belong here anymore.

He had sold his New York-based company in 2007 just before the world economic crisis would erupt the following year. He was fifty- eight years old. His friends called him a lucky bastard. Maybe. Despite his boasting about his business acumen to Élise, he was forced to sell the business. Helen had just died. Lily pleaded with him to quit his job and sell his company. He was looking at the possibility of triple bypass surgery for the blocked arteries they found on the angiogram. He was anxious all the time and depressed. He was overweight and drank a lot. But his company was doing great. And then everything came crashing in on him when he had his heart attack and his cardiologist read him the riot act. So he quit. But was that the right decision?

His former colleagues and business associates threw him a lifeline by inviting him to participate in conferences and consulting. It wasn't the same as going to work and building a thriving business. Was sixty-two really that old?

Aren saw many wrinkled and silver-haired men pushing strollers. These days you could never be sure if they were grandparents, parents, relatives, or even the nanny. The world was changing so fast. It was hard to keep up.

His daughter Lily was starting to talk about raising a family with her partner Tessa. He hadn't given it much thought before one way or the other. But as he sat in the park he wondered, would being a grandparent fill that void he felt? Was it the same as having a life partner?

His thoughts turned to Élise. It had been two weeks since he saw her. He replayed their Sunday together every day when he went on his hikes. *Why hasn't she reached out to me?* Hadn't he given her a road map? He told her it was her move. This was the twenty-first century. Gender roles had evolved or so people kept insisting. He was sure she felt the same connection that he did. Why on earth wasn't she doing anything about it?

He pulled out his phone and stared at her number. He wondered if she would pick up the phone or would his call go to voice mail.

"To hell with it," he muttered. He scrolled down his call list and found the number for an old girlfriend Catherine. He pressed the number.

.oOo.

On a Monday afternoon, Élise met Fanny as usual for their Zumba class. She didn't chat happily away with Fanny as was her habit. In fact, Fanny was surprised to see Élise so quiet and withdrawn.

"So you're coming to my house for the Fourth of July, right?" Fanny asked.

Élise was looking out the window. "Yeah, sure," she said.

Fanny noticed Élise was preoccupied. "What's wrong?" she asked.
"Nothing," Élise said impatiently.

"Oh, there's something,"

"Class is going to start," Élise said.

The instructor switched on the warm-up music. The rhythmic guitar resounded in the opening bars and then "Good Feeling" by

Flo Rida began. She led the class in a series of choreographed body stretches and lunges. The music switched then to the Korean pop hit "Gangnam Style." Fanny noticed Élise tripped on the first grapevine steps. "*Hey, sexy lady, op, op, oppa Gangnam style*" the chorus began. The choreography required a horseriding step. Élise was consistently offbeat. The instructor noticed too. "That's all right," she yelled. "Keep it going! Shake that thang! Act like you got it going on, girl." That was the signal to get everyone revved up. Élise didn't react. She was lost in her own world.

Fanny tried to get Élise's attention during the various routines. "What's wrong?" she mouthed. Élise would shake her head emphatically and then proceed to fumble the choreography. After class, Fanny saw Élise packing up her things hurriedly. She took out her phone to look at it and then thrust it back into her bag. Fanny approached Élise and tried to engage her.

"Okay, what's going on? You messed up royally on the combinations today. You don't do that. Spill. What's up?"

Élise looked up at Fanny and bit her lip, letting Fanny see her distress.

"Oh baby, what's wrong?"

"I don't know. I—I met someone."

"You did? And you didn't tell me? Chica!"

Fanny switched into a tirade of Spanish. Élise chuckled.

"So what's the problem? He's not married, is he?" Fanny asked suspiciously.

"Oh, no, no, no. Why would you even think that?"

"Well, you know that happened to Gloria. She said her boyfriend told her he was divorced and that he took custody of the kids every other week. Bastard! He was playing her! He wasn't even separated from his wife. Separate bedrooms in the same house don't count!"

Fanny stopped her rant long enough to notice Élise was no longer paying attention. She focused her attention back on Élise.

"So if he's not married, and you're sure about that, what's the problem?"

"Well, when he came over, we—"

"You had sex? *¡Ay, Madre de Dios!*"

"Well, no. We kissed."

Fanny hesitated and then sputtered in laughter. "You kissed. And—that's it?"

Élise let out a breath and then said, "Yes."

Fanny laughed again. She saw Élise was serious and stopped laughing. "So okay, what's the next step?"

Élise looked around the studio. They were alone. She returned her attention to Fanny. "I'm not sure. He said I should come up to Vermont and stay with him."

Fanny's eyebrows lifted dramatically.

"Oh, wow! Really? So when are you going? He's legit, right? I mean—"

"Yes, he's an engineer. Well, he's retired," Élise explained.

Fanny gasped and then she closed her mouth. Élise glared at her. "Sorry, go on," Fanny said.

"Anyway, I've seen his LinkedIn page. We even have some connections in common. No, he's fine. It's just—"

"Just what?"

"I don't know. I wasn't looking for a man. He's the kind of person you give him an inch and he take a mile."

"You know I never completely understood that expression," Fanny said absentmindedly. She then took in her friend's continuing distress and sighed. "You know, it's not that complicated. No one says you have to marry the guy or get down and dirty with him between the sheets if you're not into him. Although, there's absolutely nothing wrong with getting down and dirty. Times have changed. You'll still be the wonderful you if you let him go down on you between the sheets. Just remember to go to confession. I hear Father Alan is really sympathetic about these things."

"God, I hate you," Élise said in exasperation.

Fanny laughed. "Call him. Why don't you plan to spend the Fourth of July with him? I'll forgive you for missing my party, but you owe me.

You can spend some time with this guy to see if you really do connect." Fanny gathered up her things and was dragging Élise by the hand.

"What's the hurry?" Élise said.

"We're going shopping," Fanny announced.

"Shopping for what?" Élise asked, genuinely baffled by what Fanny had in mind.

"Oh, well you can't get sexy with this guy without the right costume. I know just the thing. Call him right now. I'll wait for you downstairs and we'll drive in my car." She grabbed Élise's phone.

"What are you doing, Fanny?"

Fanny scrolled through Élise's call list.

"What's this guy's name? "Is this him? Aren? Aren Karajian? What kind of crazy name is that?"

Élise scowled. "Give me back my phone!" she yelled.

Fanny pressed the button to initiate the phone call and returned the phone to Élise.

.oOo.

Aren

I was sitting in a conference room with four other people. We were discussing the upcoming photovoltaic conference and presenting new designs in inverters and monitoring units and marketing strategies for smart grid technologies. I was going to participate in the panel. My phone rang, and I glanced at the ID display.

"Élise," I said, evenly. I didn't realize until the moment I said her name, how angry I was with her. No, actually I was furious. *Why has it taken you two weeks to pick up the fucking phone and call me? I should just tell you I'm busy and hang up.*

"Oh, Aren, hi. I-I'm interrupting—"

It was the way she said Aren with a soft "a" and the slightest hint of a trilling r. She was afraid. I could hear it in her voice. Was she afraid that I might reject her or afraid of finally making a move? *What's it going to be sweetheart? If you invite me to the art museum or a damn opera I'm going to hang up on you.*

"It's okay. What is it?" I replied.

"Oh, I-I—I was thinking if you're free for the July 4th weekend, I-I could come up to visit. I mean visit you. If—you're free. It's last-minute notice—"

"As in you stopping over to say hi while visiting other people or you mean staying over at my house?"

I glanced at my colleagues. They were talking among themselves, not really paying attention to me.

Élise sighed. "Visit as in stay over at your house—if that's all right with you."

"Hmmm, I have to think about it. I made tentative plans. Can I get back to you? I'll call you right back."

"Aren, wait—"

"I'll call you right back."

Élise

I stared at the phone. I could feel my heart pounding so hard, I thought it would leap out of my chest. "I made tentative plans," he said. I put my hand to my forehead. "*Merde!*"

Aren

I put away my phone. My colleagues paused their conversation and looked at me.

"Is everything all right," one colleague asked, "You seem upset."

"Yeah, I just need to step out for a few minutes. I'll be right back."

"Sure," they all said.

I walked out of the conference room and walked to the end of the hall. I pulled out my phone and stared at it. I scrolled to find Catherine's number and pressed it. I let it ring a few times and then left a voice mail. "Sorry, babe. Where are you? I'll send you a text. I hate sending those goddamned things. Anyway, call me or text me back when you get a chance. Thanks."

I opened the nearby exit door leading to the staircase landing with a window. The window had a view of the parking lot. I composed a message to Catherine and sent it. I then called Élise.

"Bonjour! Holà! Hello! Sorry, I'm not available to take your call. Please leave a message at the sound of the beep," said Élise's voice on the voice response system.

"Shit!" I yelled, and then I remembered I was being recorded. "Oh, Élise, I'm sorry I missed you. I wanted to tell you to come. Come all right. I'll text you. Or you can call me back."

"End record message. Press #1 to review the message. Press #2 to send," said the voice response system. I pressed the #2 button. Then I typed out a text and email message that said:

Élise, if the offer still stands, I would really love for you to come.

I walked back to the conference room. Whatever rage I felt before had now transmuted to panic.

.oOo.

Élise and Fanny had just walked inside of Fanny's house. Élise had been silent during the whole ride. She had switched off her phone after talking to Aren.

"You know, honey, maybe he had a family obligation or something. That happens. Why don't you check your phone? Maybe he left you a message."

"I feel like an idiot," Élise moaned.

"All right, do you want me to check for you?"

Élise nodded her head and burst into tears. "I'm so stupid," she cried.

Fanny hugged Élise tight. "Come on. Give me the phone."

Élise handed her phone to Fanny. She dried her tears. Fanny

switched on the phone.

"Hey! He left you a voice mail and a text message," Fanny said excitedly. She handed the phone back to Élise. "Here."

Élise read the text and then retrieved the voice mail message that Aren left. She looked up at Fanny.

"Well?"

"He wants me to come," Élise answered.

"Well, that's great! Isn't that what you wanted? Why do you look so sad?"

"Maybe the telephone tag was God's way of saying: 'Don't rush in. *Cuidado.*'"

"You don't need God to tell you that. All relationships require care and attention. You know that."

"If I go out there, he—well, he'll have expectations. What if I can't? I'm not a love goddess."

"Of course, you are. Why do you have to accept the pornographic version of what a love goddess means?"

"Because that's what people, men expect. You say so yourself all the time."

"All right, just reserve a room. If things don't go right, give yourself an out. No harm no foul. Go ahead, call him. I'll go in the kitchen and make us a smoothie. Pear, kale, and ginger?"

"And—"

"A shot of cayenne pepper. Got it. Now go."

Élise waited until Fanny was in the kitchen and then called Aren. Aren picked up on the first ring.

"So we have a date. Good. When are you coming?" Aren asked. "Oh, well—" Élise stammered.

"Okay, why don't you come Thursday? We'll get an early start on the long weekend. Now I have to get back to my meeting. I'll see you next Thursday, okay?"

Élise caught her breath and then said, "Okay, Aren."

"Bye, honey."

"Bye, Aren."

.oOo.

Élise sat in her kitchen with Fanny. They were looking at a pair of panties made of delicate silk and lace fabric with a double strand of pearls that served as an opening. Fanny had ordered this for Élise.

"Fanny, this isn't underwear. I'll be exposed."

Fanny took a sip of her tea and laughed at her friend. They had known each other for over twenty years. Their lives went in different directions once Fanny settled down and got married and started raising a family, but they remained close. The one thing they didn't talk about was sex, or more specifically, Élise's sex life. So when Élise confirmed her trip to visit Aren, Fanny went into combat mode.

"Leave it to me. I will hook you up. I know just the place for the lingerie. I have to order it, though. We have time."

"Fanny," Élise said. "I don't want to spend mad money on lingerie."

"Oh, no. Leave it to me. Just give me your size. Better yet, I will measure you. It has to fit just right for maximum effect," Fanny said excitedly.

"Fanny, don't go crazy. I just thought I should have something a little sexier than my cotton pajamas," Élise said. She was laughing.

"*¡Ay Caramba!* You better stay over at my house after we go shopping for other essentials. Stay for dinner. You can cook. You know how I hate cooking. You owe me."

Fanny clicked her tongue. "*Mira*, Élise. You're going up to visit a man. What do you expect?"

Élise looked at the crotchless panties and groaned inwardly. They were really beautiful to look at, but the thought of actually parading about in that slip of nothing—

"I can't do it," Élise said finally.

Fanny knit her brows. "Do you like this guy?"

Élise shrugged. "I don't know. I mean he's nice. Really nice. You know, I would love it if we could just hang out and take walks and play Scrabble," she said dreamily.

Fanny's tea dribbled all over her face as she sputtered in laughter. "Right. You're going all the way up to Vermont and asking for my advice on lingerie so you can take walks and play Scrabble?" Fanny scoffed. "¡Ay Dios! Mira. I don't care how old this guy is. He's a man. He will have expectations. That doesn't mean you have to put out, if you don't feel right about it. But don't kid yourself. As much as you like to pretend, you're Mother Teresa, you've got a banging a body. Okay? Just saying. This is me. Remember?"

"So what do I do?" Élise asked.

"Be yourself. But be honest. I mean do you like it when he touches you? Do you like his kisses? Because if you don't like his touch, don't even bother going to see him. The trip will be a disaster. Do you understand what I'm saying? Don't waste his time or yours."

"So, I don't have to wear this thing," Élise said in relief.

"You know what, querida? You should feel sexy for yourself. Just like everything else that you do." Fanny reached for Élise's hand and squeezed it. "I tell you what," she said. "Wear it a few times in the apartment. Get used to how you feel in it. And when you see this guy, you'll know if it feels right to let him see you in it. Okay?"

Élise nodded. She looked at some of the other items Fanny bought for her like the silk nightgown and the satin camisole and tap pants. Fanny must have spent a small fortune.

But her eyes went back to the beautiful crotchless panties. What is the point of wearing something like that if it isn't to openly invite sex? *Why does everything have to come down to sex?* Élise thought about the conversations they had over the years about sex. Maybe because it's an essential part of life. But it was more than that. Seduction was an essential part of a sexual relationship right alongside desire. How ironic that she could devote so much of her academic study on poets known for their eroticism and that simple fact eluded her. She could talk about eroticism but it was not something she lived or experienced.

Deep down inside she was coming to terms with that frigidness her ex accused her of. She was loving and attentive, but that was not enough for him.

Élise realized that the crotchless panties weren't for Aren's benefit. They were for her benefit. Fanny was right. The point of wearing something like this was to help her feel when the moment was right.

"Fanny, am I doing the right thing?"

"Yes, and I'm proud of you. If all that happens is that you just hang out, then I think it will still qualify as a success. You need to be reminded that you still got it going on."

"Got it going on?" Élise repeated and then she laughed. "What?"

"Oh, I was just thinking of how funny your accent is when you say that."

"Yeah, well, it's not like your accent is any better. And you took accent improvement classes."

"Uh, so did you. Remember? That's how we met." They both exploded into laughter.

"Show me a picture of your man again," Fanny said. "He's not my man," Élise said quickly.

"Yeah, yeah, yeah. Show me a picture."

Élise scrolled through her phone and found a photo taken at the jazz club. She also found the first photo she took of Aren on the hiking trail against the backdrop of wildflowers. She passed the phone to Fanny so she could see the photos.

"You know, he's not bad-looking. He's pretty buff," Fanny said. "Oh, I don't care about that. He's a really nice man."

Fanny started to laugh again. "Honey, you're not driving four hours by yourself to go up to Vermont because he's a nice man."

"But he is."

Fanny rolled her eyes. Élise was showing her the silk pajamas she intended to pack.

"You know what, Fanny," Élise said, "I don't really know what I want to happen when I see Aren. Maybe I just want to find out if I am ready to be intimate with someone. I'm scared to death just thinking about it. But I want options. I doubt very much I will be prancing naked around his cottage. I will think about backup clothing so I'm prepared." Fanny finished her tea. "That was really good tea by the way,"

Fanny said. "It smelled divine."

Élise smiled. An idea had popped into her head.

"I'm glad you liked it. I picked it up at a tea place Aren introduced me to in Vermont. You know if you don't have to head back home, do you want to come with me to the mall? I want to pick up a few things. We can stop by Lululemon. My treat."

"Oh, Lululemon! Yeah, I'm game. I have been eyeing their new line-up of bras and tank tops. The colors are fabulous!"

Élise smiled knowingly. A sale at Lululemon was an occasion to drop everything, leave work early, and go buy a cute exercise outfit. She glanced at her hands.

"Fanny, maybe I should make an appointment for a manicure."

"Yeah," Fanny said picking up her purse. "And a pedicure," she mused. "But you can do that the week before you go. You should get your hair done too and get a wax."

Fanny motioned Élise to get her purse and grab her keys.

"I'll drive," Fanny said. "We'll talk about the planning details on the way. Let's go! Lista?"

Élise followed Fanny out the door.

.oOo.

Élise

I packed the car the night before my trip to Vermont. I took Fanny's advice and did any heavy lifting or chores before my spa appointment. I decided not to go to the hair salon and instead just opt for a relaxing head massage and deep condition with a trim. I could blow out my hair when I got home or bring the blow dryer with me on the trip. So when I woke up on Thursday morning to begin my four-hour drive to Vermont, I felt ready. I looked out the window and saw the heavy rain. For a moment I thought it was an omen warning me not to go. *See it through,* I said to myself. I got dressed. I made myself a banana and kale smoothie and toast with almond butter. I made coffee and filled my travel thermos. I grabbed my water bottle and my purse. I took one last look around my apartment and then walked out the door.

I ignored the "recalculating" warning on my GPS. I ignored the indications on the illuminated map and followed instead the directions Aren emailed me last night. The weather forecast for Massachusetts said it would be partly cloudy with chance of rain in the afternoon. In Vermont, they predicted heavy rain. I left my apartment at 10:00 a.m. to fill the gas tank and pick up last-minute items. My goal was to get to Aren's house by three o'clock. Give or take.

"Two-ish," I had said.

"Are you coming at two or are you coming at three?" he pressed.

"I said two-ish. Traffic is unpredictable . . ."

"If you follow my instructions and you leave on time, you should get here by two o'clock. So what time are you coming?"

God, he was so cranky. For a moment, I thought why do I want to do this? Are we going to fight the whole weekend?

"Aren, if you're having second thoughts, it's okay. I don't want—"

"I want you to come, okay?" he said.

Aren was so vague about our itinerary. When I hung up the phone with him, I was thankful that I reserved a hotel room at the hiking spa resort. I didn't tell him. I would just play it by ear. My Putumayo collection of world music was playing as I drove. It rained steadily, but I didn't have much of a problem until I approached Western Massachusetts. The traffic slowed to a crawl. The rain had worsened to a torrential downpour by the time I exited Route 495 and got on the back roads to New Hampshire. The traffic slowed to a crawl because of the trucks. As I approached the bridge over the Connecticut River that bordered Vermont, the windshield wiper could barely keep up with the rain. I slowed my speed down to thirty miles per hour just so I wouldn't crash into the car in front of me. There were a few smart aleck drivers who decided I was too slow and passed me. One got pulled over fairly quickly by the Vermont state trooper. The other one, well, I couldn't see anything. Who knows what happened? Sometimes I veered off into another lane and then a driver would honk, which spooked me. I started to panic. I reached Ludlow, Vermont. Aren's house was another fifty miles away. Every time the car ran over a huge puddle, I could feel the car lurch and the tires skid. My hands were gripped on the steering wheel. The car slowed to a crawl.

I could make out the signs for a ski resort. I just pulled into the lot, but I must have driven over something, because now it was making a terrible noise. It was Bromley ski resort in Peru, Vermont. *Maybe I should check into a room and wait out the storm.* I sat in my car watching the downpour and listening to the thunder. I searched for my phone and called Aren.

.oOo.

Aren

On a rainy Thursday afternoon leading up to the July 4th weekend, I stood in my cottage surveying my handiwork. My cleaning lady had come at the beginning of the week, so I was going around sprucing. I had just touched up the bathroom, put fresh sheets on the bed, and refreshed the overpowering Diptyque reed diffuser. Élise had commented on it, when she was over, so I made a point of ordering more. I was deliberating whether or not to prepare the guest room. My phone rang.

"Aren?" Élise said. Her voice sounded shaky. She sounded upset. My heart stopped for a moment. *Oh, God, no. Please don't bail.*

I took a deep breath to calm myself and then I said, "What's up, honey? You're still—"

"Oh, yes. But the rain is so heavy. I can't see. I'm not such a good driver. I just wanted to let you know that I have been delayed. I'll just wait out the storm. It shouldn't last much longer, I hope. If it does, I can book a room and come tomorrow."

"Where are you?"

"Oh, I just pulled into a ski resort. Bromley, I think. I couldn't read the signs. There's so much rain."

"Listen, sit tight. I'll drive out to you now. It should take me an hour depending on the road conditions." *She had taken a detour, but I didn't want to upset her more.*

"That's silly. You don't have to do that."

At that moment, I just wished I could hug her tight. She pushed past her comfort zone to come and see me. She got rewarded by near misses on the highway and getting caught in a bad downpour. I believed her. If she were a confident driver, this would be nothing. But she wasn't and she was scared. I could hear it in her voice.

"I do," I said solemnly. "Just lock yourself inside your car. When I get there, I will call you first and then knock on your window. Okay, sweetheart?"

"Thank you, Aren," she said with relief.

There were only a few cars in the lot when I arrived. I listened to the weather report as I drove. There were reports of flash flooding exactly in the area where I found Élise. Thank goodness she was able to reach the resort and just stay there. I pulled up alongside her. I honked. She waived. I got out of my truck and immediately tapped on her window. I was now soaking wet. I motioned for her to roll down her window.

"Is everything in the trunk? You stay there and I will unload your stuff into my truck."

She nodded. I quickly transferred things out of her car to my truck. I noticed her car was parked at an odd angle. When I was done, I knocked on the window again.

"Okay, Élise, all set," I said. "Let's get you out of here."

She opened the door, tentatively, perhaps fearing the rain would carry her away. I reached for her hand and pulled her out. She had pulled up her hood, but I pulled it down. Her hair was loose and starting to frizz in the rain. I was so happy to see her. I hugged her tight. She seemed so much thinner than I last remembered. She was shivering. I ushered her into my truck and turned up the heat.

"Hey," I said, "can you give me your keys so I can re-park your car? I'll move it so it's a little closer to the building."

She nodded. "Can you also let me know if you notice anything? I'm not sure if I ran over something when I turned into the lot."

I re-parked the car and quickly ran to my truck.

"I didn't notice anything. When the weather clears up we can have it checked. Got everything?" I asked before driving away.

"Aren, is it safe to leave it here?

"It will be fine. We can come back later tonight or tomorrow." I picked up her ice-cold hand and kissed it.

"You're actually here, Élise," I said enthusiastically. "You're cold. I'll get you home in a flash."

I reached over and brushed my lips against hers. That she didn't immediately respond didn't bother me. It was what I expected. She was nervous. I put on the music from the Buena Vista Social Club CD— one of her favorites—and drove.

Élise

When Aren and I drove up the winding gravelly path to his cottage, I was both relieved that we arrived safely and then anxious about how the rest of the day would unfold. I was happy Aren came to get me in his truck. I'm not sure his Prius would have been able to cut through the flooded roads. Aren and I didn't talk on the drive back. I appreciated that he played the Buena Vista Social Club CD. It provided a pleasant contrast to the otherwise gloomy day. That he played the CD let me know that he understood I just needed to regroup. I don't know why the rain was messing with my head. And now I was stuck at his cottage. My car was parked forty-five minutes away.

"Élise, I'm going upstairs to take a quick shower," Aren said when we walked inside of the cottage. "Why don't you hand me your bags so I can bring them upstairs? While you're downstairs, you can unpack your crate of special goodies. I can't wait to see what you brought. Okay?"

"Okay," I whispered.

Unpacking calmed me. I knew where everything was and so I went into auto mode while Aren showered.

Fifteen minutes later, Aren came downstairs looking refreshed after his shower. His gleaming hair was slicked back. He was wearing a long-sleeved white t-shirt and a pair of gray slim-fitting sweat pants. He looked relaxed.

"Okay, your turn," Aren said.

I found my bags neatly stowed under the window sill. I was glad he didn't put them on the bed or next to the bed. We didn't talk about where I would be sleeping. I knew there was a spare bedroom and a full bath down the hallway. I guess if he put my bags in his room, the expectation was I would share his room. Expectations. In the bathroom, I looked at my reflection. The blow-dried style I had this morning when I left was gone. My hair was bushy. I chuckled. I grabbed my shower cap and the shower gel I brought with me and took a long hot shower. There were body jet sprays as well as a hand sprayer and full rain showerhead.

It was all delicious. I looked across the room and saw the tub. It was so inviting. I crossed the room and indulged in a quick soak. I didn't notice any bubble bath.

When I was done, I toweled off. I brushed my teeth and applied my favorite facial products. I pulled on a set of clean underwear and slipped a caftan from Morocco over my head. I applied some hair lotion to my hair and twisted it into a bushy updo and then I made my way downstairs.

Soft instrumental music was playing.

"There you are," Aren said. "I'll get the tea going. Did you enjoy your bath?" he asked.

"I did, thank you."

Go in and make yourself comfortable on the sofa. I'll bring out the tea and the ginger biscuits you like.

"Okay," I said gratefully. I was happy he remembered that I liked ginger biscuits with tea. I grabbed my crate of goodies and brought them with me to the sofa. Aren joined me minutes later. He set the tray with the assortment of tea, mugs, and the hot water on the coffee table. He settled next to me on the sofa. I reached for the hibiscus tea and a mug and filled it with hot water. Aren set a small plate in front of me with ginger biscuits. We enjoyed a few sips of the tea and then turned our attention to my crate of things.

"Let's see what you brought," he said as I pulled my small crate close to me.

Aren pulled out the potpourri sachet bag I made for his drawers. It was filled with cedar and balsam fir. "What's that?" he asked.

"It's for your drawers so your clothes smell nice."

"Hmm, that's original," he said. It wasn't a gag gift. I spent time making them. I knew this was not something he ever bothered with. But I had some crazy idea he might appreciate it. Aren looked at me and then patted my hand. "Thank you," he said.

Aren felt around inside the crate and pulled up a pack of his favorite brand of cigars from Honduras, El Rey del Mundo, and a bottle of Haitian Barbancourt rum.

"God, you're an angel! I love it!" Fanny's husband Enrique suggested I do this. Thank goodness I listened.

I reached for my mug of tea and took a few sips and then set it down. The temperature was perfect. I settled back on the sofa. Aren draped his arm loosely around my shoulder and kissed my temple. He brought my hand to his lips and kissed it and then brought it to his chest.

"I'm so happy you're with me, Élise."

Tears started to roll down my eyes. I didn't realize it until Aren wiped them with his thumbs. "Oh, what's the matter, sweetheart?"

"I—oh—I don't know," I said.

Aren leaned back on the arm of the sofa. "Come here," Aren whispered.

I didn't even think. I just curled up against him and just let the tears run freely. We didn't talk. I didn't fuss when he undid the twist in my hair. I let him touch my hair and massage my head. That felt good, actually. It calmed me. I could feel his hand traveling from my head to my face to my shoulders and then to my breast. I could feel a faint stirring of arousal as his hand lowered and started to lift my caftan and caress my leg. I sighed.

"Aren."

"Shhh," he said. He kissed my forehead again. "Relax," he said. My lids were feeling heavy. I could feel myself drifting off to sleep. "I love you," I heard a voice say.

"Too soon," I murmured.

The last thing I remember was the sound of laughter.

.oOo.

Élise

When my eyes opened, I could see a beautiful rainbow sunset over Lake Champlain. I focused my attention on that sight. Aren was snoring, but it wasn't bad. It was kind of cute. His arms were wrapped tight around me. I could barely move. A lot of thoughts flooded my mind all at once.

It was hard to know what I thought or felt. Then one unified articulable thought settled in my mind: car. What about my car? The heavy rain had cleared. If we hurried, we could get my car before it was totally dark, but of course, I would have to follow him in the dark. I fidgeted a little in Aren's arms so he could loosen his grip.

"Aren," I said softly. He stirred a little and stopped snoring. I tapped his chest gently and called his name again. I tried again and said, "Aren, wake up."

His eyes opened, slowly. He blinked a few times and then he stretched his arms before settling them again around me. He kissed my nose.

"Good morning, sunshine," he said with a chuckle. "Aren, it's not morning."

He sighed dramatically. "I feel refreshed." He looked at his watch. "It's seven. Let's have breakfast for dinner!"

"Aren, it stopped raining," I said. "Maybe we could go get my car?"

He smiled at me. With his finger, he started to trace the contours of my lips. *Did* he *hear what I said?*

"Aren, I'm worried about my car. It's in a parking lot. Anything could happen. I can't afford to lose my car."

He looked at me. I couldn't read the meaning of his look. But he said, "You're here with me. Your car is fine. I parked it near the entrance. Nothing bad is going to happen to your car. Okay? Trust me. Just relax."

"Oh my God, you're doing it again."

"What?"

"You're trying to control me."

"Honey, it's late. We just zonked out. I don't want to drive out there. I certainly don't think you should drive in your car at night in unfamiliar terrain, especially if you're feeling anxious."

"But I'm feeling anxious because my car is abandoned."

Aren kissed me. I didn't respond. He kept kissing me, my lips, my nose, my cheeks, my neck. His kisses tickled my neck. I giggled.

"I want to cuddle with you. I don't want to drive anywhere. Trust me, Élise. It's not in my interest that your car gets sabotaged."

I looked deeply into his eyes. He kept telling me to trust him. But he didn't trust me. But then I hadn't given him much reason to trust me. I was the one who kept running away. There was so much we didn't know about each other and still needed to learn about each other. Aren could be incredibly pushy and annoying. But from everything I was learning about him, he was well-liked. He wasn't a creep or sleazy.

"I don't like not having my car. If you were in my shoes, you wouldn't be happy either. But can we make a deal? If we don't get along, you'll take me immediately to get my car?"

"Deal," Aren said quickly. "And you promise to relax and trust me?"

"You promise to respect my feelings? Trust has to be earned. Okay?"

"Okay," Aren said. "Kiss me now?"

"Oh my goodness! You never stop," I said.

"Sweetie, I dig your mind, but it's not your mind I want to connect with. He put his hand on my chest and then slipped it between my legs. I gasped.

"Even when you're mad at me, I can connect. When you shut down and go inside your head, I can't follow. You feel me?"

I nodded. I shifted my body so I could reach his face with mine. I wanted to kiss him, not because I was burning with passion or feeling frisky. I came to see him to find out if there was something between us. Aren was right. I didn't let myself feel. Even now I wasn't sure if I could be intimate with him. It was an academic thing for me, not a physical one. And so I kept my gaze on him as my lips approached his. I pressed my lips against his for a moment then lifted my face.

"More he said."

I pressed my lips against his and this time opened my mouth but I didn't engage my tongue. He pressed his mouth hard against mine at first, which I didn't like. But he relaxed and softened his lips. I liked the smell of his skin. I touched his face with my hands and with my lashes, butterfly kisses. I touched his hair. He moaned softly. I withdrew instinctively.

"Touch me," he said. "Don't be afraid."

I liked the way Aren responded to my touch. I liked the way he coached me. "Touch me here." Or, "No, honey, that's a sore spot for me." Or, "I don't feel anything if you touch me there." But maybe more than his kisses, I liked the way Aren held me. I felt safe. I felt protected. After we cleared up the tea, we made sandwiches and heated some miso broth. We strolled into the garden and then settled in for a night of TV watching. I was relieved Aren didn't complain. We watched *Game of Thrones Season 1*. A lot of the teachers had started to watch it when it premiered in April. I waited until mid-June to start watching. We made mint tea and then settled in to watch. I curled up next to him.

Aren yawned when the show was over. He stretched his arms. "So do you think you'll be up for more episodes?" I asked. "How many are there?"

"Ten."

Aren smiled. "Oh, sure—that means one episode per day," he said. "Great! You'll stay ten days. I love it!"

I didn't answer. I had no idea what the future held for us. But if we could hang out like this every day, then I had no problem sticking around. But that's not what Aren was expecting.

We cleaned up. Aren stood behind me and wrapped his arms around me. He kissed my cheek.

"I think it's bedtime," he whispered. I could feel my pulse starting to race. My feet felt heavy as if bolted to the floor.

"Why don't you go upstairs and get ready for bed?" he suggested. "I'll straighten up here and then I'll join you upstairs, okay? You won't lock me out, right?" he chuckled.

The thought had not really crossed my mind that I could or would lock him out of his room. The bathroom was another matter. I nodded in agreement.

"Good," he said.

Slowly, I climbed the stairs and walked into Aren's bedroom. I pulled out my toiletry bag and headed into the bathroom. After I finished my nighttime regimen, I applied a generous amount of argan oil onto my hair and wrapped it with a silk scarf. I removed my caftan and put it in a drawer Aren reserved for me. Most of my clothes were still packed. I didn't want to get too comfortable. I looked through my bag. I had packed a couple of satin nightgowns, a pair of silk pajamas, and my long-sleeved cotton pajamas. I opted for the nightgown. It was something I bought for myself long before I met Aren. It was pretty and comfortable. I hoped Aren would appreciate it without going crazy. The crotchless panties were at the bottom of the bag. I heard a knock on the door.

"I am finishing up," I said. "I'll be right out."

"No worries, Élise. I brushed my teeth downstairs. Take your time." I took one last look at my reflection in the mirror. I closed my eyes and said a quick prayer and then I walked out of the bathroom. Aren was already sitting up in bed. The lights were dimmed. His chest was bare. He reminded me of Sean Connery sporting his hairy chest in those iconic James Bond 007 movies. My knees grew weak—from anxiety. "I just want to put away my things," I said quickly. I set my toiletry bag down and put it in the drawer. I was trying to be subtle about the deep breaths I was taking. It was so quiet in the room. I could feel Aren's eyes boring through the back of my head. I stood up, holding onto the drawer chest for support. With bare feet, I made my way to the bed. Aren smiled at me.

"That was some green mile," he said. "What?" I said.

"*Green Mile,* ever watch the film? It's a wonderful movie about an unjustly convicted man facing execution. The reference to 'green mile' is the walk to the electric chair."

"Oh," I said nervously. I think I heard of the movie. I didn't see it though."

"I'm sorry, I was teasing you. I know you're nervous. He patted the space next to him. "Come here. I can't promise that I won't bite you, but I can promise I'll be gentle."

I gulped hard. Aren laughed.

Aren turned down the covers. "Come on. Get in."

I removed my robe and slid into bed. I clutched the covers.

Aren brushed my cheeks with his fingertips. He lowered his face to mine and kissed my cheeks. "You're beautiful," he said. He slid down and lay on his side watching me. He reached for the extra blankets at the end of the bed and place them on me. "Are you warm enough?"

I nodded. "Yes," I said.

Aren lifted my gown and parted my legs with his. He rested his hand on my hip. "Are you okay?" he asked huskily.

"Yes," I squeaked, or at least that's what it sounded like to me. He didn't do any more than that. We had reached a plateau for now. I hoped.

He slipped down a strap from my nightgown and kissed my shoulder.

"I have to pinch myself that this beautiful woman is in my bed and I can touch her and she can touch me." He searched my eyes. I blinked several times. He laughed. "Sweetheart, I am going to kiss you. Whatever you got going on in your head, let it go. Okay?"

Before I could finish the second syllable of "okay" his lips were on mine. It started as a few light pecks, loud pecks, and then he opened his mouth a little wider to open mine. The hand that was on my hip was now caressing my breast. He pinched. He teased. He was nibbling my ear and talking, his voice buzzing. Everything seemed to be happening in slow motion but all at once. He was tugging at the hem of my nightgown. I froze.

He kissed my lips gently.

"Sweetheart," he murmured. "I want to see you and touch you. Don't be afraid."

I raised my arms so he could lift my nightgown gently over my head. He put it on the floor next to his side of the bed. Then he began a trail of kisses leading to my breast. My nipples were standing erect. I chuckled.

"What's so funny?" he asked.

"Oh, I—I was just laughing at my body. My nipples are standing up!"

"Okay, stop talking. Your body and mine want to have a conversation and your mind is a distraction."

I laughed out loud. Aren ignored me and focused on the nipple he began to suck. I gasped. He was gentle at first and then started to move his tongue in different ways and then I don't remember any thought I had other than *Wait! I thought we were going to go slow.*

Aren was taking control. In truth I was relieved. I wasn't confident to initiate anything. He was leading me down a garden path, a neglected garden path, and breathing life.

"Stay connected to me, sweetheart," he kept saying when I drifted away into my thoughts. *How did he know?* He kept telling me to stop talking, but he kept talking to me, encouraging me with his words the way a photographer talks to a model to elicit the right emotion, the right expression, and the right moment to be photographed.

"Beautiful," Aren kept saying. He sat up with his back against the wall and guided me to sit inside of the V space of his legs. "I'm going to make you feel good, baby," he said. I just followed his voice. My back was against his furry chest. But I also felt a long and deep raised scar. He was kissing my neck. I turned my head.

"Hey, you're messing with the choreography," he said. "Aren," I asked, "do you have a scar on your chest?"

"Mm-hmm," he said as he continued to kiss my neck. And then he paused. "Do you want to see?"

"You don't mind?"

"No. Turn around."

I now sat facing him. My legs were wrapped around his hips. Aren angled the night light so I could see a long vertical scar decorated with a heartbeat line tattoo with a date. *March 11, 2007.*

"Oh my God!" I said. With shaking fingers I traced his scar. "Does it hurt?"

"No. Sometimes it itches. Certain fabrics irritate it. But otherwise, it gives me no problems."

"You did mention you had heart surgery, but I never connected the reality of the surgery."

Aren lifted my chin to look into my eyes. "Does it bother you? Does it freak you out?"

I touched his scar again and traced the design of the tattoo. "No," I said. "The date is the date of your surgery?"

"It's the date my cardiologist said I was going to make it. I made a decision on that day to live life to the fullest."

I instinctively wrapped my arms around Aren and held him tight. His story touched my heart. I kissed him as passionately as I could.

Aren broke from the kiss, panting. "Whoa, woman!"

"Oh, did I kiss you too hard?"

Aren smiled. "Just give me a second to adjust. You had the pilot light going and then you turn up the heat full blast!"

"It was just a kiss, Aren."

"Oh, I don't think so," he said. He slid down on the bed with me. We were lying on our side face to face naked. We kissed. We caressed each other. We fell asleep in each other's arms. Maybe Aren hoped for a robust love-making session. Maybe that would come. But I was lying naked in Aren's bed giving and receiving love and attention. This was huge for me. If Aren and I never saw each other again, I would still treasure this moment with him. I didn't have a visible heartbeat line tattoo. My tattoo was invisible. The date would be today the day I decided I would be open to love.

.oOo.

Aren

The birds seemed to be singing especially loud when my eyes flew open on Friday morning. Élise was deeply asleep. We were spooning. I kissed her shoulder lightly. She stirred but didn't wake up. Her skin was so soft and fragrant. I caressed her round butt and her hips. I could feel my dick stirring to life.

"Down boy," I said. "She's not ready yet." I chuckled. I couldn't say for sure whether yet was as soon as she woke up or in a few hours or even tomorrow or the next day. But I felt like she reached a milestone. We reached a milestone. I gave her pleasure and she accepted it. She might try to pretend last night didn't happen, but it did. Her body responded to mine. Her body enjoyed my touch, my kisses, and my voice. Patience was needed. My dick would be tunneling inside of her soon enough. Just thinking about being inside of her made me go rigid again. I had to stop thinking about us. I needed to go pee. I looked at Élise again. She looked so young and innocent.

"Soon, baby, you'll be mine," I whispered. And then I got up and padded over to the bathroom. I would go for a quick jog around the neighborhood and come back.

.oOo.

It was eight o'clock when I brought up freshly brewed coffee to the bedroom. I sat down on Élise's side of the bed and kissed her.

"Good morning, sleeping beauty," I said. "Wakey, wakey! Let's not waste the day."

Élise was still and then I saw her lashes start to flutter.

"Hmm?" she said. She opened her eyes and looked at me. She smiled so sweetly. I kissed her.

"I brought coffee. Time to wake up," I said.

Élise slowly sat up. She reached for her robe which miraculously was still at the end of the bed.

"Baby, I have already seen you naked. Why are you putting on your robe?"

"Aren, it's daylight. I can't just be naked and drink coffee in front of you."

"You're impossible," I said. I kissed her neck. "And sexy as hell."

She made room for me to sit down next to her. I handed her a mug of coffee and we looked at the newspaper that I picked up on the way back from my jog. I loved this. We worked on a crossword puzzle together. I checked the chess moves section. She looked at the Living Arts Section.

I took a quick shower. Élise refused to join me or let me join her. *Patience. Patience.* I thought for sure Élise would insist on immediately going to Southern Vermont to retrieve her car. But she surprised me.

"Aren, I called the resort and explained what happened. They were very helpful. I gave them the license plate number and told them I would pick it up at some point. They have my number. So I think for now everything is good. We can figure out later when it's convenient to drive down to Peru. Why is there a Peru, Vermont?" she asked.

"Beats me," I said. I didn't much care. What I cared about was that Élise cleared our schedules and we didn't have to devote an hour to retrieve her car. I was happy.

"Let's take a picnic and check out some waterfalls," I said. "I hope you brought a sexy swimsuit or else I'm going to throw a tantrum." That was an empty threat.

We hopped into the truck. We decided to visit four waterfalls. Moss Glenn Falls and Bingham Falls were both in Stowe. Moss Glenn Falls had a 125-foot drop that was stunning. The hikes were easy enough for Élise. The Big Falls in North Troy had a scenic pool in the forest. It was perfect for swimming. We ended our visit to the waterfalls in the afternoon at Bolton Potholes in Bolton. We secured our own pothole, a mini water cave. We splashed around like children. I stole a few kisses from Élise. She never looked more alluring in her dashing bold blue swimsuit. I dubbed her "La Sirène" after one of the Haitian goddesses she talked about.

It was after eight o'clock when we returned to the cottage. We stopped at a farm-to-table restaurant in Burlington on the way home.

.oOo.

Élise

I spent a fantastic day with Aren on the Friday leading up to the 4th of July. I always enjoy waterfalls so I was happy when Aren proposed to make a trip to visit the various waterfalls in Vermont. He wanted to visit all of them. I just wanted to take time to visit a few and enjoy the scenic ride. We ended our journey by having dinner at a wonderful farm-to-table restaurant on the way home. Fanny called me and yelled at me for not checking in with her.

"Are you okay?" Fanny asked. "I haven't heard from you in forty-eight hours. You didn't even answer my texts," she said in a huff.

Aren could hear Fanny's voice. "Élise is fine. She's very much alive. I can attest to that," he yelled so Fanny could hear him.

"I see," Fanny said. "Am I interrupting anything?" she asked sheepishly.

"Oh, we're on our way home. We had a great day," I said breezily. "I guess so. Listen, querida. You're not off the hook. You better find some time from el hombre and spill some details. Okay?"

"Love you too, Fanny," I said and quickly ended the call. "Who was that?" Aren asked.

"Oh, that's my best friend Fanny," I explained. "She was just worried because I hadn't checked in with her."

Aren glanced at me and then returned his attention to the road. "So are you going to tell her that I am 15/10 or 10/10?"

"Hmm, I think I'll tell her that I rate you a seven."

"What?!"

"Well, if I give you a perfect rating, then there's no motivation on your part."

"I guess you don't grade on a curve."

"Oh no, I never do that," I said.

"So tell me, honey, how's it going for you?"

"I guess I'm happy."

"You guess?"

"I don't know. I want to take each day as it comes. Today I spent a phenomenal day with you. Thank you."

"You're welcome, sweetheart. I had a wonderful day with you. It will be a perfect ten when we make love."

Somehow, I hadn't thought about our amorous time last night. Did it really happen? Did I dream it? I could feel Aren's eyes on me.

He lifted my skirt and patted my bare legs. "We're almost home."

I stared out the window. It was dusk. The road was quiet. I turned my attention to Aren's Pandora's menu and selected Steely Dan. *Where are we going? Do we have a future? How long does it last?*

We walked inside the cottage arm in arm. During the last leg of our trip, many thoughts flooded my mind. Maybe there was no answer to my questions. What I was left with was something my acupuncturist would say to me. "Accept the gift in the spirit it was given to you." From the moment Aren rescued me from the terrible rainstorm, he showed me nothing but kindness and attention. For however long I had to spend with him, I decided I would do my best to meet him halfway. No one had to know the salient details of what did or did not happen between us. All I could hope is that when the time for me to leave would come that we would have no regrets about the time we spent together.

.oOo.

Aren

Élise made us some ginger tea after hanging up our wet clothes. I was in a great mood, but I was also tired. I could feel her eyes on me, watching me carefully.

"Aren, why don't I run you a nice hot bath? I picked up some bath salts when we stopped at the store."

"Wait. Élise Douchet is proposing to take a bath with me?"

"No, Élise Douchet is proposing to give you a bath."

"Is there a catch?"

"Catch? Of course not. I'll go upstairs and get the bath ready, okay?" I could hear her taking a quick shower and then running the bath.

I quickly cleaned up and then used the downstairs bathroom. When I went upstairs, I brought up two nightcap cocktails I quickly made and put them in the mini-fridge in the bedroom. I then walked into the bathroom where I found Élise wearing the beautiful robe she had on the night before minus the gown underneath. I wrapped my arms around her and gave her a sloppy wet kiss. She scowled.

"Oh, Aren!" she said in disgust. "That was awful!" I laughed. "Hey, be nice!"

I quickly stripped off my clothes. Before I was able to put a toe in the water, Élise insisted I take a shower first.

"Oh come on!"

"No, really. Take a quick shower. Use your brush. In fact, here, I'll brush you and then you take a shower and then take a bath."

I groaned and complained but secretly, I was enjoying Élise brushing my skin vigorously. My skin tingled in a good way. She walked toward the shower and turned on the water testing the temperature.

"I hope it's not too warm for you. But you can adjust it."

I stepped in and took a shower, lathering up, and then rinsing. I felt super clean. I shut off the water and stepped out. Élise was standing with my bathrobe and helped me put it on.

"Well, thank you, darling." I kissed her quickly. She led me to the bathtub. In truth, I probably had used the tub once before: the day I moved in. I don't know what possessed me to install a bathtub. I never took baths. But Élise urged me on. Thank goodness I installed handlebars. I stepped in carefully. It felt really hot, but not uncomfortable. I sat down and inhaled the fragrance of the water.

"This feels good, baby."

"I'm glad," she said. "Lean back. I'll massage your shoulders.

Élise massaged my head, my face, my shoulders, and my hands. I felt like I was getting a special. But I loved the way Élise was giving me attention. She found the knots in my muscles. She told me funny stories. I felt relaxed and just happy. I sighed.

"Is anything wrong?" she asked.

I looked at her. "Yes, please get into the bath with me."

"Aren, I wanted to show my appreciation. This is your time."

"Okay, this is my time. I appreciate your appreciation. Now get in the tub."

She didn't argue with me or make excuses. She slipped off the robe and got in the tub with me. The tub was big enough so that she could sit facing me, but instead, she positioned herself with her back against my chest. I instinctively wrapped my arms around her waist and squeezed her tight.

"Thank you," I whispered.

While we talked about our day and made plans for the next day, I caressed her body. Maybe giving me a bath to relax me, also relaxed her. I caressed her breasts and she accepted my touch. Everything felt natural. We were two people who really liked each other and cared about each other. I felt her attraction to me.

"You know who you remind me of?" she asked. "Who?" I asked suspiciously.

"Hmm, Sean Connery. He had the best dimples. And he had a hairy chest like yours. Very sexy."

"Oh, you think I'm sexy, huh?"

She smiled. "Oh, in that Sean Connery kind of way," she said slyly. "I always thought I looked like Omar Sharif, you know from *Dr. Zhivago*."

Élise fluttered her lashes.

"Yes, I can see that," she confessed.

I could feel a momentum building up slowly between us. If I could pace things right, we would be sharing a smoldering passion.

"Okay, sweetheart," I said. "Let's drain the tub and get out of here."

Élise smoothed oil and cream over my body and I did the same for her.

We left the bathroom hand in hand. I motioned for her to get into bed. I quickly retrieved the nightcap cocktails out of the fridge and set them on my nightstand.

"What's that?" she asked.

"Oh, a rum flip," I said. "I thought it would be nice to have a little nip before bed. Take a sip."

She took three sips and then set the glass down. "What do you think?" I asked.

"It tastes like egg nog, but with a kick."

I laughed. I set my glass down. I positioned myself in the center of the bed and guided Élise to sit facing me with her legs extending long facing the wall. I was overcome with desire for her. I kissed her open-mouthed and then introduced my tongue. She hesitated and then tentatively introduced her tongue. My tongue left her mouth and found her breasts. Her pulse was racing. Her hands were in my hair. She was rubbing my scalp. Her skin was soft and supple. My mouth found her opening. She gasped from shock and then she moaned. Everything about her was delicious.

"I love you, baby. I'm not going to hurt you."

I brought her hand to my dick. "Touch me. Make me feel good. "I'll show you how." I coached her. I told her how fast and how hard she needed to stroke until I was hard. I placed a pillow under her hips to get the angle right. *Oh, I'm coming in!*

"Look at me," I said to encourage her. "Keep your eyes on me. Connect with me." I started to thrust. I thrust slowly with long intervals. When she started to respond, I thrust more vigorously. Her eyes rolled back in her head. She was squirming and writhing. But I could feel her gripping me hard inside of her and I collapsed on top of her shuddering along with her. We were sticky with sweat and our lovemaking. It was all I could do to crawl out of bed quickly and get a washcloth for us. Élise was drifting off to sleep. I washed her and wiped my dick. I brought the cloth back to the bathroom and then crawled into bed. I pulled Élise to my chest. As sleep claimed me finally, I remember saying, "I love you, Élise."

.oOo.

Élise

The sound of birds singing woke me up. I lay still to listen for a while and then I turned to look at Aren. He was still asleep. His arms were still around me. That made me smile. But I needed to use the toilet. I tried to wriggle out of his grasp without waking him.

"Where are you going?" he said in a gruff voice. "I have to pee," I said chuckling.

Aren released his hold on me. "No dilly-dallying. Get your ass back in bed, ASAP."

I got up quickly and went to the toilet. I examined my face in the mirror as I washed my hands. My hair had morphed into a super fro! I would deal with that later. I brushed my teeth and returned to bed. Aren was gone. I took the opportunity to find my scarf and hair lotion and wrap my hair. Hopefully, that would whip it back into shape. Aren padded back to the bed and slipped right next to me.

"Why are you wearing a scarf?"

"Because my hair looks like a wild bird's nest."

"But I love your wild look."

"Yes, well, a scarf helps preserve the health of my hair."

"Okay, enough of that. I'm horny."

I laughed. "Now?"

"Uh-huh."

"Aren, did you take something while I was away?"

"Let's find out," he said with a sheepish grin.

Aren's energy was so different. He wasn't rough, but he wasn't gentle. He was insistent.

"I want you now," he said. He then stood up next to the bed and pulled my legs to wrap around his hips. He thrust forcefully, rubbing me inside with his fingers. It was all happening so fast. But what I felt was intense pleasure. He then positioned himself on the bed and set me on top. "Take me for a ride," he said.

Aren placed his hands on my hips lifting me up and down until I could do the rhythm on my own. Aren was saying all kinds of words: a mixture of crass vulgar words and words of love. Then I felt that pressure build. I could grip him better and squeezed as hard as I could.

"Élise!" he yelled and then shot his seed inside of me.

"Oh, baby," he said kissing my face. "You fuck like a goddess." I laughed. "Stop!"

He kissed my shoulder. "You're my love goddess," he said. "I love cuddling with you and being romantic. But sometimes I just need to fuck—you."

"Oh," I said. I didn't know what to do with that information. He pulled me to his chest and pulled up the covers.

"We'll take a snooze and then get up. It's early. It's not even seven."

"Okay," I yawned.

"I love you, baby," he said.

"Me?"

"Yes, Élise. You. All right, let's sleep."

When I woke up again, I felt awake. Aren was caressing my body. "Wake up, sleeping beauty," he said. I smiled.

"Good morning, sweetheart," Aren said. "Did you sleep well?"

"Yes, I did, thank you."

I started to get up. He stopped me.

"Good. Are you ready for some poking?"

"Poking?" I sputtered in laughter.

"Yes, sweetheart. I want to poke you and then take a shower and get on with the rest of the day."

"I don't know. Poking doesn't sound very pleasant."

"Oh, that's what you say. You know nothing."

Aren swung his legs to the floor and pulled me up out of bed. Frisky Aren was back. But he was more affectionate and loving. He took his time with foreplay and then he angled himself inside of me. There was no mad thrusting. Just connection. I liked that. His hands were gripping my hips to secure his connection.

"We're made for each other," Aren said. "I love you. Don't fight it."

.oOo.

Aren

I had just stepped back into the room after taking a shower. "Aren, your phone rang," Élise announced.

"Who was it?" I asked.

"I don't know. I didn't pick up your phone."

"Why not?"

"Aren, I'm not in the habit of answering other people's phones without permission," she quipped.

"You're joking, right?"

"No. It's your phone."

"Well, I got nothing to hide."

"Well, I don't know. It could be private."

I looked at the earnest expression on Élise's face. She was curious, but she wasn't going to interrogate me. Aha! A test.

"Okay," I said. I walked over to her and started nuzzling her neck.

The phone rang. I kept kissing her.

"Aren, shouldn't you answer your phone?"

"It's my phone. If I don't feel like answering it, don't worry about it."

She made a face.

"You're jealous," I said to tease her.

"How can I be jealous of someone I'm not aware of? You flatter yourself."

"Uh-huh. Well, I'm curious."

I walked over to my nightstand and looked at the caller ID. It was Lily. I smiled. She had left a text message asking me if I was all set for the weekend. I looked up. Élise was watching me. For a second I thought about torturing her, and then I realized if she got messages first thing in the morning and didn't immediately volunteer who they were from, I would be annoyed.

"Relax, honey. It's Lily, my daughter. She wanted to make sure I had plans for the weekend."

"Oh. Well, you know if you want to spend time with her, that's okay—"

I walked over to Élise and kissed her nose. I loved her nose. It was actually very delicate and complemented her small full lips. I quickly texted Lily.

Hanging out with É. All set. Happy 4th.

I showed Élise my message before sending it.

"Aren, we haven't talked about this, but I guess now is a good time as any. What are we?"

"Hmm, I think we're human beings. Specifically, your genitalia suggest you're a woman and my genitalia suggests I'm a man."

"Ha, ha. You know what I mean. I don't want to complicate your life. I don't know how I'm supposed to act. What are the rules?"

"You're funny."

I led her by the hand and sat her down on the unmade bed. I pulled over my cube cushion and sat in front of her, still holding onto her hand. "Élise, would you believe I'm new at this too? Sure, I have had a few relationships with women since Helen died. For the most part, I've been content with sex visits and booty calls. I haven't been interested in companionship. It's different with you. I think I want to build a life with you."

I could see Élise's face turning gray. Why was this so surprising to her?

"Aren, I don't know what I want," she said. "Before I met you, I made peace with being alone. I'm used to it. I don't know that I want to build a life with anyone at this point in my life."

"Sweetheart, why did you come? Don't get me wrong. I'm happy you're here. I want you to be here. But what did you expect?"

She took a deep breath. "You know I booked a room at the hotel where I stayed last time—just in case. I mean, what if we had a big fight or we didn't click? I didn't want to be stuck."

Her admission made me laugh. "So did you cancel the room?"

"No, I have the room until Sunday. I want the security." I kissed her forehead.

"You know, if I were in your shoes, I might have done the same thing. In fact, I'm pretty certain that I wouldn't have spent the night—if it were anyone but you. Okay, I'm not going to mess up this good thing we have between us with all sorts of demands. Just know: I'm not seeing anyone on the side. I do have a lot of friends, male and female, and maybe some leftover romances where it ended a long time ago on my end. I want to spend more time with you. I don't know for sure where we will end up, but I'm willing to work to forge a path. Is that something you might want?"

"I like you, Aren. More than you realize. Maybe even more than I realize."

She was fluttering her eyelashes, but she wasn't biting her lip nervously.

"That's it?"

"Mmm-hmm." I laughed.

"You're a nut. My coconut."

"Ugh!"

I stood up, pushed her down on the bed, and started kissing her. The phone rang again, but I ignored it. And so did Élise.

.oOo.

On Saturday there was a balloon festival going on at Silver Spring Lake, so I took Élise on a balloon ride after spending the day swimming and kayaking. This was why I lived in Vermont—a dazzling blue sky against the backdrop of rounded green mountaintops. The air tastes sweeter than anywhere else. Later that night she insisted on looking through my photo albums.

I made a fire in the great room. We looked through photo albums. I talked to her until the wee hours of the morning about all the events in my life. She actually listened. Like her, I was not born in the US. I had moved to the United States with my parents as a child. She loved the stories I told her about growing up in Kazakhstan. It was all so exotic for her. But perhaps her greatest generosity was listening to my stories about Helen. It was rare that I could get through my story about Helen and a woman would not then begin to comfort me with sex. Élise sat next to me wide-eyed, soaking in every detail as an impartial listener. It was a luxury. Most people aren't really interested in the past—especially if it entails a tragedy.

"So Helen didn't live here."

"No. We bought this place as rental property. Her parents had a great place in Lake Winnipesaukee where we vacationed a lot. Lily moved out to Vermont first. And then when Helen died, I wanted to be closer to Lily. Would it make a difference if Helen had actually lived here?"

"I don't know, maybe. I get the feeling she was a larger-than-life presence."

"She was. And so are you."

Élise sighed.

"Élise, I have talked all night about me. What about you?"

"Aren, I told you my life story."

"No, you haven't. Who broke your heart?"

Élise smiled enigmatically. Mona Lisa had nothing on her. "It's all forgotten now."

"Clearly, not," I insisted.

"Clearly, yes." She yawned and looked at her watch. "It's late. You promised we could go antiquing tomorrow. I'm going to take a quick shower and meet you later, okay?"

I sat stunned as Élise kissed my cheek and then disappeared out of the room into the bathroom. By the time I cleaned up and got ready for bed, Élise was curled up in the bed wearing a pretty but not especially sexy nightgown. I crawled into the bed and slipped my leg between hers in a fitted spoon.

"Are you mad at me?" I asked.

She turned around to face me. "No, Aren, of course not."

"So why are you wearing this?" I said, slipping the strap of her nightgown down her shoulder.

She chuckled. "Oh, I got it especially for you when we went shopping. Don't you remember?"

It was my turn to chuckle.

"You are a very beautiful woman. I mean it. Why the hell do I need you to be wrapped up in this thing? You have nothing to hide from me, sweetheart. Take it off."

"Oh, Aren. Really?"

"Please. I want to feel your skin against mine. I hate lace. It's scratchy."

"Fine," she sighed. She sat up and pulled off her nightgown. "I guess that settles that," she said. She sank back onto the bed and resumed our spooning position. I was stroking her breasts and nuzzling her neck.

"Élise?"

"Yes?"

"Are you ever going to tell me about your past loves?" Élise glared at me and then turned away from me. "Élise."

"Stop it!" she screamed. "Do you want me leave?" She sat up and looked at me.

"I don't understand Élise. I tell you everything. You're keeping this devastating hurt that impacted your life from me."

"I told you about my family and the terror we experienced in Haiti. That's huge."

"But that's not what broke your heart."

"How do you know that? My relationship with Olivier—"

"That's his name. You've never mentioned his name before."

Élise slapped her hand against her forehead and screamed: "*Putain! Merde!*" She got out of bed and went inside of the bathroom and then came right out wearing a bathrobe.

"Where are you are going?"

"I don't want to sleep with you. I'm going to the pool house. I don't want to be in the house with you."

I blocked the door. "Élise, let's be adults about this."

"Get out of my way, Aren."

"I want to be close to you," I said. "I need to get rid of this guy."

"He's gone, Aren. Are you listening to me? He's gone. I don't talk about him."

"You save his letters. You keep his pictures."

"How the hell do you know?"

"When I came to visit and changed in your bedroom, I noticed a stack of cards and letters. On top was a framed photograph."

"You-you spy on me?"

"No, I noticed it. I didn't go snooping. It was right there on your shelf."

"Stop, Aren. I'm serious. What you think you're looking for is not in that part of my past. If you think that, then you don't understand me. My time with Olivier was a disturbing time in my life, but that's not the cause of who I am. Maybe at best it was a symptom. If I have to have one more discussion about this, I'm done. I don't want to go back. Why can't you understand that? You can't possibly be jealous. Is that what this is about?"

"If you keep blowing up every time I mention him or that period in your life, then the scab has not healed. I want to love you. All of you, not just the part outside of the bandage. Even the gross scabby thing hiding beneath the bandage, I want to see it. I want to kiss it and make it better and make you whole."

"So you're a magician and an engineer," she sneered. "Aren, I'm not broken. And if I were, you couldn't fix me."

"You don't know until you have shared everything with me. I love you."

"Stop it! We've spent sixty hours together. That's nothing."

"It's a point in time along the curve of infinity. I know what I feel. Stay here."

"Aren, why do I have to tell you everything? That's not intimacy. That's just your being controlling."

"But that's who I am. That's what I'm trying to explain to you. I don't know how to function otherwise."

"Oh, God."

"Make love to me, Élise."

"Now? In the middle of an argument?"

"Yes."

"Are you crazy?" she shouted.

"Hmm, yes," I said. I reached out and caressed her face. "I'm mad at you," she said.

"I know. You can kick me. Just make love to me, Élise."

I walked back to the bed. I bent down and pulled out a position wedge and placed it on the bed.

"You choose the positon," I told her.

Élise shook her head perhaps in exasperation.

"Use me to work out your rage. You have so much fire and passion inside of you. Rock my world. Bring on the volcano. I can handle it, sweetheart."

I walked up to Élise and untied the robe. I started weaving around her in attempted strikes.

"Stop it, Aren."

"No. Fight back."

"No."

"You think I'm frail. I'm much tougher than you think."

I tried to land a few sidekicks which Élise blocked. I put up my fists and started to spar.

"Come on. Your best shot."

Élise tried her best kickboxing moves and I blocked them. At one point I made her stumble. She got up and got aggressive. We shoved each other. I had her pinned on the floor and with her knees she pushed me hard so that I fell back against the bed. I could feel her breath on my face like a furious lioness. And when she dropped herself on top of me, she pressed down as hard as she could. She was strong, but I was stronger. I flipped us so that I was now on top. She could roll away from me, but it would take a lot of effort.

"Make love to me."

And the sweet gentle Élise was replaced by an incredibly strong warrior who had legs of steel and gripped mine. She grabbed my dick and sucked forcefully.

"Oh, god, yes!" I breathed. "More! Touch me."

"No, I want my pleasure first."

"Okay, take me. Take what you want."

Élise sat astride me. I brought my hands to her opening and fingered the way she liked. She moaned.

"Élise," I cooed. "Do you want me, baby?"

"Yes," she cried.

"You want my dick inside of you grinding inside of you, ripping you apart?"

"Yes."

"Then take me."

I watched as Élise twisted and shifted in all sorts of angles to get the right friction until she found her rhythm.

"Go, baby. It's just us." I grabbed her hips and then moved her up and down while she rocked her pelvis and used her muscle to squeeze my shaft."

"Squeeze me. That's right. Squeeze."

We rocked and convulsed together and then collapsed in ecstasy. "That's what it's about," I said with satisfaction. "I love you. Now sleep, honey. We can be sweet and gentle in the morning if you want." Élise lay her head on my shoulders. She fell asleep instantly.

I held her tight as she slept.

"You're mine," I said out loud. *I'm going to break you free.* I shut my eyes and fell asleep.

.oOo.

Élise

What began as a treacherous journey filled with anxiety ended up being a marvelous blip in my otherwise uneventful life. I couldn't say Aren was the love of my life, *l'homme de ma vie*. But I wasn't looking for happily ever after. Happy for now was actually very nice—nicer than I ever imagined. On July 4th, we stayed in bed most of the day, a *grasse matinée*. We read the paper and worked on crossword puzzles together. We had a sumptuous breakfast in bed, featuring poached eggs, café au lait, and delicious jams on fresh-baked bread we picked up at the bakery. Then we spent the evening in Shelburne enjoying an open-air concert by the Vermont symphony and later watched the fireworks display. It was my last night in Vermont with Aren and we slept in the loft of the pool house so we could watch the sunrise over Lake Champlain. We cuddled and fell asleep instantly. It was perfect.

I wanted to end my wonderful visit with a short morning hike with Aren. We sat on the wraparound deck sipping our morning coffee. Most of my things were packed. I just had a few odds and ends to pack before my trip home. I was lost in thought so I wasn't sure I heard what Aren said.

"Stay?" I repeated. "Stay," Aren confirmed.

"Hmmm," I said. I was sad to be leaving, but I was also ready to leave. If I stayed, would I be committing myself to a relationship that I didn't necessarily want? If I left, would I be slamming the door at a gift, an opportunity? From the moment I arrived Aren told me every day that he loved me. He had already asked me if I was open to exploring a path of a loving partnership. I didn't answer him then. But that's what he was asking of me now by asking me to stay. Was I open to his love, not just sex, but a loving relationship with him? Aren wanted a package deal with me. *Was I willing to let him be my man? What's that line in the Eminem rap song "Lose Yourself" that my students always sang?*

> *You only get one shot, do not miss your chance to blow*
> *This opportunity comes once in a lifetime*

.oOo.

Aren

"Stay," I said to her simply. I didn't want to hear excuses about commitments and conflicts. I felt such a strong connection to her. Did she feel the same?

"Okay," she whispered.

"Hallelujah!" I cheered and reached over and kissed her. She chuckled.

CHAPTER 5

CAN'T GET ENOUGH OF YOUR LOVE, BABE

L'amoureuse²

> *Ses rêves en pleine lumière*
> *Font s' évaporer les soleils,*
> *Me font rire, pleurer et rire,*
> *Parler sans avoir rien à dire.*
> —Paul Eluard

I could listen to Élise recite this poem a thousand times and never get bored, always finding new meaning and subtleties. Her deep breathless voice, the consonants sounding more like the low hum of a bee delighting in the sweet fragrance of a beautiful flower.

Her voice, the sound of my lover whispering and cooing words of love. I still marvel at the perfection of each line of the poem that sums up that miraculous feeling of being in love with a woman who eclipses my existence. Who stands on my eyelids, her hair entangled in mine, who makes me laugh and cry and laugh again and then makes me talk even when I have nothing to say.

"Aren, if you could wish on a star and change the course of your

---

2   And her <u>dreams</u> in the <u>bright</u> day
     Make the suns <u>evaporate</u>
     And me <u>laugh</u> cry and <u>laugh</u>
     Speak when I have <u>nothing</u> to say

life, what would you wish for?"

I thought about that question and the first response I initially gave. I was such an ass. What would I wish for? I would wish to be stuck in a magical time loop so I could relive over and over again the twelve days in July I spent with Élise. We went cycling, swimming, and kayaking. I took her shopping in Manchester so she could get proper outdoor clothing and gear, including decent hiking boots. We made love every single day throughout the day. All right, sometimes we just cuddled and spooned with each other. But as far as I was concerned, we were making love. And Élise was happy to be with me. Her eyes sparkled like diamonds when she looked at me. She didn't have to say she was in love. Her face and her eyes were so eloquent on that subject. And I delighted in her company.

I would sing Van Morrison songs and my favorite selections from the American songbook like "Under My Skin" in the middle of the grocery aisle when we would go shopping. I'd throw tantrums in public if she didn't kiss me on demand. I wrote poems and love letters, posted them to her apartment in Boston, and bragged to the postmaster that that was what I was doing. She was like a little girl enthralled by the magic and the fanfare.

We made love under the stars and woke up together to watch the sun rise.

All good things come to an end eventually, so they say. I cried when it was time for Élise to go home. She said she needed to concentrate on the paper she was going to deliver at an upcoming conference. I was going to be traveling.

"So we'll just touch base when our schedules free up. A month isn't so terribly long, Aren," she chided.

The trip to Bromley Mountain to pick up Élise's car was quiet. We played music. She sat as close to me as possible and laid her hand on my lap as I drove. I was in a bad mood. Actually, I was angry.

I insisted on replacing her windshield wipers as a delay tactic. Or maybe I just wanted to show her that I worried about her making the long drive back to Boston alone. She didn't like to talk while driving so I couldn't talk to her during the drive even though she had a hands-free phone. I was dying. I couldn't breathe.

"Aren, please don't do this," Élise pleaded as I refused to let her get into her car. I had her pinned against the car, and I kept kissing her, pressing myself hard against her so she could feel me.

"Call me when you get home. Promise," I said gruffly.

"Yes," she said. She brought my face close to hers and kissed me passionately. It was sweeter than fresh water. My soul needed that. Yet my heart was still breaking.

"Thank you for doing that," I murmured.

She took advantage of that moment to quickly open the door and lock it. She rolled down the window enough so I could kiss her. But I could not reach inside and unlock the door. She knew me well.

I stepped back and watched as she pulled out and made her way back to Boston. That was it. No goodbyes. No "I'll see you soon." It was a gorgeous, sunny Tuesday afternoon. I walked slowly back to my truck. I got in and sat in silence for seconds, minutes.

A clicking sound startled me. Someone was tapping on my window. "Sir, are you all right?"

A young woman was looking at me with concern. I smiled, blankly. "Yes," I answered in a flat tone.

I wasn't all right, but I started the truck and waved as I pulled out onto the road back toward my cottage. On the way home, a policeman stopped me. Apparently, the young woman was concerned that I might not make it back. The policeman followed me back to my house. How humiliating. I picked up the phone.

"Hey, Dad, what's up?"

"Nothing. Can't I call to check in on my daughter?"

"Sure, Dad. But you don't usually call me in the middle of the day. What's up?

"Can you come over, Lily?"

"Now? What's wrong, Dad?"

I broke down. "I… just come over, okay?"

"Sure. Sure. I'll be there in a couple of hours, okay? I love you, Daddy."

"I love you, too."

I threw the door open to receive my daughter and melt into her arms. She hadn't seen me this distraught since her mother was initially diagnosed with terminal cancer ten years earlier.

"Talk to me, Daddy."

"I'm just an old fool." I was sniffling. We sat on the sofa, father and daughter. I laid my head on my daughter's lap, and she gently stroked my mostly salt-and-pepper hair. She was studying me the way she always did, marveling at my Central Asian features that contrasted with her Nordic appearance even though we shared the same blood.

"I said goodbye to Élise," I said, sighing. "Who's Élise?"

"This incredible woman I met. I spent the most wonderful twelve days with this woman."

"Ah, that's what you were up to. Well, did you break up?"

"No. We have to work on our own projects. We won't see each other for another month."

"Well, Dad, you'll see each other, then," Lily said cheerfully.

"I told you: I'm an old fool. I don't want to be away from her for a month."

"Does she feel the same way about you?"

"I don't know."

"I see. What's she like?"

I stood up, walked over to my laptop, and called up some photos. I brought the computer to the sofa and lay it on her lap. Lily saw hundreds of photos of an attractive brown-skinned woman, my Élise. She especially liked the one where Élise was wearing sunglasses and staring off toward a lake, her long silver strands swirling with the wind. Lily paused at the photograph of me giving Élise a piggyback ride through the woods. There was also a funny photo where Élise was coming out of the water wearing a relatively conservative bikini. I was bursting with pride then and now with how fit she was. With her it was discipline, not vanity. In the photo, Élise was trying to cover up her face to avoid the camera's eye. Her gray hair was plastered against her head. Her brown skin seemed to soak up the sun's reflection. Lily looked up at me. I could feel myself wordlessly seeking her approval. I had never sought her approval for anything. Clothes didn't count.

"She seems like a very special lady," Lily finally said.

"She is."

"Then I'm happy for you."

Lily opened her arms and held me while I wept inconsolably. "Dad, is she one of those 'out of sight, out of mind' people?" Lily asked.

I stopped crying and thought for a moment. "Yes, in some ways or at least where I'm concerned, she does have that tendency."

"You're pushy and controlling," Lily said. "She stayed with you in this cottage for almost two weeks."

"What are you getting at, Lily?" I said.

"Dad, you have to do what you always do. Wear her down. If you think a month is too long, then come up with a scheme to shorten the time. Come on, Dad, you know how to play this game."

I sat up. "You think so?"

"Dad, did you ever watch that movie with Heath Ledger—*Ten Things I Hate About You*?"

"No. What an odd title for a romantic comedy."

"Well, some of these movies have great dating advice. Come on. Let's make popcorn and watch the movie."

I was dubious about Lily's movie suggestion, but she was onto something. I was not going to let Élise slip away. I would have to wear her down. The more outrageous, the better.

CHAPTER 6

BACK TO BOSTON

Élise was opening the door to her apartment when Antonio opened his door and poked his head out.

"Holá!"

"Holá," Élise replied.

"Where have you been? Even the postman has been going crazy. You didn't forward your mail. Is everything okay? By the way, I have a big box that I signed for you."

"Yes, I'm fine," Élise said breezily. "Come in." Élise had not yet put away her bags from her extended stay with Aren. She had stepped out to do some quick errands and get groceries.

Antonio walked quickly toward Élise and helped her with her grocery bags. He looked closely at her. "Did you go on vacation?" he asked. "You look rested."

"Thank you. I guess I did go on vacation." Élise was making her way to the kitchen. "Want some tea?"

"Sure."

Antonio sat at the table and watched as Élise happily prepared tea. She was humming. He thought he recognized the tune: the theme song from the Brazilian telenovela they loved to watch together on Youtube. The song was "Jura Secreta." Antonio laughed, as if let in on a secret.

"What?" she said.

"I don't believe it," Antonio said softly. "What?"

"You're in love."

Élise laughed. "No, I'm not!" she protested. Her face revealed the most radiant smile he had ever seen on her face.

"*¡Dios mío!* It's true." He laughed. "I'm not in love."

Antonio snorted. "You met someone. That's why you were gone so long. I thought you said you were going up to Vermont for the weekend. That wasn't a weekend. You were gone two weeks!"

"Twelve days."

"That's two weeks. So tell me. Diga me."

"There's nothing to tell."

"You insult me. I thought we were friends. Wait, it's that gentleman friend of yours who borrowed my bicycle. It's him!" he said excitedly.

"Yes, it's Aren. I spent the holiday with him in Vermont. We had a lot of fun."

"Fun. What kind of fun?"

"You know, we went swimming and kayaking and hiking and—"

"You made love?"

Élise's face flushed maroon. Antonio laughed. He reached over and patted her hand.

"It's a wonderful thing, that magic between a man and a woman. Never be ashamed of it."

"Oh God, there you go again."

Antonio chuckled as he received his cup of tea. Élise handed him the sugar bowl, and he helped himself to two lumps of sugar.

"So was this a fling or are you two going to see each other again?" Antonio asked.

"I guess. I mean, we need to take a break so I can focus on my paper for the conference."

"Mira! You have been presenting a variation of the same paper for the last—"

"Oh, don't start."

"You find a man, and you use the excuse of a conference to keep your distance? So maybe he didn't please you that much—"

"Oh, can we stop talking about this?" she said quickly. "He's not married, right?"

"No, he's a widower and has an adult daughter. She's thirty-four."

"Have you met her yet?"

"No, actually. She lives in Vermont. They don't live together, but she's close enough that they see each other."

"How long ago did his wife die?" Antonio asked. "Hmm. Four years ago. She had cancer."

"I'm sorry for him. So, in that time he hasn't had relationships?"

"Oh, he seems to have dated a lot. I mean I didn't interrogate him."

"What does he do for a living?

"Oh, well he was trained as an engineer. He went to MIT. He had a solar energy business and sold it not too long after his wife died. He's retired, but he still has projects he works on."

"I see. Well, whatever it was that you did or did not do with this man, clearly you had a good time. It shows all over your face. But be careful, querida. There's no such thing as a free ride," Antonio said.

"Great. Is this your way of encouraging me? Because it's not working."

Antonio smiled wistfully. "Listen, querida. Just remember: we're all human beings. We make mistakes."

"He said he doesn't have women on the side. I believe him."

"All right. Maybe he's telling the truth. I don't know the man. I'm not trying to poison you against him. It's just that you have high expectations of people, and I just want to warn you that not everyone can live up to your ideals. It doesn't mean they're bad or that they're trying to harm you. Just open your heart and be ready to forgive—if this guy deserves it."

"It's funny how these things happen. I wasn't looking for anyone. I was fine being on my own. And when I got home last night, I felt so lonely. I didn't tell him that. But it was so hard for me to fall asleep," Élise sighed.

Antonio patted Élise's hand affectionately.

"You know I've been praying for you for so long."

"Oh God, no—"

"Have faith, querida. God sent me to watch over you."

Élise started to laugh. Antonio rolled his eyes in exasperation. "Didn't you say you have a box for me?" Élise said, wanting to change the subject.

"*Insolente*! That's your problem."

"Yeah, yeah, yeah. Go get that box."

.oOo.

Élise waited until the evening to open the box. It was shipped from Holistic Wisdom. *Hmm, I don't remember ordering anything, Maybe it's some kind of spa gift from the resort.*

She opened the interior box and saw the huge, beautifully gift-wrapped box with a card.

She opened the card and found a $100 gift certificate.

HOLISTIC WISDOM GIFT CERTIFICATE IS HEREBY AWARDED TO ÉLISE DOUCHET FROM AREN KARAJIAN.

"Hmm," Élise said out loud. She read the card, and it said:

So the adventure begins, my love.

Élise smiled. She pulled out the large gift-wrapped box and opened it. Inside was a cellophane blue microfiber wedge-shaped cushion. She laughed. It was one of Aren's sex cushions: a combination wedge and ramp: The Liberator wedge.

"Oh my God, what have I done?" she sighed, shaking her head. Later that night, Élise was reclining comfortably against the Liberator wedge. She picked up the phone on the second ring.

"Hey, Aren," she said brightly, genuinely happy to hear his voice. "Hey, sweetie. What are you up to?"

"Ah, well, I got this incredible present that was delivered to me. It's a reading cushion. I'm using it right now as I sit up in bed and read."

Aren loved the way she said "cushion," exaggerating the "kew" sound.

"What? You dodo, it's a love cushion."

"Meh. It works fantastically as a back support while I'm reading. I love it. Thank you."

Aren laughed.

"Well, what about the gift certificate?"

"What about it?"

"What are you going to get?"

"I don't know. I checked online. There wasn't much I was interested in."

"I hate you."

Élise chuckled. "Aren, is it really necessary for you to have all these props to make love?"

"Well, yes, if you want to have red-hot sex."

"Oh, okay. Whatever you say."

"You're hopeless. Do you miss me? I can be there in the morning."

"No, Aren. I need some alone time."

"Ugh! What else do you have to tell me?"

"Well, I read some of the letters you posted. They're beautiful."

"Really?"

"You know, for an engineer you have a wonderful sense of poetry."

"Why is that so surprising?"

"I don't know. Maybe because you're so sharp-edged, I assume you don't have an artistic side."

"Ah, but why does my being an engineer mean I'm not an artist? Science people dream as much if not more than literary types. Our imagination and creativity are boundless, like the energy we try to harvest."

"Hmm, I guess you're right."

CHAPTER 7

───

LONELY NIGHTS

───

T he month of separation was not quite as awful as Aren had feared. He and Élise talked every day, sometimes three times a day. They traded stories and encouraged each other with their respective projects. And they laughed. "I miss you, baby," Aren said.

"Aren, please don't get mushy. I hate that."

"How can you say that? You don't even know what mushy is. Sheesh! God gave you brown skin to help warm up that cold heart of yours."

Élise laughed.

"I'm glad I amuse you."

"Well, why else would I put up with the blathering nonsense of an old man?"

"Ha! That is so cold. Are you sure you weren't born in the North Pole? I think the time you spent in Canada ruined you. You need to reclaim that Caribbean sun to thaw that frozen heart of yours."

"I think I have to work on landing harder blows. You came back too quickly."

"I'm a tough bird. So now are you going to give me some hot sex talk?"

"No!" Élise shrieked, indignantly.

"Ah, come on. The FBI isn't interested in our sex talk."

"You're a dirty old man."

"Kind of lame, but it's a start. Now, shall I talk about how I want to ram—"

"Oh no, I'm hanging up. Bye."

Aren exploded into laughter at the sound of the line going dead. He texted quickly.

Keep it up, sweetheart. You' ll be mine soon enough. In your dreams, old man, she texted back.

.oOo.

TWO WEEKS LATER

"Baby, I just got your flowers. No one has ever sent me flowers before, not even Lily. I love them. Thank you. I love tulips."

"Did they make you smile, Aren?"

Aren chuckled. "Yes, Élise. I'm smiling now."

"Good. So what's this article you sent me? I can't make heads or tails of it."

"That's it? I'm gushing over the flowers you sent me, and then it's all business with you?"

"Uh-huh."

"You're hopeless."

"I know."

"I miss you. Do you miss me?"

"Aren, we talk every day. I don't get a chance to miss you."

"My bed is screaming out for you, darling. You know I had a dream about your ass. Oh, you were rubbing it all over me and I just—"

The line went dead. Aren erupted into laughter. Élise was laughing too.

.oOo.

Rrrrrrring!

Élise fumbled for the phone.

"Élise."

"Huh?"

"Wake up, baby."

"Aren? What time is it?"

"It's six o'clock in the morning."

"Is something wrong?"

"Baby, I had a great idea. You know, there's a team I've been consulting with that's working with the government of Morocco to design a smart grid solar project in Casablanca."

Élise didn't register what he was saying. All she knew was that she had stayed up late working on her paper and she was tired and frankly annoyed to be woken up so early.

"Aren, I need my sleep. Can you call back later?"

"Honey, didn't you hear what I said? You could consult, maybe translate. This could be a great transition for you. You said you were tired of teaching. And—"

Aren struck a nerve. She didn't recall openly admitting she was dissatisfied with teaching. She was too busy defending her teaching. School was getting boring, but it provided her a comfortable life.

"Aren, could you please stop. What, I'm supposed to drop my responsibilities? My students—"

Perhaps Aren was so caught up in his vision for Élise that he missed the irritation in her voice. He spoke as if she agreed.

"Listen, this is great. I can coach you on your presentation skills. You're a natural. I wanted to talk to you now so I can start making some calls—"

"Aren, I can't function right now. I need to sleep. Bye."

Élise didn't go back sleep. She was actually angry. She didn't know why. She got up and went to the bathroom and then decided to take a shower and go for a walk around the Arnold Arboretum. Her phone rang again, but she didn't answer. After her walk, she stopped at her favorite café and ordered a café au lait and a croissant.

It was noon when she returned to her apartment. She looked around her place. She loved it. Her life? It was okay. She grudgingly admitted to herself she liked having Aren in her life but in small doses. He had the tendency to want to take over. It was kind of scary.

She picked up the phone when he called. "Yes, Aren."

"Don't be like that, baby."

"Why are you plotting to change my life?"

"I thought you said that's what you wanted?"

"When did I say that?"

"Élise, when we were first looking at the stars and you talked about how you would like to do more humanitarian work. And then I have been reading some of your papers, and it clicked."

Élise chuckled. "Just like that? You wave your magic wand, and presto, I change my life?"

"Well, not exactly. I told you. I have to talk to a few people. Coach you and get you up to speed. But you would be perfect for some of the projects I know about in Africa and Latin America. You could be a liaison or even project manager. You're great with people."

"Aren, that was just fantasy and what if. That doesn't mean I want to give up my life."

"Élise, why are you so hell-bent on perpetuating an existence that's not particularly inspiring to you? You could do so much more."

"I'm fifty, Aren. I'm old. You say so yourself all the time."

"Élise. Your mentality is old. You want something, go after it. You're wasting precious time and energy that you could apply toward an exciting career that uses your God-given talent, hard work, and education."

"What, you think teaching is not good enough?"

"Not good enough for you. Not now. That phase of your life is over."

"Aren, I know you mean well, but I don't like people bossing me around. You know I think what I do is important. It's rewarding." She drew a breath. "All right. This conversation is over."

Aren laughed. "You're a big baby, you know that?"

"And you're an arrogant, pompous, know-it-all ass," Élise spat back.

"Ooo, she's using the big, nasty words."

"Screw you!"

"Love you too," Aren said.

Élise screamed before ending the call.

Élise was still staring at her phone when she heard a quiet but insistent knock on her door.

"Querida, it's me," Antonio called out. "Are you okay? Open up! I have your spare key and I will open your door if you don't answer."

Élise got up quickly and opened the door. Antonio rushed in and hugged her.

"Are you okay? I heard you scream and then silence. My blood ran cold. I needed to make sure you're okay."

Élise led Antonio to the kitchen. She urged him to sit down. She was going to make some mint tea.

"I'm sorry. Aren and I—we were arguing."

"¡*Por Dios*! That's not like you to lose your temper. Did he, did he betray you? That was a scream of rage."

Élise handed him a mug of hot tea. She set a small dish with two cubes of sugar and a teaspoon.

Antonio dropped the cubes of sugar into his mug and stirred. He inhaled the fragrant mint leaves and then set the mug down again to cool. He turned his attention to Élise. "Gracias," he said.

"*De nada*," Élise sighed. She sat down. She looked at her hands and then looked at Antonio. "No, it wasn't ugly. He made me mad, but he didn't do anything wrong. I think he thought he was trying to help me." Antonio took a sip of his tea. "Querida, since when does someone trying to help you result in your screaming. He hit a nerve, didn't he?"

Elise sighed. "Yes, he called me early this morning about an opportunity to work with the government of Morocco as a translator for a solar energy project Aren is consulting on."

"Querida, that's what you studied, to be a translator. That's perfect! Your man calls you first thing in the morning about bringing you in on a project he's working on and you get mad?"

Élise swallowed hard.

"Well, I wasn't really awake when he called at six in the morning. And then as I thought about it, I became resentful. He is always disparaging my work as a teacher. I care about what I do and it hurts when he keeps attacking what I do. And then he called saying that I had an old mentality for not wanting to change. I accused him of trying to control me. We said some nasty things to each other, and then I screamed."

Antonio took a sip of his tea.

"Élise, you're my friend. I don't know much about Aren. If you say he is controlling, I believe you because a man who has experienced his level of success has to be controlling. It doesn't end at work. That's how people like him see the world. But querida, the opportunity you described fits you to a T. Traveling to Morocco. Using your language and people skills to help a nation improve their lives, that should be your life. Don't lash out at the man for speaking the truth."

Élise could feel her eyes smarting.

"You know, I'm always teasing Aren about being old. But I'm the one who's old. I don't want to change. Yet, I'm frustrated by where I am. I feel like I have accomplished very little and time is running short. You know Aren has a scar from his open heart surgery. The scar goes from his sternum to his breast bone. It's frightful looking, actually. But you know what he did?"

Antonio shook his head.

"He added a heartbeat tattoo with the date of his surgery. He says his new life began on that day. I still think he's incredibly pushy and arrogant. But I also know he looks forward. He goes after what he wants and doesn't apologize. He always reminds me life is short and to seize the moment."

"Well, that's a gift to have someone like that in your life. He has stared at the face of death and come out on the other side. I don't want to lecture you. We can love each other passionately and still not agree. Do you understand what I'm saying? You will always be you. Aren may be pushy, but he can't change who you are. Maybe you need to trust yourself more. That man cares for you deeply. You think he doesn't see you as his equal, but I think he does."

Antonio drank the rest of his tea and patted Élise's hand.

"Okay, querida, I'm going to go. Maybe you come over later—dulce con leche?"

Élise smiled broadly. "Thank you for listening to me, Antonio," she said.

Antonio blew a kiss. "*Como no*, of course. Later."

Later that night Aren called again. She was in bed reading the French novel *Elle s'appelait Sarah* by Tatiana de Rosnay that was later translated as *Sarah's Key* and turned into a recent film. She was thinking of presenting this historical fiction about the holocaust and its consequences on subsequent generations to the present to her advanced French studies class. She was in her cotton pajamas. A cup of ginger tea rested on her nightstand. She hesitated before picking up the phone. After the third ring, she answered.

"What?"

"I love you."

Élise had to laugh. "Why do you keep saying that? You don't know me. We had two great weeks. We talk on the phone. What do you really know about me?"

"That I love you. You have a great heart. You're funny, principled, and independent and fuck like a goddess. Ah!"

"Is that the sum of what you supposedly love about me that I 'fuck like a goddess?'"

"Sweetheart, the physical love is extremely important to me. It makes me feel alive. But surely you know I love all of you: your wit, your charm, your grace, and beauty. You make me deliriously happy."

"How? I feel like you want me to have some glamorous job. You're always putting down my teaching like I'm a loser. I feel like I'm on the receiving end of your contempt and your lust. That's not what I call love. For the record, I don't need sex to feel alive."

"*Ich bin ein Dummkopf!* Sweetie, is that what you think? I wish I were there with you right now. You know why I called you at six this morning?"

"To be annoying."

Aren laughed. "Well, okay, maybe that. But I was up and I was thinking of the project and I thought how wonderful it would be to have you on my team. We could work together. Are you listening to me? I want you to partner with me. To share my life."

"Aren, this is too much. We haven't known each other that long."

"That's true, but it doesn't change how I feel."

"Aren, are you sure we should continue to see each other? We're moving so fast—I—"

"Well, I haven't seen you in over two weeks. But yes. We're good for each other. And right now I am so desperate for your body, that I'm thinking about making the drive tonight to see you. Do you miss me?"

I actually do miss this crazy man. How is that possible? But he's too much.

"You have the maturity of a teenager," she quipped.

"That is so cliché, *ma chérie*. Why can't you admit that you miss my dick tunneling its way inside of you? You know, I still haven't washed my sheets—"

Élise held her head in her hand. "Please stop. You're so gross! I can't believe you."

"Oh yes, you can. You love it," Aren laughed.

"Aren, you have washed your sheets, right?" *If this is Aren's idea of a torrid romance, I'm not sure I want this.*

"I'm pleading the fifth—my right to not self-incriminate."

"*T'es fou! Loco! Verrückt!* You're crazy!"

"Your conference ends on August 8th. Why don't I come up to Boston and meet you?"

"I don't know, Aren. You're disruptive."

"Please. I miss you. I can't stand this separation. It's bullshit. You could have still prepared for your conference without keeping me away."

"I need to concentrate. I can't do it if you're hanging around and distracting me. Besides, you said you were busy too."

"Not so busy that it requires that I be away from you for a whole month."

"Aren, I don't want to fight with you."

"Then say yes."

"You are being pushy and controlling. You expect me to change my life to suit you. Is this not the very reason why we are arguing, why I want to put some distance between us? You are wearing me down. Is that your strategy?" she said.

Aren noticed Élise's accent was getting more pronounced. Perhaps he was wearing her down, but not in a way that benefited him. She wasn't annoyed. She was furious. There was a long pause. Aren sighed. "You know what, sweetheart? You're right. I have been trying to wear you down. I am a pompous know-it-all ass. But you know what else I am?"

"What?" Élise said.

"I'm your man. Your conference is coming up and you're feeling stressed. I can help you. I can give you feedback. I can help you format the paper. I don't want you to push me away. Give me a chance to show you I support you."

"Aren—"

"Sweetheart, I get it. I don't like it, but I get it. Let me come to Boston and stay with you. I promise I'll behave. If you want to banish me to a designated spot in your apartment, I'll stay there. No more wise cracks from me about your teaching. I promise."

"I do want to see you, but I don't want to see you until after my conference. Please don't just pop up for a visit. You'll never leave. But after the conference—"

"I'll meet you in Boston?" Aren asked.

"Yes, for a few days. But remember, I can't give you my undivided attention. School starts at the end of August, so I have to prepare."

"All right. And if you do ever want to consider the consulting job, just let me know. I won't push it."

"Thank you, Aren."

"So - I'll meet you in Boston after your conference?"

Élise thought for a moment. *This is status quo ante. We had always agreed that we would plan to see each other after my conference. Aren wanted either for me to come back to Vermont or let him come to Boston now. I have to keep him on a tight leash or he'll have me in chaos.* Élise let out a sigh of relief.

"Are we good now? Can we do our good night kissy routine?"

"But why do I have to do the kissy noises?" Élise complained.

"Because you're the best, especially when you throw in the French. Spanish is even better. Go ahead. I'm listening. *Je t'*écoute, *chérie.*" She laughed.

"I'm waiting," Aren said huskily.

Élise kept laughing, but there was silence on the phone. "Aren?"

"I'm waiting."

"Agh! *Querido, mi amor, hasta pronto. Soy tuya para siempre.*" on."

"Ooh, I like that! Oh, wait. You forgot the kissy noises. Come

"Good night, Aren."

"Good night, baby. I love you."

"Aren?"

"Yes, sweetie."

"I don't want to fight with you. If you can't respect what I do, if you disparage my work or distract me so I can't work, then this thing, this connection we have isn't going to work. I love our time together. I look forward to your calls. But I don't like feeling bad about myself when you undermine me. Do you understand? I'm not going to just drop everything to please you. We're at different stages in our life. You know that."

There was a long pause and then Aren spoke.

"All right then. I will try to be the man you need me to be. Just don't give up on me. I love you."

CHAPTER 8

<<<<<<<<<<<<<<<<<<<<<<<<<<<<<<<<<<<<<<<<<<<<<<<<<<<<<<<<<<<<<<<<<<<<<<

A NEW PERSPECTIVE

<<<<<<<<<<<<<<<<<<<<<<<<<<<<<<<<<<<<<<<<<<<<<<<<<<<<<<<<<<<<<<<<<<<<<<

Baltimore Comparative Literature Conference

Whe Élise arrived in Baltimore for her conference, she saw all the familiar faces of her colleagues she had known and collaborated with over the years. They were in a sense as much her family as her own family. Every year they got together in different cities and exchanged papers in a vain attempt to seem relevant in a rapidly changing world where Romance language departments were having to give up their budgets to make room for more "relevant" languages like Arabic or Chinese. Who spoke German anymore, especially since high schools started cutting away at language programs? Some colleagues had given up and tried to go into the corporate sector with mixed success. Going from university-level instruction to high school—albeit an elite school—was a bit of a demotion for Élise. She could acknowledge that to herself. What she lost in prestige, she won in security and stability notwithstanding the political battles she endured with getting plum assignments and titles. She didn't have to worry about rapacious cuts. Her school at least paid for her to travel with students every other year to France or Spain. Occasionally, she could add trips to countries outside of Europe or Canada like Cuba, or Montreal, Canada, or Senegal, Africa. She led a trip to the Philippines which was so successful there were ongoing discussions about establishing a permanent program.

As she participated on the different panels and attended lectures, she wondered how long she could keep doing this. All the squabbling with Aren forced her to admit to herself at least that she was tired of teaching and tired of the whole cloistered academic life. But at fifty, what kind of new career path would be open to her, especially in this economy? She thought about Aren's proposal. It did seem interesting. But how could they work as a team as partners? *He would be micromanaging me and second-guessing me. What a nightmare! And even if that weren't the case, I don't know how I feel about mixing a personal relationship with a business relationship.*

"Is this seat taken?"

Élise looked up and was initially startled to see a man asking to share her table. She was at a café near the campus.

"Oh, yes, of course. I'm sorry. I was lost in thought." She looked around and saw the place was getting busy.

"You don't have to rush off. You look kind of preoccupied. You got a lot of paper. Are you a teacher?"

"Yes. But I teach in Massachusetts at an independent school. I'm here for a conference."

"A conference?"

"Yes, um, a colloquium for French professors."

"Oh, I wondered what language that was. I'm no scholar, but I figured it didn't look like English. Are you American? You kind of got an accent."

"Well, I have traveled a lot. I am an American citizen, but I was born in Saint Martin and grew up in Montréal, Canada."

George's face lit up. "Oh, I know where Saint Martin is."

"Do you?"

"Yeah, I worked on a yacht crew for a summer, and we went there. Real nice people."

Élise smiled absently and then took a sip from her coffee. "So are you here for a long time?"

"Um no, actually, I have one more day, and then it's back to Boston."

"Too bad. You seem like a really nice lady."

Élise smiled and then began to pack her bag. She looked at the man. She held out her hand in a gesture to shake hands with him.

"I'm sorry. I never properly introduced myself. My name is Élise Douchet."

George shook her hand.

"That's a very pretty name. It suits you. My name is George Marshall."

"Nice to meet you, George. Well, I should be getting back."

George quickly scribbled a number on a napkin and handed it to her.

"You seem like a very fine lady. If you would like some company or someone to talk to or you get bored with your colleagues, give me a call."

Élise couldn't suppress her chuckle but then quickly stopped. She didn't want to hurt his feelings.

"Thank you, George. That's very kind of you."

"So you're not going to give me your phone number."

"I'm afraid not," Élise smiled. Then she dug inside of her bag and pulled out a program.

"Um, you'll probably ditch it, but here is a copy of our program. You seem like you might be curious about the world. Here's a way of getting insight. Anyway, it was nice chatting with you. Thank you for making me feel welcome in your city. I appreciate that very much."

George stood up and let Élise pass. When she left the café, he perused the elegantly produced program and found Élise's name and the topic of her paper.

When Élise got up to deliver her paper on the last day, she was happy to see George in the audience. She fretted a little, wondering whether she had stupidly led the man on since she knew she had no intention of pursuing any friendship with him. But he seemed to be paying attention, which gave her a lot of confidence.

"Good afternoon, friends and colleagues. The topic of my paper is the comparative study of late nineteenth century French poet Paul Éluard and mid-twentieth century Chilean poet Pablo Neruda. The paper analyzes each poet's response to the political crisis and wars of his day. Both poets were influenced by the French Surrealist movement and lived through the Second World War."

Élise had been speaking for twenty minutes when she noticed one of the facilitators had approached her and asked if she could answer an urgent question from one of the attendees. She was caught off guard. Usually, there was Q&A following the presentation. For a moment she wondered if this might be a surprise interview, a prospective university interested in her work. She relaxed her shoulders and nodded to the facilitator.

"Where is he?" she asked, not immediately identifying who the questioner was.

"Oh it's me," the voice said seemingly out of nowhere. "Thank you for taking my question. Yes, now can you comment on Kafka's notion of *Aufmerksamkeit?*"

She always had nightmares of flubbing a talk. And now her worst fears were coming true. Of all the disasters Élise imagined for this conference or in her professional life, seeing Aren at her conference asking an absurd question was the furthest thing from her mind. Her instinct was to scream in rage. *Go with it.* A voice inside of her said. *This is your show. Don't let him control you. You know your material.* She said a little prayer and then calmed down.

"Excuse me, what does that have to do with today's talk on the poetry of Paul Éluard and Pablo Neruda?"

"Hmm, well, Paul Celan, who would later translate the works of Paul Éluard, was influenced by Kafka's belief that attentiveness is the natural prayer of the soul. Is that not the basis for which you can establish a comparison between these two poets, Patoja?"

It was the reference to Patoja rather than the random questioning that made Élise flush with embarrassment. Of course, everyone picked up on the significance of Patoja, which was the pet name the poet Neruda used for his third wife throughout his most passionate love poetry.

What kind of horrible game was Aren playing? Did she stumble into some kind of *9 1/2 Weeks* psychosexual drama? Aren, who professed love to her, was now actively humiliating her in public. But is that what was really going on?

Élise surveyed the room. Hers was the last lecture on the last day of the conference. Many conference attendees were anxious to leave. Or, that is what she thought. Instead of glazed-over stares, she now had everyone's rapt attention. What was motivating Aren's question? He was a man of science, not a man of letters. Was he really trying to sabotage her? His comments revealed the sometimes hours of conversations they had discussing poetry. He asked her about her paper and was fascinated by the story of these poets, Neruda and Eluard these were men of their times who not only wrote bold poetry, but who also inspired others through their fight for freedom of expression.

Neruda was famous for his sexually explicit love poetry. Of course, that was not the focus of her paper. She planned to focus on the role of communism and how participation in the Spanish Civil War and World War II affected both poets. She found herself launching into an exposé of Neruda's "Ode to Daily Life." Élise started to read an excerpt of the poem. She had not prepared to present the poem, but she did have it in her materials.

Slowly dies he who becomes a slave to habit repeating the same journey every day,
   he who does not change his march,
   he who does not risk wearing new colors,
   he who does not speak to those he does not know.

Élise paused after reading the first stanza.

"Perhaps the others might enjoy hearing the other part, Pantoja." Aren said.

"Yes," please someone called out. There were giggles in the room but everyone wanted to hear the poem.

Slowly dies he who avoids a passion, he who prefers either getting things down in black and white or dotting his "I's", to experiencing a whirl of emotions; particularly those that make the eyes shine, those that turn a yawn into a smile, those that make the heart beat before error and feelings.

In a time of tremendous global upheaval, Paul Eluard and Pablo Neruda expressed through their poetry the importance of passion as essential to life. Political regimes could come and go but the passion that stirs one's soul was essential to a meaningful life.

Aren succeeded in getting Élise off-topic. But maybe she chose the wrong topic. Or, maybe the impertinent question was a commentary about Élise and her life path. Élise used the poem to segue back to the initial topic. *Phew!* She thought. The lecture didn't turn out the way she planned, but the audience was with her, listening. But Aren kept raising his hand and calling out questions. With each answer she gave, she was illustrating the very point the poets were making. This was turning into a master class, a colloquy between teacher and student. Finally, he yelled out his request that she choose a poem he had written for her that approximated Neruda's penchant for attentiveness. Everyone's attention was fixed on Élise, waiting to see what she would say.

Did she tell Aren she kept his poems with her like a treasured photograph in a worn wallet? Was life imitating art? She couldn't help but smile. Aren's poems were silly. They were passionate. They were loving. They were ordinary and extraordinary just like life should be. Just like Paul Eluard, Pablo Neruda, and Paul Celan who translated both poets, said life should be. At that moment what was real was morphing into the surreal. Her emotional life carefully tucked away was now exposed. What was supposed to be an esoteric academic discussion was now an entertaining topic of analysis. She felt like a newscaster delivering the news while their child is running around in the background live on camera. Life happens. And maybe what was most extraordinary is that her colleagues were more interested in connecting with the personal rather than an impersonal academic analysis.

"Go ahead, Élise," a colleague said from the front row. "We promise to give you five stars on the evaluation."

Everyone laughed.

Élise reached for her bag and pulled out a sheet of paper. "So what's the poem?" someone called out.

"Une Femme d'un Certain Âge, by Aren Karajian." Élise announced.

Today I took Élise *to buy her first pair of jeans.*

She thinks jeans are worn by twenty-somethings and not by une femme d'un certain age.

But when she puts the jeans on, she is transformed. I see the possibilities.

She will no longer be une femme d'un certain age.

She will become just une femme, my femme, who hikes with me along the Appalachian Trail.

My femme who will be free to dig the garden and wipe her muddied hands on her jeans.

Free to come down from her pedestal and just be with me. For this femme d'un certain age, the best is yet to come.

Our love is rich beyond measure. Not even Bernie Madoff can touch it. Like a rose in the desert, she is my Arab spring.

Everyone cheered and applauded. The lecture concluded.

.oOo.

Élise

And so it is the man of science and the woman of letters who are locked in an existential struggle. The man of science is pulling the woman of letters towards nature, abundance, love, and freedom. The woman of letters has drawn lines and boundaries and looks at life from an ivory tower, content to observe from afar and above. I accused Aren of being annoying, but having him in my life has forced me to be bold, at least to confront what is bold. Aren was maddening, but he made me happy. I fell and he picked me up, literally. I keep pushing him away, but I don't want him to go away—not permanently. Sometimes I do need a break from him.

Did he upend my presentation to punish me for limiting his stay with me in Boston? I don't know. What did Aren know about Paul Eluard, Pablo Neruda, and Paul Celan before we met? Not much. But in that surreal exchange, Aren revealed he had been listening to me. He had read my papers. He had done a little bit of extra reading. He was paying attention to me. He did want to engage with me in my world. He did want me to engage with him in his world. At a different time what happened today would have devastated me. I would have fallen into a heap and wept. This would have been the end of our budding relationship. Instead I felt exasperation, but I could see the humor. This wasn't about me or my career. This was about us and whether we had a future. What an interesting perspective.

Aren greeted me with a triumphant smile when the room emptied. "Do you know what you've done?" I asked him.

He shrugged. "I helped you deliver a memorable presentation. They're going to pull out their dusty copies of poems by Eluard, Neruda, and Celan and they're going to think big thoughts." He chuckled.

I rolled my eyes. "Big thoughts?" I scoffed. "Are you punishing me for not letting you stay with me longer?"

"I shook things up. You kept your cool. You kept it moving. You knew your stuff. Your next paper will be about something else besides communism and surrealism. The conference attendees will be on the lookout for you. In marketing, they call it guerrilla tactics."

Aren helped me gather up my things. "Let's get naked, baby," Aren murmured seductively.

I laughed. "Do you have an off switch?"

"If I do, I don't want to know where it is," Aren said.

"What makes you think I want anything to do with you after the stunt you pulled?" I said.

Aren looked at me with a serious expression. And then a grin appeared on his face.

"I know this fabulous tea room in DC, The Peacock Alley Tea. They serve wonderful macarons, I hear. In my experience, nothing can't be resolved over a cup of tea. Will you join me?"

Was I going to go on this merry-go-round ride again? It was making me dizzy.

"I don't know Aren," I confessed. "I don't like crazy. I don't want to be adventurous. Maybe you were right the first time we met on Precipice Trail. I shouldn't push beyond my level of experience. It can be dangerous."

Aren smirked. "But you're not a novice anymore. You can handle the challenge."

Are you worth it Aren? I sighed. "Tea. Can we try tea and conversation?"

"As you wish, my lady," he said. We walked out of the conference hall arm in arm.

CHAPTER 9

A PERFECT GETAWAY

Élise

W hatever lingering resentment I may have felt toward Aren after my French conference was over, we struck a truce. The next morning, we woke up in Aren's hotel suite in Northern Virginia. We ordered room service and enjoyed our continental breakfast on the balcony. We were both wearing our hotel bathrobes.

Aren reached for my hand and kissed it. "Let's go to Puerto Rico," he said.

I smiled. "That sounds nice. For Christmas maybe?"

"In three days," he said.

"What?"

"We can book a quick getaway trip to Puerto Rico. There's a flight out of Boston on Tuesday and we come back on Friday—or whenever you're ready to come back," Aren said.

"This is insane, Aren."

"That means it's a great idea. Come on. After next week I'm going to have to compete for your attention against a horde of hormonal teenagers. Indulge me, please."

"Yeah, sure. Whatever you say," I said sarcastically.

.oOo.

Jamaica Plain, Massachusetts

Aren was watching me pack a suitcase for our trip to Puerto Rico. We were leaving the next day.

"I'll be fucking your brains out," he said. "You don't need any clothes."

"How about deodorant?" I said.

"Why? We can bathe in the ocean. Who cares?"

Maybe in the movies good-looking lovers could spend endless days with each other without ever practicing basic hygiene. *L' horreur!* What's that expression the young people say all the time? Aren must be tripping.

"Aren, have you been checked for dementia?"

"Hmm, I hear they have excellent drugs in San Juan." I laughed heartily.

My younger brother Fred met us at the Miami airport to share a drink on the way to Puerto Rico. We reserved a bungalow with a private pool a few meters away from the path to the beach. We arranged to have some groceries delivered ahead of time. A prepared meal would be waiting for us in the refrigerator. When we arrived, we wasted no time making use of the sumptuous tub and then collapsing on the bed for a nap. Outside it was pouring rain. When we woke up, it was sunset. The rain had stopped.

.oOo.

While Élise was in the bathroom, Aren busied himself laying out the bedroom gear he brought with him. Like a host making sure the dinner table is perfectly set, Aren was making sure the staging for their lovemaking was just right.

"What are you doing, Aren?"

"What does it look like I'm doing? I told you I intended to fuck your brains out."

Élise laughed. Aren looked annoyed.

"I don't see what you find so funny. This is serious."

"Oh, I'm sorry," Élise teased.

Aren eyed the negligée Élise was wearing. It didn't fit with the scene he was trying to create. "Take that thing off," he said.

"Oh come on, Aren. This is pretty."

"I don't want pretty. I want raw."

"Argh!"

"Argh yourself. Take that thing off and get over here. Now," Aren said.

Élise stuck out her tongue and then giggled. They were role-playing. "I'm going to drag you by the hair if you don't get over here right now."

Élise rolled her eyes and removed her nightgown. They were lovers, and yet she still felt shy standing naked in front of him if they weren't actually in the act of making love. She walked over to him. He strapped a belt around her hips with a dildo hanging from it.

"Oh my goodness! You changed the script. What am I supposed to do with this?"

"Whatever you want, sweetheart."

"Oh no. This is weird."

"It's not weird. Everything is in your head. The good and the bad."

"You want me to violate you with this thing?"

"No, I want you to pleasure me with this thing."

"No, no, no. I can't."

"All right, remember how I showed you how to massage my perineum? You know that lump just behind my sac?"

"Yeah."

"Well, now I need you to go inside. Please."

"Why?"

"Because it feels good. And it's how I stay healthy. It's therapy for my prostrate. I can do it myself, but it's nicer if I have a beautiful woman who I happen to be crazy about do it for me. Yes, it might be gross. Maybe I fart, maybe I don't. You're my lover, you can handle it."

Élise clucked her tongue. "Okay."

"Good girl. Now, take some of this lubricant and spread it over your finger."

Élise poured some lubricant and spread it on her middle finger as Aren instructed.

"Now let's walk over to the bed and lay on the wedge. Don't worry. We have the throw, so if it gets messy, we're not going to ruin the sheets."

Aren positioned himself so that he was lying on his side.

"Now, you can position yourself in the front or the back, whichever way you prefer. I want you to start introducing your middle finger slowly into the hole and angle it up until you feel a bump. I'll guide you."

"And then what happens?"

"Well, you're going to massage it for me, and if you do a good job, I'll probably cum, especially if you give me a hand job at the same time."

"I don't think I'm that coordinated."

"Oh, you underestimate yourself. But you know, that's okay. What I want is for you to feel comfortable doing it. The more you do it, the better you will get, and the better I will feel."

"Hmm."

"Ready?"

"Not really. Can I talk you out of this?"

"Nope. It's showtime."

Élise slowly guided her finger into Aren's rectum ever so gently, gliding her finger as deeply as possible, and began massaging gently.

"You can rub harder, baby. It feels good."

Élise focused all her attention on the massage. The room was quiet except for the faraway sounds of the beach and Aren's increasing breaths.

"Harder," he choked.

Élise's finger was getting tired. She remembered he wanted her to stroke him. At first the rhythm was a little disjointed as she tried to figure out how to do both, but eventually Aren's reaction was the best guide. He was starting to convulse. She panicked and quickly withdrew her finger and penetrated him with her dildo and continued to massage his penis.

Aren gasped. "Oh my God!" Before she could even react Aren had turned around and penetrated her shallowly but deep enough to spill his seed all over. Élise was shocked. This was the first time she had seen him completely beyond himself. He collapsed on her and lay still against her, panting.

"Oh, I needed that. Thank you."

"Aren?"

"Yes."

"Is the butt thing more pleasurable than being inside me?"

"I prefer to experience it as part of the many ways of making love to my woman."

"Aren, if this has to become a regular feature of our intimate time, we might have to break up. I don't like this. The massage is fine. I understand that. The strap thing, no."

"You want to know a secret?"

"I don't know. It depends on the secret. I could get nightmares." Aren chuckled.

"You're the first woman not to give me a hard time over it. You're funny. You're so prim and proper outside of the bedroom. There are things about sex you still find completely weird, but you don't really object, especially if I make a direct request."

"Hmm. Did Helen do this for you?"

"In the beginning she did, at least before Lily came along. And then she stopped."

"Why?"

"I don't know."

"Why didn't you ask her?"

"I don't know. It was easier just to do it myself."

"You know, Aren, if you like that so much, how do you know you're not gay? Or bi or whatever they call it these days?"

"You've never been with a woman?"

"No."

"Not even curious?"

"Not really."

"Hmm. Well, a male acquaintance introduced me to this."

"Really?"

"He didn't penetrate me with his dick. I just couldn't quite cross that line, but I experienced the most intense and exquisite pleasure. I can get hard just thinking about that experience. Does that weird you out?"

"It should, but it doesn't—as long as you're sure you're not harboring some secret fantasy about a threesome with a guy."

"So that means you're open to a threesome with a woman?"

"No."

Aren laughed.

"You're my coconut. Come here."

Aren rolled on top of Élise and started kissing her and sucking on her tongue. She could feel the pull in her lower abdomen, her pelvic floor muscles tightening. Aren helped her unstrap the dildo so they could move more freely on the platform wedge and find a position to their liking.

"Oh!" Élise groaned afterwards, completely and utterly spent. Aren rolled to his back. Élise lay her head on his chest. She caressed his scar tenderly.

"Come on," Aren said, "let's take a quick shower."

They jumped out of the bed, stepped into the shower, and scrubbed each other, taking special care to wash their genitals. Then Aren led Élise by the hand back to the bed. They wiped the throw down with a wet washcloth, and then without further ceremony, they assumed their sixty-nine position and devoured each other.

.oOo.

Élise

Was Aren part of some ancient sex cult? The quick romantic getaway I thought we would have in Puerto Rico was turning into a mind-blowing daily sexual ritual similar in frequency and devotional energy to the Catholic Liturgy of the Hours. At least one sexual session involved elaborate staging with Aren's magic sex cushions and intricate choreography. Yes, there was tremendous pleasure, but it came with a powerful intensity. If during my stay with Aren in Vermont he was gentle and "went slow" to accommodate my lack of experience, now he was more demanding. He wanted to break down barriers. So now oral pleasure involved swallowing. It happened once.

"Oh no!" I cried. "You horrid man!" Aren chuckled.

"It's good medicine. It will keep you young and strong. It's rich in vitamins and essential minerals," he said confidently.

I shuddered. "No! It's disgusting. Please don't tell me it's in my head."

"It is the biggest turn-on to see my woman take my seed."

I jumped off bed. "Ugh! I have to go rinse my mouth. Oh, God!"

Aren laughed but followed me into the bathroom. He watched me scour my mouth with Listerine and the hydrogen peroxide I always carried. I repeated the process three times. He brushed his teeth too and then led me back to bed again.

"Can we stop now?" I said. I didn't want to go through another round of sex.

"I can keep going, honey."

I believed him. "What were you like when you were eighteen?"

"Sexually frustrated."

"*Quelle surprise!*"

"Come on, let's spoon. I want to feel your ass against my dick."

"You know I hate that word."

"Figures. Anyway, thank you. I'm telling you, you fuck like a goddess."

"What does that even mean?"

"It means you know how to give me pleasure and keep me wanting more. I hope I do the same for you."

"Hmm. I don't think I'm as needy and greedy as you are."

"Probably. Okay. Let's nap a little, and then we can eat. And then we can do whatever you want."

I curled up against Aren, rubbing his stubbly face with my hand. I caressed his chest scar and heartbeat line tattoo. Aren said he only looked forward. I was looking ahead of me and I was getting nervous about what could await me on the other side. If Aren kept breaking down my barriers, what would be left of me?

CHAPTER 10

IT'S THE REAL THING

Elise and Aren returned from their Puerto Rico getaway and walked into her apartment laden with suitcases and shopping bags. She stood on her toes and kissed Aren affectionately.

"Why don't you relax," Élise suggested. "I'll put everything away and make us some soup."

"You know, I don't think I'm even going to protest. I'm beat. You wore me out last night and this morning."

Élise rolled her eyes. "Go on. There are fresh sheets on the bed. Take a shower. Relax. Take a nap."

"All right."

Aren followed Élise into the bedroom to drop off his bags. He gave her an affectionate hug and then released her. He looked around the room. Even though it was jam-packed with books, it was actually very serene. Her bed was a little fussier than he would have liked with a ridiculous amount of pillows and coverlets, but oh so inviting. He quickly undressed and went to the bathroom. While he stood under the shower, he relived the incredibly sexy weekend he had spent with Élise in Puerto Rico.

Aren

That Puerto Rico getaway trip was a brilliant scheme. It was even better than the two weeks we spent together in Vermont. Puerto Rico was all about rollicking fun and deep intimacy. We did all of the usual touristy pilgrimages and fit in lots of beach time. Élise could go topless on the private beach without worry about intrusion. But the prime objective of the getaway trip was sex. Élise had exceeded my expectations.

We were developing synchronicity. I didn't have to beg or cajole her for sex. A look, a touch, or a word was enough for her to sense my desire and satisfy it. We could talk about anything, no matter how personal or potentially embarrassing.

Élise had slipped into bed and pulled up the covers to her waist. She was topless and wearing a very intriguing pair of panties I had never seen before. I pulled the covers back to expose her white silk and lace crotchless panties trimmed with pearls. "Oh! You dirty woman. I love it!" My shaft stood at attention, immediately.

"Aren, are you sure it's okay for you to keep taking those pills?" she said with concern. "We don't always have to have sex. I do actually enjoy your company," *Élise* said one night after intense lovemaking.

"You don't get it. I feel so alive. It's bad enough with getting older your bones ache and you're a little slower than you used to be. You forget things more easily. But when I'm with you and we're having crazy sex"—*Élise* rolled her eyes—"I feel at least in this department I'm still in the game. I don't take more than three."

"Aren, that's too many."

"I don't do it every day. In fact, usually I can skip a day."

"Maybe we should plan it more. You know, schedule it."

"You're serious."

"Sure, why not?"

"Okay. Every day, preferably in the morning and in the afternoon."

"Hmm, not at night?"

"You know, honey, I wouldn't mind getting more sleep at night."

"I'm sorry."

"Don't be. We're talking now. Sometimes at night it's fun. But it's better for me if we do it earlier in the day."

"Okay, but Aren, you don't have to prove anything to me. I really like cuddling."

I returned my attention to *Élise's* exquisite silk and lace panties. I was mesmerized by the double strand of pearls bordering her opening. *Élise* chuckled.

"I thought you said lace was itchy," she teased.

In my best Groucho Marx impression I said, "I don't know. Let's find out!"

I was whistling. Anytime I thought of any moment with Élise during that trip I would just start whistling. I toweled off after my shower, brushed my teeth, and then walked back into the bedroom. I felt refreshed but at the same time exhausted. I pulled down the bed covers and got into the bed. I inhaled the fragrance of the freshly laundered sheets—heavenly—and promptly fell asleep.

.oOo.

Élise checked in on Aren an hour later. He was still asleep. He was snoring. She chuckled at the way his mouth was open. His strong nose and chin formed a silhouette in the growing shadows of the room. Élise lingered for a moment, lost in thought. She heard a soft knock on the door.

"You're back!" Antonio said. "Yeah."

"Here's your mail."

"Thanks."

Antonio remained at the threshold. "So are you going to invite me in?"

Antonio noticed a pair of men's shoes next to the door. "Ah, you have company."

"Well, he's actually asleep."

"You tired him out, huh."

"Would you stop?" Élise said impatiently. Antonio started to laugh.

"All right, querida. Why don't you both come over for dinner? Don't order out. I promise not to make a nuisance of myself. But if you're going on long getaways with this man, I want to meet him."

"Fine."

"Don't worry about anything. Just bring yourself. Eight o'clock. Is that too late?"

"No, it's perfect."

"All right. See you later, chica."

Élise went back into the kitchen and put away the soup she had prepared. She could bring it over to Antonio's as an appetizer. Then she walked over to her desk and went through the mail Antonio had given her. She answered some email messages and then stood up. She walked to her bedroom, undressed, and then stepped into the bathroom. She took a quick shower first and then drew a bath. She lit candles and poured in her favorite bath salts before stepping in. She sighed with pleasure. She lifted her legs and admired the pedicure she had gotten while she was in Puerto Rico. In fact, she had gotten a spa treatment the day before, so she was feeling especially relaxed and pampered.

"Can I join you?"

Élise looked up at the door and saw Aren's head peeking in. She smiled.

"Sure." Élise moved forward to make space for Aren.

Aren dropped his robe and stepped into the tub. He winced a little because the water was a little too hot for his taste, but it was manageable.

He grabbed her and brought her close against his chest. He kissed her neck.

"So where shall we go next?" he murmured, stroking her breasts.

"I don't know. It would be nice if we could really plan a trip. I mean spur of the moment is nice, but it doesn't leave much room for real exploring."

"I don't know. I'd say we did a fair bit of exploring—of each other." Élise smiled. She looked up at him.

"Aren, you know once I start teaching, I won't really be able to take off on a whim."

"I know. I know. I hate it."

"How do you just take off like that?"

"I'm my own boss, and with technology, I can be anywhere and everywhere."

"Nice life," Élise said a little enviously.

"It would be nicer if you were sharing it with me." Élise froze. Her eyes darted back and forth.

"Aren, when you were in your other relationships, how did you end them? I'm not asking why, just how did you tell them it wasn't working?"

"I told them exactly that: it's not working."

"Just like that and the relationship was over?"

"Yeah, pretty much. I mean, don't get me wrong. Sometimes the woman would say, 'It's not working for me.' Or sometimes she might give me an ultimatum—that was one instance, and I said no. If it was casual, then sometimes it was enough that one of us stopped calling each other. Oh, and a lot times I would say, 'Hey, I have a heavy travel schedule coming up, so I won't be around.' And then I wouldn't call them or return their calls."

"Oh my God. That's what you said to me. You were traveling."

"Yes, but you're the one who said you needed some time to yourself to focus on your paper. And then I crashed your conference."

"Hmm."

"Hmm, what?"

"Is it just the sex, Aren?"

"It is the sex, but it's not just the sex. You know that. I'm attracted to you sexually. I never made a secret of that. But I also like hanging out with you. You're hilarious."

"Pfff!"

"I love when you do that," Aren said. Élise chuckled and then grew serious. "So we're a couple."

"Oh, yes. I'm glad to see you have finally accepted the truth. Why is that a surprise? I thought that was established when you came out to Vermont."

"I know. It's just I'm not sure what I'm supposed to do or how to behave."

"Don't change. You're perfect. We're perfect. Well, we're almost perfect. I want you to quit your job and work with me."

Many thoughts swirled around Élise's head. *Oh, no, no, no. I can't depend on Aren or any man for my livelihood. What happens if the relationship fizzles? What happens if he says "Honey, this relationship is not working for me"?* She shook her head.

"I like my job."

"Liar," Aren replied.

"Well, it's not always rainbows and unicorns. Every job has its downsides. That's not unusual. I have a rewarding job."

"You have been working for over twenty years. You have savings and a pension. I could invest some money for you, and you would never have to worry about money. And you just spend your time with me, having fun, making love, traveling, and working with me."

"Is that really what you want?"

"Mmm-hmm."

"And then what do I do when you grow tired of me?"

"I won't. I know a good investment when I see one. We're perfect for each other. I can't believe it sometimes."

Élise marveled at the enthusiasm in his face. He was so sincere, almost zealous. She shook her head.

"It's scary sometimes to listen to you," Élise said. "There's no such thing as perfection, especially in relationships. People break up all the time."

"Well, if you want to get all pissy about it, fine. You're right. But the odds are in our favor. We're older. We have led our separate lives and pursued our careers. We don't have children to create stress in our lives. We're not struggling to make ends meet. And we're fundamentally simple people. We're alike in so many ways. It amazes me. As far as I'm concerned, you're an Afro-French Caribbean Armenian."

Aren kissed Élise's temple. She looked up at him and smiled. "What am I going to do with you, Aren? She covered his mouth with her hand. "Rhetorical question."

She wriggled out of his grasp and stood up. "Come on. The water is getting cold. We have a couple of hours before we need to present ourselves across the hall. We've been invited over for dinner."

"Oh."

"Yes, Antonio wants to meet you and give you the third degree." Aren chuckled.

"Fine. Okay, let's get dressed. Maybe you can try on that gorgeous dress you picked up. You are so hot."

They stepped out of the tub and passed the full-length mirror. Élise stopped for a moment to look at herself. She had wrapped a towel around herself in sarong style. Her hair was slightly damp and curling. Aren was standing behind her, his hands on her shoulder, looking at her reflection.

"What do you see, Élise?"

"A graying woman. Should I color my hair?"

"Funny, when I first met you, I thought that was the single best improvement you could do for yourself. Now I've accepted it as part of you. And you know it's soft and you style it so well. It's just a hair color. If you want to change it, fine by me."

"Ah, so you think I should color it."

"Oh no! Don't start!"

Aren kissed her cheek and then darted into the bedroom.

.oOo.

Aren, Élise, and Antonio were sipping wine after dinner. Élise at one point stopped in midsentence.

"Baby, what's wrong?" Aren asked suddenly with alarm. "Your face is covered in red splotches."

"Oh, my face feels really hot and itchy."

Antonio got up and knelt in front of Élise to examine her. "Querida, you're breaking out into hives. Are you allergic to something? Maybe the wine?"

"I don't know. I've never had a problem with wine before. And I'm not allergic to chicken. Maybe my biorhythm is off with the recent traveling."

"All right, well, maybe lay off the wine. I'll get you some water and a hot washcloth. I'll add a drop of tea tree oil. It'll make you feel better."

"Thanks. I'm sorry for being such a bother."

"No worries, querida."

Aren moved closer to Élise and put his arm around her and kissed her head.

"Do I look awful?"

"Hmm, you're not quite the clear-skinned bombshell I'm used to shagging all the time, but you're still hot."

"Gee, thanks," Élise said sarcastically.

Antonio returned with a glass of water and the washcloth. By the end of the evening, Élise had recovered.

At the door as the three exchanged their goodnights, Antonio shook hands with Aren.

"Aren, it has been a pleasure getting to know you. Élise is a great woman. Take good care of her, okay?"

Élise rolled her eyes.

"I will," Aren said and then shut the door behind him.

CHAPTER 11

HOT STUFF

Lily was lying on the sofa, spooning with Tessa. The fireplace was lit, and everything was cozy. They were actually in her father's cottage. He was staying with Élise while they sought refuge in his cottage from the flash flood caused by Hurricane Irene. The power lines were down at their house, but they were at least spared the worst of the flooding.

"Hmm, do you think we can talk your father into staying with Élise so we can take over his cottage?" Tessa asked, kissing Lily on her neck.

Lily chuckled.

"It is a nice cottage, isn't it? Well, don't get too used to it. He fully intends to share his little paradise with his new main squeeze," Lily said. "Main squeeze, huh? You know, don't get me wrong, but I never ever would have figured your dad for, like, jungle fever."

Jungle fever? What was Tess getting at? Yes, Dad did tend to date a physical type but in general, Dad was open and friendly to everyone.

"Dad has traveled all over the world. People are people to him. Plus, he has been on the receiving end of a lot of prejudice because of his dark complexion. But I will say Dad does appreciate good-looking women.

Élise is good-looking. I haven't met her in person, but in the photos, she seems like a very friendly and down-to-earth person. It's wild, she has like granny hair and a killer body like Halle Berry. In fact, she looks likes Halle Berry with silver streaks in her hair. Anyway, most of the photos I have seen of her she's wearing a swimsuit or shorts. She gives me hope that I can still look attractive at fifty."

"Wait a minute, she looks like Halle Berry? Is she kind of screwed up?" Tessa joked.

"Well, I don't know," Lily said not understanding Tessa's oblique reference to Hollywood gossip. "I think Élise has her head screwed on tight, according to Dad. She teaches at a prep school in Boston. She teaches French and Spanish."

"So you like her?"

"I don't know. I haven't met her. Dad has been pretty cagey, but I think this one might be serious. I talked to one of his friends who met her, and she passed the Nick and Cynthia test."

Tessa started to giggle. "What's so funny?"

"Oh, remember that time we went to their party and your dad was dating this investment banker from New York? Every sentence began with the latest deal she just negotiated. God, she gave new meaning to the word self-centered. How in the world did your dad end up with her?"

"What was her name? Catherine Manning, I think. I don't know. I can't say that I completely understand my dad's taste in women. She kind of looked like my mother because of the blonde hair, but that's where all resemblance ended. Anyway, I'm glad that one didn't last long. She didn't make him very happy."

"You know, I don't think I have really ever seen your dad happy. I mean I know he took your mom's death pretty hard, but he's always seemed kind of hollow."

"Tess, the funny thing is, I think he improved a lot after mom died. It was the sickness that really sucked up his spirit. He hated seeing her go through all that pain. And then the open-heart surgery and selling his company. He had a lot going on. No wonder he seems hollow to you."

"Hmm."

Tessa held on to Lily a little tighter and rubbed her nose in Lily's fragrant hair. They lay silently for a while, listening to the crackling sounds from the fireplace.

"So what do you want to do for your birthday, babe?" Tessa asked. "Hmm, I might be up for a birthday party if you make my favorite meal and bake the cake."

"Ah, man—"

"Come on. It'll be fun."

"Who do you want to invite?"

"You know, I want to keep it kind of small. Let's invite Sherry and Liz. Mike and Kelly, Barry, Sandy, and Piper."

"You don't want to invite your dad?"

"Oh, he's already in the count. Dad is not one to pass up a free meal—especially if you're cooking."

Tessa smiled.

"Okay. So maybe he'll bring his new main squeeze."

"Maybe. Now let's stop talking about my father's love life and let's focus on us. I'm feeling neglected."

"Really?"

"Yeah."

"Oh well, I guess we need to take care of that right away, baby."

"Damn straight," Lily said as she brushed her lips against Tessa's.

They quickly undressed each other and gave in to the surge of passion growing between them.

CHAPTER 12

CONNECTIONS

E lise was sitting in the kitchen with her mug of maté tea. It was a late night, and she was working from her laptop, going over next day's lesson plan and grading some assignments. Her laptop signaled she was getting a message. She checked her inbox.

A Facebook friend request from Lily Karajian.

"Oh," Élise said out loud.

She checked the profile and read the message. She accepted.

Five minutes later, she got a LinkedIn request to join Lily's professional network. Lily was a real estate agent in Vermont.

"She's very persistent. Like her father," Élise said, chuckling. Then an Evite came through. Élise laughed. "What now?

Lily invites you to a dinner party on Saturday, September 17."

Élise scrolled through the list of invitees. Aren listed himself as tentative and then indicated in the note: "Waiting for Élise's response."

"That man!" Élise sighed, and then she responded yes to the Evite.

.oOo.

Lily ushered Élise and her father through the door of her Arts and Crafts-designed house.

"Oh, it's wonderful to finally meet you," Lily said. "Dad talks about you all the time."

"Thank you, Lily. Thank you for inviting me," Élise said.

Élise handed her coat to Lily and took in the view of the picture-sized west-facing window with a muntin pattern. It had a built-in bookshelf and overstuffed chairs.

"Your house is so cozy. I love it."

Wow, Lily is the spitting image of her mother. If I searched long enough, I might be able to find traces of Aren in the contours of her lips.

"Come, I'll show you around. Hon, come over and meet Élise."

Tessa walked up to Élise and greeted her warmly with a kiss on the cheek.

"Hi, I'm Tessa."

"Hi, I'm Élise. It's nice to meet you."

"So Aren says you teach French. I have a few French-Canadian clients, actually," Tessa said.

"Really? What do you do?"

"Oh, I'm a tax accountant. I have a specialty in international tax."

"Ah, sounds interesting," Élise said.

Élise was introduced to the other guests and very quickly got into lively discussions. Élise thought how different her experience was when she met Aren's friends. Here, no one put her on the spot. Everyone was welcoming. There was no awkwardness. It was refreshing. Most of the guests at the party were in their twenties and thirties. They were professionals and at the beginning of their careers. Élise enjoyed the energy of this diverse crowd. Everyone seemed so comfortable in their skin. Élise marveled at how confident Lily and Tessa were as a couple. As a teacher of teenagers, Élise had witnessed the sometimes awkward coming out of students as gay and navigating relationships in a strong heterosexual culture. It was changing. It had changed a lot from when she first started teaching.

"Dinner is served," Tessa announced ceremoniously.

Everyone stood and approached the table. Tessa served a wonderful butternut squash ravioli with seared tuna and a fresh garden salad. The table was set beautifully and elegantly. Aren sat next to her. He kept his hand on her knee during the entire meal. He kissed her cheek occasionally and smiled. Every sentence he began with "Élise and I" or "Élise." Even when he talked about something he was doing or speaking about him and Lily, he somehow brought the conversation back to himself and Élise. Everyone roared with laughter when Aren described his date with Élise at the Public Garden.

"He took you on the Swan Boat?" Lily exclaimed. "Yes," Élise replied.

"We did the Ducklings Tour too. Élise didn't know anything about *Make Way for Ducklings*. I had to buy the book for her and we were able to identify the buildings in the book." Aren leaned over and kissed Élise. Lily marveled at how much her father touched Élise. He was continually rubbing her neck or stroking her arms. The more he did it, the more relaxed he seemed. Her father had an ornery side. Her friends had met him often enough to just accept it as part of his personality. That night, Lily saw a different side of her father. He was patting people on the back, asking them about their jobs. He was offering advice and networking opportunities. He was jovial. He enjoyed one cocktail which he nursed before dinner. He didn't complain that she had diluted the alcohol content. "Thank you, honey," he said when he took a sip. He set it down and then wrapped his arm around Élise. It was fascinating really. At first, she thought Élise was the passive one in the relationship. But it wasn't that really. She just wasn't that overtly demonstrative. But she had the most amazing smile when she looked at him. And when he spoke, she gave him her undivided attention, without being fake. She was in the moment with him. It was sweet.

As they were all seated in the living room, sipping their coffees and liqueurs, Barry raised his glass.

"Happy birthday, Lily. You don't look a day over fifty. No, oops! I mean thirty-f—"

"No, no, Lily doesn't look a day over twenty-nine," Élise said. "Don't worry, Lily, I got your back," she said, chuckling.

"Barry, you're fired as my friend. Élise, you're my new BFF."

"Hey, what about me?" Tessa said, pouting.

"Oh honey, you're my main squeeze. But I gotta have a BFF." Everyone laughed.

"Thank you, everyone," Lily said a little tearfully. Everyone there was part of her inner circle. Some she had known in school, like Barry. Others she had met since moving to Vermont like Tessa. She was delighted that her father was there to share this moment with her. They had both been on a long journey and it felt like they had reached a beautiful safe haven.

"I had the best birthday," Lily said gratefully. "I'm excited that Dad has a fantastic woman in his life." Élise beamed with joy to be included in Lily's circle. "But, geez, Élise," Lily continued, "he's turning into the Energizer bunny. Every time we talk, he has these elaborate plans. You gotta get him to slow his roll a little. I want him around for a long time."

"Don't worry, honey. Élise gives me good stuff to keep going," Aren said.

Élise's complexion deepened. Aren laughed and everyone else joined him.

"Way to keep the old man young, Élise," Barry said.

"Oh my God," Élise said as she buried her hot face in Aren's shoulder as he laughed.

"All I can say is God bless *Cosmopolitan Magazine*. Woo-hoo," Aren said.

"Dad, if Élise gets any redder we might have to admit her to the hospital."

Aren kissed Élise's hot temple.

"All right, everyone, I'll bring out the cake," Tessa announced.

.oOo.

After the party when Lily and Tessa had cleaned up, they sat in bed and discussed the evening. Tessa leaned over and kissed Lily.

"Happy Birthday, sweetie. I hope you had a great time."

Lily smiled. "Thank you. The party was wonderful. You outdid yourself. I keep telling you need to ditch the tax accounting business and open up a catering business."

"Oh, no. I do the cooking out of love. I can't imagine putting all that effort for strangers, no matter how much they paid me." Tessa noticed a faraway expression on Lily's face. "What's on your mind, honey?"

"Oh, I'm sorry. I was just thinking of my dad."

"Why, he was in rare form tonight. I think that was the first time I saw your dad genuinely enjoying himself. He was actually mingling with people."

Lily chuckled. "Yeah," she agreed. "He did seem happy, but—"

"But what? Didn't you say before that your dad has been through a hard time and it hasn't been easy for him to break out of his depression?" Tessa said.

Lily ran her fingers through her hair and knit her brows together, absentmindedly.

"You know, Tessa, I don't ever remember seeing my dad like that with anyone, not even my mother. He touched Élise the entire time they were here."

Tessa blinked a few times. "Well, they're dating. Isn't that what people do?"

"No, this is different. It's like she's his narcotic." Tessa laughed.

"No, I'm serious. She calms him. He's not so irritable."

"Well, that's a pretty good narcotic," Tessa said.

"Yeah, but they only met a few months ago. He's really into her like I have never seen him before. What if she breaks his heart? She's not like his other girlfriends."

"Honey, they're grown-ups. This is the euphoric stage of the relationship. Everyone goes through this. Let them enjoy this phase. Élise doesn't strike me as a gold digger. I kind of like her. If she had been my language teacher, I would have become fluent in French and Spanish. She's got something. I see why your dad likes her."

Lily eyed Tessa suspiciously. "What?" Tessa asked.

"You have a crush on Élise."

Tessa erupted into laughter. Lily sat with a stony face. "Oh, come on, babe," Tessa said.

"All right," Lily said grudgingly. "Maybe it's not a crush. But she has a magnetic personality. You know that French expression '*attachant?*' That's Élise. She's very loveable."

"Isn't that a good thing?" Tessa asked.

"I'm just afraid that my dad is going to become so attached to her that he will stop paying attention to me. I have never had to compete with anyone for my father's attention. And now for the first time, I feel like I could become a third wheel."

Tessa looked at Lily with compassion. Turning thirty-five was a milestone for Lily. They had started to talk about raising a family whether through adoption or assisted reproductive technology. For now, they were just talking. Having a family was not a priority for Tessa. For Lily it was different. Time would tell.

Tessa slid down on the bed and pulled Lily to her breast. "Come here, sweetie," she cooed.

They lay together for a few minutes and then Lily fell asleep. Tessa's intuition told her Élise would usher great drama into their lives. It would eventually work out. How the drama would unfold or get resolved was as yet a mystery. Élise was a beautiful woman. Tessa understood perfectly why Aren would pursue her relentlessly and then keep her at his side. *Aren Karajian you're a lucky bastard.*

Tessa yawned. *So the adventure begins.* She yawned again and then promptly fell asleep.

CHAPTER 13

PAPERS

Aren was sitting in his chair reading the newspaper, yawning. Élise was hunched over a pile of papers. It was 11:00 p.m. He got up and walked over to the desk where she was working. He had set up a workstation for her at his cottage. "Honey, how much longer are you going to be?"

"I don't know. It's taking me longer to get through these papers. Goodness, some of them are dreadful," Élise said.

"Well, wouldn't it be faster if you reviewed them online?"

"I can't stand reading papers online. I have to print them and mark them up."

He picked up one paper filled with red marks. "What grade are you going to give this one?"

"B."

"With all these marks?"

"Well, the analysis was well done, and even the sentence structure is good. There's just a lot of grammatical and punctuation errors."

"Sweetheart, if you used the program I developed for you and graded them online, you could have the papers autocorrected. That would free up your time to do the substantive review."

"I know, but—"

"Honey, you're not making any sense. It helps no one if you are so bogged down by correcting stupid errors that you don't have time and energy to devote to the big stuff. Do you want me to show you how to use it?"

"No, I can do it."

"I don't believe you. Show me a paper you haven't printed out yet." Élise called up a document and then opened it up.

"Scoot over," Aren said. He pulled up a stool and sat next to her. He typed in some macro commands and created some new rules. Then he hit the "enter macros" button. Élise watched in wonder as the program counted up the errors and classified the type of error, such as syntax, punctuation, word choice, spelling, and grammatical. The program even provided the correction for how to fix the error.

"Wow!"

"Baby, your time is precious. This is a tool to help you optimize your teaching. But your students have to take some responsibility too. Now maybe you still have to review the results, but tell me this isn't faster than what you're doing now."

Élise rolled her eyes.

"Don't be like that. I'm selfish. I want to be in bed with you now, not watching you slave over some snotty-nosed kid's work."

"They're not some 'snotty-nosed' kids. The fact that they come from privilege doesn't make them less deserving of compassion. Your wife Helen went to a prep school."

"All right," Aren sighed. "I'm just grumpy because you're working so hard and those kids have no idea how hard you're working for them. Meanwhile, I am deprived of your attention which I desperately crave."

Élise removed her glasses and rubbed her eyes gently. She reached for Aren's hand and kissed it.

"Doudou, chéri. That's what it means to be with children, even teenagers. Teaching is a vocation. I didn't give birth to them, but my students are my children. I am responsible for preparing them for the future. They are precious. The time I take away from you is for a good cause. Don't be jealous, okay? If you were working on a project that could transform people's lives and take them out of misery, I would not resent the time you had to be away from me."

Aren kissed Élise affectionately. "What did I tell you? I'm selfish.

If I were on a project, you would be right there with me and we would be working together side by side."

Élise chuckled. "Oh, you're silly. I'm not a scientist."

"You know what? You're smart and teachable. I could train you to do anything." He glanced at the computer screen. "You could master this program, it's just that you think you're cheating your students if you don't slave over your work."

Élise sighed. "Aren, I'm curious. Do you like children? Yes, you love your daughter. I'm just wondering how you survived being a parent."

"The whole parenting phase of my life seems like a blur. I was lucky. Lily was the best-behaved child. Anyway, that part of my life is over, thank God!"

Élise had a wistful expression on her face. Apart from her reference to students or an occasional reference to Fanny's children or the children in her neighborhood, they rarely talked about children. They lived a life absent of children. Or, more precisely, he lived a life absent of children. It didn't bother him at all. Élise loved children, especially toddlers. If they were in a store, children would stare at her because maybe they weren't used to seeing someone like her. She was always very patient and kind. They always ended up smiling at her. That's what he loved about her. She was at her core, a very kind and generous person. *Thank goodness we don't have grandchildren. I would never have private time with Élise.* Aren thought about Lily's growing interest in having children. *Yikes! At least with Élise's students, it was time-limited. There were vacations, school breaks, and graduations. I can wait to be a grandad. Take your time Lily.*

"Come on, sweetheart. Your eyes are all glassy. You need to sleep. You can get up in the morning and finish. I won't even give you a hard time for not coming out with me. Okay?"

Élise packed up the papers and shut down the computer. Aren was in the bathroom drawing a bath. Élise looked at Aren quizzically when she entered the bathroom.

"Come on. You're tense. I thought a hot bath might relax you."

Élise smiled. "Thank you. That's really sweet."

"I am joining you."

"Oh, I see."

"I'm going to overlook that underwhelming response and chalk it up to your being tired," Aren chided.

Élise shook her head and began to undress and then stepped into the tub. Aren lit some candles and then joined her. He pulled her back against him. He kissed her cheek.

"Feel good?"

"Hmm," she moaned with pleasure.

They were quiet for a while. Aren was massaging her shoulders and back and stroking her breasts. She could feel his penis slowly coming to life and bumping up against her butt.

"Aren, is it okay if we just relax—I mean not have sex?"

"Why?"

She chuckled nervously.

"Well, I don't know. Lately, I feel like my body is on demand 24/7."

"Sweetie, I don't get to see you during most of the week. This is my time with you."

"I know, but it's like we don't cuddle anymore. It's more and more sex."

"But you enjoy it."

"Yes. But I like just cuddling too."

"Well, we were cuddling."

"No, that was foreplay."

"Same difference." Élise let out a guffaw.

"Now, what's so funny?" Aren asked in irritation.

"I think we're quarreling over who has control over Élise's body."

"What?" Aren replied.

"Never mind. I can't explain it. I'm feeling loopy, I guess." *If I told Aren how utterly exhausted, I really feel, he would lecture me about using or not using the program. All I want to do is curl up and sleep. Something is off in my body. I don't want to tell him. He'll just start to panic and I don't want that. If I don't snap out of it, maybe I'll go see the doctor.*

"So can we get back to what we were doing before?" Élise sighed in defeat. "Yeah."

Aren held her tight and then started fingering her. His breathing accelerated. He was kissing her, and her nipples stood erect. She winced at Aren's touch. Her breasts were feeling tender lately. He quickly positioned her so he could enter her, and he rocked back and forth and up and down, sending waves of water onto the bathroom floor.

Élise was surprised by the intensity of his desire. When he slipped out of her once he felt the release, he sighed and kissed the nape of her neck and then bit her hard.

"Merde!" she yelled.

"I don't know what it is," Aren said. "Lately, I'm hungry for you."

"Well, I'm not food. Cut it out."

Aren chuckled. "It's a love bite."

"Yes, it's a bite. I'm not sure about the love part."

"Come here, let me kiss it and make it all better."

He drained the tub and stood up with Élise and dried them off quickly. They brushed their teeth and then went to bed.

Aren noticed Élise was quiet and impassive. He pulled her to his chest and kissed the red mark on her shoulder. Tears welled up in her eyes. She started to cry.

"Sweetie, why are you crying? My God, you're sobbing." A sinking feeling in the pit of his stomach started to grow. "Did I hurt you?"

Élise continued to weep. She looked up at him. He was desperately trying to wipe her tears.

"It hurts Aren, b-b-but,"

"But what sweetie? Tell me."

"I—I don't know why," she sniffled. She paused to catch her breath. "I don't know why I'm crying. Maybe it's hormonal. I just have to cry. Maybe I'm overtired."

"Go ahead, baby."

Aren held Élise tight against his chest. The salt of her tears made his scar itch a little, but he did not let go of her. She cried herself to sleep. And then Aren kissed her forehead and fell asleep instantly.

CHAPTER 14

⬦⬦⬦

NOT SUCH SECRET THINGS

⬦⬦⬦

Elise's back lay arched over Aren's latest BDSM liberator wedge cushion mounted on top of the black microfiber platform.

Her hands were bound to microfiber hand clasps attached to the wedge. Sexy black kitten blindfolds covered her eyes. Aren sat comfortably facing her, supported by another wedge cushion against his back, allowing his feet to lay flat on the floor. Élise's slender legs wrapped around his hips as he built a steady rhythm, thrusting inside. They were shaking from pleasure. Aren released Élise's hand clasps so she could flip her body and lie with her back against him in a yoga fish pose. Then he continued to thrust from behind. The head rush from leaning so far backward made her let out a blood-curdling scream.

Just then Lily and Tessa walked through the front door. It was unlocked as usual. Aren and Élise had invited them over for dinner. It was casual, so they hadn't fixed an exact time for their arrival. The two women stood in the main room, frozen in their spots in reaction to the scream. They stared at each other. They heard cries and loud weeping noises.

Lily gasped. "Oh my God! Is that Élise?" she whispered. "Tessa, what should we do? Should we call the police?"

"Babe, let's be calm about this," Tessa answered. "Maybe they just had a bad fight. It happens."

"Tessa, what if she's hurt?"

"Well, has your dad ever exhibited violent tendencies?" Lily gulped. "I don't know."

"Okay, let's take a deep breath. We'll go upstairs. We'll check." Tessa took Lily by the hand, and they crept quietly up the stairs.

They heard loud slapping noises, animalistic grunts, and more weeping. When they reached the top of the stairs, Lily screamed.

.oOo.

"What the hell are you doing here?" Aren yelled.

Élise looked up, doe-eyed in the midst of the commotion.

Lily stammered but couldn't articulate any words. She turned around and ran out of the house. Tessa followed.

.oOo.

"Aren," Élise said. "We forgot the time. We told them to come."

"Holy shit!" Aren said. "Right. What do we do?"

"I don't know," Élise said worriedly.

She stood up and removed the cuffs from her ankles. "Do you think they're traumatized?"

"I don't know, sweetheart. I mean, they're adults. I just don't understand. We were so loud, couldn't they figure out what was going on? I mean, why come up the stairs?"

.oOo.

Lily

Catching your parents "in the act." Isn't that the phobia all children have? Or maybe it's one of those first-world problems. I never understood how families in different cultures could crowd into one sleeping room.

How do the children not catch their parents in the act? But here I was, thirty-five years old, a successful real estate agent in a committed relationship with a woman, and I found my father in a compromising position. Compromising? Well, he was having sex with his girlfriend, a grown woman of fifty. But it was, dare I say, how they were going about the act that horrified me. They were acting out some kind of BDSM scene. I'm sure if I shared the story with friends, they would fall over themselves laughing. Old people do have sex, but kinky sex? But she was screaming—did my father hurt her? My father was the most loving and caring man I have ever known. How could he treat a woman like that? My father is an animal, a beast? I have to hold my head together so it doesn't unravel. Clearly, there are things that one wishes one could unsee—that I wish I could unsee and unknow.

.oOo.

A quarter of a mile away from the cottage, Lily was sitting on the side of the curb hyperventilating. Tessa was sitting next to her, rubbing her back to calm her down.

"Jesus Christ! That was my father," Lily cried.

Tessa was silent. Lily repeated herself. After the third time, Tessa spoke.

"Honey, whatever else we can say about your father and Élise, they're not exhibitionists. They didn't know we were there. I think they forgot we were coming. We've done that before."

"Oh God, Tessa."

Baby, when it's red hot between us, we have had neighbors three doors down complain about us. It's sex, baby. And they love each other."

"Tessa, I mean—"

"If it really freaks you out that much, we can go home. I can call your dad and apologize and explain. I'm sure he understands and is probably as mortified, if not more."

"No, he's not. You heard him. He was furious. Oh my God, did you see how he was treating her?"

"Babe, I hate to break it to you, but um, Élise was loving it." Then Tessa erupted into laughter. She laughed so hard she started cry.

"What is wrong with you?" Lily snapped with indignation.

"I think your dad has been watching way too much porn. He's not so young anymore. He needs to tone it down." And then she laughed again. She was clutching her belly.

"Tessa, this is not funny. It's sick. I mean, Élise had ankle cuffs on."

"They were pretty nice. We should find out where they got them. And you know that platform thing they were grooving on was amazing."

"Go to hell! I'm sitting here trying not to throw up over what I saw, and you're making jokes?"

"No, I'm serious. Your old man was basically showing us sex is still magical no matter how old you are. Well, it helps that the woman he's banging is hot. Did you see her ass? And her tits? She's gorgeous. Now we know the whole prim and proper French teacher thing is a façade. We have blown her cover sky high," Tessa giggled.

Lily felt her stomach tightening. She could taste the bile rising to her throat. She wanted to heave. She stood up suddenly.

"I'm going to take a walk."

"Where are you going?" Tessa asked.

"I don't know. There's a bar a mile away. You can find me there in an hour."

"Sure you don't want me to come with you?"

"No, I'll be all right," Lily said and continued walking. "Okay. You have your phone, right? It's charged?"

Lily pulled out her phone and held it up while nodding. Tessa watched as Lily walked away quickly in the direction of town. Tessa walked in the opposite direction, back toward Aren's house.

.oOo.

Tessa rang the doorbell and then walked inside. Aren and Élise were standing in the living room, dressed in sweats. They exchanged worried looks when they saw Lily was not with Tessa.

"Where's Lily?" Aren said.

"She said she needed to walk. I'll pick her up in an hour at the bar."

Élise bit her lips nervously. Tessa noticed her face was a little thinner than usual.

"Don't worry, Élise. Lily and Aren have always joked about his sex life, but she's never had to see it up close and personal. Well, no child ever wants to see a parent getting it on."

"Yes, I understand. But I feel so bad about it," Élise said. Aren put his arm around Élise and kissed her temple.

"Tessa, why did you two come up the stairs?" Aren asked with a hoarse voice.

"Um, well, when we walked in, we heard a scream. We thought— and then as we got near the room, some of the other noises seemed to be consistent with our fear."

Aren stared at Tessa in exasperation. He closed his eyes and took a deep breath.

"Tessa, for the record I have never abused a woman. Ever. I know sometimes with L—"

"Don't say another word, Aren. I'm sorry. You're right. We're family. Don't say what you're thinking. All right?"

Aren nodded. He turned to Élise and kissed her.

"You didn't, we didn't do anything wrong, chérie." He smiled sadly and then left the room. Minutes later he came back with his boots.

"Aren, where are you going?" Élise asked.

"I have to find her. She's still my baby. I don't like the idea of her running around distraught even in this small town. That's how bad things happen to people. I'm taking my phone. You two stay here."

"Okay," Élise said.

Aren walked up to Élise, kissed her, and whispered, "I love you." Élise smiled as she watched him walk out the door.

Élise looked at Tessa. "Do you think Lily is okay? Maybe I should run after Aren and go with him."

"You know what? Aren is right. This is a daddy and daughter conversation."

Élise marveled at Tessa's clear-headedness.

Tessa studied Élise's expression. She chuckled. "When you have a career looking at how people and businesses manage their finances, you learn a lot about human motivation and behavior. Very little surprises me. I apologize. I let my imagination run wild. I'm sorry."

"Do you think less of me?" Élise asked. Tessa smiled.

"No. Though I must say there's a reason why we're programmed to enjoy sex. You got it going on, girl," Tessa said.

Élise smiled weakly.

"Well, come on, let's make some dinner. Your face looks thin. Are you losing weight?"

Élise touched her face. She didn't have much of an appetite lately. "Oh, you know how it goes. The weight goes up and down. I'm sure when winter comes the weight will come back on."

.oOo.

An hour later, Aren returned with Lily. Both of them had bloodshot eyes from crying. Élise and Tessa looked at each other but said nothing. Dinner was a quiet affair. Afterward, they played some backgammon and then snuggled up on the sofa to watch a Netflix movie.

When it was time for Lily and Tessa to leave, Élise was surprised by the warmth of the embrace Lily gave her. It brought tears to her eyes.

"We'll see each other soon, okay?" Élise said in a weepy voice. "Just us. We can have lunch, my treat."

"I'd like that," Lily said.

"I'll call you this week and we can talk, okay?" Élise said gently. Lily smiled.

Tessa and Élise hugged each other. "Thank you, Tessa," Élise said.

.oOo.

Later that night, Élise and Aren were lying entwined in each other's arms. They had made love to each other again that night, but this time the session was gentle and tender. Élise was radiant and happy. She made loud kissy noises all over his face and licked him like a puppy.

"Cut it out, woman!" Aren said, the affection in his tone belying the grumpy expression. He looked at her. "Élise?"

"Yeah?"

"Am I too rough?"

Élise was quiet for a moment. *How do I answer the question without triggering some kind of crisis? Sometimes we do tread a fine line.*

"If by rough you mean, are you hurting me? No. Absolutely not. If you're asking me if things are intense between us sexually? Then yes, very much so. Frighteningly so, sometimes. But then, you don't force me to do anything I don't want to do if I have made up my mind I don't want to do it. There's a limit to what I'm willing to submit to. Although sometimes, I admit, I have trouble identifying that limit. Have I answered your question?"

Aren ran his fingers nervously through his hair. He fixed Élise with a steady gaze.

"Élise, what I feel for you is like a hunger. I've said it before. It's crazy sometimes. When it gets really hot between us, sometimes I think I'm capable of just biting your head off. Not because I hate you. It's just the opposite. I want to devour you. Own you. Control you. It's how I experience the passion."

Élise erupted into laughter.

"It's not funny, Élise. I'm being serious."

"You can't possibly be serious. You're not making any sense. I love you, but I don't worship you. You're not a god."

"But that's how you make me feel. Like I'm omnipotent."

"I think those male enhancement pills have addled your brain, amigo."

"Maybe I'm not explaining it well. But I think you understand what I mean. Anyway, I'm realizing that maybe I should show more tenderness toward you. You have been trying to tell me, but I haven't wanted to listen. I like tenderness too."

Élise had a flash of an earlier conversation between them in the bathtub when Aren said cuddling and foreplay were the same thing. For Aren intimacy seemed to always result in sex. There were nice and gentle ways of going about it and there were bold and sexy ways about getting there. For her tenderness was the cuddles, the walks in the garden, dancing, and the exchanged smiles. So what did he really think tenderness was? *Clearly, we have different love languages.* She looked at him. "All right, Aren. Are we good now?"

"Yeah. I love you so much. You know that, right?"

Élise lay her head against Aren's chest and played with his furry hair. Then she kissed the scar on his chest.

"I love you. I don't say it very often. But I think you need to hear me say it."

She looked up, and tears were rolling down Aren's face. She smiled, tenderly wiped his tears, kissed him, and then hummed his favorite lullaby, and they both fell asleep.

In the morning, Élise woke up first and turned to Aren, who was still asleep. She leaned forward and planted an open-mouthed kiss on his lips, breathing life into him. He slowly woke up.

"Huh?"

"Hi."

"Hi. Is everything okay?"

"Mmm-hmm," Élise purred, breaking into a radiant smile. "I want to make to love to you. Do you have to pee?"

"Hmm, I think I can wait." Élise smiled.

"You're so beautiful. Come here."

Without the benefit of Aren's wedges and platforms, they managed to maneuver themselves on their sides so Aren could ease himself inside, with Élise's right leg to support him. No talking, lots of laughing and loving caresses and kisses until they both exploded inside of each other.

CHAPTER 15

AUTUMN LEAVES

Élise

It was only once the school year commenced and my life began to take on its usual patterns that I realized I had passed the summer without seeing Fanny. We still spoke on the phone, but I was no longer available to hang out with her now that Aren was in my life. It was Aren who suggested we go on a fishing trip together. "Brilliant!" I said, hugging him. We were going away Columbus Day weekend so we settled on getting together the weekend before.

We drove to the north shore to Gloucester on Cape Ann. It's on the Atlantic Coast. Fanny, her husband Enrique, and their children Jorje and Manuel came. Antonio also came along. It was an Indian summer. The temperature hovered around 65°F. We caught striped bass and flounder. Later, we went whale fishing. In all the time I had lived in Massachusetts, this was my first time seeing this magnificent site of dolphin pods and whales frolicking in the water. As much as I was enjoying the wonderful sights and the sea air, I could feel myself getting queasy from the rocking of the boat. I gripped the rails to steady myself.

Aren's voice startled me.

"Are you okay, honey?"

"Oh, maybe I'm a little sea sick," I said. "I think maybe I'll go back below deck and lie down. I just need to reorient myself."

Aren had taken me sailing before and I didn't have this reaction.

Maybe I was just coming down with something. I passed Fanny on my way back toward the boat cabin. Thank goodness she didn't pester me with questions. I was sure once I had a chance to sit and rest a little, I would feel better.

On the way home, we stopped and picked up some fresh cod, haddock, and swordfish. We would divvy them up when we got back. Fanny announced she would be making a Columbian seafood stew specialty, cazuela de mariscos. Mmmm, it is one of my all-time favorite dishes. Fanny was an indifferent cook—except when it came to preparing a Columbian specialty. I couldn't wait. I helped Fanny prepare the ingredients, but I didn't stay in the kitchen. The smell of the butter, cream, and coconut milk made my intestines roil.

It was six o'clock in the evening when Fanny served the stew. In the end, I couldn't eat the stew. I took a few bites of the haddock. I didn't touch the shrimp or the clams. I ate some of the tamales and the platanos.

"Are you okay, Élise?" Fanny asked. Usually, I was the first one to ask for seconds.

"I'm sorry, Fanny. I think I am coming down with something. It all looks amazing, though."

Aren looked at me and then turned his attention to Fanny. "Compliments to the chef," he said graciously. "This is amazing.

You'll have to visit us in Vermont and teach me how to replicate this. I love it."

"Hear, hear," everyone at the table said. Fanny looked so happy.

After dinner, we all sat on the deck of Fanny's house. Everyone was enjoying some rum. I drank ginger ale. Ever since that evening at Antonio's, I have been avoiding alcohol. Even at Lily's birthday party, I stuck to ginger ale. It was safer.

I didn't say very much. The truth was I didn't trust myself to speak. That loopy feeling, I had been having returned, but this time with a headache. Fortunately, it passed after a while. Aren, Antonio, and Enrique disappeared to help with the boys' homework. Later the men would come back and smoke cigars. That was my cue to stand and help Fanny clean up.

I started to rinse the dishes and load them into the dishwasher. "Dinner was fantastic!" I said.

"Hmmph!" Fanny said. "What? You don't think so."

"No, I think the stew was amazing," she said. "But you didn't eat, querida. Are you okay? You're not your usual bubbly self."

"I'm okay. I must have picked up a bug somewhere, and I'm having a hard time shaking it off."

Fanny gave me a stern look.

"Élise, go see a real doctor. Not your woo-woo practitioners with their scary needles. A real doctor. Promise me, okay?"

I nodded and then we talked about our day on the fishing boat.

Fanny spoke animatedly and I was glad to be able to listen. "He's a good guy," Fanny said finally.

"Yes, that's what I keep telling you."

"He's crazy about you." Fanny said with a chuckle. "It's the cutest thing."

I did the *Kanye shrug* and Fanny erupted into peals of laughter. "What are you doing for Thanksgiving? Why don't you both come over for Thanksgiving?"

I chuckled. "Thanksgiving is a long time away. We were talking about possibly going away maybe travel to Mexico. Aren has friends who live there. We were thinking of either staying with them or renting something on our own."

"I see," Fanny said. "You're a woman of leisure now."

"Leisure? No, I'm still working. But Aren has a much for flexible lifestyle. I'm just going along for the ride."

"Querida, this is much more than a ride. Aren is serious."

"Well, I'll get back to you closer in time, okay? Maybe Aren would prefer a family-style Latino Thanksgiving."

It was nine o'clock when we got back to my apartment. I let Antonio sit in the passenger seat. I sat in the back with the window open. The men found something to talk about and I dozed during the drive home. When we arrived at my apartment building, Antonio invited us over for some tea.

"You go on," I urged Aren. "I have school tomorrow and I need to get some sleep." I kissed Aren quickly and hugged Antonio before rushing off to my apartment. I quickly undressed and crawled into bed in less than ten minutes. Whenever it was when Aren returned to my apartment, I didn't hear him.

.oOo.

The Wednesday following the weekend fishing trip, Aren woke with a start. It was a cool and brisk October morning. Élise was wearing a pair of silk pajamas. In Vermont, she tended to hug the blankets to her. She was always cold. That morning her arms were draped loosely over the blankets. She was sleeping deeply. She had overslept.

Aren shook her gently. "Élise, wake up." She stirred. "Huh?" she said.

"Baby, you overslept. If you don't get going, you're going to miss your class."

"What?"

Élise was having a hard time focusing on what Aren was saying. She felt like she had a hangover even though she had not had one drop of alcohol in over a month.

Aren noted her haggard expression. "Are you okay? Maybe you can put on a movie for your class. You don't look like yourself."

Despite Élise's protests, Aren decided to stay for the week. They would be flying out to Chicago on Friday afternoon as a jumpstart to the Columbus Day weekend and celebrate Aren's birthday. He used her music space as an office while she taught. Usually when he stayed longer than a weekend, he got really bossy and fussy, which annoyed her. But this morning, she was grateful he was there. She felt awful. She sat up slowly, blinking. Her head was spinning.

"Maybe I'm coming down with some kind of bug. Something has

been going around school."

"So stay home," Aren said.

"No, I think a hot shower will do the trick. But if you don't mind, maybe you could drive me. I'm tired."

"All right, honey. Go. I'll make some toast. Coffee?"

"Hmm, dry toast, please, and skip the coffee. Maybe I'll have some yerba maté. I'm feeling kind of loopy."

"You got it."

Aren was back in Élise's apartment by 7:30. He made himself some breakfast assam tea, and brought it with him to his improvised study. He thought he would work on a project proposal, but his mind went blank. He couldn't focus on the proposal because he was worried about Élise.

Things were good between them, he thought, but he couldn't shake this nagging feeling that something was off. Élise was behaving strangely. She was fastidious about the care of her teeth. Lately, he noticed there was blood when she brushed her teeth. When he questioned her about it, she got mad and accused him of spying on her. And then later she said: "Oh, I just brushed my gums too hard." *Hunh?*

It was little things he noticed. She complained about being tired. She didn't have much of an appetite. She was menopausal but when she had a recent period that lasted all of one day, she complained of severe cramps. Aren thought of the course of Helen's cancer that ultimately took her life. *God please don't take Élise away from me.* Maybe he was panicking for no reason.

.oOo.

Élise

By noon, I was feeling better. I played the first thirty minutes of a movie and then divided the class into discussion groups. I had no energy to teach. The students seemed to enjoy the break from routine. Throughout the day I felt low-grade cramping and bloating in my lower abdomen. In truth, I had been feeling like this off and on for a few weeks. But today was just the worst. Maybe I had a urinary tract infection. Fanny had mentioned to be careful now that I was sexually active.

Aren picked me up when my classes were over. I cancelled my office hours. I eased myself into the passenger seat. Aren stroked my face.

"You look miserable," Aren said. "Let me cook tonight. You still seem kind of out of it."

"Thanks. I'm just tired. I think a good night's sleep will do wonders."

"All right," Aren said.

We had an early supper. I only spent an hour preparing for class. I took a warm bath that eased a lot of my symptoms. Aren prepared hibiscus and ginger tea while I got ready for bed. I felt better. Aren curled up with me and I was asleep by eight o'clock.

.oOo.

Aren

I lay next to Élise and watched her sleep. She really needed me to take care of her today, and I was glad to be there for her. I decided to stay in bed with her. I reached for a book and started to read. At nine o'clock my phone rang. I looked over at Élise. She didn't stir.

"Hello."

"Hi, Dad."

"Hi, Lily. What's up?"

"Just wanted to check in to make sure we're all set for this weekend?"

"Yeah, why?"

"Well, I spoke briefly to Élise today. She was kind of weird on the phone. Is everything okay between you?"

"Yeah," Aren said in genuine surprise. "Yeah. I mean she had an off day today. She's asleep now, and you know what a night owl she is."

"Okay. I just want to check in."

"Thanks, baby. You're my girl."

"Yeah, yeah, yeah. That's what you say to Tessa."

"Well, she is my girl."

"You're a slut, Dad."

I laughed. "Okay, I'll see you on Friday. Love you."

"Love you too."

I ended the call and looked over at Élise. She was still deep asleep. I lowered my head and brushed my lips against hers. "I love you," I whispered. I turned the lights out and spooned with her. "Feel better," I whispered.

.oOo.

In the middle of the night, Élise got up and went to the bathroom. When she got back to bed, Aren was awake. She slipped in next to him and lay on her side.

"I'm sorry. I didn't mean to wake you up," she said. "No, that's okay," Aren whispered. "Are you all right?"

"Yeah."

Aren looked at her back. "Are we okay?" he asked. Élise turned her head. "Oh God yes. Why?"

"I don't know. You've been kind of grumpy, lately."

"Well, I haven't been feeling well," Élise explained. "Is that all?"

"Yes! When did you get all sensitive?" Élise teased.

Something about the way Aren was speaking signaled her she should take him seriously.

"Come here," Élise said, gesturing him to lay his head on her chest and hold him. She kissed his hair and started humming his favorite lullaby. She could sing the words now, and she sang them. She heard the soft rustling of his snores. She chuckled. She felt the urge to pee again, but she didn't want to disturb Aren. Eventually, she fell asleep. In the morning, she woke up just before dawn with a dire urge to pee. Aren was still snuggled up against her, but she managed to wriggle out of his embrace and race to the bathroom. When she returned, Aren was awake. He went to the bathroom.

Élise was lying on her side when Aren returned. He slipped back into bed and spooned with her, caressing her.

"You have an hour before you need to get ready for school," he murmured in her ear.

She felt his erection. She wasn't in the mood at all. She was hoping she could leave a little earlier and do some prep work. He was already fingering her and stroking her breasts, which were feeling tender this morning.

"You know what, Aren. My body hurts. I'm in pain and I'm exhausted. Can we just hold each other for a little bit before I have to get ready for school?"

Aren studied Élise closely. "Are you hiding something from me?"

Élise sighed. "I'm not hiding anything from you. I've told you the truth. I'm not feeling well."

"I love you, Élise." She smiled.

"Why don't you ever tell me you love me?"

"I do! Besides, why do you place so much value on words? I'm devoted to you. What more do you want from me?"

"Hopelessly devoted?"

"Let's not get carried away."

"Maybe I want you to be carried away."

"That's not who I am."

Aren rolled himself on top of Élise and looked at her. She still seemed tired. Her face seemed thinner than usual. Nothing major, but he was now noticing it.

"I need to hear you say you love me."

Élise clucked. "Oh, Aren. Okay. I love you. I love you with all of my heart. I love fighting with you. I love listening to your snores in the middle of the night. I love the way you make love to me. I love your touch. I hate it when I have to sleep alone. I'm always thinking about you, even when I'm furious with you. I don't fantasize about anyone but you."

Aren smiled. "Really?"

Élise rolled her eyes. "Enough."

"Okay." He kissed her lips affectionately. "Get ready. I'll make breakfast and drive you. If you hurry, I can get you to school by seven and you can do some work."

Élise smiled and stroked his cheeks and kissed him passionately. "Baby, if you keep that up, you're going to be late, and then don't blame me."

She smiled and then got up, showered, and got ready for school.

.oOo.

Aren

Later in the afternoon, Élise called me.

"Hi, Aren. I just wanted to let you know that I just made an appointment to go see the doctor. I was talking to one of the students, who says there's a nasty stomach virus going around campus. I don't want to take a chance. Anyway, the appointment is at three this afternoon. I can get a ride to the doctor's and then take the T subway home. Don't worry, okay?"

"All right. See you later then."

I felt both relief and guilt when Élise ended the call. I felt relief because maybe there was an underlying bug that was causing Élise's malaise. That would explain a lot. I felt guilty because I wasn't taking her complaints about fatigue seriously. If she was fighting something, then she wouldn't have energy. She was pushing herself beyond her limits just to teach. A bug I could deal with, a more serious illness, I didn't even want to imagine.

When Élise returned home, I was in the kitchen. I noticed the worried look on her face.

"Hey, sweetheart. How did your appointment go?"

She sat down. "Oh, okay," she said. "They're going to run some tests to make sure I don't have diabetes or some digestive disease like diverticulitis."

I could feel the color draining from my face.

She smiled at me. It wasn't one of her dazzling light bulb smiles or a sheepish grin. She was putting on a brave face for my benefit.

"It's okay. He's just being thorough. Actually, besides being tired, he thought I looked really healthy for a fifty-year-old. Woo-hoo!"

"Are you hiding something from me?" I asked, perhaps a little aggressively. My Spidey senses were tingling. "Maybe we should cancel our trip this weekend."

"Oh no, Aren." she said quickly. "I don't want to cancel our trip. Lily has been looking forward to this and so have I," she insisted. "I'm feeling under the weather, but even the doctor said there is a bug going around. If I actually do have something, it's a mild case. The worst symptom is that I'm not very hungry and some intestinal issues. I can live with that."

"Well, I don't want you to be skin and bones," I said gruffly. That uh-oh feeling was slowly ebbing away. My Spidey senses weren't tingling anymore.

She reached over and placed her hands over mine.

"Stop fussing, Aren, okay? One more day and then we fly out to Chicago and celebrate your birthday."

"My birthday is not for another two weeks," I said to be contrary. "Oh, don't be such a fuddy-duddy. We have a public celebration in Chicago, and then we do something special, just the two of us, on your birthday."

"Promise?" I said.

"*Mais oui, chéri*, of course."

I sighed. She was being charming to deflect from whatever was really going on in her mind. She was probably right that whatever health issue she was experiencing wasn't too serious. But something was up. Whatever it was, she still wanted to be with me and celebrate. So okay, I was going to give her space. When she was ready, she would tell me. "You know you haven't called me chéri in a long time," I said, making an exaggerated pouty face.

Élise got up from her seat and hugged me. "*Ah, chéri du mon coeur.*" Élise made loud kissy noises and showered my face with kisses. I laughed. I pulled her onto my lap.

"You're not allowed to get sick, okay?"

"Yes, sir."

CHAPTER 16

WINDS OF CHANGE

O n a blustery and windy October afternoon, Aren, Lily, Tessa, and Aren's friend Boris and his wife Silvia walked into a trendy pizzeria on Dearborn Street in Chicago. As they waited to be seated, Élise was overcome by the strong smell of cheese that made her swallow back the bile rising in her throat.

"Oh no, I can't eat here. I'm sorry," Élise said.

"Oh, well we can go somewhere else if you like," Lily offered. "No, no. It's okay. I have been dealing with this stubborn stomach virus. And on top of that, I'm probably still dehydrated from the flight. I'm going to go back to the hotel. You guys have fun. I'll meet up with you later."

Aren looked at her with concern. She whispered in his ear. "Don't worry. I'm going to take a nap and relax. I love you, okay?" He winked at her. She smiled.

"Okay. I'll see everyone later," Élise said to the group. "Bye, Élise," everyone called after her.

Fortunately, the hotel was only a few blocks away. She was grateful for the brisk wind that perked her up as soon as she stepped onto the sidewalk. By the time she reached the hotel, she felt much better.

Aren texted her: *R u ok?*

She texted back: **s** (smile.)

Five minutes later as she was about to step into the shower, she was overcome by nausea and ran to the toilet and vomited. The heaving and cramping from her abdomen terrified her. "Oh my God!" she said as she sat naked on the bathroom floor, her head still hovering over the basin. When she felt certain that the wave of nausea had passed, she stood up shakily and cleaned up. She took a deep breath and then stepped into the shower. Afterward, she felt better and slipped into a bathrobe and lay down.

Élise was still fast asleep when Aren returned to the hotel room. Of course, Élise was the topic of conversation once she returned to the hotel. Tessa and Lily went into high gear speculating over what might be wrong with Élise. They didn't buy the stomach flu story.

"Dad, sometimes abdominal pain can be linked to something else, like ovarian cancer."

"Oh for crying out loud, Lily!" Aren snapped.

"You know what, Aren? You're making yourself sick speculating. Why don't you take her at her word? If there's something wrong, I'm sure she'll tell you," Boris said.

"Thanks, man." To Lily and Tessa Aren said, "You see there. Boris is right. Stop stressing me out. You're making me ill."

"Dad, don't be so dramatic," Lily chided. "Not everything is about you, Dad. Just create a safe space for her to open up. She really loves you, Dad. Don't fuck this one up. I like her a lot."

Tessa looked at me. Tessa studied Aren and asked: "Would you walk away from Élise if there was something wrong with her?"

The table went quiet. The waiter arrived with their order. I didn't get to answer the question. But why the hell did she even ask that question?

.oOo.

Aren

I found Élise asleep when I got back to the hotel. She was wearing the hotel bathrobe. I caressed her face. Sometimes I could see the little girl she once was with a sweet face and sweeping lashes. She stirred and opened her eyes.

"Oh, hey," she said. "What time is it?"

I glanced at my watch. "Just after three. How do you feel?"

"Better."

"Sure?"

"Yes."

She looked better—more like herself. I started to undress. She was biting her bottom lip.

"What are you doing?" she asked.

"What do you think I'm doing? I'm getting into the bed with you." Élise scooted over and made room for me in the bed.

"What time are we meeting everyone for the theatre?" she asked. "We need to be there by seven thirty," I replied.

"Okay. Can we order room service?"

"Sure."

I slipped her robe off. I stroked her breasts. My hands made their way between her legs. I began fingering her the way she liked. She sighed. I sucked on her neck and started rocking back and forth. Very quickly I felt her arousal.

"That's it, baby. I'm here. Can you climb on top of me?" Élise smiled and then straddled me.

"Oh, I packed the liberator wedge," she said suddenly remembering. "Should I go get it?"

"We're good. Stay with me," I said. This was usually her least favorite position, but at least this way I didn't put any weight on her belly, which seemed to be causing her such distress. She could control the movement. I was stroking her as she rocked back and forth. She quickly climaxed.

We slept for a bit and then ordered room service. We showered together. When we met up with the group later that night, Élise was her usual effervescent self, charming everyone.

.oOo.

After the successful evening out the night before, Aren got up early to go for a run and left Élise to sleep in. While he was out, Élise did get up to go to the bathroom. On her way back to the bed, she stretched her body and then immediately crumpled to the floor. It was the sound of Aren opening the door that brought her to. Aren was looking down at her with a panicked expression.

"Élise, what are you doing?" he asked.

"I don't know. I was on my way back to bed and then I heard you open the door."

"You fainted?" Aren asked.

"I don't know," Élise confided.

Aren helped Élise to her feet. He grabbed her bathrobe and helped her put it on.

"Honey, this isn't normal. Thank God I came back when I did. What if you were alone?"

Élise nodded. "I'll follow up with the doctor's office when we get back. Maybe the tests will reveal the reason why I'm so out of sorts."

Aren had a sick feeling in the pit of his stomach that he refused to give voice to. "Let's take a shower. We'll both feel better." Aren stripped and led Élise by the hand into the shower.

.oOo.

They spent the morning visiting Aren's brother and extended family. Then they separated so Aren could visit with his mother along with Lily. Tessa and Élise ducked into a tearoom for an hour.

"Do you mind if I don't go with you to the museum?" Élise asked.

"Hmm. Still not feeling well. Have you seen a doctor?"

"Yes," Élise said in exasperation. Tessa chuckled.

"Well, what did the doctor say?"

"He said it could be a lot of different things, including a mild case of the stomach flu."

"Did he run any tests?"

"Yes, Tessa. I'm not a child. I don't need people second-guessing how I manage my health."

"Aren't we a little prickly today." Élise sighed. "Enough. I'm leaving."

"Élise," Tessa said, suddenly reaching for her hand. "Wait. Don't be like this. I care about you. And you're just being stubborn."

Tessa pulled out her phone, scribbled down a number, and handed it to Élise.

"Here's the name of an internist. She's a good friend of ours. She runs a clinic nearby. Please go see her. She can see you now or at least her nurse practitioner can check you out."

Élise sighed heavily and then nodded. "I'll see you later, then."

Élise walked out of the tearoom café in a huff. She walked aimlessly for a while. Then, she stopped inside of a building and pulled out the number Tessa had given her. She dialed the number.

"Dr. Maggie Vanderhof speaking."

"Oh, hello, I'm sorry, I'm actually speaking to Dr. Vanderhof?"

"Yes," the voice said, chuckling in reply.

"My name is Élise Douchet. I'm just passing through town. I'm having some kind of health issue that is not resolving itself. My friend Tessa Poole thought you could help me."

"Yes, she called me half an hour ago. She's worried about you."

"*Mais ce n'est pas possible*," Élise muttered.

Dr. Vanderhof chuckled. "I don't speak French, but I gather you're not happy that she called me in advance. I don't know. Seems like she cares about you."

"Yes, well, Doctor. I take my privacy seriously. It's a bit overwhelming to have people nagging me."

"Is that right?" Dr. Vanderhof said. "Yes," Élise said primly.

"Fine. We understand each other. So are you coming to see me?"

"I suppose so. Where are you?"

Élise typed in the address on her phone and made an appointment to meet in an hour.

.oOo.

Élise arrived at a pleasant Victorian house painted in purple and orange just outside Chicago. A woman a few years older than herself greeted her at the door.

"Hello, you must be Élise. I'm Dr. Maggie Vanderhof."

"Nice to meet you," Élise said.

"Come in, dear. It's chilly out here."

Dr. Vanderhof ushered Élise into a cozy office off the main foyer. It was crowded with apothecary shelves filled with hundreds of bottles and jars of pills, potions, creams, and powders. Élise looked puzzled.

"You're a doctor?"

"Well, yes, but my main practice is as a medical intuitive."

"What's that?"

"Well, I trained as a medical doctor, and then I got into an alternative healing track where I heal people by helping them listen to their body."

"You're joking."

"No, I'm afraid not." Élise laughed.

"You've got a good, earthy laugh. You're not going anywhere." Élise laughed even more. "I'm sorry. I just—"

"That's okay. I'm used to it. Look it at this way—I am a great conversationalist. Tessa has already paid your fee. This session will cost you nothing. While we're talking, I'm going to ask you to write down your doctor's name and number. After our visit, I'll contact him or her. And if possible, if you're able to access your medical records online, you can do so on this computer and print it out. I'll look it over. How does that sound?"

"Weird."

"Yeah, I know. Oh, and just be still for a second, I want to check your polarity. Hold out your hand."

Élise held her hand out face down. Dr. Vanderhof waved a magnet over her and asked Élise to resist the force of her hand in the opposite direction.

"Well?" Élise asked.

"The good news is I don't detect any parasites. But you do have blockages. Do you have constipation?"

"Yes," Élise said.

"Well, let's talk a bit more and then I'll do an examination and address any issues I can. You don't have to undress."

Dr. Vanderhof sat behind her desk and pulled up a form and began asking questions and noting the responses on the computer. She already had preliminary information about Élise regarding address, date of birth, and occupation during their initial telephone call.

"When was your last period?" she asked.

"I don't know. I mean it has been pretty erratic. It comes and goes. But I had a really short one in August. It lasted a day and then another that lasted half a day, but I had bad cramps with that one. I guess I'm in menopause."

Dr. Vanderhof nodded. "Are you having sex regularly?" Élise bit her lips. Dr. Vanderhof chuckled. "I see."

The exam lasted forty-five minutes. For Élise it was more of a therapy session than a medical consult. During that time, Élise talked mostly about her relationship with Aren and her worries about the future with him. She was a little more forthcoming with Dr. Vanderhof about her past relationships and her career as a teacher. At the end of their session, Élise stood up. She felt actually really good. Better than she had in the last two weeks.

"Now I'm going to give you these vitamins and a nutritional supplement. I have indicated when you should take them. It will help with some of your intestinal issues. Also, you might want to lay off any sugar and dairy. And definitely no alcohol."

"Really? I'm not dying?" Élise said with relief.

"No, far from it. But you do need to rest. You're a strong woman, but you're not twenty-five. You need to respect your body. Get more sleep."

"So I'm a hypochondriac?"

"No, you're not. But I won't lie to you. There is something I'm picking up. I have a hunch of what it might be," she said ominously. "I promise to get back to you today when I have looked at your labs and tracked down your doctor."

Dr. Vanderhof handed Élise a brochure. "Oh, and here."

"What's this?

"It's my bio. I know you think I'm a quack, but I really am a doctor. I just happen to use this modality for healing."

Élise chuckled. "Well, thank you so much for seeing me on short notice. That was very generous of you."

"You're welcome."

The two women shook hands. Dr. Vanderhof watched Élise step into the taxi waiting for her just outside the entrance. She heard the fax machine signaling an incoming fax. During her session with Élise, she was able to contact her doctor's office. They said they would fax her latest lab results. Dr. Vanderhof plucked the fax from the machine and quickly scanned it. Élise's kidney and liver function were above normal. Her cholesterol level was a little high but nothing worrisome. She glanced at the hCG level.

"Wow!" she said out loud.

She looked at her watch. Élise said she would be going straight home. Dr. Vanderhof decided she would wait an hour before trying to contact her. She looked at the cover page of the fax. There was a starred message.

Please contact Dr. Schuler's office immediately!

.oOo.

When Aren returned to the hotel, Élise was in an exceptionally affectionate mood. She wrapped her arms around him as soon as he walked in the door and showered him with kisses with extra-loud sound effects.

"I missed you!" she said.

"Wait? What have you done with my Élise? Never mind, forget her. Let you and I get acquainted," Aren said, raising his eyebrows. Élise laughed.

They sat down and talked about his visit with his mother. They would schedule another trip before the end of the year so he could introduce Élise to his mother. She nodded in agreement. She talked about the whacky doctor she visited that afternoon, and that just made Aren laugh. But what did any of it matter? Élise looked like herself again. They made plans for the next day.

"Aren, why don't you go in and take a quick shower and then set up the room? Then I'll go in and get ready. I picked up something naughty and nice for you while I was out and about."

"Really?"

"Yep. Now go ahead."

Élise quickly went through her shopping bag and pulled out some beautiful lingerie. Well, it was probably more for her benefit than his since beautiful lingerie always put her in the most receptive mood. She had picked up some new perfume and had been able to get a quickie pedicure while she was out.

When Aren came out, Élise stepped in. She also grabbed her phone. She and Lily had planned a special surprise dinner at his favorite restaurant the following night. It wasn't a complete surprise to Aren, but they had kept the details from him.

Élise had just stepped out of the shower and wrapped a towel around her. Lily called, and they finalized the next day's itinerary. Then she quickly slipped into her negligée. Her phone rang again. It was Dr. Vanderhof.

.oOo.

Aren was busily staging the bedroom for lovemaking. He took an extra dose of the Capatrex pill just in case. He heard her speaking in soft tones on the phone. He smiled, wondering what kind of surprise she had in store for him. Élise stepped back into the main bedroom compartment and approached the bed.

Aren looked at Élise's face as he pulled her down on the bed. She had a strange expression. He and Helen had that look of shock when the doctor announced Helen was not going to beat the cancer and would die in a few months. Élise was fluttering her eyelashes and biting her lips. Her chest heaved rhythmically.

"What's the matter, sweetheart?" he whispered, choking with emotion.

"I'm pregnant," she blurted out.

Aren froze. His eyes darted aimlessly. Then he gasped. "W-What!" Élise remained silent. Her eyes were fixed on her hands on her lap. "H-h-how?"

Élise still didn't look at Aren. "I'm fifty," she muttered. "It never occurred to me I could get pregnant."

"But sweetheart, I thought you were going through menopause. You haven't had regular periods since we have been together."

Élise was on the verge of tears.

"I-I don't know what to say," she stammered.

Aren jumped to his feet. He took a deep breath, and then he started to pace the room. He sat down again and joined his fingertips together and brought them to his nose.

Aren looked at Élise. "When did you find out?"

"Just now. I was speaking to Dr. Vanderhof, the doctor I saw this afternoon. She called my doctor in Boston, and he confirmed for her the results from the lab of a positive pregnancy."

"But honey, you saw your doctor in Boston on Wednesday. Why wouldn't they have tried to contact you sooner?" Aren lifted her chin. "Talk to me, sweetheart. What are you hiding?"

Élise's eyes glistened with unshed tears.

"The doctor's office left a message on the day of our flight. I panicked. You know, I have not been feeling well for a while. I decided I didn't want to celebrate the weekend with potentially bad news. I decided I would follow up when I returned."

Aren nodded. "How do you feel?"

"Dr. Vanderhof gave me a nutritional supplement that I took, and

I feel so much better now."

Élise registered the look of complete shock on Aren's face. Tears started to roll down her face. Hours earlier she had talked about her relationship with Aren and how much she loved him. There was something about Dr. Vanderhof that she seemed to reveal her deepest emotions and the experience seemed to unburden her. And now she was responsible for crashing Aren's world. *It's my fault. I have ruined us.*

"Oh no, do you hate me?"

"Come here." Aren kissed Élise tenderly on the forehead. "Of course, I don't hate you. I love you."

"I'm scared, Aren."

"Let's go to your doctor when we get back to Boston. Get tested again. Maybe they can provide more information about the baby. We'll figure it out."

"Aren," Élise said. And then the enormity of Aren's words finally dawned on her. "What are the chances that I am carrying a normal, healthy baby?"

"Let's get tested. We'll know for sure then."

Aren had a flashback of when his late wife announced she was pregnant with their daughter. It was scary and exciting all at once. Now, faced with the same news, he was horrified. How could this happen? Aren looked at Élise's panic-stricken face and wanted to comfort her now more than anything. She was sitting beside him, but she was so distant, emotionally distant. He pulled her into his arms and lay on the bed spooning with her to the deafening sound of silence.

CHAPTER 17

HEY, THAT'S NO WAY TO SAY GOODBYE

Élise

Aren and I sat across the desk from Dr. Adam Schuler. He was examining an ultrasound test. He handed it to me. I gasped. Tears started to run down my face. I had never seen a sonogram before. I wasn't prepared to see a clear image of a baby. Aren took the image from my hands and I just wept from raw emotion.

"That's our baby," I sobbed. Aren wrapped his arm around me and I could feel my tears soaking his shirt.

"Well, Doctor?" Aren asked impatiently.

"The baby has a strong heartbeat. It looks like you're eleven and a half weeks pregnant. If I order a genetic sampling test, I can confirm for you the sex of the baby if you want to know. It's called the chorionic villus sampling test or CVS. We could do it next week when you're in your twelfth week, but there are other important tests we need to do." There was so much information. So many questions. I was grateful Aren was asking questions. My mind was on information overload. I was almost three months pregnant. How did I not know?

"Is it—I mean the baby… developing normally?" Aren asked.

"As far as I can tell, yes. It looks like at some point there might have been a twin. That happens sometimes with older women. They tend to double ovulate."

203

Double ovulate? Twins? Dr. Schuler kept talking, but I didn't listen. I couldn't focus on what he was saying. I could see the color drain from Aren's face. He looked deathly pale. The lines in his face deepened. We exchanged looks of shock. Twins?

"Aren, we had twins? We had two of them?" My throat burned and I started a fresh wave of tears. I was sobbing again. Aren held me tight. "I love you, sweetheart," Aren said. His voice was so shaky. He focused his attention on Dr. Schuler.

"Dr. Schuler, do you think you could stop talking and give Élise and I a chance to absorb the enormity of what you're telling us? What's the matter with you? Don't you see that we're not a young couple? This is coming as an enormous shock to the both of us. Show some compassion for God's sake."

Dr. Schuler cleared his voice. I could see his face redden.

"Yes, well, as I was saying, everything seems to be right on target in terms of milestones. Élise's hCG levels are over 250,000. That's consistent with the end of first trimester stage of pregnancy."

"Okay, isn't that good news?" Aren asked. Dr. Schuler shook his head.

"I have to be honest with you. The chances of a woman of advanced age like Élise having a normal child are pretty low. I mean if this were a donor egg situation with a youthful mother providing the egg, I would say this is a normal pregnancy. But Élise has never given birth before and she's, well, fifty. The risks are very high for a chromosomal abnormality like Trisomy 13, 18, or 21."

Dr. Schuler directed his attention at me. "It's possible you won't even go past the first trimester. You have been there before, Élise."

Dr. Schuler's voice cut me like a knife. I died a thousand deaths at the moment. He was telling me I might not make it past this first trimester. Many years ago I tried IVF. I decided I would do it alone. I wanted a child. But it didn't work. I miscarried in my sixth week. There was no one to comfort me. No one knew I was even trying. The memories came crashing in on me. My chest hurt. My throat ached. Hot tears just spilled from my eyes. I hadn't told Aren about that phase in my life. I had buried it. And now he knew.

Aren gave me a mournful look. I didn't see any bitterness, just tenderness.

"Don't worry," he said, rubbing my shoulders.

As I sat with Aren's arms around me, I started to calm down a little. The raw emotion was giving way to more clear thoughts and feelings. "Aren, I don't want to lose my child. Our child. This is a gift from God."

"Shh, honey. We'll take it one day at a time—" Dr. Schuler tightened his lips.

"Well, that's what I need to talk to you about. We could schedule a level II ultrasound in week fourteen, but there are a lot of false positives. I recommend amniocentesis. You have a tiny window in which to do the amniocentesis between the fifteenth and eighteenth week, but there are serious risks associated with the test, assuming you get that far."

"No—God!" I screamed. "Stop talking!" I started sobbing. This was all too much to handle all at once. "I want to go home."

Dr. Schuler looked at us. Or at least I could feel his eyes on us. I couldn't bear to look at him. He stood up and headed toward the door. "I'll leave you two alone," he said. "You have a lot to discuss. I will be right outside."

.oOo.

Aren

I wanted to throttle Dr. Schuler with my bear hands. I wanted to wipe that supercilious grin from his face. *If he is so caring, why didn't he counsel* Élise *about the risks of pregnancy for menopausal women?*

Élise and I drove back to her apartment in silence. She made some tea and served it in her best china. She sat down. I held her hands. I took a few sips of the earl grey tea, my favorite. It didn't calm me, though. I swallowed hard to keep the rage inside of me from spilling over.

I was shaking uncontrollably. In the time we had been together, I had never raised my voice at Élise. I complained. I whined. I was grouchy. But yelling at her was not something I did or at least not consciously. And now I could feel the rage roiling inside of me. I was frightened. I was on the verge of exploding at her.

"Honey," I said, "I'm sixty-two years old. Well, I'll be sixty-three in a week. I don't want to raise a special-needs child. You're not that young either, Élise. Do you want to spend your older years caring for a special-needs child? It'll kill you. It will ruin us."

Élise looked at me soberly. All of the hysteria she exhibited at Dr. Schuler's office was gone. She was calm.

"So you'll leave me if I don't terminate the pregnancy." It wasn't a question.

"I didn't say that."

"But that's what you mean." Her clipped Caribbean accent seemed so reproachful.

I was silent. We were on dangerous ground now. *My relationship with Élise is unraveling before my eyes.* Hot tears were streaming down my face. I took a deep breath.

"Is it having a baby that upsets you or having a baby that has special needs?" Élise asked. "If the baby were normal and healthy, would you— would you help me raise our child?"

"Élise, I don't know. This is coming at me so fast."

"I didn't do this on purpose. I was stupid. I underestimated my body."

"Sweetie, you didn't get pregnant by yourself. I was right there with you. Never in my wildest dreams did I think this was a possibility. I failed you."

She was weeping uncontrollably. The emotional intensity between us was unbearable. I held her and kissed her temple.

I sighed heavily. *What do I do? What do we do?*

"Shhh," I said to Élise. "Let's have the test, okay? Dr. Schuler said in four weeks we could have the test."

"But Aren," Élise said, "I could lose the baby from the test."

My head hurt. I just wanted to shut myself in a dark room and disappear. I couldn't stop my tears. *Why is this happening?* I stood up and knelt next to Élise. I lay my head on her lap. I looked up at Élise plaintively.

"One day at a time," I said.

.oOo.

Élise

Aren stayed with me the first few days after our visit with Dr. Schuler. We celebrated his birthday quietly with no fanfare. We agreed to tell Lily and Tessa. They came to Boston to celebrate Aren's birthday and then returned home to Vermont.

I took a few days off. We just went for long walks in the park. We didn't eat much. We didn't talk much. We cuddled a lot. Neither one of us had any libido. By the end of the week, Aren announced he needed to go back to his cottage. I think I needed some alone time so I didn't make a fuss when he left. Thanks to the supplements Dr. Vanderhof gave me, I was able to manage the pregnancy symptoms I had not previously recognized. I was grateful for the distraction of teaching. I started to use Aren's program to help me grade student assignments. He was right. It saved an enormous amount of time. The program enabled me to give more useful feedback. The time I saved I could put toward more rest time. No supplement could remove the fatigue. My body craved sleep and now I was in a better position to accede to its demand.

"Is it safe for me to exercise?" I asked Dr. Vanderhof during a telephone call. I didn't feel comfortable asking Dr. Schuler this question, but I trusted Dr. Vanderhof.

"By all means, exercise," she said. "But take it easy. You have nothing to prove. Take breaks during Zumba. Do the easy steps, you know, the cumbia. Just do that. I don't care if it's a salsa or merengue. Stick to cumbia and what's that other one?"

I ran through a mental list of the types of dances we did in Zumba.

"Bachata?"

"Yeah, that one. They always use that one during the slow downs."

"I didn't know you were such a Zumba aficionado," I teased.

"Heinh, Zumba is my stress reliever. I get more out of it than yoga."

She paused for a moment. "You know, you might want to switch to yoga instead of Pilates. Stick with gentle yoga and focus on breath."

"During my lunch breaks, I walk. When Aren is here, we walk."

"That's great," she said. "And you and Aren are managing, okay?"

I thought about my first visit with Dr. Vanderhof and I how I talked nonstop about Aren. I was so hopeful. I could feel myself tearing up. I gulped. Before I knew it, I was weeping.

"I see," she said. "Under the best of circumstances, pregnancy is a game changer. I can't give you advice about your relationship. What I can do is just encourage you to maintain your health for your sake and for the sake of your baby. That's the most important thing you can do."

I kept crying. I still heard and understood everything Dr. Vanderhof said. I was so grateful for her words. When I was able to speak, I said,

"Thank you so much."

I heard a knock on the door.

"Oh, that's probably my friend at the door. I have to go," I said quickly.

"Call me or email me if you have any more questions, okay? You're not the first woman to have a change of life baby. You're not old. Get that out of your mind. You're stronger than you think. Bye, Élise."

"Querida, open the door please."

I ended the call with Dr. Vanderhof and ran hurriedly to the door.

Antonio strode into the room and looked at me.

"I heard you crying, querida," he said. Antonio took me in his arms and held me. I thought I was done crying. Just being in his arms stirred the emotions in me and I started to cry again.

"Come on. Sit down. I'll make us some tea," he said.

I sat down on the sofa and took deep breaths to calm down. I could hear the kettle whistling and Antonio opening the cabinet to pull down the mugs. It took him a while to come back to the living room.

"Antonio?" I called out.

Antonio came out with a tray with two glasses of water and two mugs of tea. He set the tray down on the coffee table.

"Querida, I walked by the Lady. I noticed a picture I have never seen before. What's going on?"

After Aren left, I put the ultrasound picture on the altar. Every day I offered a petition of prayer for my baby. I looked at Antonio.

He took my hands in his and kissed them. "¡Madre de Dios! You're pregnant!"

I nodded.

Antonio plopped next to me and took several gulps of water. "D-Does Aren know? He's the father, right?"

I smiled. "Who else?" I looked down at my lap. "He knows, Antonio. But I don't think he's happy." Antonio looked at me sadly. "Did you break up?"

I shook my head.

"No, we're taking each day as it comes. I think he needed some time alone. I needed time too. There are some tests—"

"Is the baby, okay?"

"We're not sure. There are tests that will give us more information. My doctor is concerned about genetic defects. So is Aren. I'm entering my second trimester—"

"How long have you known?" Antonio asked.

"You know that trip we made to Chicago? That's when I found out. And then we scheduled a meeting with my doctor here in Boston. So maybe a couple of weeks."

Antonio nodded. I was glad I didn't have to keep this a secret from him.

"I haven't told Fanny. I don't know how to tell her. You know Antonio, Dr. Schuler doesn't even believe this pregnancy is viable. I'm terrified of losing the baby. I'm terrified that the tests might show there's something wrong with the baby."

I started to heave.

Antonio pulled me into a tight embrace.

"You are not going to go through this alone, querida. Okay?" He stroked my hair and said a small prayer in Spanish appealing to the Virgin Mary. "You have to tell Fanny. Don't keep this from her. She can help you."

I nodded. Antonio released me and I sat upright and reached for my mug of tea. "Thank you, Antonio," I said.

Antonio sat with me and talked about all kinds of things, about everything except my pregnancy. After an hour, I started to feel sleepy. "Do you mind?" I said to Antonio. "I feel tired. I just need to take a nap."

He kissed my forehead. "Of course, querida," he said. "Come over for dinner, okay?"

"Gracias," I said.

.oOo.

I decided to go to a Sunday Zumba class. Now that school was in session, Fanny and I didn't meet up for classes the way we did during the summer. I had spent so much time away that my instructor made a special point of saying hello and welcoming me back to class. I remembered what Dr. Vanderhof said and I just tried to move to the beat. I didn't worry about remembering dance steps. I was enjoying the music and I was having fun. My favorite part was the cool down. We were moving slowly and doing stretches. It felt good. I looked in the mirror and noticed Fanny was standing there. I'm not sure how long she had been standing there. We all clapped at the end of class. I picked up my things and joined Fanny.

"Class is over, Fanny," I teased. Her eyes were brimming with tears. I realized then Antonio must have told her. I had mentioned I would go to Zumba when we had dinner together the previous night. He must have called her after I left. Those two were incapable of keeping any kind of secret.

Fanny hugged me. I missed her. She reached out and touched my belly. My flat abs were gone. Tears started to roll down her face.

"It's true. Oh my God!"

I nodded. "Are you ashamed of me?" I asked.

"No, you *estupida*! Don't let anyone tell you otherwise. I wish you had told me, sooner. I can help."

I swallowed hard.

"I was afraid. I didn't know this was possible. We tell young people to be responsible and me—" I couldn't finish.

Fanny wiped my tears. She smiled.

"Come on. I'm following you back to your place. We'll talk, okay?"

I nodded.

When Fanny came back to my apartment, I brought the ultrasound image to her. She traced the image of the baby with her finger. "*Que lindo! Que lindo!*" she said. She reached out to touch my belly. She closed her eyes and hummed a little. Then she opened her eyes.

"It's a girl," she announced.

I laughed. "It's too soon to tell," I said.

"Okay," Fanny said skeptically. "What do you think?" she asked. "I try not to think about it, but—but, I think it's a girl too. It's a just feeling. Antonio thinks so too."

"Mmm-hmm!" Fanny said triumphantly. "What does Aren think?"

I shrugged. "We don't really talk about—" I sighed. "I don't think—"

We looked at each other. Whatever she saw in my eyes, it stopped her from going on a rant about Aren or some friend in a similar situation. Instead she said:

"Pack up a few things. You're staying with me for a few days. I want you to rest and be free from worry for a couple of days, okay? You're tired. I see it in your eyes. I'm going to whip you up some power juices to rev you up!"

"That sounds nice, Fanny, but—"

"No buts, chica. We'll stop by Antonio's. I'll invite him over too. It's just a couple of days. Come on. Pack up. I'm going to Antonio's now. You better be over there in twenty minutes with your bag. Chop, chop!" I laughed. I needed her to boss me around. I had decisions to make and sitting around feeling sorry for myself didn't help. I picked up the ultrasound and put it in my purse. It took me ten minutes to throw some clothes into a bag and then lock up.

I replayed Fanny's reaction to the ultrasound in my mind. "¡Qué lindo!" she said. Yes, it was wonderful. In all the drama, I had not focused on the wonder of carrying a life inside of me. I needed Fanny to lift my spirits and remind me that what was happening to me was not a travesty, but a marvelous thing.

When we got to Fanny's house, Enrique and the boys came out to greet me with hugs and kisses as if they hadn't seen me in a very long time. I felt welcome. I touched my belly and said in my heart to my baby: *We're going to be okay. I promise you.*

.oOo.

Later that night, Élise woke up and was unable to go back to sleep. She looked at the digital clock in the room she was sleeping in. It was ten o'clock. She had been asleep for a couple of hours. She decided to get up and maybe sit out on the deck with a cup of tea. Perhaps the fresh air would help her go back to sleep.

Fanny's house was quiet as she padded down the stairs. She noticed a light in the kitchen.

"Oh, hi Enrique," Élise said. "Did I wake you up?" he asked.

"Oh, no. I just woke up and couldn't go back to sleep. I thought maybe I would make some tea and sit outside."

"Are you sure? It's kind of chilly now," Enrique said. "I have the kettle going. Just stay here. If you're really warm, I'll open the window."

Élise chuckled. "Okay."

Enrique brought out an assortment of herbal teas. He chose chamomile. Élise chose ginger tea. She brought the steaming cup to her face and enjoyed the feel of the steam. She set the cup down. She noticed Enrique was watching her.

"Élise?" Enrique said. "Yes?"

"Have you thought about how you will explain your pregnancy to your school administrators?"

Élise blinked in surprise.

"No, I hadn't seriously thought about it, to be honest."

"Mira," he said. "You know we focus on business law at our practice but employer and employee relations do come up a lot. Usually, the issues may involve harassment or discrimination," Enrique said.

"Yes," Élise said, not entirely following where he was going with the conversation.

Enrique registered Élise's confusion.

"*Entonces.* A lot of schools have morality clauses," he said slowly. "Élise, your being pregnant, a single mother, could violate you morality clause. Have you looked at your contract?"

"What?" Élise sputtered. "Oh come on, Enrique. This is the twenty-first century. I mean, several years ago the insurance paid for my IVF cycles as a single woman. How is this any different?"

"Honey, this time sex is involved. Depending on how the moral turpitude clause is written, pregnancy outside of marriage could be a material breach and override your tenure or employment."

"Enrique, this is an independent school with no religious affiliation."

"Right, did you have to have a meeting with the headmistress and the HR director last time? You need representation. Even if they don't fire you, they might try to pull something."

"Oh, please. We're all friends."

"Yeah, I bet," Enrique said sardonically. "This is the real world. Your employer is not your friend or your family. I don't care how nice and friendly they seem. Élise, I love you. You're family. I'm happy for you, but I don't want you to be caught off guard."

"You and Aren didn't schedule booty calls at school even in the parking lot, right?"

Élise gasped. Her eyes blinked wildly.

"B-But I would never do such a thing," she protested.

"Just checking. The point is you and Aren had a sexual relationship outside of marriage. I'm sorry I didn't speak up sooner. Fanny was fussing over you. I didn't want to bring this up. But I would have eventually spoken to you, because this could be a problem for you. If you were still teaching at a university, I wouldn't worry too much. But teachers of elementary and secondary schools tend to have a higher threshold."

"What do I do?"

"You're going to finish your tea. I got your back. I'll send you a request for personnel records by email tomorrow. Just fill in the names of the relevant administrators and send it to them. Email is fine. Just copy me, okay? Use my law firm email. We'll talk more tomorrow. Okay?"

Élise nodded. She sipped her tea silently. In truth, the thought had crossed her mind about the moral's clause. She just didn't want to think about it. She sighed. *One more stressor.*

"You're good. The important thing is that we start preparing and we come up with strategies."

"I'm going back to bed," Élise said. "Gracias, Enrique. I have a lot on my plate, but I'll just have to handle each crisis as it comes. At least I have a little bit of time with this one, right?"

"You'll be all right, Élise," Enrique said. "Get some rest."

"Thank you for the tea," she said then she padded up the stairs to the bedroom.

.oOo.

Aren

At Élise's insistence, I canceled our plans to celebrate Thanksgiving at a remote resort in Isla Holbox, Mexico. I thought going to an island paradise would be exactly the thing we needed to deal with the stress and the monumental changes in our lives. Élise was terrified, however, of the effects of extended air travel on her fragile pregnancy. She was entering her second trimester. She had a little belly now. She spoke to Fanny and Antonio on a daily basis. I noticed they stopped saying "Say hi to Aren." We celebrated Thanksgiving with Lily and Tessa. They knew the situation. They didn't pepper us with questions.

.oOo.

On a Sunday afternoon in early December, Dr. Schuler called with the results of the level II ultrasound. Élise and Aren were spending the weekend in Vermont. Élise put him on speaker phone so Aren could listen.

"We have the results of the test."

Aren held her hands. Élise held her breath.

"There's a 15 percent chance the baby may have some anomaly related to her heart. A 1/25 percentage chance of the baby being born with Down syndrome. You still have time to take the amniocentesis and know for sure."

"Doctor, how long do we have before we run out of time to—" Aren didn't finish his sentence.

"You have two weeks," Dr. Schuler said.

"Thank you," Élise said quickly and then ended the call.

Aren hung his head dejectedly. Élise was shaken by what Dr. Schuler reported. *But it's still more likely than not my baby is fine. He didn't say anything about my individual risk.* These were Élise's thoughts. She and Aren sat in silence.

"Let's go for a walk. We can clear our minds," Élise said. Aren nodded. They put on their jackets and boots and headed out the door. They took a long hike in the woods but still kept silent. They came back to Aren's cozy cottage after an hour. Aren started a fire. Élise brought in some tea. They sat down and faced each other.

"You really want this baby, don't you?" Aren said sadly. "What Dr. Schuler said didn't terrify you?"

Élise took steadying breaths to calm herself before answering. "From the moment I learned I was pregnant, I have done nothing but freak out and worry. What Dr. Schuler said didn't make me happy, but he didn't necessarily issue a death verdict either. There are a lot of risks. But it's still more likely than not that our baby will be okay."

"Élise, listen to me. I know you want a baby. But you're not making any sense. Even if we went through with this, we're not young. Who will take care of the child? It's not fair to bring a child into the world with all these problems and then leave them as a ward of the state."

Élise looked at Aren. From her perspective, all Dr. Schuler did was read a report of probabilities assuming the report actually assigned a percentage risk. Aren had taken the figures and accepted them as certainties, not as probabilities. He didn't fight back. He didn't argue. He didn't question how the numbers were derived. Aren didn't want the baby. That realization burned inside of her.

"Aren, you don't want this baby," Élise said. "If Dr. Schuler had assigned a 5 percent risk, you would still focus on the risk rather than the greater possibility that the child is okay."

Aren swallowed hard.

"I don't want to lose you."

"I can't terminate this pregnancy. We've done the research. I understand all of your arguments. I really do. But I can't do it. If it means I have to raise a special-needs child alone, then so be it. I've been alone most of my adult life. I can do this."

"Honey, we have a beautiful life waiting for us. We can be happy. Children are hard work even under the best of circumstances. There's a reason why young people were biologically designed to bear and raise children. You have no idea what you're letting yourself in for."

"This isn't a rational decision, Aren. This is my heart, my soul. I need to carry this baby to term to the extent I can. I'm old, but I'm healthy. I'm praying. This is a message from God."

Aren snorted.

"Aren, do what you have to do. I will not resent you for it."

"You know, Élise, even if I walk away from you, I'm still responsible for that life. I do not want this baby."

Élise trembled with emotion and then broke down in sobs. Aren stood there watching Élise fall apart in front of him, and he couldn't seem to go to her and take her in his arms. He needed her to get out. He waited for her tears to subside.

"Élise, I need some time to myself."

From the moment they became lovers, Élise had dreaded those words. She always expected it would come to this. She just never thought in her wildest imagination that a pregnancy, her pregnancy, would result in the end of their relationship.

Élise nodded. She packed up her things and got in the car. Aren drove Élise home. He helped her bring her bags to the apartment.

"Thank you," Élise said quietly as she stood with Aren in front of the door. He kissed her forehead lightly and then turned to open the door. "I'm sorry," Élise whispered dejectedly as Aren walked out the door and continued down the stairs without a backward glance.

.oOo.

Aren

After I dropped Élise at her apartment I sat in my car. I could see the light in her apartment. She didn't seem to be moving around. Thirty minutes after I dropped her off, the lights went out in her apartment. Did she go to bed? Did she go to Antonio? I don't know. She didn't try to call me or text me. I turned my back on her, literally and she let me walk out of her life.

So you'll leave me if I don't terminate the pregnancy.

It wasn't a question. She thought it all out and she made her choice. She let me go. I bent my head over the steering wheel and I started to cry. I sobbed.

I felt so drained. There was no way I could make the long drive back to the cottage. After what I did to Élise, I'm not sure I could stand to be alone in the cottage. I turned the ignition and started to drive, but I only drove to Jamaica Pond, five minutes away from her apartment. I decided to walk. Maybe the cold crisp air would clear my head. I did two loops and then returned to my car. I checked my phone. It was eight o'clock. I still didn't feel stable enough to drive back to the cottage, but where could I go? Zach. I could call Zach. He lived in Newton. I could call him and ask to crash at his house. He wouldn't pepper me with questions. I just need a quiet space to think. I don't know what to do. "Is it having a baby that upsets you or having a baby that has special needs?" Élise asked. "If the baby were normal and healthy, would you—would you help me raise our child?"

I don't know, Élise. I just want our life back—but it's gone. I could feel the panic rising in me. I didn't trust myself to speak. I texted Zach.

Z – It's me Aren. Can I crash at your place? I'm in trouble.

.oOo.

Lily

Lily stared at the text message from her father.

L – Need to go away. Could you keep an eye on the house for me? Empty refrigerator. Throw out trash. Call Élise. She needs you.

Lily did not immediately react to the text. *Why wouldn't he just call me?* She checked to see if he left a voice mail. Nothing. She dialed his number, but it went directly to voice mail. She checked her calendar for the day. She had a closing at one o'clock and a house tour at three. She thought about driving over to the house immediately. It was only a fifteen-minute detour from the office. He didn't say exactly when he had to leave, but she couldn't imagine he would actually take off without seeing her, especially after leaving such a cryptic message.

Lily found the door locked when she arrived at her father's cottage. She rang the doorbell, but there was no response. She walked around to the garage and peeked through the window. The Porsche and Prius were inside. The truck was gone. She immediately went back to the front of the house and opened the door with her key. She walked around the cottage calling out "Dad?" She checked every room and he wasn't there. She went to the kitchen and noticed mugs of tea. Mold had started to form. She took her phone out and tried to call him. He didn't pick up. Lily checked the time. It was ten thirty. She needed to be in the office by eleven to prepare for the closing. She thought for a moment and then called Élise. She probably was teaching, but maybe she could excuse herself briefly to take her call. Her call went to voice mail. A few minutes later, Élise texted back, *"Can't take your call right now. I can talk when I get home."* Lily gasped.

"What is going on?" she said out loud.

Lily went back into the kitchen and rinsed out the mugs and loaded them in the dishwasher. She would stop by again after the open house. Maybe her father would be back by then or at least have answered her messages.

When Lily returned to her father's cottage at the end of the day, everything was exactly as she left it. He hadn't left any messages other than the one she received. She walked to the kitchen and sat on the stool. She took a deep breath and called Élise. It was four thirty. Élise would be done with her classes and would be home. Élise picked up on the third ring.

"Hello, Lily," she said.

She sounds strange, Lily thought.

"Are you okay, Élise? What's going on?" Lily paused for a moment and then she said, "Oh, my God! Where's Dad?" She was overcome with emotion.

"I don't know, Lily. He dropped me off at home two days ago, and then he left." Élise said sadly.

"He left? What do you mean? You broke up?"

"Yes," Élise said.

"But where is he?"

"I don't know, Lily. I have to get off the phone. This is really upsetting for me, okay?" Élise ended the call.

"What?!" Lily screamed. Her heart was beating fast. She covered her face with her hands. She could feel her eyes stinging from the tears. She pulled out her phone and tried to call her father. The call went to voice mail. She then sent a text. "*Please Dad, let me know ur all right. Please. If you don't want to call me, just send a text to let me know ur alive. Please. Please do that 4 me.*"

Minutes later Lily received a text from her father.

Can't talk. Need to think. I'm okay. Sorry to worry you. Please look after Élise.

Lily stared at the text in shock. She immediately called Tessa. "Babe, I'm at Dad's house. Something terrible has happened. Please come. Now."

She didn't wait for Tessa to respond. She ended the call. She sat down on the floor and wept.

CHAPTER 18

‹‹

THE HOLY OR THE BROKEN HALLELUJAH

‹‹

O n December 31st, Élise scoured her apartment from top to bottom. A CD of a Mexican choir singing Handel's *Hallelujah Chorus* was playing. It was a present from Antonio. Actually, she had been working on her big cleanout over the Christmas holidays. The work was pretty much done. The only thing left was to reorganize her files and throw out paper. She found the folders containing her fertility charts. The last time she had looked at them, she was going through her depression about turning fifty. That's when she decided to book the hiking spa trip. That trip led her to meeting Aren. And now she was in her second trimester of pregnancy.

She looked at the post-it note: *To review in 2012.*

Élise quickly glanced through her old fertility charts. Then she thought about when she might have conceived her child. She knew it must have taken place in that week between wrapping up the conference in Baltimore and traveling to Puerto Rico and then the first few days of their return to Boston. Then a memory came flooding back to her.

On an especially hot and sultry afternoon after a sudden rain storm in Puerto Rico, the day before their departure, Aren and Élise were facing each other on the bed, their limbs entwined as he entered her.

"Oh," she sighed.

They lay like that for a while, slowly building up to a rhythm, with Élise thrusting her pelvis against Aren. She switched her position so that she was now lying on top of him, but her back was now facing him. He pounded her buttocks and massaged her anus, sending her into paroxysms of joy as she gave herself over to the rush. She collapsed her torso onto the bed, flipping herself over until she was lying next to him. They were panting.

"Oh, that was amazing, baby. It's getting better and better," Aren said.

Élise thought about that time with Aren. And then another memory came to her. It was the night she wore her silk and lace crotchless panties. She giggled. The infamous crotchless panties made their debut during that Puerto Rico getaway. Aren was always insisting she be naked during their lovemaking, she never seem to have a chance to wear anything sexy. On the night she wore the panties, they had already had sex. Prior to that, *Élise* didn't have the confidence to wear the panties in front of Aren. She hadn't owned her sexuality yet. That night she didn't wear them to seduce Aren. Rather, she wore them precisely because she felt sexy and she thought it would be a nice treat for Aren to play with. That was the night they talked about the practical side of their intimate time. It wasn't an awkward conversation. It was loving and respectful. She remembered the teasing and the raucous laughter as Aren playfully and artfully navigated his way to her opening without destroying the panties. That's the memory she wanted to hold onto. She and Aren were passionate and playful lovers.

But a tiny voice told her the X-rated version of her memory with Aren is probably what led to the pregnancy.

"Honey, we are animals. There's nothing wrong with that. And there's nothing wrong with wanting your man and pleasing him and wanting him to please you," Aren said.

"Hmm, I don't know. I still can't believe sometimes that I let you do the things you do to me. It's scandalous."

Aren kissed *Élise* softly.

"If the only way I can get you to have toe-curling sex with me is for you to have selective amnesia, then go right ahead. As long as your body works its magic and muscle memory when I need it to. I don't mind multiple personalities. It makes me feel like I have many different women."

Aren kissed the tip of her nose. He arranged the sheets over them and held her tight against him. *Élise* shuddered suddenly.

"Cold?"

"No. I just had this gush of your semen come pouring out me. It is so gross!"

"Hey, that's my essence you're talking about."

"Yeah, a gooey mess. I should get up and shower."

"Nothing doing. You're going to stew in it with me. I love it when you stink of me."

"Oh no, no, no, no."

"Just shut up and go to sleep. We'll pick up where we left off. I definitely want to try that X-rated position from the Cosmo guide. Oh, your ass is so mine."

Élise smiled sadly as she remembered that moment. Even now it was hard to reconcile the wanton woman with the serene mother-to-be she was now. It was only five months ago. All that love and passion gone. Poof! She found herself thinking about Edgar Allan Poe's poem, "Dream within a Dream."

> *Take this kiss upon the brow!*
> *And, in parting from you now,*
> *Thus much let me avow—*
> *You are not wrong, who deem*
> *That my days have been a dream;*
> *Yet if hope has flown away*
> *In a night, or in a day,*
> *In a vision, or in none,*
> *Is it therefore the less gone?*
> *All that we see or seem*
> *Is but a dream within a dream.*

She smiled to herself. There was nothing in that file that would help her now. Whatever knowledge or closure she hoped to gain by holding onto it was achieved. *So why hold on to it now?* She thought for a moment. Aren was always telling her to digitize her documents. She didn't need these files for herself. But maybe sometime in the future they might be helpful to someone else. Or, maybe when she was much older, she might want to revisit her past to assess her life. She reached for a pen. She drew a line across the original note and wrote:

To scan/digitize in 2012.

When the baby was born, if she could allow herself to think that far, she would feel ready to close this chapter of her life.

A soft knock on the door startled her. "Hello?"

"Élise, it's me, Antonio. I'm going to the market. Do you need anything?"

"No, I'm fine, thanks."

"You're coming over, right? Lily called me and threatened physical harm if I let you spend New Year's alone."

Élise smiled.

"Yes, I'm coming. Just make sure you have some yummy hot chocolate for me."

"You got it, querida."

Élise listened to Antonio's footsteps fade away through the door. She stood up and walked over to the stereo and decided to play one of Aren's favorite Leonard Cohen songs, "Hallelujah." But his voice reminded her too much of Aren, so she selected the version sung by Velvet Underground.

I did my best, it wasn't much
I couldn't feel, so I tried to touch
I've told the truth, I didn't come to fool you
And even though it all went wrong

I'll stand before the Lord of Song
With nothing on my tongue but Hallelujah

There was not a day that went by that Élise did not think about Aren. Every change in her body with the life growing inside of her reminded her of the man responsible for this enormous change in her life. She was lonely. Her heart was broken. Yet, there was no bitterness. Aren never lied to her or betrayed her. He was faced with a challenge that he could not overcome. He always told her he loved her, but that love was not enough to overcome his rejection of her pregnancy. Élise could accept that they were no longer a couple. Thankfully, Lily stepped in and was becoming a wonderful friend. But she prayed every day that Aren would at some point try to connect with their child.

Please, Aren, find it in your heart to love our baby, your child.

CHAPTER 19

ACT OF RECONCILIATION

O n the feast of the Epiphany, January 6, Élise found a box in front of her door. It was postmarked from Armenia.

She opened her door and walked into her kitchen. She reached for the shears and opened the box. Inside the box was a five-by-eight metal replica of an Armenian khachkar cross-stone with a base. It was similar to the one Aren had in his paradise garden in Vermont. She smiled. The stone was inscribed with "Holy Mother of God."

She looked inside to see if there was a note. There was a postcard with Armenian cross-stones from the Haghpat Monastery. The card explained that khachkars named after the Holy Mother of God grant happiness to families and mothers. But there was no personal note from Aren to say, "I love you. I miss you," or "I'm thinking about you." She so longed to hear Aren's raspy voice call her *baby*.

Élise sat in the kitchen and watched the snow fall from her window. She thought about the meeting she had with the headmaster, the Romance Language Department Chair, and the Director of HR. She was thankful for that impromptu conversation she and Enrique had months ago about the morality clause in her employment contract.

Enrique did all the talking. The meeting allowed her to really think about what was important to her. Aren had tried so hard to get her to quit her teaching job. Maybe this was an opportunity to do something different. She liked teaching, but it was no longer a priority.

Her apartment was paid for. She had very little debt. She had savings. If the meeting went well, her vested and unvested pension were safe. She could get by.

In the end, Enrique and Élise had both been right. The headmaster, John Golden, was not going to terminate her contract. However, according to the Department Chair, Claudia Kaminski, certain students had been talking to their parents and a whispering campaign was spreading throughout the school. It didn't escape Enrique's notice that there was some rivalry between Élise and the Department Chair. The headmaster wanted to discuss how this was affecting student morale. Also, some parents actually demanded to know the truth and suggested if it were indeed true that Élise was pregnant out of wedlock that they may withdraw their children from the school.

"What?!" Élise gasped.

"Calm down," Enrique cautioned.

Let it go, Élise told herself as she sat and listened to the proposals being bandied about concerning a leave of absence or administrative leave. *Let it go*, Élise kept saying to herself. She managed to maintain a serene expression for the remainder of the meeting which concluded with no immediate action being taken against Élise at least for the remainder of the school year.

For now, she wasn't really showing. She wore a girdle and had started wearing flowing clothes with elastic waistbands. Most would attribute weight gain to the holiday festivities. But she wouldn't be able to hide the pregnancy for much longer.

Élise touched the khachkar again, lovingly, and prayed that wherever Aren was, that he was okay. She stood up and wiped the tears from her eyes. She had a lesson plan to prepare, but she felt exhausted. She walked to her bedroom, lay on the bed, and fell asleep instantly.

.oOo.

Haghpat Monastery
Northern Armenia, Lori Region

Aren Karajian decided to make a pilgrimage to Armenia over the Christmas holidays. No one, not even Lily, knew where he was. If asked, he would have probably been unable to say exactly what drew him to the Lori Region or what he hoped to find in this thousand-year-old great walled complex at the Holy Cross of Haghpat Monastery. It was perhaps a symbolic place for Aren, since the complex had withstood several earthquakes, had been taken by siege and burned by enemies, and had been subjected to the marauding assaults of the Mongols. Despite all that, the monastic fortress endured, continuing to be rebuilt or added onto over the centuries. Priests held vespers and still served mass, sometimes for a gathering of one or two elderly congregants.

Aren would slip into the chapel quietly and listen, hoping for an answer, perhaps. Every morning after vespers he walked along the gardens, noting the hardened and frost-covered earth. He visited the khachkars in the garden. He prayed, "Holy Mary, mother of God, watch over Élise. Lend her the strength I have been unable to give her. If it is your will that she gives birth, do not abandon her. Protect her and her baby—our baby."

Every day he prayed like this. Of course, the church faithful who watched him, recognized the telltale signs of the lament of a sinner. That was just the first step to the sacrament of penance and reconciliation.

What mortal sin have I committed? Aren challenged in his prayers and supplications. *Lust? No, Lord, passion. Passion is what I felt for* Élise— *still feel for* Élise. *I lacked chastity. But I haven't been chaste in years. You would punish* Élise *and me for impurity? But we were committed to each other. Yes, I know. I left her. When she needed me most, I left her to carry the burden of pregnancy. She's not young. She could die. And I'm here and I don't know what I'm supposed to do. I lacked the virtue of fortitude. I'm a coward in the face of adversity.* Élise *refused to accede to my wish. Is this what this is about? My pride? I hate you, Lord. Why did you let me fall in love with this woman? Why?*

The solitary priest who diligently said mass, observed the unkempt man in the frozen garden who tortured himself endlessly in a gibberish of English he could not understand. Yet, he did understand.

As Aren sat in the frosty monastery gardens, he thought about his wife Helen. He stayed with Helen through the end of her battle with cancer. It was difficult, but he had stayed the course with her. He found the strength.

I loved Helen. I honored my commitment to her and our marriage. But it took a lot out of me. And Élise? *I left her. Why?*

Maybe because Helen's death, however tragic, followed a logical course. He understood the odds and the progression of the disease. And when she died, there was finality. With Élise there were so many unknowables. Who knew how this would end? And even if he never saw Élise again, if her baby—their baby—survived, he would still be linked to this other life.

I don't want this. I so do not want this.

Aren was lost in thought until he felt the firm but gentle touch of a hand on his shoulder. His eyes slowly turned upward, taking in the black cassock of the priest and his long gray beard and kind hazel eyes. They exchanged a long and silent look. The priest started to recite the general prayer of absolution. It took him a while to figure it out. And then he remembered the religious rites. He needed to confess. Which part of it? And now?

"I'm sorry," Aren said in a broken voice to the priest. He said it in English.

"Go home," the priest said in Armenian. "Go home and seek reconciliation."

The priest offered another prayer and then touched Aren's cheek lightly. He turned around and walked back in the direction in which he had come.

Aren

Oh God, how do I fix this?

"Go home and seek reconciliation," the priest said.

I sat on the frost-covered bench shivering. The priest's words played over and over in my head. But was it really that difficult to understand what he was telling me? Whatever answer or solution I was seeking, I was not going to find it in a monastery in Armenia. *Shit! I have to go home. I can't run away. I'm sixty-three years old.* Ich bin ein Dummkopf! It was easy to walk away from Élise. I cried. I made myself sick, but I still walked away. Even if Élise forgave me, what we had, that beautiful connection is dead. I killed it. I kept telling her to trust me— My eyes burned with unshed tears. She let me push her boundaries. She trusted me and then I repaid her by turning my back on her. Was I crying for her or for myself? Did I love her? Do I love her? Yes. Yes!

"What kind of love is that?" Élise's voice called out to me.

"Seek reconciliation," the priest said. To reconcile means you admit something is broken and you have to change in order to build a new relationship. How do I fix this? I can't. What if Élise agrees to let me spend as much time with the child as I want, but refuses to take me back as her lover? I don't think I could survive that rejection. I made Élise think it was really about the sex, when it really wasn't. *God, I'm crying again. I miss everything about her. Everything. Why did I do this?*

I looked up at the sky. The sun would set in one hour or so. I looked at the khachkar cross-stones around me. If Élise loses that baby, I will never see her again. What did she say about her ex? She said she erased him from her memory. She said he was gone. That's what Élise would do to me, erase me from her memory. I can't win Élise back. I have to earn my way back by helping her through this pregnancy and raising the child. But even Élise wouldn't force me to raise a child. That's why she could let me go. She wants me to love the child, our child. That child is a part of us.

"Is it having a baby that upsets you or having a baby that has special needs?" Élise asked. "If the baby were normal and healthy, would you—would you help me raise our child?"

I just wanted Élise to myself. I didn't want to share her. I don't want to share her. She was my prize for being a faithful husband until death do us part. And then I had a heart attack and then bypass surgery. I thought I paid enough. I was selfish. I was cruel. I was arrogant. But the woman I love knows my dark underside. She has seen my demons. Seek reconciliation means I have to change. I have to do right by our baby. That baby was conceived in love. We still love each other.

I stood up. The temperature had dropped several degrees. As I walked out of the monastery, I passed a khachkar dedicated to the Holy Mother. Élise had a devotion to the Holy Mother. *Tomorrow I will visit the Holy Mother of God Church in the holy city of Vagharshapat. My journey home will begin there. I will need all the help I can get to reconcile with* Élise.

CHAPTER 20

GROUNDHOG DAY

On a chilly Wednesday morning on February 2, 2011, Punxsutawney Phil, the infamous groundhog, did not see his shadow, thereby announcing that spring would come early. As Élise swung her legs to the floor, taking care to find her balance, she felt hopeful. The worst of the morning sickness was over, and she still had a viable pregnancy. Viable!

The faculty and students were being incredibly supportive about her pregnancy. She was wearing a lot of skirt and sweater ensembles with long, flowing cardigans or Japanese haori jackets to deemphasize her protruding belly. She was looking decidedly more bohemian in appearance thanks to the large, clunky, and colorful wooden beads and bracelets. Her students teasingly called her "Tierra Madre."

She joined a hiking club so she could have company during long weekend hikes. She continued with her Pilates but hired a private coach to modify positions to accommodate her pregnancy. She also committed herself to a yoga regimen of deep breathing and meditation. Each waking moment was focused on bringing about the most optimal outcome for her baby. That's all that mattered. She Skyped regularly with Dr. Vanderhof, who shipped her regular packages of supplements and reviewed her food diary online and sent suggestions. She had been steadily minimizing dairy, red meats, and simple carbohydrates and ramping up raw food consumption. She drank coconut water by the gallons, as well as mint tea at night. She snacked on pumpkin seeds and bee pollen. Try as she might, it was hard to digest regular meals.

The worst of the nausea had passed, but in its place was this thick build-up of saliva. She had to modify her teaching so as not to talk as much. There were so many challenges.

.oOo.

On Groundhog Day, Élise looked forward to getting home a little early. She planned to try out a belly-dancing class in Newton and wanted to rest before going. When she walked up the stairs to her apartment, she froze.

Aren met her at the top of the stairs. He marveled at her. She was radiant and, in many ways, seemed younger than when he had last seen her three months earlier. Her hair seemed so much thicker and longer. Her belly was now obvious, but it made her look ripe and exotic. The pregnancy didn't seem to drag her down. On the contrary, it breathed life into her.

"Aren," Élise called his name in that wonderful lilting accent he adored.

Élise took in his gaunt and almost skeletal frame. He looked like he was returning from a war prisoners' camp. He was disheveled and unshaven and hadn't bathed in a while. She had missed him so much when he left. And now standing there looking at him, she knew she didn't miss him anymore. But it saddened her to see him so miserable. She smiled as she opened her arms wide to hug him tight.

"I missed you so much," Aren said, breaking down into tears. "I'm sorry. So sorry."

"I know. It's okay." Élise broke from the embrace and stood back to stroke his face. "Lily has been wonderful to me. I don't know what I would have done without her. She has been a good friend."

Élise then dug in her purse and gestured to the door. "Come in."

Aren stopped to pick up the flowers he had set by the door for her and followed her into the apartment. He stood at the threshold, watching her remove her coat and set down her bag. She was biting her lips and fluttering her eyelashes. He set the flowers down on the dining room table and walked toward her, placing his hands on her shoulders.

"Do you forgive me?"

Élise sighed. "Aren, you have always been honest with me. Brutally honest. I can't fault you."

"Can I stay with you?"

"Oh, I don't know. I'm kind of gross now. You don't want to be with me in this state," Élise said lightly. Her light hazel eyes glinted like steel.

Aren reached out and touched Élise's belly.

"I'm very late. But I'd like to be there for you now, if you'll let me."

"Aren, I don't hate you," Élise said firmly. "We're good. The baby is good. There might be a heart defect, but they can operate a few months after she's born. A lot depends on how she develops in the next few weeks."

Élise was speaking rapidly but with confidence and hope for the future. But she wasn't talking about their future as a couple.

Aren just stared at her, realizing so much had changed between them. She had gotten stronger from their separation while he could barely pull himself together. He was frightened of losing her. Aren started taking off his clothes. Élise watched in horror.

"Aren, don't do this. I can't, okay. I—" Aren knelt at her feet and cried.

"Aren, please get up. I don't need a man who cries and feels sorry for himself. If you want to be in my life, then stand up and be a man. Own up to your responsibilities. That's all I ask. I don't want to dwell on the past. I'm over it. I have to be. I have to focus on what is important: me and the baby."

"So?"

"So, I don't know," Élise said. "Okay."

They looked at each other. "Do you love me?" Aren asked. Élise sighed heavily.

"Aren, you're a wreck. I need to nap a little, and then I have to go to my dance class. You know where the bathroom is. Clean yourself up. Your clothes are where you left them. If you want to stay, then do your part. There's laundry to be done, food to cook, rooms to tidy. The outside steps need to be de-iced. Make yourself useful. I'm not ready to share my bed with you again. I-I'm not sure if I ever will be ready. Do you understand?"

Aren took a deep breath. "Yes."

"All right then. I'm going to lie down. I would give you another hug, but you really do need to go take a shower and then soak in the tub. If I weren't so tired, I would scrub you myself." Élise chuckled.

"I love you, Élise."

"I know."

Élise then turned around and waddled slightly as she made her way toward her bedroom and shut the door.

Aren looked at his thin, naked body and shook his head. He picked up his clothes and walked toward the bathroom. He heard a knock on the door as he emerged from the bathroom. He walked up to the door and opened it.

Antonio was standing there stony-faced. "Where is she?"

"Élise is resting. Maybe you can come back later."

Antonio stepped inside and slapped Aren's face. While the slap was indeed painful, the swiftness of the action from the elderly gentleman took him more by surprise.

"You son of a bitch! *¡Maldito hijo de su puta Madre!* ¡Pendejo!" Antonio sneered.

Aren took a deep breath. He waited until Antonio was finished with his stream of profanities.

"Are you staying for good this time?"

Antonio challenged. "Yes, if she'll let me."

"What do you mean, if she'll let you? What kind of a man are you? *¿Pero qué coño?* You stand by your woman even if it means she makes you sleep with the dogs until her anger is spent!"

Antonio shook his head, sucking his teeth.

"Oh well, I knew you would come back. And I knew she would take you back. That's how these things go." He looked at Aren closely. "You look like shit. What happened to you? No, never mind. It doesn't matter."

"Are you finished now?" Aren asked.

"Yes, I just needed to tell you off. I feel better now. You want to come over for some tea? I can make you a sandwich. You look hungry."

"Oh, so we're friends now?" Aren said with a fake laugh.

"No. But if you're going to make yourself useful to Élise, you might as well take care of yourself. Come on. She is probably hiding in her bedroom praying you'll leave so she can sneak out and not have to deal with you."

"You're crazy. You know that."

"Maybe. Come on. Give her some space. She has a lot to figure out." Over sandwiches, Aren found a temporary refuge in Antonio's cozy apartment exploding with a profusion of bold red and orange colors and plenty of ceramic tiles, lush green plants, and Colonial Spanish furniture. Antonio had a thing for roosters, so they were everywhere. "By the way, Élise had a visitor a few weeks ago. Actually, just after the new year."

"Visitor?"

"Yeah, a man. Good-looking black man."

"Her brother?"

"No. I know her brother. This wasn't her brother."

"Well, who then?"

"I don't know. She was kind of vague when I asked about him. All she said was that he's from South Carolina and he was visiting from out-of-town on business."

Aren felt sick.

"Are you shitting me?"

"No."

"Why are you telling me this?"

"To get on your nerves," Antonio said smugly. "Oh, for crying out loud," Aren snapped.

Antonio shook his head. "Whatever his intentions were, I don't think she has a romantic interest in him—yet. Élise is a woman. She's vulnerable. You burnt a bridge with her. I just hope you're a good enough engineer to quickly rebuild a new one before she has a chance to build a dam and cut off all access. *Comprende, amigo?*"

"Yeah," Aren said hoarsely. "Good. More tea?"

"No, I better get going."

Aren stood up and walked toward the door. "Thanks, Antonio."

"You know, Aren, I got to know your daughter Lily and her friend Tessa. She's an amazing woman. And she's devoted to you even though she's probably disappointed. But you know I'm one of those people who believe the apple doesn't fall far from the tree. You had a bad season, but you're not a bad person. Do better. You can do better."

Aren smiled wistfully. "All right. See you."

"*Adios, hermano*," Antonio said as he shut the door behind Aren. "Oh wait!" Antonio called out, opening the door again and crossing the hall with a bag, handing it over to Aren. "What's this?"

"Oh, *bruheria.*"

"What?"

"Oh, I have been making vegetable broths for her. There are some special herbs from Mexico and Peru I like to throw in there."

"Isn't that dangerous?" Aren asked suspiciously.

"It's bruheria, I tell you. Listen, her doctor says she's doing great."

Aren shook his head skeptically and then made his way back to the apartment.

CHAPTER 21

WINTER LADY

For the first couple of days, Aren slept on the sofa. Élise took pity on him eventually and allowed him into her bed. But he knew that sleeping was all that was going to happen. Over the following days, he cooked and cleaned for Élise and drove her to her classes. He installed a bathtub grab bar and treads inside the tub to minimize the risk of her slipping, and a new high-efficiency washer and dryer and a dishwasher, all with a sanitary cycles.

Aren accompanied Élise to the Y for her early-morning water aerobics classes. He used that opportunity to swim laps and relax in the sauna. While Élise taught classes, Aren started running every day in the afternoons. He got involved with the Armenian Church. He caught up with friends. While Élise took her maternity yoga classes, Aren meditated. He set time aside during the day to work on his writing. At night when Élise was sleeping, he caught up on emails. Dinners were simple affairs. Too simple, he thought. Sometimes it was just a roasted sweet potato and a lettuce leaf.

"Honey, you have to eat more than that."

"I can't, Aren. I start to throw up if I eat too much. Don't worry, I have Antonio's magic potion that's chock full of vitamins."

Aren scowled.

"Well, if you don't mind making smoothies, that goes down pretty easily and you can add flax seeds," Élise said.

"Élise, does the doctor know about your eating habits? I mean the doctor, not the quack you saw in Chicago."

Élise shot him a withering look.

"Aren, I know you mean well, but please don't disparage my judgment where my baby's life is concerned. I'm fighting for her, okay? And the only way to do that is to be the healthiest person I can be."

Élise burst into tears suddenly. Aren panicked and stood up and held her.

"I'm sorry. I'm an ass. Don't cry. I won't bring it up again. I'm just concerned, okay?"

Élise nodded.

"Would you like me to make a smoothie? Banana and—"

"Blueberries, and throw in a scoop of Maca-Cacao powder. Thank you."

There was that dazzling smile of hers. "All right, baby."

Oh boy, Aren thought to himself. But things did get better.

Aren did his now routine four loops around the Jamaica Pond to get in his six miles for the morning. It was a beautiful place to go for a run surrounded by historic mansions and the boat house. Little children played in the snow with their playmates while the mothers, au pairs, and nannies caught up on their gossip or talked on their smartphones.

As Aren completed his last lap, he sang along with the song playing on his iPod. Leonard Cohen's "Winter Lady."

CHAPTER 22

VALENTINE'S DAY

New England had six snow storms by mid-February. Gray piles of snow towered every street corner. It was cloudy and extremely windy on the day Élise was locking the door behind her when she heard Aren's heavy footfalls coming up the steps. "Oh, did you forget something?" she asked.

"It's a little icy out there. The car is warming up. I thought I'd come up and help you down."

"Aren, I can walk down the stairs, you know."

"Hmm. Maybe. But I'd feel better if I held onto you."

Élise wanted to cluck her tongue, and then she thought better of it. He was actually being sweet. She smiled as she took his arm, and they walked down the steps. The steps creaked under both their weights as they came down the two flights of stairs. The car was double-parked in the front. Aren opened the passenger door and helped her into her seat. A compilation of piano instrumentals was playing. There was a thermos of maté tea in the cupholder. Élise turned to look at Aren as he got in and started the car. She reached over and kissed his lips softly and then drew back quickly before the kiss could deepen.

Aren had been home for two weeks now—twelve days, to be exact. They were now sharing a bed and living together as roommates. But that brief kiss reminded him of the powerful chemistry they used to have and the intimacy they once shared. The heaviness in his heart was palpable.

"Let's roll, baby," Aren said, winking. Élise laughed.

Later that night, Élise and Aren were at the table finishing up their supper of Moroccan-style pumpkin soup and fresh sautéed spinach.

"Would you like some dessert?" Élise asked. Aren was about to stand up and start clearing the table.

"No, I'll get that. Why don't you go relax on the sofa, and I'll make us some tea and bring out dessert? Go on," Élise insisted.

"Okay," Aren said hesitantly, wondering what Élise was up to.

He ducked into the bedroom and came back out with his *Financial Times* newspaper and then sat on the sofa. He placed his feet on the coffee table and began to read. Élise came out fifteen minutes later with a tray laden with tea and sliced fruit arranged around individual servings of rich chocolate mousse cake. Aren removed his glasses and sat up straight, removing his feet to make room for the tray.

"Oh wow!" he said appreciatively.

Élise knelt on a floor cushion and began to pour out the tea. She was wearing her kimono with the extra-long sleeves, which made the whole ritual of pouring out tea especially elegant. Aren smiled.

"Happy Valentine's Day," Élise said, reaching inside her kimono to present him with a card.

He reached over, kissed her cheek, sat back, and read the card. "Thank you, sweetie."

Élise hesitated, not knowing what to do next.

"Um, I didn't actually get you a card or present," Aren said. "Oh, well, that's all right, Aren. I mean I didn't really—"

"Well—" Aren pulled out an envelope from the side table and handed it to Élise.

"What's this?"

She read the flyer folded inside the envelope. "Well?" Aren said, hoping she would say yes. Élise started fluttering her eyelashes rapidly.

"Well, I guess. I mean, if you don't mind being embarrassed doing the tango with the old gray-haired pregnant lady, then it's on you."

"Good. It's settled. The first class starts this Friday night. We can have an early dinner at the Spanish restaurant on Moody Street and then go to our class."

"Okay."

That evening Élise played some Cole Porter songs on her piano. He realized as he watched her that during the time they had spent together before he left, she didn't play very much for him. They were usually too busy doing things that he enjoyed most: hiking, going out to restaurants, sitting in the garden, or making love. It was amazing that she could have this talent and only now was he getting to enjoy it. Instead of turning their backs on each other when they slipped into bed that night, Aren opened his arms and invited Élise to tuck in the crook of his arm and cuddle with him—not as a prelude to sex but for the sheer pleasure of being close. Nervously, he brought his hand to her belly.

"Is it all right?" he asked.

"That would be nice. I think she might like it if you spoke to her too."

She lifted her nightgown and placed his hand on her naked belly. He adjusted his position so that now he was leaning on his elbow and looking down on her and caressing her belly.

"Wow," he said.

"I know. I'm huge."

"You're not, Élise. And even if you were? Who cares? You're still a beautiful woman, and you're carrying life."

Aren remembered at that moment the terrible things he had said to her about not wanting a child.

"I'm sorry—"

Élise covered his mouth with her hand.

"Don't. Aren, I'm glad we can be friends again."

Aren kissed her forehead and then lay flat on the bed, putting his arm around her.

.oOo.

The Friday-night tango dancing lesson was a big hit for both of them. For Élise it was a wonderful opportunity to work through her insecurity of being unattractive. Her palazzo pants with the halter top and the flare silhouette were not only comfortable for her but won a lot of praise from their fellow dancers. And when she danced with Aren, she was reminded of how wonderful it used to be to move rhythmically with him and to feel safe in his arms.

"Oh, I ache all over," Élise said when she and Aren walked through the door after their dance lesson. "My feet are killing me."

"Come on. I'll draw a bath for you." Élise smiled.

She undressed quickly and slipped on her robe. She walked slowly into the bathroom and lit up at the sight of the lit candles and the fragrant bathwater.

"I know you like really hot water, but it's not good for you right now." Élise clucked. Aren chuckled.

"Madam, your bath is ready." He untied her robe and held her hand as she lowered herself into the water, holding on to the grab bars.

"I feel so old and incapacitated," Élise admitted as she settled herself in the tub.

Aren stroked her cheek.

"You know, except for your boobs, your butt, and your belly, you're not that big, really."

"Oh!" Élise gasped. Aren smiled.

"That's what it means to be pregnant, sweetheart. I was kidding about your butt."

"Gee, thanks."

Aren picked up a brush and started gently rubbing Élise's back. "Oh, that feels good."

Aren brushed her skin and then started massing her shoulders and feet. When he was finished, he helped her out of the tub, drained it, and then handed her a warm bathrobe.

Élise sighed in contentment. "That felt great."

They quickly readied for bed, throwing on pajamas. Aren turned to Élise.

"Let me brush your hair."

"You don't have to do that."

"I'd like to."

"It's gotten really out of control. I'm afraid to put any chemicals in it to straighten it out."

"Leave it to me."

Aren reached for a bottle of oil on the nightstand and poured some in the palm of his hand and rubbed vigorously and then massaged her scalp before taking the brush to her hair.

"Ah," Élise purred.

Aren kissed her neck and her temples. "Such a beautiful woman." He sighed.

Élise looked at him, not knowing what to say. He picked up her hand and kissed it. "Thank you for letting me do that. For letting me take care of you."

"I've been pretty ungrateful, haven't I? I'm s—" Aren covered her mouth with his hand.

"One day at a time, we said."

Aren leaned over and kissed Élise's belly. He cooed loving words to the baby in Armenian and English and rubbed Élise's belly affectionately.

Then he slid down on the bed and turned to Élise, opening his arms wide, waiting for her to turn off the lights.

"I had a wonderful time tonight, Aren. Thank you," Élise said, yawning.

"You're welcome."

He held her tight against him and then fell asleep. Élise turned to look at him. She planted a soft kiss on his chin. Still in his sleep state, he kissed her back.

On Saturday, Aren and Élise returned to the apartment after a brisk afternoon walk through the arboretum. There was a light covering of snow—enough to make the arboretum look like a magical wonderland, but not enough to make the walk difficult for Élise. Aren marveled at how the woman who was always complaining about being cold had now turned into a human furnace. She didn't wear heavy coats. A pashmina was the extent of her outdoor clothing. The fresh cool air gave her skin a beautiful radiance. They stayed out for a long time.

.oOo.

Aren

"Hungry?" I asked her when we returned to the apartment. "Meh, not so much," Élise replied.

It worried me how little solid food Élise ate. Even though she complained about being "big" she really hadn't gained that much weight. Dr. Schuler voiced his concern, but Élise ignored him. It was kind of infuriating. But in all other metrics, she was doing great. I guess those mysterious tonics from Antonio and the supplements from Dr. Vanderhof were working.

"Come on. I'll warm up that bruheria tonic Antonio whipped up for you."

Élise smiled as she followed me into the kitchen. I made myself a sandwich while Élise helped herself to a second serving of the vegetable broth.

"Élise?"

"Yes, Aren?"

"I was thinking maybe you could come with me to Sunday services." The spiritual journey I began in Armenia continued when I returned.

I made regular visits to Watertown, the hub of the Massachusetts Armenian community. When I was at MIT, I always went there to pick up yogurt and other Armenian goodies. After all these years very little had changed. I also started attending mass. I went early on Sundays so Élise could sleep in. Now that I was starting to bond with the baby, it occurred to me I should introduce Élise and the baby to my faith and culture. It's odd that I never thought of it while Élise and I were together. Whether Élise and I were intimate or not, she was now a part of my family. I wanted to share this with her and the baby.

.oOo.

Élise

Aren asked me to attend services at the Saint James Armenian Church. Of all the things Aren could have asked me, that was the last thing I ever imagined he would ask. At first, I stared at Aren, not completely registering what he was asking.

"You mean the Armenian Church?"

"The same," he said.

"Oh."

"What's wrong?"

"I don't know. I don't want to make trouble for you. I think the congregation will give you a lot of grief if I show up."

"I don't care," Aren said.

"Maybe I care. I don't really want to go somewhere where I'm not wanted."

"Who says you're not wanted?"

"They'll stare at me."

"People stare at you already all the time."

I ignored that comment. I wasn't sure what he meant. "I don't know, Aren."

"Well, I won't force you. It just would mean a lot to me if you would come."

I did feel weird about going to a service at the Armenian Church. But I also felt honored that he wanted to share his faith with me. It's not something we ever seriously discussed. Yet, we're both raised in religious households.

"Hmm. What time?" I asked. "There's a service at ten thirty."

"Do I have to make nice with the priest?"

"Probably. We may or may not be invited over for coffee."

"Great. Okay," I asked. I wasn't sure if that meant coffee at the church or at the priest's house. Either way, it would promise to be an interesting experience.

.oOo.

Élise survived her first foray into the Armenian Church. It was awkward, exactly as she expected. But people were polite. Aren stayed close by her side and introduced her to some members. She actually appreciated the service. It wasn't terribly different, liturgically speaking, from the Catholic services she had attended as a child. For Élise it was an opportunity to learn about Aren's heritage for the benefit of their unborn child. Still, it was strange to reconcile obstreperous Aren with devout Aren. She was finding she liked devout Aren very much. There were many more trials ahead for her with the pregnancy as she neared the third trimester. Dr. Schuler was talking about the baby having heart surgery in utero. The thought terrified her. If Aren was embracing his spiritual side, so much the better.

CHAPTER 23

POKER NIGHT

Aren

Poker night at Zach's house! What a treat! Élise encouraged me to go out so she could enjoy her quiet time. While I was happy she was okay with my being away for the evening, I worried. At ten o'clock, I pulled out my phone and called her.

"How you doin', baby?"

"Aren, this is your time to be with your friends. You don't have to worry about me."

"Are you in bed?"

"Yeah."

"How's the swelling?"

"Better. Don't worry about me, okay?"

"I'll be home in an hour, all right, baby?"

"Okay."

I ended the call. My friends were staring at me. "What?" I said.

"What are you going to do, Aren?" they asked in unison. "About what?"

"Your situation. You and Élise are back together again—" Zach clarified.

"Guys, I came to play cards, not talk about my personal life."

Zach pursed his lips and began to deal cards. I looked at my hand and cursed. I folded. I lost that round.

"Your mind is elsewhere, man," Zach chided. "I know."

"Is she all right?"

"Yeah. I just don't know if we're all right."

"What do you mean?"

"I mean I'm back, but I'm not really back. I'm still on probation." The men chuckled.

"Well, I can't say that I blame her," Zach said. "Don't start with the guilt trip, Zach," I snapped. Zach shook his head.

"I'm not. I'm amazed you came back. I'm not sure I would have, if I were you."

"Really?"

"Yeah."

"But I love her. I'm just not sure that she loves me the way she used to."

"I hear you," Zach said. "Well, if she starts ignoring you and lavishing all her attention on the baby, then you can go. You will have done your part. Lots of people break up when the sex dries up."

How depressing. "Is that really what life is about? If your sexual needs aren't met, just move on?"

The card playing stopped. Everyone turned to look at me.

"Okay, okay. I mean sex is an important part of a relationship. But things change when there are children."

Zach rolled his eyes dramatically. "Yes, Aren, isn't that what I said?" I thought about the poets Élise presented at her summer conference. Their perspective made more sense to me now. It's not really the sex.

It's the attention or lack of it. That's what causes people to break up.

"How many?" the dealer asked.

I held up two fingers. I discarded two cards and I drew two cards. I stared at the cards in my hands, but I didn't see them.

"You know Élise and I had a phenomenal relationship. If she didn't get pregnant, I would have been happy to continue with Élise the way we were. But she is pregnant. Even if I hadn't messed things up, things would have changed. I always thought the magic between us was the sex. But it wasn't. It was the attention. She made me feel like I was the only one, the only thing that mattered. And now she's going to have a baby that's going to demand that of her. And I can't begrudge the baby that right. But that magic between us is still there. I mean, I'm still in the dog house. But I'm in the dog house because we still love each other." Zach had a glazed-over expression. "Okay, you lost us," Zach said.

"I know. Well, I'm just taking it a day at a time. I owe it to her to try and make this work."

"Don't be such a boy scout."

"Maybe you're right," I blurted out without thinking. I felt tired. I stood up suddenly. "All right, guys. Later. See you next week."

When I opened the bedroom door, the lights were turned on, but Élise had fallen asleep with a book in her hand. I quickly undressed and brushed my teeth and then got into bed. I reached over and turned off the lights on her side of the bed and then snuggled up to her, holding her tight. Her breasts were now these exquisite orbs. I started to caress her. I reached for her crotch, which was now heavily forested. Her vagina was wet. She moaned softly as she began to wake up. I kissed her cheek. "I'm dying for you, baby, but my dick is not cooperating right now."

"Aren, let's not complicate things right now, okay? You don't have to prove anything to me."

"All right," I whispered, stroking her breasts once more, and then kissed her. "You're so beautiful."

I wrapped my arms tight around her, and then promptly fell asleep.

CHAPTER 24

STITCH IN TIME

The things which are impossible with men are
possible with God. (Luke 18:27 [KJV])

Aren

One month after I returned, Élise was admitted to Children's
Hospital to undergo fetal cardiac intervention on the baby's
heart. This was not a decision we agreed on, initially. Élise
wanted to wait until after delivery. I was able to convince Élise that
fetal surgery would give our baby the best fighting chance for long-
term survival. All those good things Élise was doing for herself would
help the baby heal while in utero. I was learning not to disparage Élise's
alternative health methods. It was working for her.

The week leading up to the surgery, I found myself fasting and
visiting the Armenian Church daily. I was terrified of losing both Élise
and the baby. Antonio was the one who came through for the both
of us. He was happy to come with me for daily mass. He found ways
to encourage Élise to eat to build up her strength for the surgery. The
surgery was successful. The next big hurdle was convincing Élise that
she takes a leave of absence and go on absolute bed rest.

"I can do this, Aren. Maybe I go on Skype, and have virtual classes.
Maybe go in part-time."

"No. You don't know how to give part of yourself to your students,"
I said. "They'll call you at strange hours. You'll stay up to correct their

papers. Hell, you still help students who are now in college. Forget it."

"Aren—"

"It's not forever, Élise."

"God, what am I going to do for three weeks?" she said.

.oOo.

Fanny

Sometimes when you have a strong friend, the one who always seems to have the answers and seems so in control of their lives, you forget how strong a friend you really are. From the moment we met Élise and I just loved each other. We were like sisters. Or at least that's the way I looked at her. I accepted her aloofness as part of her personality. When she first confided in me about Aren, I thought: *Aha! I have finally cracked her shell.* But it was when I learned the news of her pregnancy that things changed between us. She let me see her vulnerability. She let me see the crazy and didn't hide it from me. I was no longer Fanny the good-time loyal girlfriend who gave sex and love advice. I became Fanny, wise and trusted friend and experienced health professional. She opened herself up to me, Enrique and the boys. When Enrique said: "Élise, you're family," he meant it.

When Aren came to me to ask for my help to convince Élise to undergo the fetoscopic surgery, the anger I felt toward him no longer mattered. What mattered was that I was a pediatric nurse. I had seen children born successfully after this procedure. But it was very complicated. I knew what to say to her to make her see reason. When Aren came back, Élise was getting close to the deadline to opt for the procedure. ¡Por Dios! Aren chose the right moment to re-enter Élise's life. She needed him and didn't realize it. She convinced herself she could wait until after the baby was born. But Aren and I knew that whatever she thought of Dr. Schuler, on the issue of fetoscopic surgery he was right. She also needed to stop working. Even her woo-woo doctor in

Chicago said as much.

"Aren," I told him during a phone call, "maybe you should think about installing a stair lift."

"Oh come on, Fanny!" he said. "She's not disabled."

"Listen, Aren," I counseled. "I get winded going up those stairs. Maybe that's why Antonio is so strong. But as the pregnancy increases, it's going to be tough for her to climb the stairs. It's not her balance I worry about. It's the oxygen. If she's laying off Zumba, then she shouldn't be climbing the stairs."

There was silence on the phone while he thought.

"Well, I can do some research and have them professionally installed. It can't hurt to have a back-up."

It annoyed me to no end that Élise's doctor never brought up the stairs. But then again Élise probably never thought about it either. She was used to them.

CHAPTER 25

◇◇◇

ÉLAN

◇◇◇

Aren

One week after the fetoscopic surgery, Élise was lying comfortably on the sofa and crocheting a blanket for the baby. She was using the wedge sex cushion I ordered for her as back support.

I was sitting in a chair across from her. I had made up my mind to do something that was going to disrupt our routine. I didn't know how she would react.

"Élise, I signed up for the Children's Hospital Boston Marathon," I announced.

She dropped her crochet. "Oh," she said.

"I'm not sure I ever told you before, but every year since Helen's death, I have run in the Boston Marathon as part of the Dana Farber Cancer Foundation to raise money. This year I want to raise money for Children's Hospital."

Somehow just saying it made me choke with emotion. Our baby now had an excellent chance of surviving because of the fetoscopic surgery.

Élise looked at me with tenderness. She patted her belly and said cooing words to the baby in French.

"Aren, that's fantastic news!" she exclaimed. "But how are you going to run for both causes? Do you wear two jerseys?"

I shrugged and then I chuckled. "I'm not sure, but I'll figure out the details soon enough. I only have a month to get ready."

She smiled wanly. "Aren, I think that's a wonderful idea, but I don't want you to collapse either. Are you up to this?"

I stood up and walked over to the sofa and sat on the floor next to her. I placed my hand on her belly.

"Sweetie, believe it or not, I just might be in the best shape I have ever been. I've lost weight. I haven't had any alcohol in months and I've been swimming and jogging."

"Okay, Aren. I support you 100 percent What can I do to help?" she asked.

"Well, I need to ramp up my training. What I haven't started to do are the long runs. I need hills and tempo training in addition to doing long runs. It's time for me to go back to Vermont. I think the fresh air would do me good as well," I said.

Élise lowered her eyes with sadness. "Oh, of course," she said. "I'll be fine here. Don't worry."

"Honey," I said, "come with me to Vermont. The fresh air would do you and the baby good."

Élise blinked several times. She bit her lip. She reminded me of the way she first reacted to my asking her out for a date at the Dobra Tea Room. *Was it only a year ago?*

"Are you sure?" she asked.

"Absolutely," I said. "If you want, we can invite your friends to visit.

I need to train, but I want to keep an eye on you. All right?" Oh, that dazzling smile of hers appeared.

"Yes," she agreed enthusiastically.

.oOo.

Aren

The last weekend before Élise and I would transition to Vermont, Élise asked me to archive some files to make space in the apartment. I came across her files on Haïti Littéraire. By now I was well acquainted with Élise's doctoral thesis on creolization and racial identity beyond negritude. But what did any of it mean, anyway? I thought about the signed photograph framed in the hallway of Élise posing with an aging member of the famed Haitian literary circle. I peeked inside a file marked "Jeune Haïti." Inside I found assorted letters, newspaper clippings, and photographs of Haitian intellectuals who had been assassinated in the 1960s during the Duvalier regime. And then I remembered the nightmare Élise had one night. She had been screaming "Tonton Macoutes." But her family was from Saint Martin. What was their real connection to Haiti?

I read some of the news articles written in French, and then the letters from her father. Apparently, Christian Douchet, Élise's father, had been a classmate of one of the men who had been assassinated. They had studied in France together and Christian eventually accepted an invitation to teach at one of the schools in Port au Prince. He arrived in 1963 when Élise could not have been more than two years old. There were letters from Élise's mother Ghislaine to relatives in Montreal and New York that explained her growing unease with the political climate and mounting violence in Haiti. Apparently, things took a sudden turn for the worst when Christian was forced to watch the public execution of his friend in 1964 in full view of school children. He protested, and was immediately harassed by the Duvalier government. The nightmares for them really began when the Duvalier Tonton Macoutes invaded his home and assaulted Ghislaine, and took Christian. He languished in prison for two years while his wife lobbied to get him out, thanks to the intervention of the French government and friends in Canada and the United States. Élise's mother sent her to live with her family back home in Saint Martin for safety. And while her father did finally escape and lived in exile eventually in Canada, he died young at fifty from complications related to Hepatitis C from his period of incarceration.

How did Élise not mention this part of her biography? I had talked so much about the experiences of my Armenian family. One set of grandparents had fled to Yerevan in the wake of the Hamidian massacres and gone to Kazakhstan. Another set found refuge in Aleppo, Syria, just before the Armenian genocide in Turkey. I had a combined family history of pain and exile. Would we pass on this trauma to our child? I set aside the files. They were important. I would make space for them.

.oOo.

Élise

That night of the Tonton Macoute invasion of our home is the only memory I have of being taken away from my home. BoBo rescued me, but that act resulted in my never seeing my home or Haiti ever again. But the feeling of deep loss came from the separation from my parents. They sent me away to keep me safe.

The last time Aren and I had been in the cottage together was when he decided to leave me. I didn't really think about whatever ghosts there might be at the cottage until we drove up the gravel driveway and Aren parked in front of the door. When I walked through the front door of Aren's cottage, I thought of one of my favorite songs from the French Armenian singer Charles Aznavour "*Non, Je n'ai rien oublié*," or "No, I have not forgotten anything."

"Welcome home," Aren said.

Was this really my home? The cottage smelled wonderful. The cleaners had obviously scrubbed the house from top to bottom. Aren escorted me to the sofa in the great room with the soaring ceilings and the view of the lake. This was where the breakup happened.

"Aren, do what you have to do. I will not resent you for it."

"You know, Élise, even if I walk away from you, I'm still responsible for that life. I do not want this baby."

I trembled and then broke down in sobs. Aren stood there watching me fall apart in front of him. When I needed him to touch me, to comfort me, he didn't, he wouldn't.

"Élise," he had said, "I need some time to myself."

Tears rolled down my eyes thinking about that night. I wiped my tears with the back of my hand and looked out the window. I heard Aren's footsteps leave the room and then return a few minutes later. Aren set a glass of water on the coffee table.

"Have a glass of water, honey," he said. I reached for the glass. "I put the kettle on, too," he said quickly. He looked like he was going to cry. My throat ached from holding back tears. I didn't expect to react this way. I reached out my hand and waited.

.oOo.

Aren

Somehow Élise and I never directly talked about the night I left her. At first she said she was over it and didn't want to revisit what happened. And even when I asked if she would join me while I trained for the marathon, we didn't talk about the night of our break-up. I remembered a line from the poem "Silence" by Marianne Moore. "The deepest feeling always shows itself in silence/not in silence, but in restraint."

Élise reached out her hand wordlessly. I walked over to the sofa and sat next to her. She didn't flinch. She waited. I wrapped my arms around her and waited. She lay her head on my shoulder and cried. She was crying for so many reasons.

"One day at a time," we said to each other. I placed my free hand on her belly. She didn't push it away. We just sat together holding onto each other in silence.

.oOo.

Élise

It didn't take long for Aren and me to establish a new rhythm in the cottage. Despite all of my vehement protests that I couldn't stay on bed rest, I actually did sleep a lot throughout the day. Aren scheduled most of his training in the morning while I slept in. But I also took short walks around the garden alone when Aren was training. I followed Aren's example and paced myself. We had that in common now. We were just focused on being healthy. We didn't talk about our future as a family. But Aren did use our time to bond with the baby. Invariably, I would fall asleep in the afternoon and Aren was free to do as he pleased. But a lot of times I would wake up and find Aren next to me or holding me and rubbing my belly. Those moments I treasured. Lily and Tessa would visit on the weekends. Later Fanny and her family came to visit me. I loved that. I didn't miss school or my students or my life back in Boston. Antonio and I talked regularly on the phone. Physically, I felt like a truck had run over me and was still on top of me—weak and battered. But emotionally, I felt at peace.

.oOo.

Aren

What I hadn't explained to Élise when I announced my intention to train for the Boston Marathon in Vermont is that my previous runs were based on my ability to fundraise, and not because I met the qualifying time requirements. In the past, I did a run/walk combination and still managed to finish the race in five hours. This time, I really wanted to race and establish a personal best. Of course, I also wanted to raise money for two important charities. The time I spent jogging in Boston and swimming daily were foundational. Now I needed to step up my game: speed runs, interval training, and weekly long runs starting with ten miles and build up to eighteen miles before tapering. Ha! I didn't have much time. But I could do it. When I would get home, I was grateful for the ready meals Tessa prepared for us. Élise was sad that she slept so much. But I also found the training exhausted me and I often had to go to bed when Élise did. But I could see the speed runs were making a difference in my time. I could extend the time before that awful cramp, the lactic threshold would kick in. By the time of the Marathon I was ready.

.oOo.

Aren

I invited Fanny and her family to visit for the weekend. We had been in Vermont for two weeks already. I knew that would cheer Élise up. I put Fanny and her family in the pool house. The pool was heated so they could enjoy the pool as well as have some privacy. Fanny and Élise took walks together. All the things I tried to tell Élise for her own good and she dismissed me, Fanny was able to tell her and get results. I didn't get offended. I was grateful that Fanny was there for Élise. Élise always teased that Fanny didn't like to cook, but when she came to visit, she cooked nonstop. It was wonderful. The visit reminded me of our fishing trip last fall. We had a great time together. I realized I was so obsessed with having romantic getaways with Élise that I didn't invest energy in building a relationship with Fanny and her family. Better late than never. Little by little, I started to see the glimmer and spark of the woman

I had fallen in love with the year previously. Now when I bundled her up to sit on the deck and gaze at the night sky, she returned my kisses and caresses. It still wasn't where we were at the height of our romance seven months ago, but it was a vast improvement over the initial weeks of my return in her life.

.oOo.

Élise

I cried when Fanny, Enrique, Manuel, and Jorge went home. Oh, they didn't see me cry, but Aren did. It was a reunion with friends. But they also brought my painting of the Lady and the khachkar cross-stone dedicated to the Holy Mother of God. Antonio had lovingly packed everything for me including a cutting from the vines that were part of the original flower arrangement Aren sent me.

During our walk, Fanny asked me why I took Aren back. She wasn't interested in whether we were intimate or any of that. For her it was a done deal: he's back. Mercifully, she spared me the rant about making him grovel and pay for all the pain and misery I went through. I did go through a lot of pain. Maybe in the end the simple answer was that I loved him. Or, maybe the Aren who walked away needed to walk away to give space to the new Aren that returned. I would always be in love with the old Aren who pursued me relentlessly and ravished my body in a scandalous way. But that's not what I wanted or needed now. The big question was not why I took Aren back. Rather, the question was did the new Aren accept the new rules of engagement or was he going to morph into the old Aren? Only he could answer that question.

I thought about all the papers I have written about the love poetry and eroticism of Paul Eluard and Pablo Neruda. But it wasn't really the sexual innuendos or the titillation of sensual descriptions. It was the devotion, the attention that fascinated me. Intimacy. Looking back, if I had not gotten pregnant, I think the old Aren and I would have found our way to intimacy the way I understood it. But it would have taken a while. Or, maybe I'm the one who changed once I became pregnant and I needed a new Aren. Either way, the Aren I was starting to fall in love with was worth the agony I endured when Aren left me.

.oOo.

Aren

The day of the Boston Marathon had record high temperature exceeding 80°F/26°C. Élise worried when I received the Boston Athletic

Association(BAA) email advising non-elite runners to defer the race until the following year. Was I up for this? Hell yes! But it wasn't going to be easy.

The halfway point was manageable. The warm temperatures made the run tiring. The water bottles at the refreshment stations at Wellesley College were warm. Ugh! But the enthusiasm from the crowd urging me on carried me forward for a few miles. At mile 20, I tackled Heartbreak Hill. I watched people just drop out from effort and exhaustion. Others sat on the sidewalks trying to recover. I just focused on what I needed to do. I didn't have a title to defend. I just had a race to finish. Everyone's personal best was affected by the high temperature.

Élise greeted me with an exuberant hug when I came through the finish line at Boylston Street in four hours and fifteen minutes—not bad for a non-elite runner of sixty-three. I was able to raise over $25,000. Élise had a talent I didn't know about. She could write killer appeal letters. We walked slowly together to the wellness tents so that I could be checked for dehydration. I basked in Élise's company. The love between us was still there. It was still strong. The passion was on a back burner. Like the marathon I had just run, winning Élise back required hard work, pacing and endurance.

.oOo.

Aren

In her thirty-sixth week, Élise began to feel contractions. It was a miracle we made it this far. Dr. Schuler certainly never imagined it. Maybe having Fanny and Antonio visit regularly and having her special tokens of devotion made a difference. Whatever it was, the scary symptoms of her pregnancy stopped. We contacted Dr. Schuler, Dr. Vanderhof, and Fanny. They all concluded the same thing. These were false contractions. This was a signal that it was time to move closer to the hospital. We packed up and drove back to Boston. We went to the hospital to make sure everything was okay. They sent us home and told us to wait until there were regular contractions at five-minute intervals. The contractions stopped, but Élise could feel the baby moving around. Dr. Schuler checked her and said, "Soon, but not yet." It took yet another week for her cervix to start fully dilating before she was admitted. It was the start of her thirty-eighth week.

In the labor room, the nurses began the IV. She declined the drugs offered to her. Dr. Schuler said he wanted to perform a C-Section. The baby wasn't in distress. Élise refused.

"It's better for the baby if I can deliver vaginally. I—"

Bile rose up to my throat. I swallowed hard. I tried hard not to panic.

"I'm scared, Aren."

I kissed her hand. "I know, baby."

We practiced the deep breaths together. I massaged her shoulders and her feet and performed acupressure to relax her. I played her favorite instrumental artists like Vangelis, Yiruma, and Maurice Jarre. When the on-call doctor came to check in on her several hours later, he signaled she was in active labor. I stayed with her until the contractions came in rapid succession. She was ready to transition. The hospital staff were going to take her to another room closer to the operating room in case there was an emergency. I kissed her on the lips.

"I love you so much, Élise, and I love our baby too."

She smiled. She was in pain and she was frightened. But she didn't want me there at the moment of birth. She was afraid something would go wrong and she didn't want me to fall apart. If truth be told, I was terrified. I tried to get her to at least have Fanny there with her and she refused.

"Just pray for me, okay? If I let you or Fanny in there with me, you will make me afraid. I have to do this alone. I know what to do. Just pray for me, okay? Promise me," she told me. "This is my Heartbreak Hill."

I nodded and watched the hospital staff wheel her away from me. Lily joined me in the waiting room several hours later. I did what Élise asked me to do. I prayed.

Seventeen hours after Élise arrived at the hospital, I felt Lily nudging me awake. It was five o'clock in the morning.

"Daddy, I think there's good news," she said.

I stood up shakily, feeling all of my now sixty-three years. I held onto Lily's hand for dear life.

"Mr. Karajian?" the young nurse called my name with uncertainty. "Yes," I replied.

The nurse smiled. "You have a beautiful healthy baby girl." I let out a huge sigh of relief. "She's okay?"

"Yes, Apgar score 7, ten fingers, ten toes, and the most beautiful hazel eyes and a thick head of dark brown hair." She laughed. "She looks like a Kardashian."

I had no clue what she meant by "Kardashian."

"Élise—"

"Um, Dr. Schuler will be right out. He can give you more details. But the baby is in the nursery, and you can go in to see her."

Before I could react, the nurse darted through the double doors. I felt a pit in my stomach. Élise *is in some kind of trouble.*

"Oh God, Lily," I said. "What about Élise? Why does Dr. Schuler have to give a separate report about her?"

"Let's not panic yet, okay? Let's wait for the doctor."

Élise would want me to see the baby, immediately, but I need to take care of her first.

"Lily, go see the baby," I urged her. "Please go. I'll wait for the doctor."

"Are you sure, Daddy?"

"Yes, please, for me."

Lily nodded obediently and walked through the double doors. Minutes later, Dr. Schuler came through the double doors. He looked drained.

I walked towards him. "Élise?" I questioned him.

"She's stable now," Dr. Schuler announced. "What does that mean?" I demanded.

"There was a complication. I don't want to get into the full details just now, but she lost a lot of blood. She came through. That's what's important. I don't know how she did it," he said in genuine surprise.

My intestines roiled. I thought I was going to lose my bowels right there.

"She refused all pain medication. At one point when I didn't think she could push anymore, I tried to convince her to allow me to do an emergency C-section. I told her I was afraid of infection. Then, I don't know, she just pushed the baby out with every fiber of her being. I think the effort was too much for her, but at least she got to hold the baby and nurse for a few minutes before she collapsed. We gave her a blood transfusion. She's responding well. Her color is back. She just needs to rest. I think she's going to be all right."

My eyes were burning from my unshed tears. I could barely speak. "You think? What the fuck kind of answer is that?"

"Please, this has been a trying ordeal for all of us. This was a high-risk pregnancy, and we all came through it." Dr. Schuler paused and then added, "During the last push she kept repeating '*Ainsi soit-il.*' That means Amen, right?"

"Literally, it means 'So be it,' but yes it is pretty much interchangeable with Amen," I explained.

Dr. Schuler nodded. His eyes seemed to tear up.

"Why don't you go see your new baby girl? I know Élise will want to know you've done that. As soon as she's awake, we'll call you."

Lily appeared on the other side of the double door, motioning me.

I stopped before I could say any more to Dr. Schuler. I walked away from him and walked through the double doors.

Lily led me to the nursery and to the baby's bed. Lily picked her up. "Daddy, look! She looks just like grandma. She's beautiful!"

The baby had a Mediterranean complexion with brown-black hair and grayish brown eyes like my mother with long black lashes like Élise. "You want to hold her?" Lily said as she gently placed the sleeping baby in my arms.

I stood transfixed gazing at the baby, so fragile and tiny and vulnerable. She yawned and balled her little fists.

I started to walk out of the nursery.

"Let's go find Mama, sweetheart," I cooed. A nurse appeared suddenly.

"Sir, where are you going?"

"I'm going to bring the baby to see her mother, my wife. Do you mind?" I intoned. I was walking purposefully, but I didn't know where I was going. "Where is she?" I demanded to know.

"Well, let me review the records," the nurse said. "Well, it looks like she's in the recovery room resting."

"Perfect. Now, if you'll excuse us."

"But sir, the baby needs to feed."

"Yes, I'm bringing her to her mother," I said dismissively.

The three of us strode to Room 312. Even now, after all she had been through, Élise's face seemed so serene underneath the thick mane of silver hair that was now braided in a single plait. I drew the chair next to her bed and sat down with the baby.

"Élise, the baby wants to see her mama. She misses her. I do too. Wake up, honey."

The nurse started to object.

I dismissed her. I knew the baby had to undergo a lot of tests, but Fanny warned us everything but the Apgar test could be delayed and she passed that test.

"Do what you have to do. In the meantime, these two need to bond with each other."

The baby started to stir. She cried.

"Shhh," I said softly as I lay her on Élise's engorged breasts. They were now wetting the paper-thin gown. The baby found her mother's breasts and began to suckle.

I supported the baby while I stroked Élise's face.

"We're here, okay?" I said. "I'm here. I'm not going to leave you." The nurse returned with the on-call doctor.

"Is the baby latching on?" the doctor asked.

"As far as we can tell," Lily answered. "She seems to be feeding all right."

"That's a good sign," the doctor said. She checked Élise. "Well, Doctor?" I queried.

"She's stable. I thought she would be awake by now," the doctor said expressionlessly. "She just may be exhausted. Her vital signs are good. The baby is feeding. We'll just keep monitoring both of them."

The doctor left, followed by the nurse, who returned after a while with a portable crib and changing table.

Lily caught my attention.

"Dad, I need to leave but I'll call you, okay?"

She kissed my forehead and the baby's and then bent to kiss Élise's warm cheeks. "You done good, girl," she whispered.

Mercifully, the rest of the day passed uneventfully. Despite my protests, the nurse did come back and returned the baby to the nursery for follow-up and additional nutrition. While Élise continued sleeping, I took the opportunity to set up her room with her favorite meditation music and healing frequency harmonics. Nurses and aides stopped by at regular intervals to deliver flowers from her friends, who were learning through the improvised phone tree called Facebook that the baby had been born.

I managed to doze for a couple of hours in the chair. When I awoke, a panic set in as I realized we had nothing ready for the baby. With all the stress related to the baby, we had a tacit understanding not to go all out on baby gear. There wasn't even a proper nursery set up, never mind a car seat. I reached for my phone and dialed Fanny. She was on standby. She would take care of everything.

"Aren, just make sure the nurses actually monitor Élise."

"Yes, they're coming in all the time to drop off flowers."

"No, Aren listen to me. Make sure they monitor Élise. If something goes wrong, they'll say it happened because she's high risk. Don't get me wrong. She's still at high risk for post-partum hemorrhage. Infection is also a risk. I don't mean to freak you out, but this is important. It can happen up to six weeks later. Just be a hard-ass and put them to their paces. That should motivate them to pay attention. I'll be there in a couple of hours to relieve you, okay? Antonio will come too. We can take turns watching over her."

"Thank you, Fanny," I said. My head was spinning. A new chapter in my life was beginning.

.oOo.

When I returned to the hospital in the evening, a pull out sofa was set up for me. I sat in the stuffed chair next to Élise's bed and read. Her room had filled up with more gifts and flowers in the hours I had been away. The nurses had come in and gradually removed the catheters, IV, and other contraptions to monitor Élise. Each time I asked questions and demanded to see what they wrote in the charts. "Is Élise okay? She doesn't have any infection? Are you monitoring her for post-partum hemorrhage?" Saying those words seemed to have a magical effect. They knew I wasn't playing around.

The baby was now sleeping peacefully in the crib at the foot of the bed. I had just changed her and given her some enriched formula. I chuckled at the baby's expression of disgust.

"Yeah, I know. You want the good stuff, don't you?"

I loved the way the baby seemed to reach out to me whenever I spoke, even when she was sleepy. She recognized my voice.

"I love you too, baby girl," I said, kissing her before settling her into her crib for the night.

It was midnight when Élise finally woke up. Her eyes fluttered open in response to the baby's cries.

"Oh, where's my baby? She's hungry," Élise said groggily. "Wait, I'll bring her to you."

Therefore "I stood up from my chair, walked to the crib, and brought her to Élise.

"Oh," she sighed. "She's so beautiful."

The baby latched on firmly and nursed. Élise, normally a very modest person, made no effort to hide her breasts. I chuckled.

"If I knew it would be this easy to get you to flash your boobs, I would have gotten you pregnant immediately."

"You did, you old coot."

"You called me a coot?"

"No, I called you an old coot."

We both laughed, and then Élise winced. It hurt my heart to see her in such pain. I stroked her face tenderly.

"Do you like her?" Élise asked shyly.

"Yes, she looks like my mother," I announced proudly. "Daria," she said.

"Hmm," I said.

"I like that name. I was thinking we could call her Daria Christiane Douchet."

"Hmm, Daria Christiane Douchet Karajian. I don't like the initials too much, but I think it has a nice ring to it."

I looked at Élise, waiting for a response.

The baby burped, and then Élise felt a light thud. The baby cried softly. Élise chuckled.

"Will you change her for me?"

Élise handed the baby to me and watched as I removed the soiled diaper, cleaned the baby, and then put a fresh diaper on her and then laid her in the crib next to the bed. I resumed my seat.

"Well?" I asked.

"We don't have to talk about that now," Élise answered, using her prim and proper tone.

I reached for Élise's hands, but she didn't respond. "Yes, we do. I want to marry you."

"I know this is not the life you want. I don't want you to feel obligated. You can see the baby as much as you like. She will be so proud to have you as her father. You have worked hard for your freedom. I'm not going to take it away from you."

I rolled my eyes.

"Is this why it took so long for you to regain consciousness? You were memorizing this pathetic speech?"

Élise pursed her lips.

I reached out and cupped her chin so that she would be forced to look into my eyes.

"Give me a chance to prove I can be a good husband and a good father. Please."

"Aren, I'm tired. I'm really tired. I don't want to talk about this right now."

I did not want to pick a fight. "Okay," I said. I watched as Élise started to settle down in her bed and pull up the covers. She sighed. I looked at her and smiled. Suddenly the mood shifted.

"It's kind of uncomfortable in this chair. Can I sleep with you?" I asked.

"This is what you call husband material? Where's the self-sacrifice?"

"Um, it got twisted up along with my back when I fell asleep in this chair."

"You're too much."

"I know. Do you need to pee?"

"Yeah," Élise said, sighing. "Come on."

I helped Élise out of bed and walked with her to the bathroom. She held onto me for dear life as she lowered herself onto the commode.

When she was finished, she shuffled back to bed and then turned down the covers so I could get in next to her. She lay her head on my chest. I slipped my arms around her and squeezed gently.

"Aren, I feel awful. I don't even want to think about what I look like. How can you stand to be with me?"

"This will pass. It's not going to be pretty or easy, but we'll get there. Okay? Now sleep, darling. In the morning we'll send out announcements and pictures."

"Oh no, with me looking like this?" I laughed.

"We'll figure something out."

"Aren," Élise said, yawning. "Yes?"

"I'm putting in the prenup agreement that Élise does not have to change Aren's diapers."

"Well, I'm going to put in the prenup that Élise has to continue her Pilates to maintain her gorgeous figure, and no matter how pissed off Élise gets at Aren on any given day, she still has to have sex with Aren. Deal?"

"I don't know. I have to go over that with my attorney. What happens if you can't satisfy me, old man?"

"Yeah, yeah, yeah. I love you too, Élise."

"Hmmph." Élise smiled as she drifted off to sleep.

CHAPTER 26

MAY YOU GROW OLD ON ONE PILLOW

Epilogue

In 2033, Élise and Aren sat in the grand Beckman Mall under a hot June sun and watched their daughter graduate with high honors from Caltech. Élise was wearing a fantastic hat that rivaled the best British millinery tradition. Aren was wearing his Tilley hat, to the annoyance of Élise.

"Do you want me to get melanoma?" he chided when she complained one time too many.

She rolled her eyes and then became silent. "I thought so," he said in exasperation.

Élise stuck out her tongue. He squeezed her hand. She punched him. The couple sitting behind them burst into laughter.

Daria had patented a special technology based on her father's initial work on photovoltaic technology. At eighty-five, Aren was going to start a venture company with his daughter thanks to a generous grant from the government. Élise had written the grant. They were all planning to settle in Costa Rica.

Lily was not able to attend the ceremony. She was recovering from a year-long battle with a rare cancer for which they had not yet found a cure. But she was hopeful. She would be participating in a clinical trial in the next few months. Lily did send her son Vartan who was four years younger than Daria and his father Stephen. Lily and Stephen met after her relationship with Tessa ended. She was still family, though. She sent her well wishes to Daria. Élise would see Antonio and Fanny on their summer visit to New England.

At seventy-three, Élise looked pretty much the way she did when Aren first met her twenty-three years earlier. She was thinner now mostly because she ate like a bird, so Aren complained. Her hair was much longer now and completely white. She liked it when Aren called her Storm. Aren had not changed very much either. His lush hair had thinned out on the top, but he still received his fair share of appreciative looks from the ladies, so he liked to remind everyone. He stayed fit by hiking with his wife. They made love every day. They had moved to California to be close to Daria when she went off to college.

Daria was stunning. She was tall with long, thick brunette hair that reached her waist. Daria had many skills and talents. What most people found endearing about her was that she was a gifted storyteller. It came from the stories her grandmother Daria told her of growing up in Kazakhstan. It came from listening to her mother talks about her grandfather's stories. It came from visiting the Dobra Tea Room with her parents and listening to the customers gossiping and sharing their stories. It was Daria's storytelling that caught a certain graduate student's attention. Vimal Srinivasan from Trinidad overheard Daria tell the story of the sun and the moon and it made him laugh. They met the previous year and already their relationship seemed serious. Time would tell.

After the graduation, Aren and Élise joined their daughter, along with Stephen and Vartan, at the Athenaeum for the commencement lunch. Afterward, Aren and Élise took Daria to a teahouse, where they spent some quiet time together. Vimal joined the family later. He approached the table and kissed Daria and then shook hands with Aren and Élise. He exchanged pleasantries with them for a while. At three o'clock, he announced it was time to leave. He had special plans to celebrate Daria's graduation. As Daria stood up, she kissed both her parents and promised to see them the next morning.

From the vestibule, Vimal watched alongside Daria the raucous flirting between Daria's parents. He felt a soft finger wiping the tears from his eyes. Daria smiled at him. He took her hand and kissed it and led her out of the restaurant.

Thank you for reading Aren & Élise.
For more information about upcoming author and book
events, please go to www.ettenigsayambooks.com
and www.ettenigsayam.com

You may also check my book through my social
media platforms and links listed below.

Facebook
www.facebook.com/profile.php?id=100085652155777
Instagram
www.instagram.com/ettenig.sayam
Youtube
www.youtube.com/channel/UCkpceYx6ujIYmmuaoF_B_mg
Blog/Newsletter
www.ettenigsayam.com
www.ettenigsayambooks.com
www.themaplestaple.com

Seraphin Stone

seraphin stone

ettenig sayam

DIVINITY IN MOTION

Boston

Mari

Ten days after the dinner party, I was scheduled to fly out to Switzerland for the semi-final round at the Prix de Lausanne, followed by an in-person audition at the U Michigan School of Dance a week later. Papa had client meetings—he always had—so I didn't ask him to come with me. Alysson and her father, Peter, would fly out with me for the U Michigan audition, but I was on my own for Lausanne. Well, not entirely. Kristina was coming from Denmark to serve as my coach and would have backstage access. Phew!

Thanks to Alysson's brilliant idea to ask her mom to reach out to David for a favor, I managed to schedule a few hours of private studio time in addition to my regular classes at the Ballet School and Dance Studio. I had hesitated to ask for David's help; it felt awkward.

"Mari, David has so many contacts. Give me a break. He can do this favor for you, and if not for you, then for my mom. They're friends."
"I don't know, Alysson—"
"Stop. I've got this."

On Sunday, I went to church with Papa, my sister Rose, and her husband Kwame in Boston. Afterwards I planned to take a Haitian dance class at the Jean Appolon Expressions (JAE) dance company in Cambridge. The drums and movement were cathartic—precisely what I needed. I didn't have time to check my phone until I got home in

277

the late afternoon and saw a text from David asking me to call. Gulp!

After a quick shower and a change of clothes, I headed to the basement where my ballet barre stood and dialed David's number.

"Hey, Mari," David said. "Thanks for returning my call."

"Hi, David," *I replied, feeling a bit less intimidated than usual.*

"So, I hear you need a favor. Tell me."

There was something about the way he said, "Tell me," that got me tongue-tied."Oh, um, yeah. I'm planning to fly to Lausanne next week for an important competition, and I just need access to free studio space so I can get some practice. I'm taking the week off school, but I am rehearsing at my dance studio. They have regular classes during the day, so I—"

"So, your school is okay with you taking a week off?"

"Well, I'm calling it 'independent study.' I plan to write an essay about the whole experience."

David chuckled. "Gotcha. I checked with my club in Boston, and they have at least one studio available between 10 AM and 4 PM, and then between 8 PM to 10 PM. Does that work for you?"

I felt all flushed with fever, embarrassed… Oh my God! Was I singing a verse from "Killing Me Softly"? Why was that song playing in my head? *Focus, Mari.* David asked me a question—does the schedule work for me? Right.

"Yes! Thank you. Thank you so much."

"And Mari, please take advantage of the gym facilities. If you want to cross-train, use the sauna or jacuzzi, or even get a special power drink or a massage. Don't let your good manners hold you back from a great opportunity."

"Oh! Um, I guess? Thank you."

"You know, you didn't have to go through Heather. You could have just asked me directly. I don't bite."

Silence hung in the air. I didn't know how to respond.

David continued. "You sound pretty keyed up. This must be a serious competition if you're flying out to Lausanne. Is your dad going

278

with you?"

I hadn't fully processed how I felt about Papa not coming. If my mother were alive, she would've come without hesitation, canceling everything for me. Ever since the economic crisis, Papa had become low-key paranoid about losing his job, and he reluctantly asked for time off. Normally, Alysson's dad would step in, but Lausanne was a big investment in time and money. Not even Tat Tat, my aunt Erica, could manage it.

"Um, no, he can't. But my old ballet coach lives in Denmark, and she'll be my coach during the competition, so I'll be okay."

David sighed. "Okay, kiddo. When do you want to come so I can let the gym know?"

"Well, January 19th is MLK Day, and I planned to take that week off to prepare. If I can come in from Monday through Friday, that would be ideal. I fly out on Sunday."

"All right then. I'll text you the gym information. Call me if you have any problems, okay? Good luck."

"Thank you, David."

"My pleasure."

I giggled, the sound bubbling up unexpectedly.

"Mari, what is so funny?"

"I don't know. It just sounded like a business transaction."

"You're silly," he said, a soft chuckle lacing his words.

"Yeah, my family calls me *tèt chaje*."

"What does *tèt chaje* mean, Mari?" David asked.

I paused for a moment. "You know, when my family uses that Haitian expression, it's their way of saying I'm flighty or scatterbrained. But if you pronounced it the French way as *tête chargée*—*Chargée*—translates to 'mental burden' or 'heavy head' in English, in the sense of feeling overwhelmed, stressed out, or having a lot on one's mind."

David was chuckling on the other end.

"I'm sorry. Was I boring you?"

"No, Mari. Quite the opposite. It's nice to get a glimpse of the

279

nerdy, scholarly Mari giving a lecture about Haitian Kréyol and French linguistics."

"Ha, ha," I said, a little miffed.

"Oh, come on. So I'm curious. What is the Haitian expression for flighty or scatterbrained?"

I took a deep breath. I wanted to give a snarky retort, but it escaped me.

"*Tête en l'air* denotes someone being flighty or scatterbrained."

"I see. You know, Mari, I actually do think you may be *tête chargée*. You have a lot going on. But I like the imagery of *tête en l'air*. It kind of fits with your *jetés, sautés,* and *brisés volés*.

My mouth flew open in shock.

"I'm impressed. You know some ballet terms."

David laughed softly. "I've been around. Okay, Mademoiselle *tête chargée*, now known as Mademoiselle *tête en l'air*. Later."

"Bye," I said, then quickly ended the call.

I stared at my phone without seeing it, wondering why my face suddenly felt like I had stuck my head inside an oven.

.oOo.

www.ingramcontent.com/pod-product-compliance
Lightning Source LLC
Jackson TN
JSHW080302170225
79132JS00005B/8